W9-CMZ-073

Harrington, Alexis
Harrington, Alexis
Bridal veil

10/17

The Bridal Veil

The
Bridal
Veil

Alexis Harrington

THE BRIDAL VEIL

Copyright © 2002 by Alexis Harrington.

All rights reserved. No part of this book may be used or reproduced in any manner whatsoever without written permission except in the case of brief quotations embodied in critical articles or reviews. For information address St. Martin's Press, 175 Fifth Avenue, New York, NY 10010.

ISBN: 0-7394-2314-2

Printed in the United States of America

Published by St. Martin's Press,
175 Fifth Avenue, New York, NY 10010.

Maggie Grover, Nikki Harrington, Lisa Jackson, Margaret Vajdos—what would I do without you? A person never had better friends and I'm grateful for your strength and guidance.

———

BFS and GC, you brought Luke and Emily to life for me. Many thanks.

CHAPTER ONE

COLUMBIA RIVER GORGE, OREGON
APRIL 1880

"HAVE YOU COME A FAR PIECE, MA'AM?"

Emily Cannon turned her eyes from the view beyond the stern-wheeler's window to look at the rotund man sitting on the bench seat across from her. He'd been trying to engage her in conversation ever since she'd boarded in The Dalles. She had done her best to discourage him, but her short replies and near-rudeness had not quelled his interest. Faint apprehension began to grow in her chest.

Even though it was a cool, gray morning, he mopped perspiration from his florid, beefy face with a large, dirty handkerchief, bumping his bowler back to the crown of his head in the process.

"Yes, from Chicago."

He looked impressed. "Chicago! Say, I spent some time there, oh, about ten-eleven years ago." He chuckled, and wiggled his eyebrows at Emily in a way that she found extremely vulgar. "I had me a hot time there, I can tell you. Or maybe I *shouldn't* tell a lady." He slapped his hammy thigh and laughed harder.

Emily clenched her teeth and glanced around, looking for an empty seat. But the boat was filled to capacity and her only chance to get away from this dreadful man would be to go outside, where rain poured down on the decks. "I'm sure the city looks quite different, then, sir, since you last saw it. We had a fire nine years ago. A four-mile-by-one-mile area burned."

"You don't say."

"A great many homes and businesses were lost. Lives were lost as well." She sighed slightly and turned her head to look out the window again. "Or ruined."

The man extended a pudgy hand with sausagelike fingers. "Allow me to introduce myself, ma'am. I'm Earl Pettit. I travel these parts selling nails and fence wire. If you need it, Pettit can get it. Har-har-har!"

Reluctantly, she extended her gloved hand. "How nice to meet you, Mr. Pettit," she lied. "I am Miss—Mrs.—I am Emily Cannon."

"And you're on your way to Fairdale. What takes you that way?" His knee brushed hers and she pulled away, pointedly rearranging her skirts.

Disturbed by the man's increasing—and unwanted—familiarity, Emily groped for an answer that would put Earl Pettit in his place. She was traveling alone, something respectable women did only when absolutely necessary. She knew very well how she must be perceived by him, a man, clearly *not* a gentleman, and one who had not taken her subtle hints that she did not wish to continue this conversation. A gentleman would have read her cues of civil but short replies and disturbed her no further. "I'm meeting my husband there."

"So there's a Mr. Cannon."

"My husband," she repeated.

"Well, that's a disappointment. Of course—a fine lady like yourself wouldn't be unattached. But I was hoping to get to know you better."

Emily gave him a wan smile but said nothing more for fear that she'd give away how frightened and nervous she truly was. Turning back to the window, she watched the slate-gray river churning alongside the steamboat's hull. It hadn't been a lie that she'd told Mr. Pettit. But not exactly the truth, either. She'd come two thousand miles to marry a man she'd never once laid eyes upon, a man who was expecting another woman, and she had no guarantee that he would be any different from this crude traveling salesman, with his garish brown-and-red–checked suit that was shiny at the knees and stained with who knew what.

Hope, fear, and misgiving over her decision had been at war in her heart for the entire week it had taken to reach Oregon. Just as she could not escape Mr. Pettit's attentions, she would not be able to escape her future husband if he turned out to be less than what she hoped.

Please, God, she prayed as the river bore her closer to her destination, *please let Luke Becker be a better man than this one.*

"I've always loved you, Belinda. Since we were kids. That will never change."

Luke Becker sat on the edge of his bed, staring down at a small, oval-framed photograph cradled in his hands. The faces of the young wedding couple in the portrait, captured forever by the photographer's flash powder, were stiff and maybe even a little frightened-looking. "I made promises the day I married you," he whispered. "But everything has gone wrong. Rose needs help and so do I. I have to break those promises now." He gazed across the expanse of the quilt that Belinda had stitched herself, at the snow-white pillowcases, at the emptiness.

From the hallway, he heard his mother-in-law. "Luke, if you're set on doing this blame-fool thing, you'd better get on with it!" With that voice, Cora Hayward could freeze the water pouring from a pump spout in July. Then, more impatiently, she added, "Luke, the day isn't getting any younger!"

No one was getting any younger, he thought. Sighing, he stood and carefully replaced the photograph on the dresser. He checked his appearance in the mirror over the washstand, tugged at his strangling tie, and decided he looked as good as he was going to. Then, with a last glance over his shoulder, he left the bedroom, closing the door behind him.

"Fairdale! Next stop, Fairdale!"

The crewman's booming announcement startled Emily Cannon bolt upright, making her bump her hat against the stern-wheeler's window, and sent waves of terror and hope through her limbs. This was it. This was when she would learn if taking the biggest risk of her life—actually, the *only* risk of her life—would also turn out to be her very worst mistake.

"Well, this is our stop," Earl Pettit said, but Emily didn't reply. Deliberately, she hung back, waiting until he'd moved along before she left her seat.

At last, when his bowler bobbed among the other men's hats among the passengers crowding their way toward the deck, she straightened her own hat and gripped the handle of her canvas Gladstone bag. The boat made its way down the Columbia River, its steam engines rumbling beneath her. She got her feet under her and tried to brush the wrinkles from her black crepe traveling suit, but it was a futile effort. After a week on the train journeying from Chicago to The Dalles, Oregon, and then hours on this boat, she knew she looked rumpled and unkempt. And it was so important that she make a good impression. Without the advantage of beauty, sometimes a good impression was all that a lady had to offer.

Almost without thinking, she once again reached into her skirt pocket to touch the letter she'd carried all these weeks and miles. It had become her talisman, and she had hung her entire future on the pale blue words written on its paper.

Miss Cannon, I do not care what you look like, or what you must do to speed your departure—please come. We need you.

The last passage, written by a hand plainly unaccustomed to holding a pen, had made up her wavering mind in Chicago. It had given her the ideal opportunity to escape, and perhaps the only offer she'd ever have to become part of a family again. So she had embarked upon this chancy venture, hoping for security, dreaming of fulfillment, and knowing that "Miss Cannon" was expected here today. But now that her moment of reckoning was at hand, one important fact nagged at her and sent shivers of dread through her limbs.

She was not the *right* Miss Cannon.

Emily made her way to the deck railing and glanced down at the water slapping the sides of the hull. Ahead, under low, mist-gray skies, a small dock came into view. As the boat drew closer, she saw a collection of buildings perched on the steep hillside, and above them a verdant forest. In fact, it seemed to her that everything on this west side of The Dalles was either gray or green. The swift-moving river and the sheer, rugged cliffs rising above it were gray, the dense trees and vegetation all shades of green. The air was clean and sharp. Nothing back home was like this.

As the stern-wheeler slowed and chugged alongside the dock, crewmen threw out lines and dropped a rickety gangway. A small gathering of people waited onshore, and Emily sought out each face, seeking a man who had, in his letters, given himself a description that would fit many.

After edging her way down the gangplank, she stood on the dock, uncertain, waiting for her trunk to be unloaded and searching the thinning crowd. Above, on the main street, a rustic little town—and it *was* small and rustic to Emily's city-bred eyes—conducted its business. Standing on tiptoe, she glimpsed a butcher shop, a striped barber pole alongside the next storefront, a druggist's, and what she thought could be a general store. Chicago might have been built on a swamp as flat as a pancake griddle, but with its multi-storied buildings and grand edifices, it made Fairdale seem like little more than a quaint smudge on the landscape.

The minutes ticked by, and a brisk east wind still carrying a breath of winter flattened her skirts against her legs and made her wish for her cloak. But it was packed away in the trunk with the rest of the few precious things she still owned in this world.

In his letter, Luke Becker had said he would be here to meet her. She felt people's stares—she should be used to it by now, but all she'd been able to learn was pretending she didn't notice. She forced herself to stand erect with her chin up.

She spotted a tall, gangly farmer and almost stepped forward. But a smiling young woman, his wife, Emily thought, caught up with him and planted a kiss on his mouth, then linked her arm in his. Kissing in public! Why, it was scandalous behavior, but no one seemed to notice. He bent his head to hear something she said and they ambled back up the muddy path that led to the main street. Another man, squat and round, with short, carrot-red hair and a cheek full of chewing tobacco, began to approach her and she held her breath, her heart thumping in her chest. Oh, God, no. . . . But he passed her to spit in the river and went up to the saloon on the main street.

A crewman delivered her trunk and still she waited. One by one the gathering dispersed.

At last the only people left on the dock were Emily and a man with an impatient-looking young girl who gripped a small bouquet. They all stared at one another. The man appeared to be dressed in his Sunday best: a white shirt, a black frock coat, and a silk string tie. He looked uncomfortable in the clothes, as if he rarely put them on. The child with him wore a blue dress edged in yards of ruffles that seemed to engulf her. On her head was a matching straw hat. After what seemed like an eternity, he approached, taking the girl's elbow to propel her along with him.

Emily drew a breath and lifted her chin. "Mr. Becker?"

The man nodded. He was so handsome—tall, with dark, curly hair—that Emily was taken aback. She hadn't counted on such an attractive man, one who smelled of bay rum and leather. Nothing in his letters had hinted at the strong jaw, the straight nose, the mouth with its upper lip that was a shade too narrow. He'd not written of dark gray eyes that seemed to hold a hint of weariness that touched her own unhealed grief.

"Miss Alyssa Cannon?" Obvious bafflement colored his question. Looking at him, her own plainness and height bore down upon her. And she saw them mirrored in his dumbfounded expression.

Emily wove her gloved fingers together to try to hide their shaking. She wished that she had not had to meet him wearing black, but etiquette was strict about mourning clothes—six months for a sister—and proprieties had to be observed. "N-not Alyssa. I . . . I am Emily Cannon." She glanced down at the young girl bearing the scowl and the nosegay of pinks. Her clothes looked new, but the girl herself was untidy, her hair barely combed. One stocking puddled at the top of her shoe and her hat was askew on her head. "And you must be Rose. What lovely flowers. Dianthus, aren't they?" she babbled. "Are they for me?"

The girl remained mute and sullen, and maintained her grip on the gray-green stems.

Now Luke Becker was frowning, too. "Excuse me, ma'am, but I'm a little confused. In your letters, you told me your name is Alyssa." His gaze skittered over her from head to foot like a cold hand. He cleared his throat. "You described yourself quite a bit differently, too."

Oh, this was even harder than Emily had envisioned. In her mind and over the long miles, she had rehearsed this moment many times. The explanation she'd imagined had sounded reasonable. But now, the frowning man with the weary eyes stole her confidence and made her plan seem as flimsy as tissue. It also went against every mode of proper behavior that she'd ever learned or taught.

"Alyssa is—was my sister." Emily swallowed again, her grief forming a knot in her throat. Could she even bring herself to say the words aloud? "She—she was killed two months ago in Chicago."

Luke Becker stared at her. "Killed . . . how?"

"A runaway wagon—" She paused again, the memory flashing through her mind of Alyssa's crushed form lying in the mud and dirty snow. Standing on a dock that smelled of creosote and river, and explaining that horrible event had not been part of Emily's mental rehearsal. Of course, he would want to know what happened. Why hadn't she realized that? "She was crossing the street." A fine, cold drizzle had begun to fall, and it seemed to Emily that Luke Becker's coloring now matched the sky's. He plunged his hands into his pants pockets.

"Well, um, ma'am, I'm very sorry to hear about it." He dropped his gaze to the planks under his boots, as if the news were another weight on his already burdened shoulders. "Really sorry." Finally, he straightened and looked up again. "But you didn't have to come all this way to tell me. A telegram or a letter would have been enough."

"I didn't just come to tell you about Alyssa, Mr. Becker." Emily drew a breath and tugged on the hem of her black jacket. It had taken every bit of courage she could muster and weeks of fretting to arrive at this moment and utter her next words. She looked into his dark gray eyes. "I came in her stead."

He squinted at her and leaned forward a bit, as if his hearing had suddenly failed. "You what?"

"You advertised for a wife and a mother for your daughter. Since my sister could not come, I did. I realize that marrying while in mourning is not proper, but the circumstances are unusual."

After a stunned moment he shook his head, then reached into his pocket and handed the little girl three cents. "Rose, go up to Fran's store and get yourself some candy. We'll be at the sandwich shop."

Rose shifted calculating eyes to Emily. "You mean you're gonna have lunch with *her*? She's not even the right one. And she's almost as tall as you!"

An old reflex, one that she thought she'd overcome, made Emily round her shoulders and stoop slightly. The child's blunt remark and bad manners astounded her. None of her pupils would have dared to speak so rudely, especially to an adult. More than that, she felt as vulnerable as a child herself. She waited for Luke to correct the girl.

But he only nodded toward the storefronts on the main street above the dock. His voice was measured and quiet. "Go on, Rose."

Rose shuffled off with dragging steps, having never surrendered the pinks she carried. She glared back at Emily over her shoulder, then stuck out her tongue and continued on her way. Luke sighed slightly as he watched her go.

The drizzle increased to rain.

"Ma'am, we can't talk about this here," he said, turning back to Emily. He said *ma'am* in a way that conveyed exasperation rather than respect, and she quailed inside.

"No, of course not. But my trunk—" Emily protested, even as rain darkened her jacket and skirt. She couldn't leave her trunk. Everything was in there: her only family photograph, Luke's letters, her mother's wedding gown. The veil.

Luke lifted his head and scanned the plank sidewalks along the stores. Spotting a group of boys playing mumblety-peg, he called to one of them. "You, Jimmy! Jimmy Edwards! I'll give you a quarter to come down here and watch this trunk until I come back."

"You can't mean to leave it out here in the pouring rain!"

Luke heaved another sigh. "They can drag it over there." He pointed to a lean-to next to the dock that sheltered firewood.

The boy scrambled down the muddy path to the dock

with his friends following close behind, and the fine points of the arrangement were worked out.

"All right," Luke said to her. "Let's go."

When Emily last glimpsed her belongings, they were surrounded by boys with knives, the blades falling perilously close as they took up their game again.

Luke Becker eyed the woman sitting across the table from him in Fairdale Sandwich Shoppe. Her spine was as straight as a rake handle, and her back never touched the slats of her chair. She stirred her tea with slow, precise turns of a spoon that didn't even clink against the rim of the cup. For his own part, he wished he could have taken her into the saloon and ordered a glass and a bottle of whiskey instead of the coffee that sat before him now, untouched.

Every eye in the place was on him and Miss Cannon. How could they miss a woman as tall as she was? There wasn't much that happened in Fairdale that went unnoticed, but she seemed oblivious. Coming from a big city like Chicago, she probably had no idea of how small-town minds and curiosities worked. He was so put out by the turn of events, it was difficult for him to be civil to her.

What was he going to do about this mess? It had been hard enough deciding to advertise for a wife, even though he had no intention of giving away his heart again. It wasn't really his to give, anyway.

That hadn't stopped the women in Fairdale from trying to pair him off. It seemed that no more than a month after Belinda's death, two or three of the unmarried females in town had begun inviting him to Sunday dinner. He'd known them when he was still a single man—known them *very* well—but that had been years earlier; he'd been a carefree young buck back then. The first year after he lost

Belinda, he'd been drunk a lot of the time, anyway, and he'd had no interest in their obvious maneuvering. Eventually, he'd realized that Rose needed someone besides her grandmother. But he hadn't thought that any of those women would be good to his girl. And that was his chief concern.

At first, he'd kept the decision a secret from both Rose and Cora. God, especially Cora. Then, after placing the advertisement in the *Chicago Tribune*, he'd come to town every Saturday, looking for a reply. He wasn't sure why he'd chosen Chicago. It just seemed that he'd stand a better chance of finding a woman who knew nothing about his past, one who would help him get a fresh start on life.

Fran Eakins, who ran the general store and was Fairdale's first postmistress, had been none too subtle with her probes into Luke's interest in the mail. She was also one of the women who'd pursued him these past three years. She'd been so obvious and persistent in her flirting that he'd begun to hate going into her store.

Ordinarily, he didn't get much mail—a farm journal or two, maybe a seed catalog or an order from Burpee. Then he had a few different replies to his ad. He pored over them, but only one woman's caught and held his eye: Alyssa Cannon's. And when her creamy envelopes had begun arriving for him, all bearing a fine hand and the faint scent of roses, Fran's eyes had widened, her dark, caterpillar brows inching up her forehead. Pretty soon she'd started asking him some pointed questions, which Luke had done his best to evade.

When he'd finally announced his plan and Alyssa's pending arrival to his daughter and mother-in-law, the storm that broke over the Becker farm rivaled any that blew through the gorge in winter.

Neither of them wanted this new person, Alyssa Cannon, in their house. A stranger, Cora had raged, handling her dead daughter's possessions, taking her dead daughter's place? Cora had turned the house into a kind of shrine to Belinda, leaving her belongings exactly where she'd kept them, as if she'd only gone into town for the afternoon instead of to her final rest. Had his wedding vows meant nothing to him? she demanded. Given his history with Belinda, he'd wondered how she had the nerve to ask.

Rose had sulked over the news and promised not to like anyone he brought home.

Their reaction had been so bad, Luke had decided it would be better not to mention in his letters that Cora lived under his roof. He knew he'd taken the coward's way out. He just hoped it would all sort itself out. Somehow.

All the nights he'd lain awake, worrying and planning, simmering over Cora's tight-lipped disapproval and Rose's withdrawal and unladylike antics . . . all those nights of planning and hoping that a new bride would lighten his lonely widower's life and help him reach his remote, unhappy, tomboy daughter. A new wife who'd described herself so vividly—petite and dark-haired—that he'd actually been looking for Belinda to get off that damned steamboat. He'd arranged a quiet ceremony with old Judge Clifton, to be conducted this afternoon in his office, followed by a little wedding dinner back at the farm. He'd told Cora to wait at home until the whole thing was signed and sealed. Oh, he'd had lots of plans.

At the very least, he'd expected someone named Alyssa, with whom he'd corresponded for several months. Instead this stiff-backed female had arrived, resembling one of the scarecrows in his cornfield—tall, skinny, and pale—with the horrifying news that his intended mail-order bride was dead and she was here to take her sister's place. Generally, it wasn't in him to be rude to a woman, but he wanted to ask her just what the hell she was thinking of.

As if reading his thoughts, Emily Cannon spoke. "I'm sure you must be wondering why I came to Oregon, Mr. Becker. It must seem very odd to you. And I admit that it was a very forward thing for me to do."

"Yeah, well, ma'am—"

She looked away, but not before Luke noticed that her eyes were the green of spring clover. "After Alyssa's funeral, I had intended to write and tell you about her accident. Then it occurred to me. You need help with your daughter Rose, and I'm a teacher of etiquette and fine needlework at Miss Abigail Wheaton's Finishing School for Young Ladies." She gave him a sidelong glance. "Or at least I–I was until Miss Wheaton was forced to close her doors for lack of funds." She gave the tea another nervous stir with the spoon and continued in a low voice, the words tumbling out. "In any event, your letters explained your difficulties and what you're looking for in a wife." She pulled a piece of paper out of her pocket and extended it in her slender hand. " 'Please come,' it said. 'We need you.' So I came."

Luke stared at his own letter, one of the several he'd written to Alyssa Cannon, now in Emily's grip. Damn it to hell, this was too much. "You read the letters I wrote to your sister?"

The lunchtime diners at the surrounding tables leaned in a little closer.

A look of mild horror crossed her even features and she dropped her spoon. "Only with her permission, I assure you! To do otherwise would be—would be—un-

mannerly, dishonorable. She shared them with me, yes.
After all, my only sister was planning to travel to the west
edge of the country to marry a man she had never met.
She wanted me to know something about you and where
she was going."

He felt color and heat rising to his face. Her explanation didn't do much to relieve his embarrassment. He
groped around in his memory, trying to remember if he'd
said anything very personal in those letters. He didn't
think so. He certainly hadn't bared his soul to Alyssa Cannon, but the mail had been private, or so he'd believed.
His reply was blunt. "They were meant for her. So was
the train ticket I sent to her. I planned to marry your sister,
Miss Cannon, not you. I asked *her* to come, not you."

Emily dropped her gaze to the tabletop, sat back, and
folded her hands in her lap. She looked like a dog that
had been kicked from here to the river and back again,
and Luke's conscience gave him a swift kick as well. God,
he even thought her chin quivered once.

"I know that I'm not Alyssa, Mr. Becker," she murmured. "But I believe I would suit. I'm not expecting
romance, merely companionship and a chance to help."

Luke said nothing and the silence stretched out before
them like a long, dark tunnel.

Emily thought about the disheveled girl and considered
her grim-faced father, and wished she could shut her eyes
and wake up to find herself back in her rooms in Chicago.
She wished she could turn back time to the days before
all the bad things had happened, before Alyssa's accident
and the demise of Miss Wheaton's school, back to a time
when Emily had been just a teacher, innocent and igno-
rant.

She felt like the worst fool God had ever allowed on
the face of the earth. Coming here had been a horrible

mistake—she must have been out of her mind when she'd made the decision. She had suffered many humiliations in her life, large and small, but none like this. How she yearned to be back in her classroom, in charge, in control. Not at the mercy of her own feckless judgment, or subjected to a girl who should be taken in hand for her abominably smart mouth and unacceptable behavior.

But with Alyssa's death and the closing of Miss Wheaton's, Emily had felt so lost in the world, the idea of staying in Chicago became intolerable. She had no classroom to return to, nothing to take charge of. She was adrift and without employment. Her impatient landlady had threatened to evict her for back rent, which Emily had no means to pay. And so she had come to Oregon in her sister's place.

Once again, though, Emily had fallen short of lovely Alyssa's charm and beauty. It had happened so many times over the years, now that her sister was dead, Emily felt vilely disloyal even thinking about it. Except it was true. She'd loved Alyssa with all her heart, but Alyssa had been everything that Emily was not: small, dark-haired, popular.

"I'm sorry I wasted your time, Mr. Becker," Emily said, shaking off the painful memories. "I will return to Illinois. If you'll just escort me to the ticket office so that we can buy my passage to The Dalles, I'll get a train back home—"

Luke put an elbow on the table and leaned forward. "Do you have the money to make the trip?"

His blunt question brought Emily up short. Not only was it unseemly to discuss finances, it forced her to reveal her reduced circumstances. Her small savings had gone to give Alyssa a proper burial. And none of the sentimental things in her trunk had any monetary value. Even her landlady had said as much when Emily had offered them in exchange for the back rent. "Well, n-no, I don't." His smile didn't quite reach his eyes. "Neither do I. Farmers don't earn a lot of cash, Miss Cannon. If I see more than a hundred dollars a year, I'm lucky. I spent the little I could spare on the train ticket you used to get here."

The pit of Emily's stomach seemed to drop to her knees. She'd long ago become a careful person, weighing her actions and the possible outcomes from every angle. But when she'd finally decided to come to Oregon, she'd closed her eyes and jumped, refusing to give any thought to what might happen if Luke Becker didn't want her. If she'd been more cautious, she was afraid she wouldn't come at all. She'd had to get away from Chicago and the bad memories that teemed in her mind like a milling crowd. But it had been pure foolishness and now she stared into the face of the consequences, both for herself and Luke. Of course he didn't want her. He was too handsome, too vitally attractive to be satisfied with a plain-featured woman who was almost tall enough to look him straight in the eyes. She felt her cheeks grow as hot as stove lids. What was she going to do now?

"I'm sorry," she began again. "I had no idea—What if Alyssa had come and things didn't work out?"

He shrugged and took a sip of his cold coffee. "I never thought they wouldn't. I had a lot of hope."

It seemed they were both guilty of the same idealistic notion.

Just then, Rose ran into the restaurant, holding a large handful of striped candy sticks. Fast on her heels was Fran Eakins, her face vermilion and her caterpillar brows knitted in a furious frown. Her shopkeeper's apron flapped around her skirts like a sail and every eye in the place shifted from Luke and Emily to the distracting commotion.

"Rose Becker, you give me back that candy right now! One thing I won't put up with is stealing."

Luke jumped up. "What the hell is going on?"

Fran, a small woman, stood on tiptoe to put her face closer to his. "I'll tell you what's going on. Your girl here stole all those candy sticks when she thought I wasn't looking."

Rose ducked behind Luke, but Fran grabbed at her arm trying to pry the candy out of her grubby hand. "Unmannered little thief!" she barked.

"Rose, is that true?" Luke demanded. "Did you take those peppermint sticks? I gave you three pennies."

"I was gonna pay for them!" Rose said, but she held more than three cents' worth in her fist. Somewhere since the time he'd last seen her, she'd lost her new straw hat and streaked her dress with mud. At least, he hoped it was mud. These days, he never knew what she might get into.

"I've had enough of your daughter's shenanigans, Luke. A week ago she took a new pencil from my place, and the Tuesday before that, she was caught soaping the windows at the drugstore. You'd better take better control of this girl pretty soon or she's going to be in more trouble than you'll know how to fix." Glaring as Rose peeked around her father's coat, Fran added, "You are not welcome in my store, Rose Becker. You're just like your father was, a wicked, black-hearted brat and a thief, too!"

Luke could take the insult to his character—it sure wasn't the first time someone had made an unflattering comment about him. He'd heard them all of his life. But he wasn't about to stand here and let this busybody attack his child, regardless of Rose's guilt. Especially since he suspected that Fran was grinding her axe over him. "Just a minute now, Fran, I—"

Emily stood, her height calling attention to itself. With her shoulders back and her chin lifted, she had a regal bearing. "Forgive my intrusion, madam, but your accusation is very harsh, and making it in such a public place is highly improper. I might add that name-calling is no way to teach a child right from wrong. It makes the name-caller look worse than—"

Fran gave her a withering glare. "I don't know who you are, Miss High-and-Mighty, but it's not my job to teach her anything. This is none of your business, anyway." She cast her hard look on Luke. "I'll add the price of the candy to your account." Turning, she flounced out, her heels pounding across the plank flooring.

Luke glanced around the room, at the rubbernecking sandwich shop patrons; at the tall, pale woman who'd come west to deliver bad news and then to marry him, and at his incorrigible, defiant daughter. This was swiftly becoming one of the worst days of his life. It wasn't *the* worst, not by a long shot. The worst day still lay in his heart like a rock. But this one was right up there near the top of the list. He threw a half-dollar on the table, far more than he owed for the check. "Let's get out of here."

They filed out to the sidewalk, into the gray drizzle, and he turned to Rose. "Stealing, for God's sake? You've got some explaining to do when we get home."

Rose said nothing, but rolled out a long-suffering sigh and flipped her wilting curls behind her shoulders.

Then there was the matter of Emily Cannon. He felt as if he now had more problems than Job. "Look, Miss Cannon, I appreciate that you stuck up for Rose, but I'm sorry you came all this way. I just don't think . . ." She met his gaze and the welter of emotions he saw in her eyes made the rest of his sentence fizzle away.

"I felt I had to try. For Alyssa, and for your young Rose, too."

For Rose.

That made him forget what he'd been planning to say. He barely heard her over the rumble and clatter of a passing farm wagon. But he heard enough.

At last he uttered, "Yes, ma'am. I think I understand."

Rose butted in, and he swore he heard Cora talking. "Well, you can't marry *her.*"

These days when Rose spoke, Luke more often heard Cora's voice and vitriol, and none of Belinda's sweetness. His mother-in-law was spoiling Rose rotten, indulging her, and, little by little, undermining his own authority. On top of that, her bitterness was boiling over onto his daughter, and that was part of the problem, wasn't it? Rose was turning into a sullen imp. Yeah, he'd sown his share of wild oats in his younger years, but he'd never been like his girl. No eleven-year-old child should be so miserable or cantankerous.

He glanced at Emily Cannon. Etiquette teacher. It seemed like a useless occupation to him, what little of it he could imagine. A girl didn't need to fill her head with foolishness like how to hold a teacup or a fan. She needed to learn practical things, to cook and sew and keep house. To be a good daughter. To be a good wife.

Most importantly, to be a good person.

What was she learning now? To lie and steal? To be disrespectful and irresponsible, a whining complainer?

Luke didn't want to marry Emily Cannon. But he sure as hell couldn't sit back and let Cora win the tug-of-war that she was waging over Rose. Even though he'd been deceived and didn't owe Emily a damned thing, when he saw the pain and uncertainty in her eyes, he couldn't find it in his heart to turn her away. And she'd risen to his daughter's defense, when Rose had been nothing but rude to her. That took a woman with integrity and steel.

Maybe, just maybe, Miss Emily Cannon, etiquette teacher, could help him turn his daughter around and teach her to be a decent young woman. He hadn't gotten what he wanted, but he might have gotten what he needed. If she could save Rose from Cora's influence, he'd do whatever it took, even if it meant marrying a woman he would never love.

"Rose, go wait in the wagon."

"Aw, Daddy—"

He fixed her with an unwavering stare. "You're already in a peck of trouble. Don't make it worse. *Wait* in the wagon."

The girl dawdled off to their wagon where it was parked down the street.

When she was out of earshot, Luke turned to Emily. "Look, Miss Cannon, I can't pretend that I'm real happy about the way this has turned out. I can't afford to send you back to Chicago. And I can't promise you anything besides a decent place to live and the respect any man would give a wife." He shoved his hand through his hair. "I guess what I mean, that is, well, I won't be any good at moonlight and roses. . . ."

Emily tipped her head slightly. "You mean love and affection."

He sighed, half-relieved, half–self-conscious at even hearing the word *love* voiced. Luke had never felt comfortable talking about personal things like that. Except with Belinda. "Yeah. I can't give you that. But you can see that Rose needs some refinement—well, a lot of refinement, I guess. I can't do it by myself. I don't know *how* to do it. If you'll help me with her, I'll give you everything else a woman should expect from her husband—my name, a home, and respect. So if you still want to get married, my offer stands."

Emily gazed out at the river for a moment, as if weighing her whole life on the point of that moment. She had kind of a nice profile, Luke thought. To his surprise, he felt a twinge of worry that she might refuse the proposal.

But she nodded and said, "I accept your offer, Mr. Becker."

CHAPTER TWO

Mrs. Luke Becker

Emily sat next to her new husband on the hard seat of his farm wagon, trying to keep her back straight and maintain her balance on a conveyance that bounced her around as though she were a bead dropped from a broken strand.

Luke sat forward, silent, his elbows on his knees, and kept the broad-chested team of horses moving along a rutted, muddy road toward his farm. The lines lay easy in his big, work-roughened hands. As soon as they were away from town, he'd unknotted his tie and opened his shirt collar, muttering a comment about "the damned noose" choking him. Now and then, Emily caught a glimpse of his throat and chest when his shirt gapped away from his body.

On either side of the path, newly green grass and Queen Anne's lace, heavy with raindrops, mingled with emerging clover. Sometimes they passed a length of fence, where a few black-and-white cows hung their heads between the weathered rails to watch them go by.

Along the way, an occasional farmhouse dotted the high, green landscape. One was set close to the road, with fresh-plowed fields behind and to the sides. Another nestled back against the edge of tall, dark stands of fir, its drive long and straight. As they drove, they climbed, and the river gorge spread out in the vista below. Despite the low, gray sky, Emily thought it was an impressive sight, a bright spot during a day filled with inauspicious events.

The dry civil ceremony in Judge Archie Clifton's office had hardly been the sort of wedding that Emily had pictured for herself as a youngster, even when she and Alyssa had played bride in the attic of their childhood home. Back then, because of her height, she'd always been forced to wear her stepfather's wedding suit, while her sister, small and delicate like their mother, had worn the family gown and heirloom veil. Of course, as time passed and Emily's future became clear, her girlish dreams of a fairy-tale wedding had all but blown away like the tall-masted sailing ships on Lake Michigan.

Then hope, a fragile and ephemeral thing to Emily, had roused itself with her desperate decision to come west. She'd been practical enough to understand that Luke Becker would not greet her with a grand show of romance. Still, although she didn't know what she'd hoped for, it had not been this.

It had all been so hurried, so undignified. Two men called in from the barbershop next door had served as witnesses. Rose had sat stone-faced in a chair by the stove. The judge, whose shaggy muttonchops made Emily think of a chow chow, had swept through a quick monologue, punctuated by his requests for their promises to honor each other as man and wife. The beautiful wedding dress that she'd brought with her, although it would never fit, lay in the bottom of her trunk with her grandmother's veil, the one part of the ensemble she'd so hoped to finally wear. But the hasty wedding had prevented her from changing her clothes or even unpacking the beautiful headpiece with its length of white silk.

Looking more like a crow than a bride in her wrinkled

black crepe suit, she had vowed to take Luke Becker, a complete stranger, as her husband. Then Luke had placed on her hand a plain gold band intended for a much smaller woman. Because it didn't fit her ring finger, it now encircled her left pinky under her glove. She'd known a flutter of panic when his warm hand had touched hers. He could claim her with those big hands if he wanted to, regardless of what he'd said about giving her only a roof, his name, and respect. He would be within his rights to do so if he chose.

Emily glanced down. Her suit was pretty much a loss to the damp weather, and she was certain that her hat was a ruined wreck. It wasn't raining hard. It simply didn't stop, and the rain's dreary grayness seeped into her heart. In the back of the wagon Rose still sulked, as bedraggled as any street urchin Emily had ever seen in Chicago. Her ruffled dress was ruined, too.

The wagon hit a deep puddle, throwing Emily against Luke's shoulder. It was a strong shoulder, hard and unyielding and very male. She pulled away as if it were a firebrand. Emily had lived in a mostly feminine world for many years—with her sister and all the students at Miss Wheaton's Finishing School—and she was unaccustomed to dealing with a man like Luke. All she knew of him was what he'd written in his letters. Three years widowed, he grew cabbage and corn on his farm, had been born in Fairdale, and was the father of eleven-year-old Rose.

As if their brief contact had jolted him into speech, Luke said, "I hope you understand about the ring. I got it from Fran's store a few weeks ago, when I thought Alyssa was—Anyway, it didn't seem like a good idea to go back there today, after everything that happened. I'll exchange it someday when I go into town."

"Of course. That's fine." She understood, better than he knew.

"Do you like ham? Cora has fixed a little wedding supper for us."

She looked up at him. He had a fine nose, not too long or too short, a strong jaw, and a broad forehead. "Really? Cora is your housekeeper?"

"Uh, no, not exactly. Cora Hayward is Rose's grandmother. She lives with us."

"Oh?" This salient point had been left out of Luke's correspondence. "I don't believe Alyssa said anything about it."

"Yeah, well, I guess I might have forgotten to mention it to her. You'll meet Cora in a few minutes." He flapped the lines in his hands and kept his gaze fixed on the path ahead as they crossed a narrow, rickety corduroy bridge. The small logs, laid crosswise, rattled her teeth and made speech nearly impossible.

None of the scenarios Emily had envisioned included having to please a live-in mother-in-law. "Does your father-in-law live with you, too?"

"No, he died before Rose was born. Cora came to stay with Rose and me after we lost Belinda." His sigh was almost imperceptible. "Three years ago, now."

They rounded a curve and another farmhouse came into view. "That's our farm. That's the homestead." She heard the unmistakable pride in Luke's voice as he turned the team into the road that led to the house.

A tidy, two-story place, it was painted sage-green with cream trim. A wide, covered porch stretched across the front and around the side. A barn with an attached henhouse stood off to the left, and at the rear edge of the cleared land, another dense forest of fir trees loomed. Those on the outer edges seemed to have thinner branches on their eastern sides, as if they'd been beaten by fierce winds over many years. Their cold, dark silhouettes made Emily shiver. A stately old oak grew in the front yard, and a swing hung from it. No other shrubbery or flowers decorated the yard.

Waiting on the porch was a large, stocky woman with a stern face and faded red hair that was parted down the center and pulled into a tight knot at the base of her neck. She stood with her arms crossed over her ample chest, gripping a spoon in one hand. Her sleeves were rolled up to her elbows, as if she'd been working hard since sunup ten years ago.

Luke set the wagon brake and jumped down from the high seat, then came around to help Emily to the ground. Rose scrambled over the wheel and ran toward the house.

"Grammy, Grammy, guess what?" she bugled. Her tangled coffee-colored hair flew behind her, and she managed to find every puddle in her path, splashing more mud on her shoes and stockings. "This is—"

"Rose, that's not your business to share," Luke called after his daughter. "We're going to have a talk, missy. You get into the house and wash up for supper, then wait for me in the kitchen."

Apparently deciding she'd pushed him far enough today, the girl obeyed and disappeared inside. Luke escorted Emily to the porch, where the scent of cooking eddied with the wind currents. Then to the waiting woman he said, "Cora, this is Emily Cannon—well, Emily Becker, now."

Up close, Emily realized that Cora was a bit shorter than she'd first seemed. But she was sturdy and big-boned, with large, work-reddened hands. She bore the faint scents of lye soap, starch, and wood smoke. Her small blue eyes, as hard and round as two marbles, missed nothing.

Cora raked her with the same rude up-and-down gaze that Fran Eakins had. "I thought you said her name was Alyssa," she said, her tone accusing. "I thought you said she was small-built and dark-haired." She spoke to Luke as if Emily were not there.

Emily refused to be discussed like a piece of furniture brought home from a merchant's shop. Not certain how Luke would explain her presence, she interjected, "Alyssa was my sister, Mrs. Hayward. I'm very pleased to meet you." Briefly, she described coming in her sister's place, leaving out the more painful details.

Cora's hard gaze fixed on her but her stern face softened just a bit, and she uncrossed her arms. "I don't much like surprises. I want to know what's coming and I had my mind all arranged to meet someone else. But I'm sorry to hear about your loss. I've buried kin—I know what that's like."

Another memory of Chicago flashed through Emily's mind, this time of Rosehill Cemetery. Of the winter's last snowfall settling lightly on Alyssa's headstone, plain and small and new. It had been just before Emily left, when she'd gone there to say good-bye. She swallowed and nodded at Cora, unable to speak.

Luke left the porch to pull Emily's trunk from the wagon. "Emily was an etiquette teacher in Chicago. It'll be good for Rose."

"*Etiquette!*" Cora hooted. Her voice sounded like a rusty nail being pulled from a weathered plank. "Well, that's about as useless as teats on a boar. I've taught that girl all she needs—" A look from Luke stopped her. Carrying the trunk on his big shoulder, he took it inside and Emily followed it with her gaze, a feeling of panic elbowing the composure she was trying to maintain. That trunk was the only familiar thing she had in this strange new place.

"Manners and gentle behavior are important for every young person, Mrs. Hayward."

The older woman waved a dismissive chapped hand. "Bah! 'Please' and 'thank you' are good enough!"

Only manners, gentle behavior, and years of enforced self-control kept Emily from replying that stealing and a sassy mouth could not be prevented or cured with the mere use of *please* and *thank you*. No matter how she might want to, a lady did not give voice to every thought that came into her head. Apparently Cora Hayward had not learned this rule, or passed it on to Rose.

Luke reappeared, and just briefly their gazes touched. Once again, Emily was struck by what she saw in the depths of his eyes. It was more than just weariness. She saw a raw flicker. Too shy to maintain their eye contact, she broke away first.

"I'll leave you to get settled, then, while I see to the stock," he said and strode to the wagon.

"Don't be long," Cora said, "I've had that ham ready to carve for the better part of two hours." She shook her head as she watched him lead the team toward the barn. "That man. Well, come on, *Mrs. Becker*, I'll show you to your room."

She yanked open the screen door and whisked Emily by a neat parlor. Emily had little time to look around. Cora continued down a short hall that led to a flight of stairs, forcing her to follow. On the second floor she noted several rooms.

"Heavens, what a big house." After years of rented rooms, where Emily and Alyssa had shared a bed until her stepfather died, this farmhouse seemed enormous.

"Luke built this place himself for my daughter Belinda, plank by plank. I never would have thought that shiftless man had it in him to build anything. Some Swedish family lived here before, but the house burned down and they decided to leave. He got the land cheap. I wondered why he made it so big—I guess he thought there would be lots of children after Rose. But there weren't. This is Rose's." They passed a bedroom that looked as if a tornado had struck it. Clothes were strewn everywhere and hung from the open drawers of a bureau. "Luke's room is in there." Cora nodded toward a closed door on the right and passed it. "Yours is this way."

Emily didn't know whether to be disappointed or relieved that she would not share her husband's bed. If Alyssa had come, would she have been led past Luke's room as well? In any case, Cora had obviously arrived at her own decision already.

At the end of the hall, Emily glimpsed her trunk standing in a clean, bright bedroom. It was far more cheerful than her room in Chicago, where her view had been of the brick wall across the alley. This one had two big windows, graced by white lace curtains *and* shades, that looked out on the plowed fields. Between the windows was a plain wardrobe. A pretty quilt and bolsters gave the big bed a cozy look. A washstand and a simple dressing table with a small mirror and upholstered bench completed the furniture. Emily sensed a woman's touch here, and something told her it wasn't Cora's.

"All right?" Cora demanded like a grumpy innkeeper.

"It's very nice. Thank you," Emily said.

"My daughter decorated this room. She upholstered the bench herself, made the quilt, and braided the rug." Emily waited for the warning not to touch anything. It didn't come but it was implied. Cora added, "Soon as you're ready, we'll be setting down to supper."

"Yes, I'll be right down."

"I usually serve meals at seven, eleven, and five. Those who aren't setting at the table on time don't eat. I'm not running a restaurant here."

"I appreciate knowing the schedule," Emily lied.

Cora held her gaze for a moment, then nodded and closed the door with another *humph.*

Emily allowed herself a quiet sigh and looked around at the cream-colored walls. As she perched tentatively on the edge of the bed, a feeling of ineffable loneliness settled upon her like a familiar old shawl. She supposed that her decision to become a mail-order bride was no worse than taking a position as a governess or a lady's companion. The chief difference was that she was legally bound to the situation and the man who'd brought her to this house. Legally bound, and morally, too, since she had given her word to God, to Luke, to Judge Clifton, and to the State of Oregon. She was Luke Becker's wife now and the people in this house should be her family.

Except they weren't. They were just strangers. And she wasn't Alyssa, so they were not very pleased to see her.

She pulled off her gloves, and with the left one came her wedding band, too small for her ring finger, too big for her pinkie. She fished out the ring and put it back on. It was loose but if Luke had to compromise, she would have to as well. Compromise was another of Emily's familiar companions.

This marriage of convenience . . . her mother's marriage to Robert Cannon had been a loveless marriage of convenience. Emily hadn't realized that early on, but it came to her after her mother was gone. She knew she was a fool to think that her marriage to Luke Becker would be any different. But she couldn't help but wish for more.

Rising from the mattress, she went to the trunk, un-buckled the cracked leather straps that encircled it, and opened the hasp with the key pinned to the underside of her jacket lapel. When she lifted the lid, the faint, linger-ing scents of her life in Chicago drifted over her, making her throat tight with longing for what had been. Amid her belongings, Alyssa's fragrance of rosewater mingled with their mother's lavender sachet, and a hard knot formed in Emily's chest. They were all gone now, her mother first, then her stepfather, and now Alyssa.

Reaching inside, she carefully lifted out the gown and veil she'd brought with her. Wrapped in layers of tissue, the small gown was simply one of her few treasured keep-sakes. The bridal veil, though . . . oh, the beautiful bridal veil. She held the elegant headpiece as if it were a price-less relic. Between the seed pearls that decorated it, silk orange blossoms had been attached with the finest of stitches. Two-and-a-half yards of lace-edged illusion, a fine, transparent tulle made of silk, fell from the back of the headpiece in an airy cloud. Although it would not have formed a long, elegant train on Emily, as it would have on Alyssa or their mother, Letty, it would have dipped below the hem of her dress. From the trunk's top tray, she picked up a daguerreotype and looked at the woman staring back at her. Tall and statuesque, Emmaline Mary-field, the maternal grandmother for whom Emily was named, wore the veil in the portrait and it brushed the back hem of her gown. Grandma Emmaline had been a seamstress for wealthy society matrons. One of them had ordered a wedding gown and veil for her daughter. When the girl eloped, the mother was so devastated, she had paid for the ensemble and then given it to Emmaline as a gift. The gown she had sold to another customer. But she had worn the veil at her own wedding. In due time, she had presented it to Letty when she married. It had always been understood that Letty's girls would wear the heirloom when they became brides.

Emily sighed again. Her stepfather had often noted that Emily was as plain as gruel but, bless her heart and God be thanked, at least she was a well-behaved plain young lady. She had clung to that, even when she had a wicked or rebellious thought, even when she'd felt like a prisoner of the very rules she clutched so closely.

That might be why the veil was so important. The veil ... to her, it meant so much more than a wedding or a husband. It represented delicate, ethereal beauty, and from childhood she'd always imagined that if she put it on, its beauty would be magically conferred upon her. For the briefest time during her trip west, she had envisioned wearing it at last. But it was not to be, and Emily had been wrong to think it would. Regardless of her grandmother's wishes, the veil was intended only for Alyssa, the beautiful one, and always had been.

And Alyssa would have worn the veil, too, if Charles Walker had not called off their engagement and left her so disillusioned and heartbroken that she'd found the prospect of becoming a mail-order bride appealing.

How cruel were the twists of their fates, Emily thought.

Alyssa had died with her youth and beauty intact, but her spirit crushed.

And Emily would never have beauty, but she would always have her gentility.

With great care, she enfolded the garments in their tissue cocoons and replaced them in the trunk. Then she brought out a black dress to wear to dinner.

Mrs. Luke Becker. She was a wife now, but she'd never been a bride.

*   *   *

Luke stood in the cool, dark barn, forking hay into the stalls. He'd taken off his good frock coat and hung it on a nail hammered into one of the posts. It was peaceful in here, with the smells of animals and feed and time. The building was old, having survived untouched by the fire that destroyed the original farmhouse and made Lars Olstrom, the previous owner, desperate to pack up his family and return to Sweden. After a run of bad luck culminating in the loss of the house, the Olstroms decided that America wasn't the grand place they'd been told, and Luke was able to pick up the land for a fraction of its worth. He'd built the new house closer to the road because he'd thought the oak tree would look nice next to it.

It was quiet in here, too, with only the sounds of strong, equine jaws grinding on feed, the occasional contented whinny from the draft horses, or a moo from the milk cow. Barn cats darted in and out, never letting anyone get close. Out here, he couldn't hear Cora blaring like a steam whistle. Even Rose usually lost her snotty attitude in the barn, when she chose to visit. Over the past three years, he'd often escaped to the peace. It was the one place he still felt comfortable, aside from the fields.

He sat down on a hay bale and leaned against the upright behind him. So, he was married again. But except for the confounding events that had led to this result, he didn't feel any different. He didn't *feel* married, or any less a widower. His new status gave him no pleasure—it felt like the business deal that it was.

His first wedding day twelve years ago had been a lot different. When he'd stood nervous and awkward before Reverend Ackerman with Belinda by his side, he could hardly believe his good luck. Beautiful, petite Belinda Hayward, the girl he'd loved since the first time he saw her in the Fairdale schoolyard, the only girl he'd ever wanted, was going to be his wife. Just as nervous as Luke, she'd slipped her icy hand into his and suddenly nothing else mattered. Even then, the mother of the bride had sat in the front pew wearing a sour look. She'd wanted someone else—Bradley Tilson, a physician's son from Portland—to marry Belinda. Luke hadn't been surprised. Most parents had warned their daughters away from Luke Becker. White trash, they'd called him, when they weren't calling him something worse.

As a youngster, his taste for risky adventures had pulled him far to the left of respectability. His friends and younger brothers had been as rowdy as he was, and the sheriff was well acquainted with all of them. Wherever deviltry occurred, he could be found at its center. They never did anything really bad—smoking behind a barn, turning some horses loose, a little petty thievery—none of it seemed serious to Luke. It had all been just for fun, and nobody really got hurt.

Luke also hadn't been above rolling in a hayrick with a willing girl whose father wasn't looking or hadn't taught her better, but none touched his heart. Except Belinda Hayward.

Even though he'd been keenly aware of their differences—after all, he grew up in a shack down by the river and his old man had died in jail—he'd wanted Belinda for his own. Back then, what Luke had wanted he'd tried for.

Cora had blamed him for running off Tilson, but then, given Belinda's condition, there hadn't been much choice but to let her marry Luke. She'd needed a husband, and Cora reckoned that even he was better than none.

His mother-in-law hadn't worried him, though. Hell, nothing could throw a wet blanket on his spirit that day.

He and Belinda, they'd start their new lives together. Then when he found out about the baby, well, hadn't he immediately promised Belinda that he'd be a good father? Damn it, what had happened?

Absently, he pulled a blade of dry grass from the hay bale and twirled it between his fingers, remembering how he'd believed that life could only get sweeter with a wife like Belinda. He lifted his head and gazed at the dark rafters over him, and a humorless chuckle rolled up from his chest. It was probably just as well that he'd been unable to imagine anything else. But if a fortune-teller had told him what the future held, he wouldn't have believed it anyway.

The years that followed hadn't been as golden as he'd envisioned on his wedding day. They'd struggled, he and Belinda, to make a go of the farm, to overcome their differences. If only there had been more private time to work things out—but in the midst of it all, even though she'd lived at her own place then, Cora had always been around, like a burr under a saddle, always meddling—

"Luke! This ham is blame near ready to hop back on the hog it came from! We're setting down to eat. *Now.*" Her voice carried easily across the yard.

Sighing, he pushed himself up from the bale and grabbed his coat from the nail, feeling as if he were many years older than his thirty-one.

Just as he emerged into the cool April drizzle, it occurred to him that Cora had baked a ham for his last wedding dinner, too.

"It was only a little prank, Luke. Leave the girl be." Cora turned to her granddaughter as she bustled between the table and the stove. "You're sorry, aren't you, Rose?"

"Yes." Rose's mumbled reply was unconvincing.

"There, you see?"

Emily had heard the back door slam, announcing Luke's return from the barn, and hurried downstairs. Now she hovered in the hall just outside the kitchen, unnoticed and unsure if she should interrupt the heated discussion taking place in there. After all, she wasn't really a member of the family. She could see Rose already seated at the table, while Cora, red-faced from the heat of the stove, served the food. Luke paced the length of the big room, around the table and back again. Once, as if from a farmer's instinct, he glanced at the heavy sky looming beyond the window in the back door.

He raked a hand through his dark hair, his very posture revealing his frustration. "Stealing isn't what I think of as a 'little prank.' " He realized that he'd done the same thing in his own youth, but this was his *daughter*. His own child. He didn't want her to grow up the way he had. "I can't figure out why you did it—I gave you money to buy the candy."

"Land sakes, Luke, you make her sound like a bank robber or a horse thief." With short, impatient strokes of a knife, Cora sliced a loaf of bread and piled it on a plate. "Leave it be and let's have supper!"

Luke frowned at his mother-in-law, then returned his gaze to his daughter and asked again, "Why did you take that candy, Rose?"

But the girl only shrugged and kept her eyes on the boiled potato that Cora spooned onto her plate with a neat flip.

In the hall, Emily shook her head.

"Go ahead and start, honey," Cora urged Rose, who already had her fork in her hand. She added with a hint of derision, "I don't know when Mrs. Becker will find her way down here. Etiquette—hah!"

"We should wait for Miss Can—I mean, Emily," Luke said.

"I'm hungry," Rose complained.

"I've waited long enough." Cora settled in her chair like a hen on a nest box and put a slice of ham on her plate.

"Aw, hell, Cora," Luke said, and sat heavily in his place at the head of the table, his elbows bracketing his dish. "It's her wedding dinner."

Emily felt her face grow warm and she wondered again if she would be able to overcome her blunder in deciding to come here. She'd had such hope. And after Alyssa's death and the closing of Miss Wheaton's, it had seemed as if she'd had no choice but to leave Chicago. But she sensed that she'd be doing battle with Cora Hayward every single day. Battling to be a wife, such as she was, and to be Rose's mother and teacher. Well, she'd faced worse events in her life and seen them through. Today she'd made a commitment in town and she must stand by it. Lifting her chin, she stepped into the big kitchen.

"I hope I didn't keep you waiting," she said, clutching to her heart the most basic rules of entering a room. At times of her greatest stress, she clung to the tenets of civilized living the way others sought solace in their faith. In her opinion, good manners were what set humans above the animals, and were all that kept the world from social and moral collapse. If one followed the rules of polite behavior, one could survive. *Show no fear* was not one of them, but she kept it uppermost in her mind as her skirts brushed the door frame. "I'm sorry if I was too long."

Luke bounced up from his chair. The sleeves of his white shirt were rolled up and the tie he'd complained of was gone. Once again, his rugged handsomeness dried her throat. Under different circumstances, she knew that he wouldn't even have acknowledged her. Despite her height, or more likely because of it, she had always been nearly invisible to men as attractive as Luke. "No, ma'am." He indicated her place at the opposite end of the table. "We're just now sitting down ourselves."

Cora's champing jaws and full mouth belied his statement but Emily took her seat and delicately put her napkin in her lap.

"You found your room? The nice one at the end of the hall?" he asked, handing her a bowl of green beans. His eyes didn't meet hers.

"Yes, thank you. Mrs. Hayward showed me upstairs."

Luke only nodded.

Serving dishes were kept in motion in a circle around the table, and Emily soon found herself with a pile of food that was mostly white: white potatoes, white bread, white gravy. The only color came from a pink slice of ham and the beans. The meat was dry and tough, the beans boiled to a pale, sickly green.

Luke pushed around his piece of ham with a noticeable lack of interest. Cora gobbled her food as if she feared it being taken from her, and Rose busied herself by seeing how many string beans she could stack on the tines of her fork. No one told the girl that playing with one's food, especially at her age, was not acceptable, and only two hours a wife, Emily didn't feel it was her place to correct her yet.

She cut her own leathery meat into small, chewable pieces and dabbed them in the gravy to give them some moisture. The meal was ruined and she knew it was her fault. She'd made them late—she'd made them wait.

But her guilt was short-lived. Cora interrupted her feeding long enough to comment, "Well, at least the ham is still good. I was afraid it would be overcooked."

Dear God, this was awkward, Emily thought. She took a bite of bread and did her best to hide her surprise over the taste of the butter. It looked all right, but it had a stale, rancid taste. No one made pleasant small talk, such as asking about her trip, or anything else about her, for that matter. She was an outsider among them and apparently was destined to remain so, at least for the time being. They showed no curiosity at all. Outright prying would be rude, but a little interest on Luke's part would be welcome. He simply kept his eyes on his plate. Didn't he want to know something about his new wife? She certainly wanted to know about him, more than she'd learned from his letters to her sister. Little things, like how much cream he liked in his coffee, or if he liked to dance. For a moment, it seemed that it was just the two of them sitting there in uncomfortable silence. Then she remembered that they were not alone, and that it was rude to ignore the others at the table.

The ability to make pleasant small talk was a basic and vital social necessity. Feeling much less confident than she was willing to show, she plunged ahead into polite dinner conversation. "The landscape in Oregon is breathtaking. I was amazed by the change from near-desert at The Dalles to the lush vegetation here. Have you always lived here, Mrs. Hayward?"

Cora sopped up some white gravy on her plate with a piece of white bread. In her reddened hand the bread looked like a handkerchief. She answered as she chewed, and Emily had a passing glance of partially masticated food. "I came out here in '60 with my husband. We left out of St. Joe and followed the Oregon Trail."

Sorry that she'd asked, Emily forged on anyway. "Goodness, what an exciting trip that must have been."

The other woman shook her head and waved off the suggestion as she chewed. "It was a blame-fool idea my man had. We had perfectly good farmland in Missouri but he got some notion that he wanted to come out here. He came into the kitchen one day and said, 'Pack up, Cora, we're going to Oregon!' And just like that, I had to go. We went through every kind of weather God put on this earth, and I had to dump half of my belongings on the trail. Every time we crossed a wide river or climbed a mountain, there went a chair, or a dresser, or a bedstead."

Emily glanced around the table, amazed by the force of Cora's oratory. Luke looked as if he'd heard it all before and more times than he wanted, but Rose jumped in.

"Grammy, tell about how the ox got sick and died," she urged, her face animated, "and got all bloated up with maggots because the weather was too hot—"

"Rose, for God's sake—" Luke began, but Emily interrupted, horrified by the girl's suggestion and her dearth of table manners.

"Young lady, that is not appropriate table conversation! In fact, it's not proper conversation at all. It is also not proper to create artistic arrangements of your food." She indicated the beans stacked on the fork.

Rose dropped her gaze to her lap, a scowl wrinkling her face. "I don't like beans," she mumbled.

"Then leave them on your plate."

"Grammy says I have to eat everything on it."

"But you're *not* eating them."

Rose's chin began to quiver, and Emily could have bitten her own tongue. She didn't know what had come over her. Maybe it was fatigue from her trip, or the hard, assessing gleam in Cora's eyes every time the other woman looked at her. Rose gave Emily a wounded glance from beneath her lashes, then suddenly jumped up and ran from the table, sobbing. Her thunderous footsteps were heard on the stairs and a moment later, a door slammed overhead.

Aghast at her own behavior, Emily's gaze bounced from Luke to Cora and back again.

"Well! Is that how things are going to be around here now?" Cora demanded. "Luke, are you going to let this woman talk to Rose that way?"

"Oh, dear, I'm so sorry!" Emily put her napkin by her plate and began to push her chair out. "I'll go to her—"

Luke stretched his hand across the table toward hers as if to stop her. His expression showed no anger, only weariness. "No, let her sit up there for a while. She has a lot to get used to. We'll just give her some time."

Stricken to the heart, Emily repeated, "I truly am sorry. I didn't mean to upset her so. I guess I'm not used to hearing stories about dead oxen and—and so on."

"Oh, boo-hoo! Doesn't anything die in Chicago?" Cora snapped. She glared at Emily with her hard blue eyes.

Emily paused a moment before answering. "Yes, Mrs. Hayward. My sister died," she reminded her. "And my parents before her. In fact, I have no family left at all. If you'll excuse me, I'm afraid I'm not very hungry."

"Mrs. Becker"? Hah! Cora Hayward sat in the darkened parlor, her jaw tight, her slippered foot pushing the rocker in which she sat at a brisk pace. She let her gaze follow the line of the furniture and Belinda's keepsakes, still on prominent display. Her sewing basket sat in the corner, its lid opened to show off her gold-handled embroidery scissors, her sterling silver thimble, and the last piece of stitchery she had been working before she died. The linen sat there, folded neatly, half-finished, and looked as if Belinda might walk in any moment to take it up again.

Cora herself had no patience for the kind of fine needle-work that her daughter had done—life was too hard and too busy for that kind of froufrou or gewgaw. *Fancy* was good for people who had nothing better to do. Get the job done and move on to the next, that was what Cora did.

And they'd been getting on well enough here, she and Rose. Her granddaughter almost made her forget that horrible night that Belinda had died, thanks to Luke Becker. If it hadn't been for him. . . .

But they'd managed just fine here at the farm. Then Luke had to bring in Miss Fancy Manners and stir up everything. And it wasn't the first time he'd done that. Whenever Cora thought she had things in place, Luke came along to upset the applecart. She'd wanted Belinda to marry that doctor's boy, Bradley Tilson. He'd worked on one of the neighboring farms that summer all those years gone now. But no, Luke Becker, the wildest boy in town, had sweet-talked Belinda and run Bradley off. Oh, Belinda had defended Luke and told Cora that she was wrong, but Cora knew better. Those Beckers were all alike, living down in that shack by the river, their father no better than the drunken logger that he'd once been, their mother nothing but a foolish, browbeaten female. Belinda could have had a soft life in Portland married to a doctor, because Bradley was studying medicine, too. Instead, she'd had to marry Luke and end up here.

Cora looked around the room. Well, it wasn't a bad house. Luke had done better than she'd expected. She had to admit that he worked hard, too. But she knew her girl had never been happy here, no sir, never. Cora had visited often enough to know. She'd tried to get Belinda to take Rose and come home. When she finally had, it was too late. Too late.

So now Cora had Emily Cannon to deal with, in a

house that Cora had come to think of as her own. Luke claimed Rose needed a mother—well, what was she, the girl's own flesh and blood, if not a mother? Better her than a stranger from Chicago with a lot of blame-fool ideas about how people ought to act and talk and eat and dress. She'd already made trouble and this was only her first night under this roof.

Cora hoisted her considerable bulk from the chair and adjusted the bun on her head. If the new Mrs. Becker thought that Cora was just going to roll over and play dead, she had another think coming.

Luke lay in the darkness, his body deep in the feather tick. The clouds had finally begun to break up and the moonlight cut a long white slash across the quilt.

God, what a lousy damned day this had been. He was dead tired but sleep wouldn't come to him. He'd tossed and turned so much the bedding was wadded into a lump. Tension wound itself around the Becker house like fence wire pulled tight, and he felt it.

Rose had closed herself in her room for the rest of the evening. Eventually, he tapped on her door, carrying a glass of milk and a lopsided sandwich that he'd made. But his girl wouldn't answer him, so he left the food outside her room. When he came up to bed, he noticed it was gone.

Emily, his wife—hah, that was a sorry kind of joke, wasn't it? He linked his hands under his head and stared at the darkened ceiling. She'd also stayed in her room after dinner. He'd already asked himself a dozen times tonight if he'd only made things worse by marrying her. And he got no answer. That tall, skinny drink of water with her black clothes, stiff ways, and city-bred notions—

he was probably asking too much of them all in bringing her here.

Still, she had to deal with Cora. Even Alyssa, if she had come, wouldn't have known about her until she arrived. He hadn't figured out a way to tell her about his scolding, domineering mother-in-law. So if Emily was guilty of trying to fool him, he supposed he was equally guilty of keeping Rose's grandmother a secret.

When Belinda died, he'd been so wrapped up in his grief, he was glad to see Cora move in. After all, what did he know about cooking and washing and keeping house? Rose had been too young to shoulder that much responsibility and stay in school. To Luke's way of thinking, educating his daughter had been more important than turning her into a housekeeper, and he still felt that way. It hadn't been easy, though. He'd taken on the job of tending Cora's property as well as his own. Her fields lay fallow but he saw to the upkeep of the house and outbuildings. And after a while he'd begun to chafe under her carping and domination, until his nerves felt as if they'd been buffed with sandpaper.

Whenever a disagreement arose between him and Cora, she threatened to move out. To keep the peace and a stable home for Rose, he would cave in like a straw house. Every time he did, she became a little more bossy, a bit more entrenched. These days, he got the impression that Cora thought this was *her* home and Rose her own daughter, and he was merely the one who put food on the table.

Sometimes he wondered why all the good things in his life had been stripped away, one by one, leaving him a nearly empty husk. Damn it, he'd changed his ways—he wasn't the no-account, shiftless fool that many had once believed. Didn't that count for something? Didn't he deserve a little happiness? He had but one true joy in his life, and that was Rose. The day she was born, she'd made a man of him, even more than Belinda had.

Just before he closed his eyes, he glanced at the dim silhouette of the oval-framed photograph on the dresser, the one of him and Belinda, two scared kids just starting out. If only they'd had more time together. He stretched out a hand to the other side of the bed and closed it around the emptiness. Three years she'd been gone and he still missed her every single day.

He wasn't a scared kid any longer. He was just worn to his soul from the bickering and the loneliness.

CHAPTER THREE

DESPITE THE STRESSFUL EVENTS OF THE DAY, SHEER EX-
haustion had claimed Emily, and she'd fallen into a deep
and dreamless sleep. She woke early with a renewed sense
of purpose and hope. Even though it was still overcast,
she saw this Saturday morning as a fresh day and she was
determined to make a fresh start.

In the hours following dinner, she'd sat in the rocker
in her room, her big shawl wrapped around her. Though
self-pity was a quality she frowned upon and warned her
students away from, she had come perilously close to indulging herself last night. So many things had happened
over which she had no control, and it seemed she had
come to the end of a long road to find not a reward, but
yet another trial. Briefly, her mind had even strayed to the
memory of her real father, Captain Adam Gray. She didn't
often think of him, but last night he'd come to her
thoughts. She really couldn't remember his face anymore—she'd been just six years old when a November
storm on Lake Superior claimed his ship. Mostly she recalled that he'd seemed as tall as a mast and had been
light-haired. And he'd brought her the most dazzling gifts
from other ports. Then he simply stopped coming home
and her mother had told her that he'd gone to heaven.

Later Letty had remarried, to Robert Cannon, and nothing was the same after that. . . .

This morning, though, things looked more hopeful. She'd begun to put together a lesson plan for Rose, focusing on her most pressing problems first—getting the girl cleaned up and improving her table manners. Why her grandmother sometimes dressed her in those engulfing ruffles and at other times let her run around like a little savage was a mystery. But Emily knew that she would have to first make amends for snapping at Rose last night.

She looked in her trunk and found a pink satin hair ribbon that Alyssa had given to her years before. She still remembered the Christmas morning when she'd opened the small package. They'd lived in the big house on Washington Boulevard then. The family had still been together—Father, at least the man she'd come to think of as her father, Mother, Alyssa, and Emily—all secure and safe in a house that had smelled of spice and pine and beeswax candles. Who could have foreseen what would happen to all of them? How could she have guessed that she, Emily, the least promising of the Cannon girls, would be the only one left fifteen years later?

She looked down at the ribbon again. It was a special keepsake, but she wanted to give it to Rose as a peace offering. All girls liked pretty things, even unmannered tomboys.

Searching through her belongings, Emily found a sheet of creamy vellum, an envelope, and her pen and ink. She pulled out the chair at the dressing table and wrote a note:

Dear Rose,
It is my sincere hope that we can become good
friends. This hair ribbon is very dear to me and I
would like you to have it.

Just two lines, but she agonized over the wording for fifteen minutes. Then she nibbled on the end of the pen, trying to decide how to sign it. Finally, she settled for *Emily Cannon Becker*. It was a bit formal but the circumstances were so odd, she decided to stick with proprieties. One couldn't go wrong with proper form. She slipped the note and the ribbon into the envelope, wrote Rose's name on it, and sealed it.

If her new life here was truly to be a new start, if she was going to fit in, she decided, she would have to learn to get along with the cranky matriarch downstairs as well. Until yesterday she had not known that Cora lived under Luke's roof, but there she was, and Emily realized that in order to reach Rose she must also win over the grandmother. She didn't even want to consider what she might have to do to win over the remote, handsome Luke.

After washing, she put on the black dress she'd worn at dinner the night before. Then she braided her hair into a tight coronet and pinned on her mourning brooch. Cautiously she opened her door and was greeted by the welcome aromas of baking bread and frying bacon. Her appetite was back after the disastrous meal last night— surely the bread would taste good, she hoped. Hurrying down the hall, she slipped her envelope under Rose's closed door, then proceeded to the stairs. With a sense of resolve, she was going back into the lion's den—her new home.

She came into the kitchen and found Cora at the huge black stove. Her calico dress was shapeless except where her apron cinched the waist. "Good morning, Mrs. Hayward."

Cora glanced at her over her shoulder. "Mrs. Becker."

Emily clenched her teeth. There was a tone like curdled

milk in Cora's voice when she addressed her, but Emily swallowed and put on a smile.

"It's good to see a break in the rain. I wonder if the sun will come out later."

Cora ignored the attempts at conversation. Finally Emily asked the question that hovered in her mind.

"Where is Luke this morning?"

"Out working in the fields—that's what farmers do."

Emily's head began to ache from the pressure she exerted on her jaws. "Will Rose come down for breakfast, do you think?"

That got Cora's attention. She turned to look at Emily. "Why? Do you want to *improve* her some more? The child cried her eyes out for the better part of last night. She's still asleep." The knife in her hand flew as she sliced potatoes into a skillet.

Emily felt herself flush. What she wanted was to make amends with the girl, but she decided not to answer Cora's sarcasm. "Maybe there's something I can do to help with breakfast."

"I've been getting along just fine all these years without help." The potatoes sizzled in the hot grease. "You can go set in the parlor until you're called."

Genuine anger flared to life in Emily's chest. After years of respectful students, she was unprepared for Cora Hayward's barefaced rudeness. No one back home would have spoken to her so. She could rise above it, though, she told herself. She had to, no matter how she longed to make a reply that would pin back Cora's ears. Something about Rose touched her heart. She wanted to help the girl, and she'd promised Luke that she would. To do that, she felt she had to win Cora's approval. She tried again. Deliberately misunderstanding the dismissal, she said, "Mrs. Hayward, you don't need to treat me like a guest. I could set the table, or slice bread, or spoon out the—"

Cora turned. "You want to help? All right." She grabbed a handled basket from a shelf beside the door. "Go out to the henhouse and gather the eggs. Mind that you don't break them."

"Henhouse," Emily repeated. She didn't know a blasted thing about gathering eggs but she'd be horsewhipped before she'd admit it. How hard could it be? Hens sat on them, and all she had to do was search under their feathers. Probably.

"That's it out there." Cora went to the window and waved in the direction of the barn, indicating a low, weathered building attached to it. "Go on now. And be sure to close the coop gate behind you so the other chickens don't get out."

Emily went to the door, struggling with an outrage that was alien to her, one that made her want to twist off the knob when she gripped it. As she went down the porch steps, she felt Cora's eyes on her.

Damn this rocky soil, Luke thought as he stood in the side yard, trying to pry a rock out of the disk harrow. No matter how many stones he pulled out of the earth, there were always more. Some of them were as big as steamer trunks and had to be hauled out with the horse team. This one was small, maybe the size of a cabbage, but it was wedged in there as tight as a shotgun groom between the bride's parents. If he'd been paying attention, instead of thinking about Emily, he might have seen it before he ran over it. He didn't know who he wanted to swear at— himself, Emily, or the rock. With a chisel and hammer, he beat on the offending stone, making sparks fly, but the thing wouldn't budge.

Stopping for a moment, he dragged his sleeve across

his sweating forehead and considered the situation. Suddenly, he heard a tremendous ruckus coming from the henhouse. By God, if the raccoon had come back again— He dropped the tools and ran toward the squat building, splashing through puddles, determined to wring the varmint's neck with his bare hands if he could catch it. But just as he reached the henhouse, he heard a decidedly feminine squeal that was neither chicken nor weasel.

He yanked open the door and found Emily pinned against the back wall by the oldest biddy in the flock. The squawking bird leaped at her in a confusion of wings, claws, and beak. Emily did her best to cover her face, but the backs of her hands were scratched and bleeding. The rest of the hens were in an uproar, all flapping around and screeching, and raising a storm of feathers and straw. Cora's egg basket lay on the floor with broken eggs running out in a river of yolks and whites.

"Ma'am!" Luke batted the hen out of the way and grabbed Emily's arm. "Come on." He snatched up the basket and pulled her outside, slamming the door on the henhouse. She stood, swaying slightly, with dirt and chicken droppings streaking her black dress. Feathers dotted her hair and skirts. "Are you all right?"

She nodded once, or at least he thought she did. The movement was so faint, he thought she might just be trembling. She sure looked dazed. "Thank you for rescuing me. I–I didn't know what to do."

"What the hell were you doing in there?" Even his own breath was short.

Stray locks of hair hung on either side of her face, and all the color had drained from her cheeks. "I c-came out to gather eggs for breakfast," she said, her voice quavering. "That one chicken, she was like a creature possessed.

She attacked me and—and— It must have been something I did, but I don't know what."

He took her slender elbow and steered her toward a rough, weather-bleached bench that leaned against the barn wall. "Here, sit down." He put the basket at her feet and stood in front of her, ready to bawl her out for straying into danger. God, he'd known her less than twenty-four hours, and she'd already caused more trouble than he usually had in a week. "Cora is the only one who knows how to handle that mean old biddy. She should have stopped you from coming out here." He put one foot next to her on the bench and leaned his arm on his knee.

Emily gazed at the backs of her scratched hands, which shook mightily. "I asked her to let me help with breakfast and she gave me the basket. She said not to break the eggs, and I dropped them—"

"You mean she sent you?" A hazy suspicion began to take shape in Luke's mind but he backed away from it, as he often did when he thought of Cora's machinations. If he pondered it too long, he'd end up having to talk to her about this stunt she'd pulled on Emily. And that would turn into another disagreement.

She reached into her pocket and dabbed at her hands and face with a black-edged handkerchief. He could see that she struggled for dignity, but damn, it was a pretty long reach when a person was bleeding and spotted with chicken shit. Then she looked up at him, her spring-green eyes vivid with a fear that he could almost feel himself. "Yes, I wanted to be useful. I'm capable, I can help. After last night and everything that went wrong . . ."

And kept going wrong, as far as Luke could tell. He rubbed the back of his tense neck. "Look, you go inside and get cleaned up. Don't worry about helping." He started to walk away.

"Mr. Becker, wait."

He turned and waited.

"I–I was hoping to talk to you about Rose's education. I know she needs guidance, but I'd like to know if you have something specific in mind. I've formulated a basic plan."

He glanced at the harrow, idle in the yard, the rock still jammed in its workings. Daylight didn't wait for anyone, and he had another five acres to plow. "We can worry about that later, too. For the time being, just stay out of trouble. Can you make it back to the house?"

She gave him a chilly look, plucked up the gooey egg basket, and rose from the bench, her movements still shaky. "Yes, thank you, Mr. Becker. I shall manage well enough."

With her back straight and her chin lifted, she glided regally across the yard and toward the back porch as if she were the lady of the manor.

"Well, Mrs. Becker, where are those eggs?" Cora stood at the table, stirring what looked like pancake batter. Her gaze took in Emily's dishevelment, and Emily knew by the twitch of her mouth that the woman was trying not to laugh. She also realized that this was exactly the result Cora had been expecting. Rose sat at the table, dressed in boy's overalls, her hair barely brushed, eating a bowl of mush. She stared at Emily with her mouth agape, as if she'd never seen her before.

"I'm very sorry, Mrs. Hayward, there will be no eggs today." Emily left the slime-covered basket on the kitchen table and walked toward the stairs, bent on reaching the privacy of her room to survey the damage done by the hen. In the stairwell, she heard muffled snorts that gave way to braying laughter coming from the kitchen. Oh,

Cora had enjoyed a fine joke at her expense, hadn't she? Though Emily had been the butt of people's thoughtlessness and sniggering during her life, their cruelty never ceased to amaze her. Did they believe the victims of their pranks and comments had no feelings? Or did they simply not care?

In her own room, Emily sat on the brocade-covered bench at the dressing table and looked into the foot-square mirror mounted over it. Oh, God, it was worse than she'd realized outside, and Luke had seen her like this. Her hair could be neatened and her face washed, but the damage to her dress was another matter. Smeared with chicken muck, dirt, and feathers, she wasn't sure if she would be able to get it clean. Crepe didn't wash well. She had only one other black dress besides her traveling suit, and four more months of mourning to satisfy. She'd have to mix up a batch of Japanese cleaning cream and hope for the best.

Going to the washstand, she washed her face and hands, and once the blood had been rinsed off, she was glad to see that the scratches were only superficial. Then she noticed the pink ribbon.

It lay on her bed as if thrown there, as rejected and forlorn as Emily had sometimes felt. Crossing the floor, she reached out to pick it up. No note of explanation accompanied it, but there was no need, really. Its return spoke volumes. Emily swallowed hard against the knot in her throat, then gently folded the length of satin and put it away in her trunk. She wasn't sure if Rose had returned the gift on her own or if Cora had made her do it.

Cora is the only one who knows how to handle that mean old biddy.

She'd probably trained the accursed thing herself—

what a dreadful example to set for a child by playing that dirty trick.

And that Luke Becker. When he'd stood over her, practically wagging his finger in her face about going into the henhouse . . . if she hadn't been so rattled from the experience she'd have been sorely tempted to kick him in the shins. That very reaction frightened her. Passionate feelings were to be kept in check, she reminded herself. A lady did not lose her temper in polite company, raise her voice, or make physical demonstrations of her anger, no matter how she might long to. Of course, the term *polite* company barely fit these people. In civilized society, an uninvited stranger would receive better hospitality than she had so far. Luke had made her almost as angry as Cora had, first scolding her, and then dismissing her as if she were an errant child. He talked to Rose that way, when he bothered talking to her at all. God above, would Alyssa have been treated the same? No, she supposed, probably not.

Beneath her fear and annoyance, though, had been a more subtle feeling. When he'd leaned close, she caught a whiff of him, of newly turned earth, hay, and soap. They were an altogether distracting combination that had been enough to make her look up into his eyes again. She lifted her gaze now and let it stray to the fields beyond her windows, to the furrows plowed in them. She could picture him behind the draft team that had brought her here yesterday, cleaving the soil for planting, his bare back muscled and straight under a clear April sky. The image in her mind was so vivid, when she glanced into the mirror she saw the color and heat it had brought to her face.

Emily sat upright, appalled at the direction her thoughts had taken. She had struggled with unseemly thoughts all her life, ones that no real lady should ever entertain: jealousy, critical views, fear, anger, impurity, curiosity. They all were injurious to the spirit, and to one's moral and physical welfare. Certainly the copious advice manuals published on proper behavior warned against these thoughts and feelings. Her ability to remember these rules and pass them along to her students had been one reason for her success as a teacher.

But sometimes, oh, God, sometimes in her secret heart, the strictures of ladylike deportment felt a bit too tight, even to her. Though she'd rather die than admit it, she'd wondered what it might feel like to walk barefoot through grass, or lounge in bed for a morning, something a person didn't do unless she was ill, or—or, just once, how would it feel to sleep naked on a hot summer night, with nothing between her skin and the sheets? But she recoiled from the questions because, aside from their impropriety, they tore at the very fabric of security around which she had built and conducted her life.

Unbuttoning the bodice of her dress, she stood and stepped out of the dirty garment. Then she pulled the pins out of her hair so that she could brush it out and rebraid it. The soft whisk of the long strands against her waist was another sensual indulgence that Emily allowed herself to enjoy. A woman's hair, her crowning glory it was sometimes called, was to be worn up in a modest style, not hanging loose in an immodest fall of curls and waves.

But right now, she decided that this particular indulgence was one she deserved. She stood in her chemise and petticoat, pulling the bristles through her hair again and again, enjoying the feel of freed locks. If she missed Cora Hayward's breakfast, so be it. She knew they hadn't waited for her.

*   *   *

The rock lodged in the disk harrow finally broke free with a hard, impatient stroke of Luke's hammer. With a heart-felt curse, he picked it up and flung it into the blackberry brambles that edged one side of the property. God, he'd lost an hour of the morning to this. At least he could finally start the plowing after breakfast. He glanced toward the sky, hoping to see a break in the clouds.

What he saw instead was Emily Cannon Becker dressed in her chemise as she passed her bedroom windows on the second floor, her hair tumbling down her back as she drew a brush through it. He caught only a glimpse, but he saw enough to recognize that its color was of ripe wheat. Luke, stunned and suddenly breathless, thought he hadn't seen anything as beautiful since a misty sunrise last fall.

And maybe it had been long before that.

Just after noon, ravening hunger finally forced Emily out of her room. She knew she was too late for lunch, but that didn't mean there was no food in the house. Wearing her last clean black dress and with her hair tidied, she was determined to face the formidable Cora Hayward. Emily had never been a coward in her life, she thought, as she came down the steps. Well, yes, she had. Many times. But she had proceeded anyway and she would do so now.

In the kitchen, Cora stood at the stove like an eternal sentinel at her post, stirring a black kettle of something with a pleasing aroma. Rose was back at the table, drawing a picture in a composition book. With a slender hold on the courage she'd managed to muster, Emily went to the sideboard and got a dish and silver for herself. Cora turned to watch her, and she felt the woman's eyes on her every move. The silver clacked against the dish in her trembling hand, and she tightened her grip.

When she walked to the stove with her empty plate, she thought of Dickens's Oliver Twist, begging for porridge. "Mrs. Hayward, I'd like to make lunch for myself. As I said earlier, I am not a guest here. I'll be happy to help myself. If you'll just show me where I might find something to eat, I'll take care of the rest." She forced herself to smile as she spoke.

Cora stared at her. Finally she said, "I've got this kettle of stew we had for the noon meal. I was just about to put up a jar for Luke. You take some, too." The offer was grudging but Emily thought she detected the tiniest hint of chagrin. Cora took the dish from Emily's hand and ladled on a healthy portion of the rich, meaty broth studded with potatoes, carrots, and onions.

"Thank you." Emily sat down at the table and forced herself to keep from slurping the delicious stew like a boor, but it wasn't easy. She hadn't eaten a substantial meal since the day before.

Cora went to the back door and took up a shawl hanging from a hook there. "I'm going out to the henhouse to see if there are any eggs left. If you want more stew, help yourself." It sounded more like a command than an invitation, and Emily drew a deep breath when the door slammed behind Cora.

Rose sat at the other end of the table, studiously intent on the picture she was drawing. Her tongue peeked from the corner of her mouth and she gripped her pencil so tightly her knuckles were white. This was the first time since Emily arrived that she'd been alone with the girl, and after the incident with the hair ribbon, she wasn't sure how to commence. Finally she decided on what seemed like a safe topic.

"What are you drawing, Rose?" she asked after savoring the last spoonful of broth.

She didn't look up. "Nothing much."

"Hmm, it looks like *something*. May I see?"

"I guess." Briefly, she held up the composition book to show Emily a drawing that revealed a fair amount of talent. Expecting a rather immature rendering, Emily instead saw a reasonably accurate depiction of the farmhouse, complete with the oak tree and the swing that hung from its bough. The perspective and proportions were a little off, but not enough to detract from the budding gift she recognized.

Pleased surprise colored her voice. "That's very nice! How long have you been sketching?"

The girl shrugged in that annoying way of hers. Her mumbled response matched the shrug. "I don't know. A long time, I suppose. Maybe even two years. Grammy says it's a waste of time."

She *would*, Emily simmered. "Painting and drawing are very ladylike pastimes for a girl. So is stitchery. Has your grandmother showed you how to embroider and sew?"

A lock of Rose's unbound hair fell over the paper and she pushed it behind her ear. "Nope. I just like to draw."

Emily slid her chair a little closer. "Well, embroidery is kind of like drawing, except with a needle and thread. You can make pictures of all kinds of things—flowers, birds, trees, even this house. In the Middle Ages, European women stitched big tapestries that told stories of great battles and family histories. There's a famous one in France called the Bayeux Tapestry. It shows the Norman conquest of England, and it's two hundred and forty feet long, just over one fifth of a mile. It's about a mile into town, isn't it?"

Rose nodded with wide eyes, obviously impressed.

"Well, the tapestry could line the fences along the road for one fifth of the way into town. All done with stitchery." She pointed at Rose's artwork. "Of course, you wouldn't have to make anything so big. But it might be easier for you because you draw so well. You could sketch your design on the fabric."

The girl's wide eyes now gleamed. "Really?"

Emily smiled. "Yes. If you'd like to learn, I can show you how to get started."

"Oh, yes, that sounds—"

Just then, the back door opened and Cora bustled in, a stack of wood in her beefy arms. "Not an egg left in that whole blamed henhouse." She cast them both a quizzical look, then bent a censuring frown on her granddaughter. The girl fell silent.

"Would you like that, Rose?" Emily pressed, looking at her downturned head. "I have all of my threads and such upstairs in my trunk, and we can begin a sampler for you."

"Um, no, maybe not," she said, mumbling again, and from her answer Emily learned more than she'd expected to.

Cora plucked an empty fruit jar from a shelf and went to the kettle on the stove. She spooned stew into it and screwed on a lid, then put it in a basket with a half-loaf of bread. She covered the whole thing with a clean napkin.

"Rose, you take your father's lunch out to him. He'll be in the fields until dinnertime today since he got a late start." Cora put the basket on the table. "Go on now, while it's still hot. And wait until he's finished eating so you can bring back the basket." Emily eyed Cora, who turned back to the stove.

Rose chanced a peek at Emily, and she smiled back at the girl. "I'll tell you what, Rose, I'll come with you. I need to talk to your father, anyway."

The older woman spun to look at them both, her usually florid face even brighter. "Mrs. Becker, it's downright muddy out there with all the rain we've been having. You're likely to ruin your shoes. The mud will suck them right off your feet."

Emily stood and said, "I have a pair of overshoes upstairs that I'll put on. I'll be fine."

Cora tried again. "Rose can't wait for you. Luke's lunch will get cold."

"No, it won't. I'll just be a minute." Emily turned and dashed up the stairs in a most unladylike manner, worried that if she took too long, Cora would send Rose off at a gallop to get the child away from her. She was fully aware that Cora wanted to keep her separated from Rose, but she wasn't sure why.

Throwing open her trunk, she tossed things out right and left until she found a pair of fleece-lined arctics that she'd worn through the snows of Chicago. She kicked off her shoes, yanked on the boots, grabbed her shawl, and bounded back downstairs just in time to see Rose going out the door, the basket in hand.

"Here I am," she called. Rose cast a last, uncertain look at her grandmother, whose jaw appeared to be so tight, Emily expected to hear her teeth crack. "It'll be good to go for a walk."

The two set off down the path to the fields. The sun had braved its way through the overcast and the afternoon was warming up. Emily pushed her shawl from her shoulders.

Rose slogged alongside her, relapsed into her silence. Determined to draw her out, Emily asked, "Do you bring your father his lunch very often?"

"Only when he's real busy during planting and at harvest time."

Cora had overstated the mud. It was good to be outside

and away from the oppression of that house. "It was nice of your grandmother to fix him this basket," Emily exaggerated. "She takes good care of you both." She knew she was leading the girl and felt a twinge of guilt. But since no one had volunteered any information about the family, this seemed to be the only way to learn about them.

"Sort of. But Grammy doesn't like Daddy much."

Emily had already gotten that impression. "Really? Why not?"

"She says Daddy was a hell-hellion when he was younger. I don't know what that is exactly, but it sounds bad. Him and his friends were always in trouble for something. Grammy says Daddy was from the wrong side of the tracks, but I don't know what she's talking about. The train doesn't even come to Fairdale. Besides, he told me he grew up by the river. Grammy says she didn't want him to marry Mama because she had a *nice* man courting her, but Daddy chased him away."

Emily lifted her brows. She countered, "Well, your father seems like a nice man, too."

"Yeah, I guess. He used to be more fun. He's a lot different now since Mama died. For a long time afterwards he didn't talk much, and sometimes he'd sit at the kitchen table at night for hours and drink whiskey. Grammy would get mad at him about it, so he'd go upstairs to his bedroom and slam the door. Or he'd go out to the barn."

Suddenly, Emily felt that she was learning more than she should know. "Does he still do those things?"

"Once in a while." Rose shrugged and repeated, "He's not the same anymore. He used to make jokes and laugh more."

Emily heard a thread of wistfulness beneath Rose's

usual sullenness. What kind of life was that for a girl or for Luke himself, she wondered, and what could she do to change it? A wife's job, she knew, was to create a comfortable, peaceful home where her husband could shed the cares of his day. She was expected to rein in a man's coarser character, and to rear children who were well-behaved, quiet, and respectful. She had taught these values to scores of young women to prepare them to lead proper lives and keep proper homes. But she had no real practical experience. Although this was not a typical marriage, surely if she bore Luke Becker's name she should do more than act as a governess to Rose. How she'd go about it, though, with Cora holding court in the kitchen, she wasn't sure. No advice manual had ever talked about the circumstances in which she now found herself.

Up ahead, Luke and the plow team came into view. The April sun was gentle but his work was hot and hard. He'd rolled up his sleeves above his elbows, and she watched, fascinated, as the muscles in his arms flexed and stretched when he pulled on the reins.

Seeing them approach, Luke halted the team. After he fished out a dark blue handkerchief to swab his damp face and neck, he reached for the canteen slung by a strap over his shoulder. Pulling out the stopper, he tipped back his head and drank, his throat working with each swallow. For a moment, he seemed almost as big as the tall, broad-chested horses in front of him, and just as powerful. His sweat-stained shirt clung to his torso and was unbuttoned halfway down his chest. He lowered the canteen and their eyes met for a single, riveting moment. Emily slowed her pace and dropped her gaze, startled by her own visceral response.

This was not the frock-coated man who had met her at the dock yesterday, or the one who had written the spare but polite letters to Alyssa. It wasn't even the man who had rescued her from the henhouse. This man was earthy and very male, and looked like the type who would drink to intoxication at the kitchen table.

This was worse than she'd originally believed. Luke Becker would challenge her every day, forcing her to fight those unseemly thoughts and frightening feelings with which she struggled.

Risking another look at him in the sun, his dark, curly hair ruffled by the spring breeze, Emily drew a breath and stepped closer, determined to keep that dark corner of her heart under lock and key.

After all, a lady could do no less and still remain a lady.

CHAPTER FOUR

———

"WE DIDN'T FINISH OUR CONVERSATION ABOUT ROSE, Mr. Becker."

Luke sat on the seat of the disc harrow and gazed at Emily while he spooned Cora's stew into his mouth. He was surprised to see Emily out here in the fields, especially after her run-in with Cora's hens. After mulling it over, he'd known there was no getting around having a word with his mother-in-law after breakfast about the rotten trick she'd played on Emily. But as always, she'd turned huffy and defensive. Nothing, it seemed, was ever her fault.

She only meant to be helpful . . .

No one could take a joke . . .

It was only her opinion . . .

Everyone was so blamed sensitive . . .

Cora always had an answer, but none of them ever included an apology.

If he was surprised that Emily had come out here, he was even more surprised to see her with Rose. But it pleased him. Obviously, she'd already begun to take his daughter in hand and get her straightened up. The sensation of a weight being lifted from his shoulders was almost physical.

She stood beside him in the mud, with some funny

winter boots peeking out from the hem of her black dress and her shawl dangling on the crooks of her arms. Damn, she had green eyes, he noticed again, probably the greenest he had ever seen. But every time she turned them on him, he felt as if his shirt was on backward or his fly was unbuttoned.

"No, ma'am, but I was hoping you'd know what to do about Rose. That's why I married—that's what we talked about yesterday."

Emily got a pinched look, the same one he'd seen earlier today. "It isn't that I don't know what to do, Mr. Becker. I just want to find out if you have anything specific in mind for Rose's development."

Gripping the jar of stew between his knees, he tore off a hunk of bread from the loaf in the basket. "It's pretty simple. I want her to stop stealing, to have manners that wouldn't shame her mother, and to be happy. And I want to be able to stop worrying about those things because I've got this farm to run."

Out of earshot, Rose walked along the creek that edged the path, searching for ducks and ducklings. Looking at her, Luke thought his heart would break. God, she was so much like Belinda, not just in her face, but in her movements and gestures, too. Except for her ragamuffin appearance, it was as if he were seeing Belinda as a child. It only made him miss his wife more. "Just don't break her spirit," he added, almost to himself.

Emily lifted her nose. "Mr. Becker, I wouldn't dream of doing such a thing! I know that accepted teaching methods often include harsh tactics and even humiliation, but I do not subscribe to those ideas. You can't reach a child's mind through punishment and fear. Believe me, I know."

His gaze shifted back to Emily, his curiosity roused.

Was she speaking from a teacher's experience or her own? Kids could be cruel, he knew. So could adults, for that matter. Maybe in her past she'd been on the receiving end of teasing about her height. A girl like her would never blend in, no matter how hard she tried.

Nodding, he pulled off another hunk of bread. "Rose hasn't been the same since her mother d—" He still couldn't bring himself to say it aloud. "Since she lost her mother. When she's not in school she's usually with Cora or keeps to herself, and half the time I don't know what she's thinking." He threw the spoon into the basket. "Hell, I guess I hardly *ever* know what she's thinking. I don't know what makes her do things like she did yesterday."

Emily's face relaxed into a small, wry smile that made her plainness almost pretty. "Young girls' hearts are often mysteries to their fathers."

Screwing the lid back on the jar, he asked, "Did your father understand you?"

She glanced down at the toes of her boots, and a shadow seemed to cross her smooth brow. "My own father died when I was six. My stepfather and I weren't very close."

He gazed at Rose again, scampering along the creek bank, showing more enthusiasm than she'd let him see in quite a while. "I don't want that to happen to me and my girl."

Emily looked up again and considered him for a moment, as if assessing his worth as a man. He resisted the urge to shift on the seat of the harrow. "I'll try to see that it doesn't, Mr. Becker."

He met her eyes, then handed her the empty lunch basket. "Ma'am, would you mind taking this with you? I'd better get back to this field or it won't be finished."

"Surely." Turning, she called, "Rose, are you coming back with me?"

Rose looked up from the creek bank and shook her head.

"Then I'll see you at the house."

Luke watched as she turned to walk back to the house. She was fussy in her ways, and everything about her would discourage a man from doing more than tipping his hat. For his own part, Luke had always preferred women with more curve than angle. Emily was nothing but angles. She was graceful, though, he had to admit that, even if she was as tall and thin as a willow sapling. Maybe because of it.

But he hadn't married her for himself. He'd married her for Rose.

That night after dinner, Emily sat in the parlor with a slim volume of Elizabeth Barrett Browning's *Sonnets from the Portuguese* open on her lap. Rose and Cora had gone to bed and the house was quiet. The divan under her bore cushions with crocheted covers, and a pretty braided rug graced the hardwood floor. The glow of the lamp, with its lovely rose-painted shade, gave the room a warm hominess. It was peaceful here, with both Cora's voice and her kitchen noises silenced. Only the soft tick of the mantel clock broke through the night sounds of the wind rustling the boughs of the big oak just beyond the window.

Yet Emily felt as if she were not alone. A presence loomed here, just as it did in her own room and in other parts of the house. The presence was Belinda Becker. Not that Emily had seen her or even believed in ghosts. But the dead woman's spirit was kept alive and well by her family.

Cora took advantage of every opportunity to point out

something around the house that Belinda had made, or owned, or collected. Having just lost Alyssa, Emily thought she understood Cora's need to hang on to Belinda's memory. Yet she spoke almost as if Luke's first wife were not dead, but merely away. In fact, Emily had hesitated before coming into the parlor, worried that she might be trespassing on a sacrosanct memory by even using the room.

But this was her home now as well, and she would not be confined to her bedroom and the kitchen. Luke had promised her respect and a roof over her head—certainly the home should consist of more than just those two rooms. And as for the respect . . .

Her gaze dropped to the text on the page in her lap.

How do I love thee? Let me count the ways.

Emily traced over the words with her fingertip and sighed. Elizabeth Barrett had written these intensely personal sonnets about Robert Browning before eloping with him to Italy. Their courtship, which began with his correspondence to her when she was forty-two, had lasted two years. She had been frail and middle-aged when she found a love so great that it deserved a book of poetry.

I love thee to the depth and breadth and height
My soul can reach . . .

What must it feel like, Emily wondered, to love so deeply and to be loved in return? This was not the kind of question that she often allowed herself to ponder. It wasn't one of her *unseemly* thoughts—the ability to love and give love in return ennobled humankind. But when her mind ran down this path she usually became dispirited and her heart actually seemed to ache in her chest.

Things were difficult enough right now, she decided, without the added burden of melancholy. Closing the book with a clap, she glanced at the clock. It was nearly ten. She'd been waiting here for Luke to come in from the barn for more than an hour. He'd left right after dinner, and she remembered what Rose had told her about him skulking around out there. She had another question to ask him, one that she didn't want to put off. But following him to the barn, especially if he was in his cups, didn't seem like a good idea. Better that she should wait here. He had to come in eventually.

Just as the mantel clock began to toll the hour, she heard the kitchen door open. That was followed by the sound of footsteps that had become familiar to her already. Tucking the book in the crook of her arm, she went to meet Luke.

He was reaching to turn down the kitchen lamp when she walked in. "Mr. Becker—"

He jumped and whirled to face her. "Goddamn it to hell, don't sneak up on a man that way!" he snapped.

Her brows rose and her mouth tightened. "I didn't think I had." He looked, well, *unbuttoned* was the word that came to Emily's mind. His shirttail wasn't flapping but it was working its way loose. One strap of his suspenders was falling off his shoulder and stubble shadowed his jaw. He closed the back door, giving her a whiff of spring night breeze. "And there is no need to use such vulgar language."

"Sorry," he mumbled. "I just didn't expect to see you up this late."

"I was waiting for you to come back inside. I want to know about church tomorrow."

"Church?" He went to the sideboard and reached behind it, producing a dark brown bottle from what appeared to be a hiding place.

"Yes, tomorrow is Sunday. What time shall I be ready?"

He took a glass from the shelf and flopped into a chair at the table. "We don't go to church. Well, Cora goes in sometimes, but I don't."

"Really . . . I think it's important for Rose. Aside from the character-strengthening benefits, it's a good way for her to become part of the community, to be accepted, and to gain a sense of belonging." She watched as he pulled the cork from the bottle and poured a half-inch of whiskey into the glass.

Luke had been in church just twice in his life, the day he married Belinda and the day he buried her. There was nothing for him to be found there. To his way of thinking, a lot of the people—like Cora—who sat in those pews on Sunday, pretending to be good souls, were anything but the other six days of the week.

"If you want to take Rose, that's fine. But don't count on me going with you. Those hymn-singing old biddies don't want me there, either." He swallowed half the whis-key, feeling its kindly heat burn its way down his throat to his stomach. Some days, like today, when the bickering and complaining got to be too much, when the memories were too sharply focused, a drink or two was all that let him find sleep at night. It gave Cora something else to crab at him about, and now he felt Emily's disapproval radiating from her in icy waves. He didn't care.

"There's a pot of coffee still warm on the stove." She plucked a cup off the sideboard and filled it from the blue enamel pot. Putting it in front of him, she pulled out the chair opposite him and sat tentatively with her hands folded in her lap. The lamplight made her skin glow like fresh cream and gave her soft mouth the tint of crushed strawberries. Had anyone ever kissed that mouth? he wondered suddenly as he stared at it. Had a man ever broken through all that starch and etiquette to plant a big, moist kiss on the proper Miss Emily Cannon? He doubted it. And if he did, what would it feel like?

"Wouldn't you rather have coffee, Mr. Becker?" Her question interrupted his reverie. Jesus, what was he thinking of? She wasn't the kind of woman he wanted. Just daydreaming about kissing another woman seemed disloyal to Belinda's memory.

"No, ma'am, I would not. I'd rather have the whiskey." He saluted her with the glass and drained it. He poured another half-inch into the glass.

"I understand that you imbibe from time to time."

"Yes, I do, and I don't apologize for it. No offense intended, ma'am, but you're here to help Rose, not to reform me." A humorless chuckle rolled up from his chest. "I suppose Cora told you all about it." He took another drink.

Emily considered first the glass and then him. The instant of silence that fell between them seemed as wide as the river. "No, actually. Rose told me." She pushed back her chair and rose from the table. "Good night, Mr. Becker."

Luke sat stunned in the low lamplight, listening to her quiet footfalls as they traveled to the hallway and carried her upstairs.

The following morning, Emily took one last hurried glance at herself in the small mirror in her room. Her hair was in place and her dress wasn't so wrinkled that it would be noticed. Thank heavens it had stopped raining, or they would be soaked by the time they got to town.

Securing her hat with its pin, she deemed herself ready.

Earlier, she had roused the none-too-pleased Rose and told her to dress for church. Whether the girl had actually followed her instructions remained to be seen. Cora had grumped in the hallway at the news, but she hadn't had the nerve to muster a full-fledged complaint. After all, how could she object to Emily wanting to attend Sunday services? She had stomped back to her room to dress, muttering something under her breath about Mrs. Becker's blame-fool notions.

Taking her Bible from her bureau drawer, Emily grabbed her shawl and gloves, then went into the hall and stopped at Rose's doorway. She found the girl slumping on her bed in another horror of a flounced dress, wearing just one sock and no shoes. Her hair was an uncombed tangle.

"Come along now, Rose," she urged from the door. "We're walking to town and we've got to leave now to make it on time."

"Why do we have to go to *church*?" Rose demanded. "We never did before. I go to school—isn't that enough?"

Emily bustled in and snatched up a hairbrush from its resting place on the floor. "School feeds your mind. Church feeds your soul."

"I don't want my soul to eat. Is Grammy coming, too?" Rose pushed her bare foot into the other sock, but made no move to put on her shoes.

Emily took some passing swipes at Rose's long, shiny hair with the brush. "Yes."

The girl pulled away from her ministrations. "I'll bet Daddy doesn't have to go! And if he's not going, I don't have to."

"He's too busy with his chores, but he told me he wants you to go." She couldn't very well relate last night's conversation, so she hoped God would forgive her for the white lie she told. "Rose, for heaven's sake, put on your shoes. Where is your buttonhook?"

With great, gusty sighs and a lot of eye-rolling, Rose managed to find her buttonhook under the bed, finish dressing, and comb her hair. Emily kept her annoyance in check with a tight rein. It wouldn't do to snap at the girl again. In the hallway, she gave Rose an appraising glance. "You've forgotten your gloves."

Rose gave her a look as if she'd asked her to bring along a milk cow. "Gloves! I don't have gloves. Just mittens for when it snows."

Now Emily sighed. No gloves—she couldn't imagine going out without them. It simply wasn't done, just as one didn't walk barefoot through grass or sleep naked in the summer. Or any other time, for that matter. "Well, there's no time to worry about that now. We'll have to get you some later."

They went downstairs, Emily first, and Rose bringing up the rear with foot-dragging reluctance. In the kitchen, Cora put out a plate of cold biscuits.

"Don't we get breakfast?" Rose moaned.

Cora shot a look at Emily, then nodded at the plate. "Grab a biscuit. We'll have an early supper when we get back. For now, these will have to do." Her violet broadcloth dress was plainly one saved for church and special occasions—it looked as if she'd brought it out of storage. It bore the same suffocating ruffles with which she'd dressed Rose, and the purple shade clashed violently with her faded red hair.

Emily put on another forced smile. "Are we ready?"

"As ready as I'm going to be, Mrs. Becker."

Emily gritted her teeth every time Cora called her that.

Somehow she managed to convey sarcasm in what would ordinarily be a respectful form of address.

When Emily stepped out onto the back porch she saw the farm wagon, hitched and waiting. Even more surprising, she saw Luke himself beside the team, wearing the same dress clothes he'd worn when she'd met him, and looking far too handsome for her peace of mind. His dark hair ruffled in the morning breeze and caught sparks of sun, making it glint with chestnut and sable lights. Her heart felt as if it turned a somersault in her chest.

"Mr. Becker, you've changed your mind?"

He shrugged, "Yeah, well, I decided I could spare a morning. Anyway, I thought you could use a ride."

Emily turned to Rose. "There, you see? Your father *is* coming along."

Rose wore a sour expression but let him lift her to the back of the wagon where he'd set up two kegs for seats. In the meantime, Cora managed to heft her compact girth up to the seat next to Luke's place.

Luke shot her a frown, but Cora stared straight ahead and made no effort to move.

"I guess I'll join you, Rose," Emily said, trying to make light of the situation. Luke handed her up to the wagon bed and she took her place on the keg next to his daughter.

"Age before beauty, Mrs. Becker," Cora murmured to her as Luke came around the wagon. Emily could hear the sarcastic smirk in her words and her blood simmered. "Age before beauty."

Luke did his best to keep his mind on Reverend Ackerman's fairly gloomy sermon, but it wasn't easy, mostly because no one else was paying much attention to the man, either. From the moment they'd walked in, Luke felt all eyes turn toward him and his family. Heads bent to whisper and a general wave of murmuring swept over the little congregation in Fairdale Church. It was especially obvious because they were sitting in the back pew and people turned to stare, not only at him but at Emily, too. Why the hell had he let her shame him into coming along today? Even while he'd stood at his mirror knotting this strangling tie *again*—he'd worn the damned thing twice in three days—he kept telling himself that he wouldn't go, not even for Rose. That he wouldn't let prissy Emily Cannon and her prissy notions of gentility force him to get dressed up and go to church. But now here he was, and it felt every bit as awkward as he'd expected.

Beside him, Emily seemed to be far more at ease. She sat with her hands folded in her lap, serene and ladylike, and appeared not to notice all the curious gawkers. Only once did she lean over and whisper to Rose, he supposed to stop the girl's fidgeting. The pew was crowded, with the four of them wedged in next to Bob Cook's brood, and now and then Luke's thigh would brush against Emily's. The sensation shot right up his leg to—well, it didn't help keep his mind on whatever the minister was talking about. She smelled nice, too, like summer grass and clean wind.

Josiah Ackerman obviously sensed that his flock's attention was wandering because the volume of his voice kept increasing. From his pulpit, he insisted, "Our hunger will be sated, our thirst quenched. The Lord visits upon us sinners only those burdens that He knows we can bear, and gives us His grace to endure until we are finally returned to His loving arms." As far as Luke could tell, that meant life was miserable but a little better than completely hopeless.

Oh, hell, now Ackerman had everyone standing up to sing, just as he'd predicted. This whole thing was turning into flat-out torture, between his tie, and the staring, and Emily with her nice smell and long leg next to his. She opened a hymnal to share with him and took up the song. Her voice, clear and sweet, raised goose flesh on his arms and scalp. He didn't know the hymn very well, but Emily didn't even need to consult the text as she sang something about "a wretch like me." He didn't want to sing anyway. He'd rather listen to her. The sun streamed through the windows and caught her in an arch-shaped beam, lighting up her hair like spun gold. He didn't know much about God; he wasn't even sure he believed God existed. But if He did, Luke was pretty sure He could hear Emily this morning, and he doubted that God would consider her to be any kind of wretch. When the song ended, she glanced up and gave him a self-conscious smile that made him smile back.

At last, the minister took pity on them all and pronounced the benediction. There was a general milling toward the doors in the back, and Luke was anxious to get away before he got trapped by the busybodies who would probably give voice to the questions they'd formed during the service. He didn't look back as he edged toward the door—he just hoped that Emily, Rose, and Cora were right behind him.

But once he'd gained his freedom outside, he realized that they weren't with him and he found himself in the middle of a group of people.

"Luke! Luke Becker! I thought that was you." He knew that voice. He'd heard it under more intimate circumstances than these. Clara Thurmon hailed him from across the churchyard and he felt as if he'd been shot in the back during his escape attempt.

He turned to face the woman who, in her girlhood, had been reasonably attractive. But the last ten years had been less than kind to Clara—her pale mustache was a new addition, and her hair was already sprinkled with gray. She was as dull-looking as one of Cora's hens. Her nearly lashless eyes bore a brittle glint behind their spectacles.

"Uh . . . hi, Clara."

"What a happy surprise!" she chirped. "I never expected to see *you* at church. I'm glad that you've decided to break away from the farm and come into town." Her sharp gaze turned a bit coy, and she gazed at him from beneath her sparse lashes. "Does this mean we'll be seeing more of you? You know, we're having a basket social here next month to raise money for a new church roof. I organized it, so you know it'll be a big success." Clara never missed an opportunity to blow her own horn, a trait that had always irritated him.

"No, I brought Rose just for today—"

Clara looked at Cora and Rose, barely taking a breath in her monologue. "Isn't that one of Cora's nieces who came with you today? My, but she's a plain thing, isn't she?" She leaned closer then and put her hand on his arm. "Luke, say you'll come. Or better yet, just come to dinner. I still make the best fried chicken in Multnomah County. I know it would win the blue ribbon at the fair if I entered. Mother would be thrilled to see you, too, and it's time you came out of mourning for dear Belinda." Clara was one of the women who'd pursued him after his wife died.

"Really, Clara, I can't—" he tried, feeling badgered.

She tapped him on the arm again and brushed her shoulder against him. "Now, now, I won't take 'no' for an answer. We had some fun, you and I, back in the old days. I know what you need—a mother to take care of Rose and good woman to take care of *you*." She actually giggled and winked at him. "If you know what I mean."

God, this was worse than Ackerman's joyless sermon.

Two years older than Luke, Clara had never married and her desperation was as obvious as her blunt invitation. In his youth, he would have taken up her offer, just for the fun of it. Now he felt himself beginning to sweat inside his suit coat.

He glanced around, hoping to find Emily and Rose so they could leave. When he spotted them, they were standing with Cora and a group of other women nearby. He listened hard to hear their conversation over Clara's prattling.

"This is Emily, an etiquette teacher Luke found to tutor Rose," he heard Cora say. "It's a harebrained idea, if you ask me, but he didn't ask. He just went ahead and did it. I don't think it'll make one bit of difference to Rose which fork to use at the table."

There was some polite, confused murmuring among the women. "An etiquette teacher? But how nice for Rose."

"You'll be staying on for a while then?"

"Well, I live here now—"

"Are you hiring out to tutor other girls, too?"

"No, I'm not a tutor—"

Emily looked defenseless to Luke, with his mother-in-law doing her best to degrade Emily's position to that of a hired hand, or little better, a servant. "Actually, what Mrs. Hayward is trying to say is—"

His anger flared to life. Cora had done nothing to make Emily welcome since she arrived and he'd had just about enough of that. He strode toward the group, leaving Clara gawping at his abrupt departure. "Actually, what Cora should say is that Emily is my *wife*. We were married in town last week." He turned slightly toward Clara, whose mouth still hung open. "Clara Thurmon, this is Emily Cannon Becker." He took Emily's elbow and nodded at

Rose. "Farm chores won't wait for chatter. We'll be going now."

Emily rounded her shoulders and turned grateful eyes on him. Cora followed them in a fine huff—he knew the signs, and he knew he'd hear about this later. Rose brought up the rear. Word of Luke's news spread through the crowd like the buzzing of a beehive on fire. He hadn't intended to make an announcement like that, but his fuse was growing shorter each day with Cora. When they reached the wagon, this time Luke put Emily on the seat up front first. Then he handed Cora into the back of the wagon, and lifted Rose in last.

Once they were on their way, Emily watched the rooftops of Fairdale fall away as they climbed into the hills above. Everything looked fresh and green in the spring sun, and for the first time since coming here Emily felt a lightness of heart. Enduring the stares at church had been such agony, she'd almost become physically ill. She hated being the center of attention, and wished that she'd never suggested coming to church. But she'd called upon every lesson in graceful living that she'd ever learned and forced herself to appear as if she didn't notice. When the service was over, just when she thought she'd get away from the terrible scrutiny, Cora had dragged her to that group of women simply to insult her.

Then Emily had seen that woman hanging on Luke, touching his arm, bragging about her cooking, leaning closer to whisper something and giggle, and the spurt of jealousy it had kindled in Emily's chest astounded her. She had never been jealous in her life. Well, perhaps once or twice, especially when Father had compared her to delicate, beautiful Alyssa and found her wanting. This, today, had been different. She'd wanted to confront that woman, slap her hands off Luke, and tell her that her behavior was appalling.

But something had happened back there in that churchyard. Not only had Luke defended her against Cora's rudeness, he'd publicly announced their marriage. It was a simple statement—*Emily is my wife*—and yet to her, it held enormous implications that both frightened and pleased her.

As they bounced along in the wagon, her gaze kept straying to him beside her. She felt Cora's daggers in her back and wondered briefly if she would ever overcome the woman's unmistakable animosity. Mostly, though, she was more aware of Luke than ever. She'd felt his leg brush hers in the pew, even though she'd tried to pull away. He'd been impossible to ignore in the churchyard, tall as he was and better-looking than any other man present. And he was her *husband*. He'd said so. He'd told them all. He had willingly admitted that he was bound to her. This amazed her. She wanted to tuck her hand in the crook of his arm, to thank him for his chivalry. But she kept her hands firmly clasped in her lap and her mouth closed. Another wave of cold and heat shimmied through her, and her face felt fiery. Wouldn't it be nice if he were really her husband in more than just name? That was silly, of course. Emily had learned a long time ago that she was not worthy of love.

For now, the masquerade of marriage was good enough. Still, she fantasized, if they really were husband and wife, they would come to church on Sundays, perhaps attend a social or two. People would eventually stop staring when they got used to her being Emily Becker. There would be cozy dinners with the three of them, Emily, Luke, and Rose. She didn't even realize she'd cut Cora out of her daydream until she heard the woman's braying, satisfied hoot from the back of the wagon. She and Rose had been murmuring on the way home, but Emily hadn't paid much attention to the conversation.

"I guess that's how much good church did Rose," Cora said, her tone triumphant.

To hide her roiling emotions, she turned slightly to talk to the girl. "Why? What did you learn in church, Rose?" She almost feared she'd stolen money from the collection plate.

"God makes you suffer and then you die." The girl looked frightened.

Cora brayed again. "That's what your idea of going to church did for the girl, Mrs. Becker."

Why on earth would she think that was funny? Emily wondered. That was a horrible image for a child to have.

"Oh, dear, no, Rose! That's not true at all!" Emily countered, although she could understand why Rose might have gotten that impression from listening to Reverend Ackerman. And if Emily were to be honest with herself, she'd have to admit that she'd had the same thought many times in her life. "We'll talk about it later."

When they arrived home, Luke changed clothes to un-hitch the team and do some chores. Cora put on her apron and went outside to get a side of pork ribs from the smokehouse. Emily, buoyed by the fantasy of marriage she still carried in her mind's eye, stood in the kitchen and surveyed the room. The table needed something to dress up its plainness. Sunday dinner ought to be some-thing special, not just food flopped on the table with no style or grace. It was a time for family to come together. Rose lingered in the hallway, still dressed in her good clothes and looking forlorn. Blast that Cora Hayward for her insensitivity, Emily thought.

"Rose, I need your help. Do you know where to find

some wildflowers to put on the table? Like the pinks you brought to me?"

The girl scuffed her shoes across the floor. "Yeah, there are some lupines on the other side of the road."

"That would be perfect! Would you change your clothes and go gather a few stems?"

"Okay." She turned wide, dark eyes up to Emily. "Do you think that Grammy is right about God?"

Recognizing the sensitive subject, Emily asked, "What did she say?"

"She says that God doesn't answer prayers. That if He did, my mama never would have married Daddy, that she never would have died, and that—that, well . . ."

"It's all right, Rose," she urged gently. "Go on."

"She says you never would have come here. She says talking to God is a blame-fool waste of time and that a body might as well talk to the wall."

Yes, that sounded like Cora, all right, Emily thought. Bitter and autocratic. "Do you ever talk to God?"

"Sometimes," the girl answered, but she looked as if she were admitting a guilty secret.

"And does He answer you?"

"No—at least I don't think so. Daddy still doesn't laugh and things around here aren't fun anymore. Maybe Grammy *is* right."

"But does it make you feel better to tell God your troubles?"

Rose looked up at her with tear-damp eyes, and Emily's heart ached. "Yes."

"Then it's not a waste of time. Believe me, Rose, God hears you. It's just that sometimes the answer doesn't come right away. Or sometimes the answer is simply *no*."

"It is?"

"Yes. No one gets everything they want." Emily was

well-acquainted with that fact. She wanted to take Rose
into her arms and give her the affection she seemed to be
missing. But Emily sensed that it might not be welcome
just yet. "You just keep on talking to God, if you want.
And if you want to talk to me, I'll listen, too."

"Okay."

Emily gave her a big smile. "Now run and get your
clothes changed, and find those flowers for me. I'm counting on you."

Rose smiled, too. "I'll bring back the biggest ones out
there."

While Rose was gone, Emily went to the sideboard and
found a lovely cutwork tablecloth and napkins with which
she set the table. Obviously, the tablecloth hadn't been
used in a long time, perhaps years. It bore sharp creases
from sitting in the drawer and smelled of the lavender
sachet tucked into the corners. Emily tried to smooth the
fold lines with her hands, but they were too well estab-
lished. It seemed a shame not to use something so pretty
for special occasions. As she put a napkin at each place
setting, she dreamed of doing this every Sunday. They
could go to church, have a real Sunday dinner with nice
table linen and flowers. In the summer, they could even
have dinner outside, she and Luke and Rose—

This pleasant reverie was interrupted when Cora came
back into the kitchen, clutching the pork to her chest. She
let out a shrill squawk louder than the caterwauling of all
her hens combined. Her eyes were wide and staring, and
she pointed at the table with her free hand. Like a specter
from a nightmare, she squawked again, raising the hair on
Emily's scalp.

"Wh-what?" Emily stuttered.

"How *dare* you?" Cora raged.

Rose came running through the back door, grasping the

stems of wild lupines. Their purple blossoms were a sharp contrast to her pale hand. She followed the direction of her grandmother's gaze and sucked in her breath as well.

"How dare you touch Belinda's belongings?" She threw the pork ribs into the galvanized steel sink and pumped water over her hands. After throughly lathering them with soap and rinsing again, she dried them, and carefully removed the napkins one by one. Then she took up the tablecloth, refolded it following the crease lines that Emily had tried to press out, and laid the linen back in the drawer as though it were a holy relic. All the while, Emily stood by, feeling both foolish and angry, and knew that her face was the color of a rooster's comb.

"I'm sorry—I didn't know—it's so beautiful I thought . . ."

"It's pretty plain that you didn't think at all!"

Luke came up the back stairs in time to hear Cora's last remark. *God, now what?* he wondered. He wanted to turn around and go out to the fields. But that would be the coward's way out and he knew it. So he walked in, and the tableau in front of him was fraught with tension. Cora glared at Emily, Rose stood like a statue gripping some flowers, and Emily looked as if she'd been caught stealing.

"What's going on here?"

"Your *wife* put out Belinda's best tablecloth and napkins, that's what! We never use her things!"

Luke had been fighting this for more than a year now. Cora had turned the house into a shrine to Belinda, making certain that the wound of their grief would never heal. He'd tried several times to put their wedding picture into a bottom drawer of his dresser, hoping that if he didn't have to look at it every day, the weight on his heart might lighten. He'd also put away her vanity set that lay next to the photograph. Each time, Cora had searched for everything and put it all back on top of the dresser while he was working outside. Finally, he'd given up.

"Cora, for God's sake, it doesn't matter that much."

"Doesn't matter!" Her face turned as red as a gobbler's. "I guess I'm the only one around here who has any respect for Belinda's memory."

Luke's stomach tied itself into a tidy knot. That had been happening more often lately, with the friction in the house increasing every day. It had begun long before Emily arrived and had only grown worse since. For the first time since Cora had moved in, Luke allowed himself to consider what life would be like if his mother-in-law went back to her own home. For three years, he'd been doing double work, keeping up his own land and tending her property, too. He'd done it gladly, knowing that having Cora here was best for Rose. But things were different now with Emily here. Two women in one kitchen could be bad business. He didn't know if Alyssa would have been a better match for this or not. But it was exactly the kind of thing he didn't want to think about. He knew how to grow crops and tend stock. This business with females locking horns made him wish he could escape to a chore in the barn.

He knew he couldn't.

He'd brought Emily Cannon here, for better or for worse, and he had to stand by his decision. He couldn't let Cora Hayward run roughshod over her; he owed her what he'd promised. His respect and protection. And he wanted his home and his daughter back.

"Damn it, Cora, you know that isn't true. We'll never forget Belinda." He held out his hands in an open appeal. "How could we? But she's been gone for three years now. I don't see anything wrong with using her tablecloth."

Cora put her hands on her hips. Strands of faded red hair had escaped the tight confines of her bun and hung from her temples. "Oh, you don't! Well, if you're going to put my daughter's memory aside, you can do without me, too!"

"What are you talking about?"

"I'll just go back to my own place and you can see how you'll get along without me."

Luke sighed. He'd anticipated this threat and he was tired of being held hostage by it. He knew Cora expected him to back off and beg her to stay. It was a dance they'd done several times before. But not this time, by God. Not this time.

He straightened and looked her dead in the eyes. "Cora, if you want to go home, I won't try to stop you."

"Who'll do the cooking and cleaning and mending?" She jabbed a thumb in Emily's direction. "Your etiquette teacher? Hah! I don't think so. She can't even gather eggs without breaking them."

He glanced at Emily, whose face was now as white as paste. He didn't know if she could do any of the things Cora talked about. "We'd manage just fine. Life is too short to be unhappy, and if you're unhappy here, maybe you'll get on better in your own house."

Cora dropped her hands to her sides, plainly flummoxed by this turn of events. "Well! It—it sounds like you've been planning this all along—"

"I hate it when you fight!" Rose sobbed suddenly. Her gaze shifted quickly between Emily, the flowers in her hand, and Luke. Then she ran to her grandmother and hid her face against her ample bosom. "Daddy, don't make Grammy leave. Grammy, please don't go!"

That was all that stopped Luke from carrying the conversation any further.

"There, there, Rose, honey. I'm not going anywhere," Cora soothed. She glanced up at Luke over Rose's head and sent him a knowing smile. "I'm staying right here."

The knot in Luke's stomach gave another twist. Maybe she was staying—for now—but things were going to change around here. He couldn't expect Emily to make any headway with Rose if she had Cora trying to cross her up at every single turn.

Emily was his wife, just as he'd told everyone in the churchyard. He didn't love her and she wasn't the woman he would have chosen for himself. But they couldn't continue this way, with Cora holding court like a queen while the rest of them danced to her tune. There would be some serious talk tonight after Rose went to bed.

"I'll be in the barn—one of the horses is coming up lame. Call me when dinner is ready," he said. Then with a last look at Emily, and Rose sobbing in Cora's arms, he went outside.

"Grammy, why don't you like Miss Emily?"

"I didn't say I don't like her." Cora made the paring knife fly as she peeled potatoes at the kitchen table. The new Mrs. Becker had gone upstairs, and she doubted they'd see her again for hours. "She just has no business going through other people's belongings. You'd think she'd know with all that fancy etiquette she keeps talking about."

"Well, then why don't you like Daddy?"

"I like him well enough," Cora lied.

Rose had pulled her chair close and sat watching her as she worked. "But you act like you don't. You say bad things about him."

"He wasn't the man I wanted your mama to marry."

"I know, but he did, and that was a long time ago."

Cora carved off a peeling a yard long, all in one piece, and threw it into a bucket. It was a silly talent, but privately she was proud of her ability to peel a potato or an apple or a turnip in one long ribbon. She'd bet Mrs. Becker couldn't do that. She picked up another potato. "I'll explain more when you're older. But for now, I'll just say that I can't forget Luke is the reason your mama died."

She felt Rose's eyes on her, big and disbelieving. "Wh-what do you mean?"

"That's enough for you to know now." She gestured at her with the paring knife. "You just remember, Rose—no one in this house loves you as much as I do. No one."

CHAPTER FIVE

THE NEXT SEVERAL DAYS WERE FILLED WITH TENSION IN
the Becker household. Emily loathed the hours when Rose
was gone to school and Luke worked in the fields. That
left her in the house with Cora, a woman plainly determined not to accept Emily's presence as anything other
than that of an unwelcome guest. At least there had been
no more ghastly scenes like the one on Sunday after
church. But that was probably because Cora had simply
stopped speaking to her.

Although Emily should be the lady of the house, she
knew she wasn't. Her position was such an uncomfortable
one. She had no right to rearrange the parlor furniture, or
plan meals, or do any of the things other wives did. Since
she didn't know which items around the house had belonged to Belinda, she was afraid to touch anything outside of her own room. And even there, the dead woman
had left her mark.

One morning following breakfast, while Cora was in
the yard beating the dust out of the hall runner and Luke
worked in the front yard mending a section of fence, Emily climbed the stairs to get her sewing basket. Her hem
had come loose in one spot and she knew if she didn't
fix it right away, the rest of it would soon follow. As she
walked toward her room, she passed her husband's closed

bedroom door. She had never seen the room and she let
her curiosity get the better of her manners. Of course, such
snooping was an intolerable breach of etiquette. But was
it really so bad to investigate the home that was now hers?
As she gripped the knob, her heart climbed to her throat
and she glanced up and down the hall, feeling like a thief.
From outside, she heard the steady *thump-thump-thump*
of Cora's rug beater, reassuring her that she was alone in
the house. Quickly, she opened the door, slipped inside,
and closed it again. Taking a couple of deep breaths, she
waited for her hammering pulse to slow. At last she turned
to look around.

The room was not as bright or as large as hers. In fact,
it seemed as spare as the plain cells that Mrs. Wheaton
had let to her boarding students, and the furniture was
almost as simple. The view from the single window over-
looked the front yard, where she saw Luke. As if feeling
her eyes on him, he looked up at the same time. She
jumped behind the curtain, her heart bumping around inside her chest again, like a bee trapped in a jar. God, what
would he think, what would he *do* if he knew she'd tres-
passed on this sanctum? Peering at him from the curtain,
watching as he worked—he pulled the wire fencing so
tight that the muscles in his arms stood out in sharp relief—she at last felt satisfied that he hadn't really seen
her in the window. The voice of common sense, the one
she'd always listened to, told her that she ought to just
leave now, while her crime was still undiscovered and her
sin not yet too bad. But the curiosity that had led her here
in the first place silenced the voice and she remained.

It seemed odd that hers, a seldom-used guest room,
would be nicer than that of the master of the house. The
bed was big, though, and took up most of the floor space.
In the corner stood a straight-backed chair with a dirty

pair of coveralls and a shirt thrown over it. She stepped deeper into the room and stretched a tentative hand toward the quilt.

Luke slept here. This was where he lay at night. What sweet memories and private demons visited his dreams? Did she, Emily, ever cross his mind? No, of course she wouldn't—it was foolish of her to even ponder the question. Her fingers trailed up to the pillow, where his head would rest. Did he lie sleepless and watch a shaft of moonlight cross the wall, as she sometimes did, reviewing the regrets of his past and fearing the uncertainty of the future? Were there nights that seemed to have no end, nights when he longed for love as she did? Or was he content to live with the memory of what had once been? She smoothed the fabric with her hand, then leaned over and inhaled the scent of him on the pillow. It was clean and male and familiar. Now she would think of him, just one door away from her, with only a single wall separating them in the darkness . . .

The depth of intimacy this image evoked scalded her cheeks, and she snatched her hand away as if she'd stroked his brow in his sleep instead of merely touched the pillowcase.

Turning from the bed, she faced the dresser, a simple oak piece upon which stood some personal items: an alarm clock, a razor, a woman's vanity set consisting of a carved cherry hairbrush and a hand mirror, and a small, silver-framed photograph. Emily picked it up. She recognized the handsome, unsmiling young man in the picture as Luke. Next to him stood a wedding-gowned girl. So this was Belinda, the woman who had such a grip on the hearts of those under this roof. In the photo, they both looked stiff and fixed. Still, there was a gleam of joy and hope that shone in Luke's eyes that even the requirements of photographic portraiture could not dim. Emily's heart contracted a bit—she had never seen that look in his eyes. Life, it seemed, had washed away those emotions and left behind the man she knew now. But plainly, the dark-haired beauty who'd stood beside him that day—and Belinda had been lovely, there was no doubt—had given him a spark of inner fire that Emily wondered if she would ever see.

She heard the back door open and slam downstairs and she jumped, feeling as guilty and dishonorable as she had when she'd read Luke's last letter to Alyssa. Footsteps on the kitchen floor, accompanied by her husband's tuneless whistling, paralyzed her momentarily. Quickly, she replaced the photograph on the dresser and eased open the door, her heartbeat thudding in her ears. Then she stepped into the hall and closed it with a quiet *click*, feeling downhearted and wicked rather than enlightened by her exploration.

That afternoon, Emily dressed as carefully as she would have for a shopping excursion in Chicago and set out for town with her small market basket. She needed to buy ammonia and castile soap to make the cleaning cream for her dress. She was surprised that Cora had neither in the house—how did she clean spots from the family's clothes? Of course, it was possible that Cora had simply denied having the supplies on hand. Emily knew it was an unworthy thought, but considering the strain between them she couldn't stop the notion from creeping into her mind. Anyway, it would be good to get away from the stifling atmosphere.

She hoped the druggist carried what she needed, and that she could avoid going into the general store.

The mile walk into Fairdale gave Emily a different perspective of the countryside than she'd gotten while riding in the farm wagon. The mild spring day was filled with the scents of freshly turned earth, new greenness, and the air was clear and full of the tang of spring. The sun cast short shadows on the road, and along the way she paused to watch lambs capering among a herd of fleecy sheep.

Life here moved at a much slower pace than she was accustomed to. In Chicago, housewives with busy households kept strict schedules. They had at-home days when they entertained visitors with teas and luncheons, and those days when they themselves called on others and attended the sick. Many were involved in church and social-welfare activities, and still had the responsibility of raising their children and maintaining their most important domain, the home, as a sanctuary for their world-weary husbands. Here, though, everyone worked and was busy from dawn to dark, the rhythm of days and seasons seeming to govern life more than did the clock or social status.

On the one hand, she found her surroundings as alien as if she'd been dropped into a foreign country; nothing in her training had prepared her for this. And yet . . . yet there was something appealing about living closer to the land, where putting on different clothes for morning and afternoon was never thought of. But twenty-eight years of ingrained social habits were as much a part of her as her eye color or the cowlick she struggled to tame every day—she wasn't likely to change now. Regardless of those rebellious, risqué thoughts she sometimes entertained.

Just as the road began its last descent into town, a cemetery came into her view. Emily wondered why she hadn't noticed it before. Perhaps because it sat on a gently sloping hillside, and spread out below was a breathtaking vista of the river that eclipsed the burying ground. Only

two or three trees interrupted the view. Too, compared to
the imposing granite angels and large family tombs in
Chicago's cemeteries, these grave markers were modest.
It was a well-tended place, though, and she supposed it
would only be proper to go inside the low iron fence to
find and pay her respects to the grave of the woman whose
spirit lived on in the Becker house. She lingered at the
gate, her gloved hands gripping two of the iron pickets.
Somewhere in the breeze-blown trees a finch twittered a
plaintive song. Emily hesitated. She'd spent years in the
shadow of the paragon that had been her sister, but she
had loved Alyssa with all her heart. The woman she now
apparently did not measure up to she would never know,
yet Belinda was honored like a saint. She closed her left
hand into a fist to feel her wedding band press against the
flesh of her little finger.

Perhaps she was being small, Emily thought, but she
turned away from the graveyard and kept walking.

"Clara, what do you think of Luke Becker marrying that
beanpole of a woman?"

Emily halted outside the open door to Fran Eakins's
general store, riveted to a spot beside a barrel that held a
bouquet of corn brooms. To her distress, the druggist's
shop had been closed and now she was forced to come to
one of the last places in town where she wanted to be.
Based on what she'd just heard, her trepidation was not
unfounded. Her heart sank. She didn't want to go into the
store—the memory of Fran Eakins's angry display in the
sandwich shop was fresh in Emily's mind. But Fairdale
was small and there weren't a lot of merchants to choose
from. Her dress needed cleaning and there was no other
way she knew of to get the job done. She'd have to deal

with Fran again. Recognizing the shopkeeper's voice, she waited to hear a response.

"I was shocked, just shocked. God in heaven, however did Luke choose such a gangling bluestocking? And when did he meet her? I never saw her in town before last Sunday."

"*I* did," Fran answered in a vinegary voice. "I saw her the day she came in on the boat from The Dalles. I knew Luke was up to something months ago. He'd been getting letters from some female in Chicago. They smelled of rosewater and were written in a fancy hand on fancy paper. I guess they were from *her*. She's pretty full of herself, from what I could tell, with her yapping about manners and all."

"If he wanted a mother for Rose, he should have chosen a woman here in Fairdale. One who knows how to take care of a man."

"You, for instance?" Emily heard an unmistakable bristling tone.

"Why not? Luke and I knew each other before he ever married Belinda. And we were more than just polite friends, I can tell you. If ever there was a man who knew exactly how and where to pleasure a woman—well, Luke didn't get his reputation as a ladies' man for nothing. Those big hands of his can be very gentle—For all his wild ways, I could have had him in a minute if Belinda hadn't gotten into trouble first." Clara Thurmon sounded both confident and annoyed. "So he had to marry her instead."

This bit of information surprised Emily—if it were true, she thought. She remembered the woman hanging on Luke after church, her manner far too familiar for Emily's liking.

"Well, if I were his wife," Fran said, "I'd keep him on

a short chain and make sure he didn't go around *pleasuring* anyone but me. And I'd take that little brat Rose in hand mighty quick. A few nights locked in her room without supper would teach her not to steal and pull pranks."

That was as much as Emily could listen to. Was everyone in this benighted town rude and snide? she wondered. Or perhaps it was just the women. Never in her life had she heard such a crude discussion between two females.

She strode into the store with her shoulders back and her head high, the same posture she'd used on the first day of classes every year at Miss Wheaton's. "Good afternoon, *ladies*."

Clara Thurmon flushed scarlet, emphasizing her mustache, and she exchanged guilty looks with Fran Eakins. Emily knew they were wondering how much she'd overheard, and she got frank enjoyment from watching Clara squirm. Fran, however, stuck out her chin, a clearly belligerent stance.

"Mrs. Becker," Fran acknowledged in much the same tone that Cora used. "What a surprise."

"A rather unpleasant one, I gather, Miss Eakins, from what I heard outside." Emily's heart thundered in her chest and she kept her hands at her sides because she knew they were shaking. She could feel her market basket trembling against her leg. She hated confrontations and usually did her best to avoid them. But just because she had to put up with Cora Hayward's rudeness didn't mean she had to accept it from strangers. Her marriage to Luke was none of their business.

Now Fran blushed as well, and one of her caterpillar brows began to twitch. Clara, wall-eyed behind her spectacles, stood rooted to the floor like a deer caught in a hunter's sights and chewed her lower lip.

Emily forged ahead, her tone businesslike and no-

nonsense. Regardless of what Fran Eakins thought of her, she suspected the woman would not pass up the opportunity to make money. "I need a bottle of ammonia and some castile soap, if you please." The air was electric with mutual disapproval, and Emily thought she could actually smell Clara Thurmon beginning to sweat through her clothes.

"I can't add anything more to Luke's account until he comes in to settle up," Fran announced, her nose rising a notch.

Emily had spent most of her years unnoticed, moving across the backdrop of others' lives, and she had never been the object of such overt hostility. Thank God what little money she had, she carried with her now. "I am paying for my purchases today."

Outflanked, Fran folded her mouth into a flat line but said nothing more. She turned to the floor-to-ceiling shelves behind the counter that held jars, boxes, bottles, and packages of all sizes, types, and colors. When she put a pint of ammonia and the soap on the counter, she said, "That'll be sixteen cents."

Emily glanced at the jar of hard candy sitting on the counter, priced at five for a penny. "I'll take five of the strawberry drops, too." She searched her coin purse and counted out three nickels and two pennies. Then she put her purchases into her basket and started to leave. Hesitating a moment, she turned and faced the two women again.

"After you two return to your kennels this evening, I hope you'll reflect on your appalling rudeness while you're gnawing on your dinner bones and baying at the moon."

Clara released the grip her teeth held on her lip and

her jaw fell open. Fran looked as surprised as if Emily had rapped her knuckles with a ruler.

Emily sailed to the door, certain that her face was as red as the other women's. It was the worst thing she had ever said to anyone in her life.

And for the moment, it felt wonderful.

The energy that Emily's anger generated carried her out of town and up the hill toward the farm at such a fast clip that she began to grow breathless. She'd even overtaken some children who laughed and ran with the joy of being released from the confines of school on such a fine spring afternoon. By the time she neared the cemetery again, she was gasping for air and had to stop. While she agreed with physicians that a corset laced too tightly was dangerous to a woman's health, fashion and modesty required that she wear one. She wore hers more loosely than some women did, but it didn't permit a lot of physical exertion. She sat down on a boulder beside the road and concentrated on taking even breaths. Reaching into her pocket, she pulled out a black-edged handkerchief and dabbed at her damp temples and upper lip.

Now that she'd walked off some of her temper, she couldn't believe she'd said that terrible thing to Fran Eakins and Clara Thurmon. After tiptoeing around Cora Hayward and pretending to ignore her sarcasm, Emily supposed her ladylike fuse had burned down to a nubbin. But a true lady was supposed to ignore gossip and rise above insults. Indeed, she was not even supposed to acknowledge that she'd heard them. Still, a private smile turned up the corners of her mouth when she remembered the looks on their faces, and in her heart she was glad that she'd rebuked those two harridans. Why should they care that Luke had married her?

Gangling bluestocking.
Beanpole.

Neither Fran nor Clara were great beauties. Fran's brows were so dark and heavy they almost joined over the bridge of her nose to create one long horizontal line. And if Emily had the kind of facial hair that Clara did, she'd seriously consider learning to use a razor. But both women were small and fine-boned, advantages that Emily did not have.

So far, her impression of Fairdale's citizens was rather negative, although she'd met a couple of nice women at church, despite Cora's deliberate attempt to mislead them about her status with the Becker family. Would she ever be able to make friends here? she wondered. Were people everywhere so shallow that they judged a person's worth solely on their appearance? God above, one would think she had a hump on her back and a sign hanging from her neck that read "Too ugly to live."

Once more, unbidden, the image of her grandmother's bridal veil rose in her mind. Although she knew it was silly, she still held the childlike belief that the veil possessed magical powers that would transform her, plain and gawky Emily Cannon, into a graceful and lovely woman. Even though she'd hoped to wear it at her wedding, she had feared trying it on in case it might not be true. Since she was already married, in name anyway, she'd never really know. She sighed—perhaps it was just as well. Her heart might not withstand the disappointment.

She glanced at the watch pinned to her bodice and realized the day was waning. Now that her breathing had slowed again, Emily rose from her hard seat and turned toward home. She hoped to clean her dress before dinner so that it would have a chance to dry overnight.

As she passed the cemetery, she spotted a small, familiar figure sitting on one of the graves beneath an elm tree. The coffee-colored braids, both coming loose, and the flounced calico dress gave away the child's identity even though Emily couldn't see her face.

She entered the enclosed burial ground, passing small headstones that bore carvings of lambs and angels, of lilies and crosses, and approached Rose quietly, not wanting to startle her. The wind carried the fresh scent of the river to these highlands, helping to dispel the lonely gloom of the graveyard. Then Emily picked up the thread of a one-sided conversation. She knew she was eavesdropping on a very personal moment, but she couldn't pull herself away and didn't want to interrupt. Rose sat cross-legged, tracing the carved letters of her mother's name with her fingertip while she spoke.

". . . don't know why Grammy acts that way. She doesn't have anything good to say about her, Mama. She didn't want Daddy to marry her. I guess I didn't, either. She's not as pretty as you were and—and I still miss you so much. I'm lonesome without you." Here her voice quavered with a forlorn longing that made Emily's heart rise to her throat and form an aching knot. She knew what it was to lose a mother and to be lonely. "But Miss Emily smells good, and she knows about things like tapestries and God. She tries to help around the house and Grammy gets mad—a few days ago, she even said she was going to leave." Rose related to the headstone the commotion about the tablecloth and began sobbing in earnest. "I hate it when Daddy and Grammy fuss at each other! And it just keeps getting worse. They act like they don't love each other. I don't know what's going to happen."

Emily's heart twisted. She wanted to draw Rose into her arms and comfort her, to reassure her. But she couldn't do that without revealing that she'd listened in.

Besides, who was she to reassure anyone? She was as uncertain and insecure as Rose. Probably more so. Her sole advantage was her age—being an adult didn't render one's heart unbreakable, but with years and experience, hers had acquired a harder shell. She realized the only way out of this situation was to back away and make her presence known from outside the fence. Quietly, she stole back to the entrance and acted as if she'd just now come by. "Rose, is that you?" she called.

The girl whirled to look at her, eyes streaming and nose red.

"I'm just on my way back from town." Emily stepped inside the fence and approached her. "Would you like to walk home with me? It must be uncomfortable sitting on that wet grass." Her offer sounded inadequate to her own ears—how must it sound to a child with a broken heart? She held out her hand and gave her a tentative smile. "I'd like your company."

Rose glanced at Belinda's headstone one more time. She didn't take Emily's hand, but she nodded and picked herself up. The back of her calico skirt bore a big damp spot, and a few of last fall's dead leaves and twigs stuck to it. She brushed at it futilely as they walked toward the road. Her stockings sagged around her ankles and she wiped her nose on her sleeve. "I was just . . . sometimes I stop by to see my mama on the way home from school."

Emily adjusted the basket on her forearm. "I went to see my sister one last time before I left Chicago to come out here. It was hard to say good-bye because I don't know if I'll ever see her grave again. It's nice that you can visit here, once in a while." She put a little emphasis on the last part of the sentence. If Rose came here too often, she would be no better off than Cora with her refusal to let Belinda's memory rest in peace.

Rose snuffled and dragged her nose across her sleeve again. Emily cringed, but refrained from asking a teacher's automatic question: Where was the girl's handkerchief?

"No one knows about it."

Emily looked down at the dark, downturned head. "Knows about what? That you come to the cemetery?"

Rose nodded.

"Why? You don't think your father or grandmother would mind, do you?"

"No. Just that it's my secret between me and Mama."

Emily understood. She was beginning to believe that Rose thought she had no one to turn to. Emily knew that Luke loved his daughter, and Cora, unpleasant harpy that she was, loved her, too. But neither of them seemed to really know how she felt. Well, Luke had freely admitted that, but she'd thought that Cora was closer to Rose. "Kind of like talking to God?"

"Yeah, sort of." Rose watched a flock of geese pass overhead, honking as they winged their way toward a distant pond.

"I still miss my own parents. My father died when I was a very little girl, younger than you are. Then my mother remarried a nice man, Mr. Cannon." Well, he had been nice enough, and he hadn't treated Emily badly. But she'd always known that he didn't love her. Alyssa had been the one he doted upon.

"And your mama?" Rose asked.

Emily swallowed. "There was a fire . . . she passed away about nine years ago." She couldn't think about it anymore today. If she did, she might actually break down in front of Rose. She understood a child's grief, and she would offer support to Rose in any way that she could. Still, for years she'd struggled to keep her emotions under control, to bury her own grief and not look back. Social custom put a great premium on the rituals of mourning and Emily had followed them unstintingly. But she felt so alone here, so friendless, that to ponder her losses would undermine her strength. She changed the subject. "How was school today?"

Rose gave her a sidelong look. "I got in trouble." The word *again* seemed to hang between them, unspoken but implied.

"Why? What did you do?"

"I pounded the tar out of Billy Reed."

"Mercy!" Emily stopped in her tracks and stared at small, delicate Rose. She couldn't hide her alarm this time. "You fought with a boy? Whatever would make you do such a thing?"

Rose stopped, too, apprehension crossing her small features. "He said my dress looks like I got it from a carnival sideshow."

"Oh, dear." Billy Reed was right, in Emily's opinion. Belinda's skill with the needle must not have come from Cora. Rose was a beautiful little girl, but the woman dressed her in the most ghastly costumes, and they were so poorly made—seams crooked, hems fraying, and ruffles, ruffles, ruffles. The dresses looked as if a child had sewn them. Emily's heart went out to Rose—enduring merciless teasing as a youngster had been a daily occurrence for her as well. She could almost understand why Rose had reacted as she had. In her girlhood, she, too, had been dressed in well-made but unflattering clothes. Alyssa had gotten the pretty colors and enhancing styles. Robert Cannon had felt that considering her size, the less attention Emily drew, the better. So Alyssa had gone about as pretty as a flower, while Emily had worn the plumage of a plain brown wren.

Still, Emily couldn't condone Rose getting into a physical fight over it. She started walking again, and the girl followed, scuffing her shoe against a rock in the road.

"Rose, ladies don't even acknowledge that kind of insult. And they certainly don't engage in fisticuffs."

"Yeah, that's what my teacher Miss Simmons said, too. But she didn't make *him* stand in the corner like I had to. Why should he get away with saying those bad things? How come I can't stick up for myself?"

Emily was about to recite a platitude regarding forbearance and propriety, then recalled her own experience earlier with Fran Eakins and Clara Thurmon. Why, indeed? Why should a person have to pretend that she was as insensate as a lamp or a doorknob when others made rude or unkind remarks, or played cruel tricks? She realized the path of her thoughts. God above, she was questioning the very principles that she had clung to for years. For a moment, Emily's orderly, idealized world tilted sharply. Then it righted itself again.

"But Rose, if we 'pounded the tar' out of everyone who said a bad thing, what would happen to us all? We would have chaos and constant wars."

"Well, maybe it would teach 'em not to talk that way and then everyone would be nice."

For a moment, she thought that Rose might have a point. Reconsidering, she eyed the girl. "Do you remember how you talked about me the first day we met?"

The corner of Rose's mouth turned down but she said nothing.

"I let it pass, didn't I? We have to live together in a civilized manner."

"So I just have to let Billy say those things?"

"When people like Billy Reed or Fran—like Billy Reed

break the rules we live by, they suffer far more than we do."

Rose's dark eyes glinted up at her, disbelief written in them as plainly as the letters carved on her mother's headstone. Even worse, for the first time, in her secret heart Emily doubted her own words. There was no comfort in the hollow bromide and she knew it. She tried another approach.

"What do you think your father would say about what you did?"

Rose's head came up. "You won't tell him, will you?"

"I guess that means he wouldn't like it, either."

Her shoulders drooped. "No."

"I won't tell him. But maybe you should."

She pondered this, then replied, "No, I don't think so. Daddy is unhappy enough."

Emily's heart gave another little twist in her chest. How much of Luke's unhappiness was she herself responsible for?

"Here." She reached into the basket on her arm. "I seem to remember that you have a sweet tooth." She smiled at Rose and handed her one of the strawberry drops. "But please, promise that you won't get into any more fights. It's just plain wrong. And you could get hurt, you know."

The sage-green Becker farmhouse came into view ahead, and Rose started to scamper toward it. "Naw, I'm bigger than Billy."

Despite her worry and disapproval, Emily felt a bubble of laughter rise in her chest that she knew she had to suppress. She couldn't very well encourage Rose's behavior.

The girl ran ahead a bit, then stopped and turned. "Thank you for the candy, Miss Emily." She was off again like a tree swallow, lithe, agile, and full of energy.

For the second time since she'd come to Fairdale, Emily's heart felt lighter. She smiled at the pretty little girl with tangled dark hair and sagging stockings. "You're welcome, Rose."

CHAPTER SIX

LUKE CAME OUT OF THE BARN AFTER FEEDING THE TEAM and flexed his stiff shoulders. It had been a long day but a satisfying one. He stood at the corral, one foot on the bottom rail, and lifted his gaze to survey the arrow-straight furrows in the fields, tinged green with seedlings reaching for the sky. This section held the corn that he'd planted earlier in the month—it needed a long growing season in this part of the country, where there were often more rainy spring days than sunny. It was usually that way until mid-June.

Of all the things that had gone wrong over the years, he'd been damned lucky with this farm. Oh, it hadn't come to him easily. He'd worked his fool head off in all kinds of weather, reached into laboring cows up to his shoulder to turn calves that didn't know which end was out, and fought the punishing east wind that blew through this river gorge and weakened fence posts and perma-nently bent some trees to the west. He'd sat up nights with the horses when they fell ill with maladies that threatened to carry them off, and dosed the hogs with Bob Cook's sovereign remedy for the scours when their insides had turned to water.

But still, he'd been lucky. The place had thrived and he hadn't been plagued by the multitude of disasters that could occur on a farm: accidents, fires, floods, pests that ate crops right down to the dirt, diseases that wiped out whole herds of livestock. He was proud of what he'd accomplished. Not bad for a kid who'd started his life in a shack down on the river, a kid everybody had expected to fail, especially his old man. If Luke wasn't happy, well, hell—who really had much happiness? He didn't think about it too often, although he had to admit that he'd hoped Alyssa Cannon would bring a little with her.

In the end, maybe it didn't matter. He knew what his job was—to make a decent home for his girl. He'd learned by his old man's example what a man's job wasn't. He wasn't supposed to lie around, drunk half the time, in jail the other half. He shouldn't tell his sons that they wouldn't amount to a pile of horse shit, or his daughters that they'd better not end up pregnant and crying on his doorstep. A man wasn't supposed to make his wife so miserable that the only way she could escape was to die, the way his own mother had.

The way Belinda had.

Luke glanced at the oak tree in the front yard, the low afternoon sun gilding its top branches. There was no going back, and there seemed to be no going forward. There was just the farm and Rose and Cora. And now Emily. He sighed and flexed his shoulders again, then unhooked his boot from the bottom fence rail. Dragging his mind away from the painful memories, he headed toward the pump behind the house, intent on getting washed up for supper. It would probably be another stiff, uncomfortable meal, with Cora continuing her war of silence. Since the episode with Belinda's tablecloth, when she'd threatened again to go to her own home and he'd called her bluff, she'd tried a different tack—instead of harping, now she rarely spoke. But her wordless demands for an apology were as loud as shouting. Damn it, he wouldn't apologize. She'd treated Emily like a stray cat, and he was tired of living this way.

He kicked at a dirt clod, frustrated by the situation. He sensed that Rose was still the pawn in the tug-of-war between himself and Cora. Rose already had enough to get used to without giving her the added burden of losing her grandmother. At least for now. But he hoped that after Emily settled in and the girl got used to her, he could tell Cora to go home. For the time being, he felt like a bogged calf, stuck in the morass of Cora's bitterness.

When he rounded the corner, he halted in his tracks, unprepared for the sight ahead of him. Emily stood at the washtub, her sleeves rolled up to expose pale, slender arms. She worked hard, scrubbing something white up and down the washboard. Her dress front was wet from neck to waist and molded itself to her upper torso. The same low rays that turned the oak to gold made her hair gleam like the sun itself. Behind her, the pair of clotheslines held the black dress she'd worn to the chicken coop and some white undergarments. The chemises, petticoats, and a corset flapped in the breeze, scraps of pink and blue ribbons dangling from them. Mixed in with them were his own clean shirts—he supposed that Cora had done those earlier because they looked dry.

Luke thought it was a homey scene, one that he realized he'd missed. The hot water in the tub raised enough steam to stick strands of curls to Emily's face and make them coil at the back of her neck. She didn't look nearly as stiff and formal as the woman who had met him on the dock in town.

Suddenly, Luke's throat was as dry as a field in August, and he swallowed hard, completely captivated by Emily's appealing dishevelment. He stood and watched her as she worked, scrubbing, wringing, rinsing.

She looked up. "Mr. Becker! I didn't see you—I didn't know you were—what are you doing?"

"I just came around back to wash up for supper." He nodded at the pump to her left.

She glanced at the pump, then looked over her shoulder at the clean wash hanging in plain view. Obviously flustered, she plunged the garment in her hand into the water again.

He smiled at her modesty. "Trust me, you don't have anything there I haven't seen before."

Even though she puckered up as if she'd been sucking a lemon, her cheeks turned a most becoming shade of pink. "That may be, but you have not seen mine."

He chuckled outright and she blushed harder, apparently realizing how that had sounded.

"No, ma'am, that's true. I haven't." He stepped closer, enjoying this softer side of her that he'd not seen before. The day in the chicken coop didn't count—she'd been frightened and Cora had pulled a rotten trick on her. This was different. This Emily was beguiling.

"Well, please don't let me keep you from your intended task." She held the chemise under the wash water as if she were trying to drown it.

He nodded and smiled again, and began unbuttoning his shirt.

She looked at him with wide eyes. "Mr. Becker, you are disrobing!"

He opened the shirt and pulled it off. She averted her gaze. "There isn't much point in washing if I'm going to keep this dirty shirt on."

He went to the pump and picked up a sliver of Cora's acrid homemade soap from where it sat on the old piece of toweling that he kept with it. Like everything she made, the soap was crude and not very good—this stuff could strip the hide off a buffalo—but it got the job done. He went about his business, pumping the cold water over his head and working up a lather.

He felt Emily's eyes on him and an old spark of a long lost feeling ignited in his belly. Suddenly he wished he could strip down to bare skin and sit in that hot washtub in the low, golden sun, and let her scrub his back until all the dirt and all the pain of the last few years was washed away. He could easily imagine her strong, smooth fingers working at his stiff shoulders, massaging his scalp as she washed his hair, and then himself leaning back against her soft breasts while she hummed to him with that sweet voice he'd heard in church.

It was such a pleasant reverie that he forgot to rinse the soap off his face before opening his eyes. The suds scalded them like liquid fire, and he let out a string of curse words that he hadn't used in mixed company in years.

"Mr. Becker, really!" The daydream came to a rude and abrupt end.

He splashed vigorously, actually worried for a moment that Cora's lousy soap had blinded him. God knew it was possible, even though he wasn't sure just what she put in it. "I've got soap in my eyes, damn it!"

"Oh, no, let me help!" He heard the pump handle work and then felt Emily's hand, cool and soft, on the back of his neck bending him forward, as she splashed more water into his face with her other hand.

At last the burning lessened. "Better?" she asked, and put the towel into his hands. She was nothing but a blur of pale hair and black dress.

He dried his face and eyes and her image focused. Her light brows drawn, she peered at him.

"I think so. At least I can see you." And a handsome sight she was, he thought.

She took a step backward. Shaking her head, she looked at the backs of her reddened hands. "That soap is pretty caustic. I've been using it for the laundry and my skin is burning. Does Mrs. Hayward make it herself?"

"Yeah, she uses some secret recipe she swears by." He rubbed his eyes with the towel, then dried the back of his neck.

"Maybe we can buy ready-made soap. It isn't that expensive."

"No, it isn't, but Cora, well, she couldn't see the point in buying soap when she can make it right here."

Emily lifted her brows delicately. "Mrs. Hayward is rather, um, strong-willed, isn't she?"

He flipped the towel over his shoulder and laughed again, although he didn't feel much humor. Emily's etiquette had made her an expert at either diplomacy or understatement, he wasn't sure which. "You mean the way a mule is strong-willed?"

Emily ducked her head and he saw the hint of a smile.

Luke reached for a clean, dry shirt hanging on the line and again felt Emily's eyes follow his movements. "I know she's not the easiest woman to get along with."

"Yes, well . . ." She let the comment hang, unfinished.

As Luke pushed his arms into the sleeves of the clean shirt, that feeling came over him again—that he was not the master of his own home. How must it seem to Emily, he wondered, that he let Cora run roughshod over them all? He sighed as he buttoned the shirt. "When we lost Belinda, I let Cora take control, I guess. I made her the boss in the kitchen and I'm the boss in the barn. I didn't want Rose to be saddled with running a house—she was only eight years old. It's been easier to let Cora have her way than to fight her over everything." He glanced up at Emily's spring-green eyes. "But maybe I made a mistake."

Emily reached into the washtub for her underwear, then let it sink to the bottom of the tub, and dried her hands on the apron tied around her slim waist. "I'm sure you did what you thought was best at the time. It isn't easy to make decisions under such stressful circumstances. I know what that's like."

He leaned a hip against the washtub. "I suppose you do."

Their eyes met and Emily looked away. He had no doubt that they shared the same thought about her coming west in her sister's place. But he sensed that she'd known sorrow in her life. He could see it in her changeable posture—when she talked about Rose or her teaching job, or anything else she felt strongly about, she stood tall with her chin up and her shoulders back. She cut quite an imposing figure when she was stiff-spined. Other times, when the conversation turned the least bit personal, like now, she stooped a little, as if trying to hide inside herself. Or trying to hide her whole self. That he'd even noticed was a surprise to Luke. Then he realized that he'd begun to take note of other little things about Emily. The way she tilted her head a bit while she was thinking, how she ducked her chin when she smiled, as if she were shy. He figured he had to be wrong about that—Emily Cannon was not a shy woman. She had an opinion about nearly everything, he could read it in her eyes. Fortunately, unlike Cora, she didn't yap about all of them.

Emily went to the clothesline and inspected her black dress, the one that had suffered through the chickens.

"When I went to town today, I saw Rose at the cemetery. She was sitting on her mother's grave, talking to her."

He straightened away from the washtub. "She was?"

She turned to face him, her chin up. "Maybe I shouldn't have repeated it—she said it's a secret between her and her mother. But I think Rose feels like she doesn't have anyone to talk to and it worries me."

He stiffened. "She told you that?"

"No, but she's dropped little hints that give me that impression."

Stung, Luke retorted, "Well, hell, she's got me and Cora."

She pulled a clothespin from her apron pocket and turned it in her long, slender fingers. "I'm not criticizing you, Mr. Becker. It's just that I've worked with children long enough to know when they're troubled. The tension in the household is affecting her, but I believe this started long before I got here. And you admitted that you don't know what she's thinking."

Luke's shoulders sagged. Emily was right. He couldn't just turn everything over to her and expect her to perform miracles with Rose. He had to take some kind of action, too. And it wasn't that he didn't want to, exactly. But for the life of him, he wasn't sure which course was best. Cora was a source of trouble in the house and he'd send her packing today if he could, but what would it do to Rose if she were to leave? His girl's happiness was more important than his own.

"I just thought you should know," Emily said. "She also mentioned that the other children at school make fun of how she dresses."

Luke winced and threw his towel over the pump handle. Kids could be cruel. He remembered being on both ends of the ridicule, giving and receiving. "Cora makes her clothes."

She tilted her head slightly and gazed at the fields. "Hmm, I think I can help with that. I could teach Rose to make her own clothes. She's old enough and we could pick out a couple of dress patterns that are more suited to a girl her size and age."

"Is she interested?"

"I haven't mentioned it to her yet. I wanted to ask you first."

"That sounds like a fine idea, Emily."

She smiled again and with the low sun highlighting her lashes and the soft curve of her cheek, she was almost beautiful. "Good. I'll get her started tomorrow."

Suddenly, the back door opened and he heard Cora bark, *"Supper!"*

Emily's gaze locked with his and he saw understanding in her eyes.

Gratitude edged its way into Luke's heart for this woman who had come west to help him with his daughter. And the prospect of easing his mother-in-law out of his house seemed less daunting because he suspected that Emily was on his side. He couldn't remember the last time he'd felt like he had an ally. She brushed at the tendrils of damp hair on her neck. He tracked the graceful, feminine gesture, and then it hit him. She wasn't wearing her wedding ring.

He knew it didn't fit properly and he was sorry about that, but it seemed to him that a woman like Emily, a stickler for proper form, would wear that ring no matter which finger she had to put it on. Since the afternoon in Judge Clifton's office, he'd wondered if he'd ever be able to accept her as more than a wife in name only.

Until now, he hadn't thought that she might not accept him as her husband.

That night after dinner, Emily slipped down the back stairs and out to the yard with a lantern. Since the farmhouse lacked indoor plumbing, no one would think it odd that she was outside at this hour. She still hadn't gotten used to visiting the necessary here. In Chicago, even after the Cannon family had been forced to move from the house on Washington Boulevard to rented rooms, they'd still had bathing and toilet facilities, although they'd been located down the hall, and shared with a half-dozen other tenant families. The privy here was dark and spooky, and while she'd never used one till she'd come to the farm, she'd heard many horror stories about the spiders, snakes, and God-knew-what-else that lurked in the depths beneath the round hole in the plank that comprised the seat.

She glanced at the western horizon, still faintly light. The evening was soft and balmy, with a sprinkling of early stars scattered across the sky. But it wasn't the call of nature that brought her out here, not the earth's or her own.

Sometime this afternoon while she'd been doing laundry out here, she'd lost her wedding band, and she had to find it. The thing fit so poorly that it hadn't been until she sat down at the dinner table that she'd noticed it was missing. What would Luke think if he saw her without it? She'd kept her left hand in her lap through the entire meal. This had been especially challenging because the pork Cora served was just as tough and flavorless as her other dinnertime offerings. It had really required two hands to saw the meat into manageable bites, but she'd speared the leathery chunks with her fork and chewed. And chewed. Now her dinner sat in her stomach like a lump of lead.

She shuffled through the damp grass, holding her lantern low, hoping to catch a glimpse of something gold and shiny peeking from the blades. She held the light over the washtub, just in case the ring remained at the bottom. But it was empty. Setting the lantern down, she dropped to her hands and knees and began feeling through the wet grass. Her fingers moved over the tender spring growth as a blind person's might, seeking their way, seeking something metal. As the minutes ticked on, panic began to rise into her chest. How could she have been so careless? Why hadn't she realized the ring might come off in the soapy water?

She just had to find it, she *had* to. A married woman couldn't go around without her wedding band. It wasn't proper. The ring hadn't been bought with her in mind, it didn't fit, and it certainly had not been put on her finger with love. But Luke had given it to her—her husband, Luke. The man with the weary eyes and the great love for his daughter and the kind heart that she longed to have just a corner of. She hated admitting it to herself, but it was true. Tears blurred her eyes and she brushed at them impatiently. If he would give her just a crumb of the regard he held for Belinda—a dead woman—Emily would be content and her own longing for him might not seem so hopeless.

Good heavens! Her head came up at the thought. Was she falling in love with him? No, no, she wasn't supposed to—that hadn't been any part of their arrangement. They'd agreed that this was to be a marriage of convenience for the primary purpose of giving Rose a decent upbringing.

But now she'd lost the ring he'd given her, one that he'd paid good money for. What would he say?

She continued to grope through the darkness, moving

the lantern ahead as she worked her way around the wash-tub in ever-widening circles, trying to retrace her steps in her memory. But all she could remember was Luke, there in the yard, looking at her underwear, and then taking off his shirt. Luke, splashing his face with water when Cora's crude soap had burned his eyes. She remembered the feel of his nape under her hand, warm and firm with tendons.

Her hands were muddy and her dress was soaked at the knees from the wet grass. There was no point in going on—she'd have to face Luke and tell him the ring was lost. She put her hand flat to the ground to push herself to her feet, and felt something sharp dig into her palm. Yanking the lantern closer, she saw a yellow gleam poking up from the mud. Thank God! With a muffled cry of relief, she plucked the band from its hiding place and wiped it off on her skirt.

Then she pressed the ring to her lips and put it back on her little finger.

Emily bided in a borderline country, a restless, edgy place where there waited a tall, slim man with dark, curly hair. His torso was bared to the sun, his dungarees hung low on his hips. He considered her with the eyes of a lover, eyes that beckoned, drawing her closer. She stood before him wrapped only in a bridal veil made of silk illusion, lighter than a spinner's web, softer than eiderdown. She walked into his embrace and his hands on her back pressed her to his warm, naked skin, while his lips traveled down her neck, from her ear to her collarbone.

You're beautiful, Emily, the most beautiful woman I've ever seen . . .

His lips moved against her nape as he spoke, his hands explored her silk-clad body, gentle, demanding, intimate—

Emily woke with a start, disoriented and sleepily aroused. Morning had barely broken—she could make out only the vaguest silhouettes of the furniture. Even in her drowsy state, the memory of her dream both embarrassed and made her long to return to it. But something had awakened her, a jarring—

Tata-tata-tata!

From the wall behind her came a sharp, rattling noise.

Dear God, what was that? She'd never heard anything like its staccato sound, and it was right next to her head. She clutched the bedclothes to her chin, her heart hammering, and she scrambled to the center of the mattress to stare at the offending wall.

Her sleep-fogged mind grappled with a fearsome notion. Snakes—they had snakes out west, didn't they? Rattlesnakes. One day in class Emily had confiscated a dime novel from one of her students. She could scarcely credit that a young woman would have an interest in such lurid, undignified fiction, and had delivered a proper lecture about proper reading material. The Brontë sisters, Jane Austen, Louisa May Alcott, these authors wrote suitable stories for young ladies. But after school, that rebellious, wicked part of Emily had made her look at the cheap volume. It had talked about rattlesnakes in the west.

Tata-tata-tata!

She didn't know what one sounded like, exactly, but there was something in the wall and she wasn't going to wait for it to break through and introduce itself.

She leaped from her bed and looked around the nearly dark room, trying to decide how to proceed. Fumbling with a match, she lighted her bedroom lamp on the dresser and flung open her trunk to pull out her black twill umbrella. It wasn't much of a weapon—the handle was nothing but Dresden china. But it had a sharp point and it was all she had at the moment. With no little trepidation, she peered into the corners looking for a hole in the plaster from which the viper might escape, holding the closed umbrella before her as if it were Excalibur. Nothing. The sharp rattle came from the wall again. That was enough for Emily. She could not fight a snake with her puny weapon.

The protagonist in the dime novel had blown off the rattlesnake's head with a shotgun after it had sunk its terrible fangs into the leg of his companion. The friend then died an agonizing death.

She should get Luke. He'd have a shotgun, wouldn't he? All farmers had shotguns, to kill things like game and, and— At least he would know what to do. Snatching her shawl from the foot of the mattress, she threw it over her nightgown and scurried into the hall, barefoot and still gripping her umbrella. Pausing in front of his closed door, she glanced fearfully at her room again as if a demon from the Pit lurked there. She tapped on the oak.

"Mr. Becker?" she murmured.

No response. She knocked again, harder this time.

From within, she heard shuffling across the floor and unintelligible mumbling. The door swung open and she found herself face-to-face with a man who almost made her forget the main reason she'd come to him. Sleep-rumpled and wearing only the quilt from his bed around his middle, Luke looked at her. His hair stuck up in places and his pillowcase had left creases on one side of his stubbled face.

"Emily, what in the hell—"

Emily felt her jaw drop at his near nakedness. What had she expected, that he'd come to the door fully dressed? She'd gotten the man out of bed, for heaven's sake. But she didn't know where to let her gaze fall—to the broad expanse of his chest, on his long muscled legs and bare feet, or on those eyes that even now felt as if they bore through her heart and down to her soul. That was silly, of course, a remnant of a feeling left over from her shameful dream. "I–I'm so sorry to disturb you."

He glanced over his shoulder at the window behind him and waved off the apology. "I overslept anyway. What's the matter? Are you all right?" he asked, his voice froggy and utterly disarming.

She tightened her shawl and spoke in hushed tones to avoid disturbing Rose and Cora. "There's something in my room."

He glanced down at the umbrella. "What—rain?"

"N-no, I think it's a snake."

He peered at her as if she'd taken leave of her senses. "A snake."

"Yes, a rattlesnake." She felt fairly confident about that. She simply wasn't equipped to vanquish the thing. "I don't know how it got in there, but I heard it in the wall. Please come. We'll need a weapon to kill it."

He rubbed his jaw as he considered her. The stubble made a sandpapery sound against his work-roughened hand. It seemed as if he could see right through her night-gown, and suddenly she realized that she wore little more than he did. Now she found herself torn between two fears—that of the serpent in her bedroom wall, and of the feelings Luke aroused in her by just standing there, look-ing at her.

"Emily, ma'am, we don't have rattlesnakes in this part of the state. Are you sure you weren't just dreaming?"

Yes, she'd been dreaming but not about reptiles. "Please, I know something dangerous is there," she whis-pered urgently.

He gestured at the quilt and she felt her face flame.

"All right, give me a minute to put on my pants."

He closed the door and Emily lingered in the hall, feeling awkward. She fiddled with her shawl again, wishing that she, too, were dressed. In a moment he emerged empty-handed, wearing only his dungarees and suspenders, and still barefoot. Somehow, this costume was every bit as unsettling as his quilt had been.

He nodded at her and she led the way to her bedroom.

Emily began poking at the wall with the china handle of her umbrella, trying to stir up the snake again so Luke could find it. Maybe he thought she was being silly, but she noticed that he hesitated in the doorway and it surprised her. A big, strong man like him, for heaven's sake.

"It's in here someplace." She gave the wall another tap.

Luke did hesitate but not for any reason that Emily could have imagined. Seeing her at his door, dressed in a thin, white gown, her long, blond braid draped over one shoulder, had stoked fires in him that caught him flat-footed. Now the rising sun bathed her in pale gold-pink and glowed through her gown, outlining long, shapely legs. How long had it been? he wondered. How long since he'd held a woman in his arms, skin to skin, felt her welcoming softness and warmth, and covered her with his body? Years ago, long before Belinda had died. And now, here was Emily Cannon, his legal wife, a woman he'd told he could offer nothing other than his home and his name . . . jabbing at the wall with her umbrella. What a picture. He had to chuckle, despite the images rolling through his mind and the feelings she stirred low in his belly.

Tata-tata-tata!

She jumped back and pointed triumphantly at a place above the white iron headboard. "There! It's up there!"

She turned to look at him. "Will you attack from here or get it outside?"

Luke rubbed his chin again, trying not to laugh outright at her proud proclamation and her question. A body would think she was discussing a military maneuver. "Emily, that's not a rattlesnake."

She backed away from the noise, her eyes wide. "Of course it is! I've read all about them. They have big fangs that pump poison into their victims. A person dies a gruesome, agonizing death!"

"It's a woodpecker."

She gaped at him and then swung her gaze back to the wall. "A woodpecker! You mean a *bird*?"

"Yes, ma'am."

"Not a snake?" She seemed disappointed.

"No." He laughed and folded his arms over his chest. "There aren't any rattlesnakes around here. It's too cold for them. There are some down by Albany, but that's about seventy-five miles south."

She let the umbrella fall to her side and wilted a little more. "Well, of all the . . ."

"That bird is just looking for something to eat. He'll give up after he figures out he hasn't bored into a tree. I'm sorry he scared you."

"A woodpecker," she repeated, plainly amazed at her own gullibility. She glanced at the wall again. "You must think I'm just a foolish, city-born ninny."

He stepped closer and took her upper arms in his hands. Her shawl had slipped to the crooks of her elbows. "No, I don't think that at all. I think you showed real bravery."

She tipped her face up to his, and the hopefulness he saw there was almost too painful to look upon. "Really?"

"Sure—not everyone would try to do battle with just a parasol for a weapon."

Now she smiled, a bit unwillingly at first, but then let go with a full-fledged grin that he felt all the way to the grieving core of his heart. "It was the first thing I could think of."

The morning sun highlighted her brows and lashes, and turned her eyes to jade. She wasn't a classic beauty, but there was something about her pink, soft-looking mouth, her straight nose, the smooth brow—oh, a lot of different little things that added up to make her a handsome woman. Beneath his hands, he felt the warmth of her skin radiate through her thin gown. It would be so easy to kiss her. She was right here, tall enough to reach without giving him a crick in his neck, yet vulnerable in a way that made him feel protective of her.

Then from the corner of his eye, he caught a glimpse of the unmade bed. It was covered with a quilt that he'd slept under many times in this room, for many years. Memories of Belinda gripped him like a cold hand. Along with them came a raging sense of guilt and disloyalty to his late wife. Instantly, he released Emily's arms and stepped back.

"I'd better get to my chores. Farmwork is a dawn-to-dark job, and I'm already getting a late start."

The spell between them was broken and, self-consciously, Emily covered herself with her shawl again. "Oh, of course. Thank you for coming to my rescue. I'm sorry I got you in here for nothing."

Her turn of phrase sent his mind down a dangerous path again, although he knew she wasn't aware of its double meaning.

Damn it, how long would this go on? Once again, he wished there was some way to finally put the past and its pain behind him. To move forward instead of letting his years drift by like dry autumn leaves. Right now, he felt stuck in a place where it seemed that all of life's clocks had stopped.

Just as he was heading out of Emily's room, Cora's door opened. The astounded expression on her face would have given Luke a good laugh if circumstances had been different. He knew very well how it looked—Emily in her nightgown right behind him, the unmade bed, and Luke barely dressed, himself.

"Well, this is a cozy turn of events, isn't it?" Cora said, putting a last hairpin in her bun. "And what would Rose think if she saw this?"

He spoke the first words that came to him, not thinking about how they would sound, only that they were the truth. "She would think that her father and stepmother share the same bedroom, Cora." He brushed past her and went back to his own room to finish dressing.

Although the woodpecker rapped on the wall a few more times after Luke left Emily's room, the sound receded to the back of her mind. All she could think of was the thrill that had coursed through her when Luke had touched her. And what Cora had apparently thought when she saw him come out of Emily's room—that they had spent the night together. It was a wicked notion, but one that she couldn't seem to banish to that place where unladylike thoughts were supposed to be dismissed.

It had been innocent enough, Luke's hands on her arms, nothing a lady could really object to. But her heart had fluttered in her chest like a trapped bird, making her breath short. Then for one horrible, wonderful instant, she'd actually thought he might try to kiss her. Not that she had a lot of experience in that regard. She didn't know the "signs." Oh, she knew all the rituals and procedures of courtship—proper but romantic love letters, carefully worded and mindful of spelling and grammar, the giving of an appropriate gift such as a book of poetry or a box of sweets, the language of flowers. But no man had ever come calling or courted her.

This morning, though, an inborn instinct that transcended inexperience or book-learned ritual had hummed within her, as if it had awakened from a deep sleep. She crossed her arms over her chest to put her hands where Luke's had been. It wasn't the same. His hands were bigger, almost large enough to encircle her arms. There had been the way he smelled—of sleep and cotton sheeting. And the way he looked, almost as he had in her shameful dream. Emily ambled around the room, lost in the reverie. Nothing had ever felt like that, and she'd wanted the moment to go on and on. But he'd pulled away suddenly, and she'd been disappointed. As she passed the dressing table, she caught a glimpse of herself in the square of mirror hanging above it and dropped her hands to her sides. Of course, he'd pulled away. He'd been married to a beautiful woman and he was a handsome man. He had not wanted to marry dull-looking Emily, and had done so simply to help Rose. He'd made no promises about love or affection. In fact, he'd told her that there would be none of that between them.

She turned from the mirror, feeling more foolish for her old maid's daydream than she did for mistaking a woodpecker for a rattlesnake.

CHAPTER SEVEN

———

THE MORNING SUN WAS FULLY UP AND CAST A BRIGHT rectangle on Emily's bedroom wall as she stood staring at her black crepe dress spread out on her bed. Wearing her corset, camisole, and drawers, she'd reached for the garment where she'd hung it in the wardrobe last night, expecting to find a clean, fresh garment.

Yesterday afternoon, she had carefully scrubbed each spot with the cleaning cream she'd mixed, expecting to wear the dress today. But her tried-and-true concoction of ammonia and castile soap, which had worked so well in the past, had not only removed the chicken spots, it had also lifted the dye out of the fabric. Blotches of dark orange now streaked the skirt and bodice. The dress was a ghastly ruin, reminding her of a tiger-skin rug she'd once seen in one of her pupils' homes. The girl's mother had invited her to tea, and on the floor of the parlor lay the big cat's striped hide. Its head lay at one end of the rug and the mouth was wide open, frozen in a permanent snarl that revealed enormous teeth. For the whole of her visit, Emily's gaze had kept straying to the tiger's unseeing green glass eyes, and, oddly enough, she had thought it seemed creepier in this unnatural state than it would have if the beast had crouched live before the fireplace.

But the tiger had long been out of its misery. She, on

the other hand, had to deal with this striped atrocity. Although she'd brought her entire limited wardrobe with her, she had many weeks of mourning left, and now only one black crepe dress that was whole. She couldn't continue to wear it, the same one, day after day. Still, years of reduced circumstances had made her frugal and careful of expenditures, and now she found it difficult to justify buying fabric for another black dress that, God willing, she would wear for only a short time and then put away.

Emily eyed the orange-spotted dress with a sigh of frustration. The rules of etiquette were very specific and rigid when it came to mourning. Maybe she could buy black dye and try to cover the blotches. In any event, she would have to continue to honor Alyssa's memory with the clothes she had, and that meant putting on this dress today.

As she pulled the dreadful garment over her head and settled its heavy folds into place, she allowed herself to remember, just for the briefest instant, the dream of wearing only her gossamer bridal veil and seeing the proof of her new beauty reflected in her lover's eyes.

"Miss Emily, what happened to your dress?" Rose stared at Emily with wonderment as she sat down for breakfast.

"Now Rose, remember it's not proper to ask questions like that," Cora said, thumping down a big platter of fried eggs and potatoes in the center of the kitchen table. "Maybe black-and-orange dresses are the latest fashion from Chicago." The tinge of mockery in her voice was unmistakable.

The low fire that had begun burning days ago in Emily flared in her chest, just as smoldering flames jumped to life when a flue was opened. She made a herculean effort to stifle a sharp reply, both for Rose's sake and because a remnant of civility remained in her heart for Cora. But she refused to be the butt of the woman's sarcasm.

"Mrs. Hayward, I would appreciate it if you confined your remarks to—"

Before Emily could finish, Luke came in the back door. A big, craggy male in the midst of females, he seemed to fill the room with his presence. He wore a work shirt with blue-and-white pinstripes and the dungarees she'd seen earlier. His sleeves were rolled up to the elbows, and Emily found herself wishing she could see the rest of his arms again. He studied both women, obviously realizing that he'd walked in on a strained moment.

"I was hoping to get the plowing finished while this good weather holds," he said to no one in particular. He snagged a blue enameled tin cup from a shelf and poured himself some coffee from the pot on the stove. "But that damned hip strap on the harness broke again. I mended it but it's not likely to hold much longer. I'll have to go into town and order a new one."

He flopped into his chair and reached for the platter of eggs and potatoes, scraping half of each onto his own plate with a knife. As he put the dish down again, he looked across the table at Emily. His dark gaze swept over her dress, and without thinking, she busied herself with buttering a piece of toast, feeling as ugly as she ever had in her life. First thing this morning, he'd seen her at her worst, in just a nightgown and shawl, her hair sleep-mussed and undone. Now this. When she took a bite of bread, she had to force herself to swallow Cora's rancid-tasting butter.

"Is this the dress that got ruined in the henhouse?"

Emily's head came up, but Luke wasn't talking to her. He was looking at Cora.

His mother-in-law touched her thick, work-reddened

fingers to her chest and wore the haughty expression of the wrongly accused. "You're asking me? How should I know? Ask Mrs. Becker. I don't know why I'm always the whipping post around here—if something is wrong, it must be Cora's fault. Cora did this wrong, Cora did that wrong."

Luke seemed ready to say more but a glance at Rose's wide eyes must have stopped him. Thank heavens he'd taken Emily's words to heart. Like a sea sponge, the girl was absorbing the tension in this house.

Instead, he poured a long drizzle of cream into his coffee and took a big drink. He followed that with a forkful of eggs and potatoes, all mixed together. Swallowing, he said to her, "Rose, since I'm going into town, you can hop a ride to school, if you want."

Rose, who'd finished eating, shrugged and nodded.

"Go get your books." She pushed herself away from the table and went upstairs.

Luke sighed, and the rest of the meal was finished in silence, and not a moment too soon for Emily.

As she helped clear the table and put the dishes in the sink, she occasionally peered out the kitchen window, watching for Luke to bring the wagon around. She had a favor to ask of him.

"Rose, let's get going!" he called.

Emily wadded up the dishtowel she held and hurried outside to the porch. There Luke waited on the high wagon seat.

He grinned at her and the sight of his smile nearly made her forget what she meant to ask. Why did he have to be so handsome? she wondered, annoyed. His good looks only underscored her own sense of self-doubt. "Emily," he greeted. "I meant to ask—did your snake finally leave?"

She didn't like being teased. In her experience, teasing was just a thinly disguised form of ridicule that made her feel inadequate or foolish. How many times had she been asked about the air "up there"? Her own stepfather had been unsparing with his little jokes and backhanded compliments.

We don't know where Emily got her height. Maybe an ostrich brought her instead of the stork, eh, Emily?

Your dance card will never be filled, my dear, but your looks contrast so nicely with Alyssa's.

But she saw kindness in Luke's eyes, realized that there was no malice in his tone. Only humor. She ducked her chin a moment and smiled back. "Yes, he did. I'm sorry I bothered you about it."

"That's all right. It's not often that I get asked to help a damsel in distress."

She felt herself flush. This was the kind of polite, flirting banter that she'd heard often enough from her seat along the wall at musicales and dances. Not that it had ever been directed at her. Oh, well, once it had been, when she'd gotten her bracelet caught on the caned side of a chair. Alyssa's dancing partner had very gallantly disentangled her, then swept her sister off across the ballroom. She had remained behind, for that dance and all the rest, feeling clumsy and graceless.

But there was no one else here now, and Luke was bantering with *her*. She clutched the dishtowel more tightly in her hands. "Mr. Becker, I was wondering if you could do a favor for me."

"Don't you think it's time you started calling me Luke?"

"Oh! Well, I didn't . . . I don't know . . ."

"After all, I've seen you in your nightgown." There was that teasing tone again, but this time she felt herself blush to the roots of her hair. "And we *are* married."

She could barely force herself to look him in the face. Her own cheeks felt so hot she thought her head might pop. She twisted the towel in her fingers, hating the fact that no words seemed to form in her head. She didn't know what to say. If she tried to respond, she was certain that nonsense would be the best she could do.

Lord, what had gotten into him? Luke asked himself. He was actually flirting with Emily, and embarrassing her to the point that he felt sorry for her. She wrung that dishcloth as if it were a chicken's neck, and her shoulders were rounded. He shifted on the wagon seat and the horses stamped restively. More and more often, he caught himself thinking about her, and now, since he *had* seen her in her nightgown, he couldn't get the image out of his head. It wasn't as if she'd been wearing some filmy little scrap of underwear, the kind of thing he'd once seen on a French postcard his brother had gotten. Emily had been covered by a spinster's high-necked, long-sleeved nightie and a shawl. Still, even in her dishevelment and wielding an umbrella, she'd carried a curious combination of dignity and allure that he'd never seen in a woman. Or anyone, for that matter. Not even Belinda. His automatic reaction to this last thought was familiar, one that he hauled with him day after day, like a dog dragging around a grubby piece of salt pork. That reaction was guilt. But as much as he'd loved Belinda, she was gone and nothing would bring her back.

"What was it you wanted to ask me?" he said, returning the conversation to less personal territory.

She gestured at that lousy-looking dress she wore. "As you can see, my efforts to clean off the dirt were more successful than I'd hoped. I was wondering if you could get me a package of black dye when you're in town." She went on to explain the torturous rituals of proper mourning for her sister. He thought she was overdoing it—after all, no one here was watching the calendar, ready to condemn her for not wearing black dresses for six full months. But he felt vaguely responsible for the ruin of her clothes. Cora lived under his roof, and if his mother-in-law hadn't sent Emily out to that coop, none of this would have happened.

He interrupted her explanation. "Black dye. I'll get it."

Just then Rose emerged from the house, carrying her schoolbooks.

Emily smiled at her and searched her apron pocket. She pulled out a piece of hard candy, which she handed to Rose. "You may eat this after lunch, but not before. All right?"

Rose took it and tucked it into her own pocket. "Yes'm. Thanks, Miss Emily."

Emily patted her on the shoulder. "Have a good day at school."

Watching them, Luke got a funny feeling in his chest, one that he couldn't readily identify. Gratitude, certainly, that Emily was good to his girl. And she genuinely liked Rose—he could see it in her face. But the feeling went deeper than that. For a moment, he almost had a sense of family, with the three of them together like this.

"I'll be back in a couple of hours," he said to Emily. Rose took her father's outstretched hand and climbed up to the wagon seat beside him.

Emily smiled again and waved as he slapped the lines on the horses' backs. "Get up now," he said, and clucked his tongue to the team.

Emily called, "Don't forget to use your hankie instead of your sleeve, and mind your teacher."

Luke turned the wagon out to the main road, and

couldn't help but grin. He wasn't sure if Emily's instructions were just for Rose, or for him, too.

"Rose, we haven't visited your mama's grave for a while. Would you like to go this Sunday after church?" Luke purposely asked the question to see how his daughter would respond.

She rolled her eyes. "We have to go to church *again*? We just went a couple of weeks ago."

"Miss Emily thinks it's important for you, and it's a chance for her to meet new people and make friends. We could go by the cemetery on the way back."

Rose cast him a sidelong glance. "Sometimes I stop and see Mama on the way home from school." She admitted this as if it were news that he wouldn't like, but it only confirmed what Emily had already told him. He didn't care if she went to her mother's grave, but a kid her age ought to have more going on in her life than visiting a cemetery.

"Well, that's all right." They rode along for a bit, the silence broken only by the clop of horses' hooves and an occasional songbird. Then he said, "You know, if you ever want to, well, talk, I—we—it would be okay."

"Talk about what?"

"You know—things, I guess. If something is bothering you." Luke stumbled along, laboring under the sudden and unpleasant sensation of drowning. He didn't know the first thing about what went on in a girl's head. He wasn't even sure he was supposed to. Hell, he hadn't been raised that way. The old man hadn't wanted to hear anyone's opinion but his own, and Luke's mother, a worn-out, quiet wraith, had known better than to speak up. But if Emily were right, if Rose felt like she had no one to talk to, he had to try.

"Do *you* ever go see Mama?"

Not for a long time he hadn't, but he didn't know if he should tell Rose that. For the first year after Belinda died, the three of them—Cora, Rose, and he—went to the cemetery every Sunday. Jesus, in good weather, Cora would even pack a picnic and they'd eat on Belinda's grave. He'd thought it was sort of ghoulish. At any rate, he discovered that instead of making him feel better, the frequent visits had affected him like vinegar on a wound. There had been days when the world looked so bleak he didn't even want to get out of bed. But men didn't give in to that kind of weakness. They just kept going, gave the world a stoic face to look at, and went about their work. There were fields and animals to tend, chores to do, mouths to feed. At night, they drank at their kitchen tables or in their barns, with the stock for company.

"I haven't been there for a while," he finally answered. "I imagine your grandmother doesn't like that."

Rose shrugged and then looked up at him. "You *miss* Mama, don't you? You still love her, even though you married Emily? Grammy says you don't."

Damn that Cora, he simmered. "Sure, I miss her, honey." How could he explain to a kid conflicting feelings that he had trouble understanding himself? "But . . . but I think that maybe life is for the living. Do you know what that means?"

Rose shook her head.

"I mean that your mama left us a lot sooner than any of us expected. Now she's gone, but we're still here. We still have years of our own lives to go on with."

Rose seemed satisfied with his answer.

Struggling to keep the conversation going, he re-marked, "Your hair looks nice today." Her wild coffee-colored hair was braided into two long, neat plaits and tied on the ends with ribbon.

She smiled and plucked at one braid, obviously pleased that he'd noticed. "Miss Emily helped me with it."

Chalk up another one for Emily, he thought.

"Why doesn't Grammy like her?"

"I wouldn't say she doesn't like her."

"Oh, I would."

Luke couldn't lie to her, but he was hard-pressed to explain their complicated domestic arrangements to anyone. "We'll work it out somehow. Try not to worry about it."

They drove down the last hill that led into town and Luke pulled the wagon up in front of Fairdale's small white schoolhouse. Children played in the yard, running and laughing, enjoying their freedom before the teacher came out to ring the bell.

"Thanks for the ride, Daddy."

"See you tonight," Luke said, watching Rose scamper down from the high seat. He looked at the other girls in the yard and saw that they were dressed very differently from his daughter. No judge of fashion, even Luke could see that she would be a target for teasing in Cora's garish flounces. Thank God that Emily wanted to help with Rose's clothes as well as her manners.

As he drove off toward Main Street, he sensed that he'd forged a little path into his daughter's heart. And it hadn't been as hard as he'd expected.

Luke walked into the general store and was immediately struck by the familiar scents of bacon, coffee, leather, and soap. He wasn't much interested in shopping, but he'd always liked coming in here. Out front in the summer, a couple of men always occupied the bench Fran kept there, and in winter, they bellied up to the stove to spit, whittle, and spin yarns. It was the way her father had run the place, and Fran had kept it that way after he died. She carried a lot of different merchandise to appeal to all of her customers, and had a knack for artful displays. Behind the counter, rows of glass jars full of peas, beans, rice, and candy lined the shelves. He supposed she'd make some man a reasonable wife, if that man didn't mind being ordered around like a flunky. Fran Eakins was bossy and insisted on being in charge—in all matters—which was one reason Luke had never been very interested in her, even when she was young.

This morning she stood behind her counter, unpacking a crate of baking soda. This was the first time he'd seen her since the day in the sandwich shop, when Rose had stolen the candy. He hoped she'd had enough time to cool off by now. "Hi, Fran. How's business today?"

The look she shot at him from beneath her caterpillar brows—well, a lesser man might have frozen dead in his tracks. He didn't wince, but he had no doubt that she was still mad.

"Luke," she acknowledged.

"I need to order a new hip strap for my team."

She set aside a box of soda and reached for a green-backed ledger on the desk behind the counter. Flipping through its pages, she ran her finger down a column, then spun the book around, pointing to his name. "I see here that you owe one dollar and thirteen cents on your account. I can't add anything to it until you pay off your balance." She paused and lifted her chin. "That includes the candy and the pencil that your daughter stole from me."

Other names on her list had sums next to them that

were ten or twenty times higher. He'd run up much higher balances in the past himself.

He stared at her, unblinking, until she finally dropped her haughty gaze. "One dollar and thirteen cents," he repeated, reaching into his pocket. "As much as that, is it?" He put a silver dollar, a dime, and three pennies on the counter and pushed them closer to her. She snapped them up like a miser counting her last coins. "Is this about Rose? Or is there a problem between you and me?"

Her chin came up again. "You and *me*—I don't know what you mean."

Fran had been as obvious as Clara in her maneuvers to snag him after Belinda died. He'd never led her on, never once allowed her to believe that he regarded her as anything more than an old acquaintance. Even in their youth, he'd had nothing to do with Fran. He just wasn't attracted to her. So he'd ignored her clumsy attempts at coquetry that she sent him from her rows of jars and boxes. That had only made her more determined. But her attitude toward him changed once he began receiving letters from Alyssa Cannon. While he'd never discussed his plans with anyone, she'd sniffed those scented letters like a bloodhound and begun giving him baleful looks. True, Rose's antics hadn't helped, but he sensed that Fran's hostility went deeper. He had to do business with her, though, and decided to let the matter drop.

"I need that hip strap, Fran, and a package of black dye."

Her manner was crisp and clipped, and she took his order with a minimum of chitchat. If she wondered what the dye was for, she didn't ask. When she offered to put his purchases on account, Luke refused and paid cash. It wasn't easy. At this time of year, he didn't have a lot of money. But if Fran was going to pucker up like a prune over a dollar, he didn't want to give her the chance to get snippy again.

He was just about to leave the store—couldn't *wait* to leave—when his eyes fell upon a bolt of blue-green fabric on a table near the door. It was the color of a mallard's head, rich, dark, and almost iridescent. He glanced down at the box of black dye in his hand. He could imagine that teal color on a woman with creamy skin and light hair, the sun falling upon her and making her gleam like a rare gem. And wasn't that church social coming up?

"I'll take some of this, too." He pointed at the bolt.

Now Fran's dark brows drew slightly. "What? That grosgrain silk? I just got that in."

"Well, it's for sale, right?"

"Yes, but what are you—why would—" She stopped herself and her nose went up, and she was all businessy again. "How much do you want?"

"I don't know. Enough to make a dress."

"For Rose?"

"No, for a woman."

All the way home, Luke eyed the twine-and-paper-wrapped package in the wagon bed behind him, cursing his impulsive purchase. When he was young, he'd been impetuous, making decisions with no thought of the consequences, and more than once he'd paid the price. As he grew older and settled down, trying to prove himself to both Belinda and her mother had made him circumspect and, well, maybe even stodgy, he supposed. Something had come over him today, though. He wasn't sure if it had been Fran's curt attitude or something less easily defined. He'd just seen that fabric and thought of how well it would go with Emily's coloring.

Huh, as if he knew about that kind of stuff.

But now he was worried. She had asked only for black dye—what if she didn't want this material? Fran had tried to sell him just six yards, but he didn't know if that would be enough. So he'd bought ten. It had cost over five dollars, a hell of a lot of money for a dress or anything else that couldn't reproduce or provide food for the table. More than five dollars for *frippery*. And as soon as Fran had made the first cut with her scissors, he'd known he couldn't change his mind.

He passed Chester Manning's farm, where he saw Chester tending his sheep. The flock looked good, as good as sheep could, anyway. Luke had never been interested in raising them himself. Last year had been hard on the Mannings. Chester had fallen off the barn roof and broken his leg, smack-dab in the middle of harvest. He was laid up for over four months, and Luke had rallied the neighbors to help bring in the Mannings' onion crop. First they'd pulled the onions, and then everyone, including Chester's wife Jennie and their six kids, had spread them out to dry. Chester had watched the work from the back of a wagon, where he sat on a divan brought out from their parlor, cursing his bad luck and his splinted leg. After the onions had dried, everyone came back with wagons and drove Chester and his crop to market.

It had been a lot of work—two hundred acres' worth—but that's what neighbors did. It was so different from the way Luke had grown up—the old man had never done anything for anyone unless he stood to gain from the deed. People who acted out of charity or human decency were all saps to Cole Becker. Even those who'd occasionally helped his own family. But Cole had been such a miserable failure as a man and at life in general, Luke had finally figured out that if his father thought something was right, it must be wrong. Over the years, Luke had discovered that was usually true. So he tried to do the opposite of what Cole would have done, hoping everything would turn out.

Chester hailed him with a wave and a call. "Hey, Luke!"

"Whoa, there, whoa." Luke pulled up the wagon next to Chester's barbed wire fence.

The rawboned man walked along the fence to catch up to him. He still limped a little—the break had been a bad one. When he came abreast of Luke, he turned up his sad, weather-seamed face to Luke's and shaded his eyes. He was only a couple of years older than Luke, but he had the look of a man who'd spent forty years in the outdoors. After the two exchanged the usual talk about weather, crops, and feed-store prices, Chester said, "We heard about your new wife. Congratulations, Luke. Jennie is meaning to come by and say how-do to her one of these days. You know, make her feel welcome."

Luke smiled. Chester didn't ask a lot of nosy questions about how the marriage had come about, or comment that it was high time he took another to wife. He merely wished him well, and Luke appreciated it. "Thanks, Chester. Emily would like that. She hasn't had a chance to meet many people yet."

The other man nodded. "I ain't forgot how you helped us out last year, so I have a little wedding present for you." He turned and gestured at his flock of sheep. "You pick yourself out a ewe and a lamb. Whichever ones you want."

"Oh, hell, Chester, you don't have to do that. I wasn't the only one who came. A lot of folks worked to—"

"Now, now, it ain't a matter of *have* to. I want to do this. Yes, everyone pitched in, and I'm grateful to each but I know that you were the one who organized 'em."

His expression was naked and earnest. "God, Luke, I'd have gone bust if you all hadn't helped out."

Luke knew he couldn't offend the man's pride by declining his offer, but he didn't want a damned sheep. "It's too much—you can't be giving your flock away like that."

In the end, though, Luke drove home with a gift he wasn't certain he should have bought, and one he didn't want baaing behind him in the wagon bed.

CHAPTER EIGHT

EMILY SAT AT THE KITCHEN TABLE LOOKING AT A BOOK of dress patterns for Rose. Not knowing what might be available in Fairdale, she'd brought with her from Chicago the latest copy of *Metropolitan Fashions*, which featured Butterick patterns. As she studied the pages, she starred with a pencil those dresses she thought the girl might like. There were several nice ones, with simple lines and pretty aprons to wear over them. Some of the dresses had a single edge of pleats or one ruffle, but they wouldn't smother Rose. And they would be reasonably easy projects for her, if Emily helped. She could order them directly from the catalog, and even buy fabric, too, if she wanted to avoid going back to the general store. Or maybe she could take Rose on a shopping trip to Portland.

Oh, that was a grand idea. She gazed at the stove, imagining the adventure. They could catch the boat early one Saturday morning, go to one of the big department stores there—she'd overheard a pair of women talking about them on the trip from The Dalles. They'd been going all the way into Portland, and they made it sound like such a busy, cosmopolitan place. One of them mentioned a particular store, Meier & Frank, in almost reverent tones. She and Rose could have lunch in a nice café or even a tearoom, perhaps, and she could show Rose that knowing how to have proper tea wasn't the complete non-sense that Cora had implied. It would be even nicer if Luke came, too—they could stay for dinner and take a late boat back to Fairdale. It would be a wonderful day, the three of them together.

Emily's reverie came to an abrupt end when she realized how expensive such a trip would probably be. The boat fare and the spending money they'd need were probably a lot more than Luke could afford right now.

Sighing, she rested her hand on her chin and looked at the Butterick illustrations again. Well, she could still order the patterns and even the fabric by mail, and avoid a trip to the general store. But she knew that eventually, she'd have to deal with Fran Eakins again. She would simply have to rise above the woman's hostility. And, for all she knew, she might have actually put Fran in her place. Probably not, though.

Just as she marked another page in the catalog, she heard the horses drive past the house and the wagon's iron wheels crunch on the gravel drive. Her heart did a little flip, giving her a fluttery sensation in her chest that nearly took her breath. She told herself it was simply because Luke was back with her black dye and now she could do something about the deplorable state of her own dress. But that was silly, and she knew it wasn't true.

She wanted to see *him* again, to talk to him, even though he sometimes made her feel as tongue-tied as a girl Rose's age. She didn't like that part. That she should even be attracted to him was a mystery. He was not the kind of man she'd envisioned for herself, when she'd had the temerity—or hopeless hopefulness—to imagine a husband. She'd pictured a pale, slim, middle-class man who wore a suit every day to his job as a bank teller, or maybe even a secretary or senior clerk. He would have dexterous hands to play a musical instrument such as the violin, he'd like to read, and he would be well-informed about current events. Getting him to church would not be a struggle—he might even serve on a social welfare committee or two—and they would lead respectable, proper lives.

None of these descriptions fit Luke Becker. He was big through the chest and shoulders, and his arms were roped with muscle and tendon that moved in a fascinating concert when he worked. He had a farmer's hands, large, callused, and rough, but she'd seen him tend the horses with the gentleness of a physician. He probably had no musical ability, he'd grown up in questionable circumstances, had a reputation for being wild when he was young, and he drank whiskey at the kitchen table. He wore rough work clothes, had a job that got him dirty and sweaty, didn't like going to church, and rarely wore a suit, although he looked very nice when he did. No, he was not the man she'd pictured for herself. Circumstances and her impulsive decision had brought her to him.

Sometimes, though, a raw flicker flashed behind his weary eyes—she'd seen it this morning in her bedroom. When the "snake" had rattled in her wall again, she'd turned to Luke to point out the location and had caught him looking at her in a way that no man ever had. It was so brief, she almost thought she'd imagined it. After all, what did she know about how men looked at women? And why should she, Emily Cannon, believe for even one second that she could evoke that flicker she'd seen in his eyes? But she was intrigued by the very possibility, even as she feared it.

She waited now, expecting to see him walk through the back door. But the minutes ticked on, and he didn't come in. Cora thumped into the kitchen to start cooking lunch, clanking her pots and pans, and still he didn't come.

All right, then. Emily would go to him.

She closed the catalog and said to Cora, "I'm going to talk to Luke." She told her as a matter of courtesy, a habit she couldn't seem to break, and wasn't sure she should.

"Tell him I'm getting ready to put the noon meal on the table and we'll be setting down in a few minutes." The reminder was unnecessary. The whole family had been trained to Cora's schedule. Rose told Emily that Cora had followed the same routine for the three years she'd been here, and from what Emily could tell, nothing ever varied.

Still holding the catalog, she opened the door and went down the back porch steps. The morning had turned overcast and the sky looked threatening, with heavy clouds pushing in from the southwest.

She approached the barn with some uncertainty. It felt as though she was entering Luke's domain, a place where females might not be welcome. It rather reminded her of the private gentlemen's clubs in Chicago, where, it was said, men gathered to play cards, smoke cigars with impunity (often not the case in their own homes), discuss business, and put deals together. It was also rumored that some of the establishments had bars with paintings of nude women hanging on the back walls. Emily knew that to even wonder about those places was indecorous, but that rebellious part of her heart, the one that asked more questions than it should, had made her try to sneak a glimpse whenever she passed one and saw men coming or going through the door. It was all so deliciously forbidden.

As she stood in front of the barn, the atmosphere was dramatically different, but the feeling persisted. She took a step closer and heard a distinct bleating sound. As far

as she knew, Luke didn't keep goats or sheep. She came
around the corner and peeked inside. A warm draft of
animal scents and clean hay wafted over her. Inside she
saw all sorts of equipment and tools hanging on the
walls—hoes, scythes, shovels, harness, horse collars—as
tidy and well-kept as the rest of the property. The structure
was built with heavy timbers, and gray light filtered in
through the high, filmy windows.

"Well, I don't know what the hell I'm going to do with
you," Luke said. He stood with his thumbs hooked into
the waist of his pants and spoke to a pair of woolly ovines,
one grown, the other just a lamb. They eyed him, too,
from their spot just inside the barn doorway. The lamb
baaed back at him.

"Oh! Isn't it precious?" Emily blurted, utterly charmed
by the baby. She stepped forward into the dark cavern of
the barn.

He looked at her and rubbed the back of his neck.
"Yeah, Precious might end up as a good Sunday dinner."

"Not if Cora does the cooking." The words popped out
before Emily had the chance to even think of squelching
them. Horrified, she clapped her free hand over her mouth
and stared at Luke with wide eyes. "I beg your pardon!
That was very rude of me!"

But he only laughed. "Well, Emily. So you do have a
sense of humor under there. I wasn't sure."

"Oh, no!" She was genuinely distressed. "It's not right
to gain amusement at someone else's expense. Especially
if the person isn't here to defend herself! It's shameful,
like, well, like gossip."

He laughed again, this time with a conspiratorial gleam
in his dark gray eyes. The broad grin lit up his face. What
straight, white teeth he had, she noticed irrelevantly. "The
only shame is that we have to eat what she puts on the

table. Besides, it's true. Cora is a lousy cook."

She dropped her hand to her side. "Perhaps *lousy* is too strong a word . . ." she proposed.

Almost simultaneously, they both shook their heads and grinned at each other. This time Emily didn't even blush.

"I've offered to help out in the kitchen, but Mrs. Hayward won't let me. She said she doesn't need help. And anyway"—she gestured at the sheep—"you aren't really going to butcher this little thing for dinner, are you?"

He gestured at the lamb. "I'm no sheep rancher—I don't know what to do with them." He told her the story about Chester Manning. "I really tried to discourage him, but I couldn't turn him down without insulting him."

"Well, why don't you give them to Rose?"

"To Rose! These aren't cats or puppies that she can feed table scraps and take to her room. They have to be grazed and watched. A coyote could come down from the hills some night and snatch the lamb, carry him back to her pups for dinner. I'd rather have him on our own table than let a damned coyote get him."

"But Rose seems to like animals, and it would give you something to work on together. It might bring you closer."

That stopped him. He glanced at the ewe and her lamb again. "Do you think so?" The sudden hopefulness she saw in his eyes made her heart ache.

Actually, Emily was just guessing. None of her students' fathers had cared about spending time with their daughters or sharing an interest with them. Luke was different. "It's certainly worth a try." She nodded at the catalog she carried. "I've been looking at dress patterns for her. I thought I'd have her choose one or two, and order them and the fabric. Is that all right with you?"

"Whatever you think is best."

She nodded again, then added, "I don't want to keep you from your work. I just came out to get the black dye so I can fix this dress."

"Oh, yeah, um—I have it right here." He walked over to a hay bale and reached behind it to pull out a large, brown-paper-wrapped package tied with twine. A long blade of hay trailed from it.

She had to tuck the catalog under her arm to take the heavy parcel with both hands. "This is the dye?"

He ran a big hand through his hair and shrugged, looking as self-conscious as a boy giving his teacher an apple. "No—well, yeah, it is, but there's a little something else in there. I saw it and thought you might like it."

A gift? She draped the catalog over the top rail of a stall, and pulled away the string and paper. A package of dye lay on top of the loveliest material Emily had ever seen. Teal silk grosgrain, yards and yards of it.

"Ohhh," she exhaled, running light fingers over the ribs woven into the fabric. She even held it to her face to inhale the scent of the new material. There was no question that it was an expensive gift, one that had cost more than her wedding band.

"It's okay?" he asked.

Her throat closed and she found it difficult to respond. "Yes. I–I've never had anything so wonderful, Luke. But . . . but why?"

Now Luke really did look uncomfortable. "Well, I felt responsible for this—" He gestured at her black-and-orange costume. "My chickens ruined your dress, and my mother-in-law let it happen. I wanted to pay you back."

That took a little of the luster off the gesture. He felt obligated to her the way that Chester Manning had felt obligated to him. The teal grosgrain was a payment to her rather like the ewe and the lamb were to Luke. "I see. Well, thank you very much. It wasn't necessary, but I certainly appreciate it." With fussy movements, she began to wrap the paper around the fabric again. It was a difficult task to accomplish without a work surface. The paper rustled against the silk, and the string fell on the floor. The sheep looked on with half-closed eyes.

"And there's that church social coming up. I thought that maybe you'd like to go."

Her head came up at this, and suddenly the atmosphere in the barn changed. He was actually inviting her out. This wasn't like the day they'd gone to church. He *wanted* to be seen with her at his side. There would be dancing at the social, and perhaps Luke would even be willing to give her a turn on the floor before relegating her to the sidelines. Her heart beat faster.

"Yes, that would be nice. I'd like that very much." She envisioned the new dress she'd create from the rich blue-green silk. They would walk into the social together, she and Luke, and she would be proud to be seen on her husband's arm. Then her joy flattened like day-old champagne, and she sighed. "But I'll be in mourning for weeks yet, and it isn't proper for me to appear at social functions."

He gave her a casual dismissive gesture. "No one knows that. People aren't sitting by their calendars, waiting for you to slip up."

She eyed him with horror. He was suggesting that she cheat on her duties? "But *I'll* know." Once again, she recited the torturous social customs that governed mourning.

He took a step closer to her. Instinctively, she tried to back up but she felt a post between her shoulder blades. He reached out to tug on her sleeve with a light pull.

"Who made up that rule, anyway? Did God hand down stone tablets to someone? 'Thou shalt wear black for six new moons' or something like that?"

He stood so close to her now, she could barely think straight. "Of course not. It's just the way things are done. Without rules, society would be in chaos." More than ever, she struggled to clutch her values to her, trying to remember them and ignore the way he looked, the scent of him, of fresh air and clean sweat. When it came right down to it, she was afraid of the feelings he stirred in her.

"But some rules are made to be broken, especially if they don't make sense."

She lifted her chin. "Are you saying it doesn't make sense to honor Alyssa's memory?"

"No, but can you do that only by wearing black in public for six months?"

Something was wrong with his logic, but at this moment she couldn't put her finger on just what it was. She couldn't think of anything except him. The watery light from the windows fell on his face, highlighting the planes and hollows. He stood just inches from her. Only the width of the package separated them. She looked into his charcoal eyes, transfixed by the raw flame she saw there.

"Come on, Emily, say you'll go. It would be nice to get away from here for a few hours. Life shouldn't be nothing but work."

"All right, yes, I'll go." She hadn't meant to give in. It was as if he'd willed her assent from her. He lifted his hands and put them on her upper arms again, just as he had earlier this morning. His touch was warm through the thin crepe of her sleeves.

"And you'll wear your new dress?"

He seemed almost eager to be with her. She couldn't help but give him the answer he wanted. "Yes."

He moved one hand to her jaw and tipped her face up to his. His fingertips were rough on her skin, raising a rash of gooseflesh that flew over her scalp and down her back. She smelled Cora's lye soap on his clothes but somehow, even that aroma was intoxicating.

"Emily," he murmured, and her lashes fluttered under his warm breath. With the same slow, gentle movements she'd seen him use to soothe the horses, he lowered his face to hers and took her lips with his own. Soft and warm and slick, the kiss was brief but set her heart to pounding like a hammer on a rock.

He released her mouth and for a sweet instant touched his forehead to hers. "Thank you," he whispered. Then he pulled away, self-conscious once again. He crossed the floor and spoke to the ewe and the lamb. "Okay, for Rose and Miss Emily, I'll save you from the stew pot."

Emily grabbed up her catalog and, clutching her package to her chest, hurried out of the barn with her face flaming and wearing a secret smile.

The kiss—God, where had *that* come from? Luke wondered irritably as he herded the sheep toward the pasture. He hadn't planned to do that. He hadn't planned much of anything that had happened today, and it was only now lunchtime. The afternoon had better be more uneventful. He walked down the muddy path with the sheep in front of him, and it began to rain. Oh, this was perfect—not much smelled worse than wet wool.

Emily had just been standing there in the barn, her arms full of silk and brown paper. He didn't know if it was the light that had struck her just so, or if loneliness and temptation had simply gotten the better of him. The next thing he knew, he was kissing her.

And he'd liked it. A lot more than he'd expected. She'd

frozen under his touch like a frightened rabbit, but beneath her surprise and hesitance he'd felt a thrumming warmth, an eager softness that he could barely imagine, much less explain to himself. He only knew that it had been there.

He stopped at the gate and unhooked its rope loop from the fence post, then pushed the sheep through the opening. He slapped the bleating ewe on the rump as she passed. "Get in there—this is your lucky day. A nice lady convinced me to save you for Rose."

Luke closed the gate again and gazed out across the land and the heavy sky. Even though the rain poured down on him in earnest now, the day didn't seem so bad after all. Among those unexpected things that had happened, two had given him the greatest pleasure. As he headed back to the house for lunch, a chuckle worked its way up from his chest.

Emily was wearing her wedding band.

And Emily, with her fussy ways and starch-stiff rules of conduct, had kissed him back.

That night at dinner, Cora considered both Emily and Luke with a calculating gaze. First she'd caught Luke coming out of that woman's bedroom this morning, and now they looked like cats that had shared a canary. Neither of them seemed to be able to make eye contact, and they were each acting as though the other one was company, all anxious and polite.

"Would you care for more mashed potatoes, Luke?" Emily extended the bowl to him.

He took it from her hand. "Yes, ma'am. Thank you."

Lord, it was just sickening. And worrisome to Cora.

"Did you like the present your father brought home for you, Rose?" Emily asked.

The girl's face lit up like a kerosene lamp. "Oh, yes!

My very own sheep! Daddy said it was your idea to give them to me."

"Now what on earth is Rose going to do with sheep, Mrs. Becker?" Cora interjected, slapping a thick glob of butter on a biscuit. "Serve them tea and crumpets?"

"I thought she and her father could spend some time together taking care of them." The tone in Emily's voice reminded her of a preacher's wife talking, snotty and superior.

Cora hooted. "You've been here long enough to know that there isn't a spare minute on a farm. It's hard work from before sunup till after sundown. Luke, for heaven's sake, tell her."

He just shrugged like a simpleton. "It sounds like a good idea to me."

"I thought you wanted Rose to learn etiquette. There isn't much need for that with animals."

"I want her to learn about a lot of things, Cora."

Rose piped in, "And Miss Emily is going to teach me how to sew my own clothes! We even picked out two patterns she's going to send away for."

Cora put down the biscuit on her plate and stared at the three of them. "Is that so?" She knew what they were up to, Luke and his new wife. It wasn't enough that Emily Cannon had come out here and moved into her daughter's house. Now they wanted to take Rose away from her, too, her only grandchild. When Cora had threatened to go back to her own house, Luke had as much as held the door open for her. After three years of cooking, washing, and cleaning for him! And Emily had been helping the girl with her hair in the mornings, seeing her off to school like she had the right, meeting her on the porch when she came home in the afternoons. She hadn't even been here a month. "Don't you like the dresses I make for you, Rose?"

The girl stared at her plate and wouldn't look her in the eye. "Well, um, it's not that. I—" She stammered to a halt.

God, what nonsense were they putting into her head? Cora wondered.

"Well, then, what is it?"

"It won't hurt her to learn," Luke reiterated. "She needs to start learning how to do some things for herself. You can take care of the sheep and do some chores around the place, can't you, Rose?"

With short, angry motions, Cora took up the biscuit again and sopped it in her gravy. "Next you'll be telling me that she's old enough to get married and move out."

"Oh, damn it, Cora, nobody said—"

"Let her have her childhood. She's just a baby!"

"No, I'm not, Grammy!"

Cora pushed half a biscuit into her mouth and spoke around it. "I guess one of these days you'll tell me you don't need me to do *anything* for you anymore. Who needs old Grammy? She's just in the way."

Rose's face had turned chalky. "No, I don't mean that!"

Cora chewed furiously. "Oh, I know what you mean, all right. We'll just throw Grammy out in the road. We're done with her." She snapped her fingers. "Just like that."

Rose's chin began to quiver and her eyes filled with tears. "No, that's not so! Daddy, tell her it isn't so."

Emily sat witness to this, appalled at the histrionics Cora was using to manipulate Rose. She looked at Luke and saw a muscle tense in his jaw.

He stretched his hand across the table toward his daughter. "Rose, it's all right. Cora, can we get through one damned dinner without a case of indigestion for everyone?"

Cora wore a look of injured dignity. "What did *I* do? Absolutely nothing! What would Belinda say about this?" she demanded. "What would she say if she knew you were trying to force me out, always finding fault with me, when all I've ever tried to do around here is help?"

Rose swiveled her head between Cora and Luke. "Daddy—tell her it isn't so!"

"It *isn't* so, Rose." He spoke to his daughter but he leveled his gaze on Cora. "And your grandmother knows it."

This family was a nightmare, Emily thought, twisting her napkin in her lap. An utter nightmare. She had never in her life felt such tension or seen such shameful behavior at the table. Though she tried to remain neutral, ultimately she had to lay the initial blame squarely on Cora's shoulders. What had started out as a pleasant conversation about Rose and her new pursuits had deteriorated to this— this *scene*.

"Why, I'll bet your mama is spinning in her grave this very minute down at Fairdale Cemetery, wondering why no one in this house loves her or me any—"

Rose began to wail and Luke brought his fist down on the oak tabletop, making the dishes clatter. "Cora! That's enough!" His words boomed against the walls like summer thunder rolling across a valley. For several seconds, the only sound in the kitchen was that of Rose's sniffling and the coffeepot perking on the stove.

Cora looked as surprised as if he'd fired a warning shot from a rifle. Emily stared at him with wide eyes. It was the first time she'd heard him raise his voice.

"Rose, are you finished eating?" he asked, and Emily could see he was struggling to control his anger when he spoke to her. The girl nodded and dragged her sleeve across her nose. Emily said nothing about it. "Then you go on outside and see to your sheep. We'll bring them into the barn tonight—I want to check on the little one."

Rose nodded and slid out of her chair. She went to the back door, and then turned to glance at Cora. But her grandmother was still watching Luke, wary as a bird watching a cat. Emily sent the girl a private smile and she slipped outside.

Luke turned to her. "Miss Emily, ma'am—"

"I have a lot of things to do upstairs, so I'll excuse myself, if you don't mind."

Luke nodded at her, and she swept from the kitchen. Curiosity, one of her more regrettable traits, made her want to linger in the hall to hear what he would say to Cora, but her better nature conquered the temptation. As it turned out, she didn't need to be close by anyway. Even as she climbed the stairs, she heard Luke's voice, and although she couldn't make out the words, his tone reflected his aggravation. Cora's replies were loud enough for phrases to penetrate the floor of Emily's bedroom.

". . . why we couldn't go on as we always had . . ."

". . . turn her away from me . . ."

Emily puttered nervously at straightening her bureau drawers until she heard Cora's heavy tread on the stairs and her bedroom door slam.

If anything had been settled, she didn't know what it was.

Later that evening, Emily sat on her bed with her wonderful new fabric spread out next to her. It almost seemed too nice to cut with a scissors.

She hadn't seen Luke or Cora since dinnertime. Cora, she believed, was still ensconced in her bedroom. Luke was probably outside, taking advantage of the lingering daylight. As upsetting as dinner had been, it didn't dim her secret joy over this lovely gift he'd given her, or the kiss that had followed. He was the first man who'd ever kissed her. The memory of it—warm, soft, unexpected— lingered in her heart and memory. It had been *exciting*. And for the first time in her spinster's life, she had not felt too tall. Under Luke's touch, she'd actually felt small and delicate. It was silly, she knew, because she was nei- ther. It had been almost as if she'd put on her bridal veil, light and gossamer. Almost.

Should she try it now? Maybe it would work. She stood and went to her trunk, where the veil laid in repose. She had just unwound it from its tissue-paper cloud and was lost in thought when she heard a timid voice call her name.

"Miss Emily?"

Emily looked and saw Rose standing in her doorway, dressed in overalls and an old shirt. A shadow of worry still clouded her small face, and Emily wished she had the right to embrace the girl, to tell her that everything would be fine. But despite Luke's gift and the kiss, she wasn't sure she believed it herself. The specter of Belinda still haunted this house, and Cora was her willing mes- senger.

Hastily, she started to put the veil away again. "Come in, Rose. I was just looking at the fabric I'm going to use to make my new dress." She indicated the silk on her bed.

The girl came closer and pointed at the length of illu- sion. "What's that?"

Emily stopped the repacking process and looked at the white headpiece. "It was my grandmother's wedding veil. My mother wore it, too, and I'd hoped—well, I brought it along with me."

"Can I see?"

"*May* I see."

"Oh, yeah—may I?"

If talking to God and to her mother were Rose's secrets, this veil was Emily's. She kept it close to her heart and her dreams. But the girl had shared her own secrets, so perhaps it was only fair that Emily return the confidence. Carefully she unfurled the veil and spread it out over the rocking chair.

Rose approached with a reverence and respect that touched Emily's heart. "Oh, it looks like something a princess would wear!" She extended a hand and Emily's breath stopped, but the girl added, "I washed my hands before I came up. Can I—may I just feel the edge?"

Emily forced herself to relax. Rose had had such a horrible experience at dinner, she couldn't bring herself to deny the request. "Of course. But it's very old, so you'll want to be careful."

Rose nodded and touched the lace edging with a single, gentle fingertip.

"There's a gown that goes with it. I'll show it to you someday."

"I'd like that! Is it as pretty as this?"

"*I* think it is. But it was made for a small woman, probably one about your mother's size."

Rose made no reply to that, but her gaze drifted to the teal silk on the bed. "That's pretty, too."

"Yes, your father picked that out himself. Didn't he make a good choice?"

"Uh-huh," the girl answered, but she was fingering the brown paper it had been wrapped in. "Are you going to keep this?"

"That wrapping? Why, would you like to have it?"

"It would be good to draw on."

There was probably six or seven feet of paper there, and yes, it would be good for that. "Yes, I believe you're right. You may have it if you'd like." Emily pulled the paper away from the material and rolled it up to hand to Rose. "There you are."

"Thank you," she intoned, plainly delighted. A person might have thought that Rose had been given a gold necklace or a year's worth of strawberry drops instead of a length of plain brown wrapping. She clutched Emily around the waist and hugged her for the length of a heartbeat.

Then she scampered out of the room, leaving Emily surprised and damp-eyed.

Heavy rain pounded down on the roof late that night as Luke lay in his bed staring at the dark ceiling. The confrontation with Cora at the table had carried him another step closer to telling her to move out. Just one thing she'd said had stopped him, and it was the same device she used whenever she didn't get her own way.

She'd invoked Belinda's name.

A cascade of blame and remorse had washed over him, and even now he felt Belinda's accusing finger jabbing at his shoulder from beyond time and loss: He'd kissed another woman today in the barn. He'd even bought her a present that he really couldn't afford. No matter how much he'd wanted to hold Emily in his arms, and regardless of how long Belinda had been gone, guilt got in the way of his desires.

The last night he'd talked to his late wife had been like this one, cold and wet, with a hard east wind that lashed the rain against the house in sheets. Well, they hadn't really talked. They'd argued. Again. Cora had come for dinner, during which time she'd reviewed what she saw as Luke's many failings.

The jabs had been subtle—the new stove he'd bought wasn't the best one, was it?

What a pity he hadn't been able to get enough money together to get a neat little surrey for Belinda to drive to town.

Ray Ellison had taken *his* wife to San Francisco for a second honeymoon. Wasn't it too bad that Luke hadn't been able to give Belinda a honeymoon at all?

She'd tried to rearrange the parlor furniture to suit herself and had criticized Belinda for doting upon Rose.

Afterward, Luke's simmering resentment had boiled over onto his wife. Why could she never take his side during one of Cora's tirades? Or give him her permission to defend himself against the fault-finding nag? Out of respect for his wife, he'd held his tongue, but a man had his limits. . . . If she didn't feel up to that task, couldn't she at least ask her meddling mother to keep her opinions to herself, goddamn it?

It had been nothing more than a rehash of other arguments, older hurts, and discontentments. He'd loved her so much, but no matter how hard he'd tried to please her, Cora always gave her reasons to be unhappy with him.

Finally, one night, that night, he'd decided he couldn't take it anymore. If he'd known what lay ahead, if he'd kept his temper under control, life might be different now. He and Belinda, the only woman he thought he could ever love, might be lying in the bed in the room where Emily now slept. They'd be listening to the rain hit the house and he might still think of himself as the luckiest man on earth.

He rolled over and swallowed hard, hoping for sleep and trying to forget the image of Belinda in her coffin before the undertaker nailed down the lid.

CHAPTER NINE

SEVERAL DAYS LATER EMILY CARRIED HER BASTED DRESS to the sewing machine in the parlor to stitch the bodice to the skirt. After dinner tonight, she would help Rose with her own new dress. Now, though, she took advantage of the quiet and solitude to work on the teal.

She'd used a pattern that she'd brought with her from Chicago but had never tried. The outfit was making up beautifully, even nicer than she'd expected. She'd willed her hands to remain steady while she cut out the pattern pieces—one slip of the scissor blades, one sleeve cut from the wrong side of the silk, and an expensive length of fabric might have been ruined. But so far, everything had gone well. She had only to attach the skirt and the sleeves, and the garment would be ready for hemming. With no full-length mirror to look into during fittings, Emily had used her best judgment as to fit and drape.

That she was permitted to use Belinda's treadle Singer seemed like nothing short of a miracle. She had expected to get an argument from Cora. Strangely enough, it had been Luke who seemed a bit reluctant. After the kiss in the barn and his gift of the teal silk, he had become distant with her. He wouldn't meet her gaze and at times seemed to be avoiding her outright. Of course, she shouldn't be surprised by that. She had probably been a clumsy kisser—after all, what experience did she have? Or perhaps he'd thought her forward for kissing him back. She wasn't even sure he still intended to take her to the basket social, but she forged ahead anyway, trying to pretend as if nothing had changed, that she hadn't noticed the rejection. She ought to be accustomed to rejection by now. How odd that it still hurt after all these years, that she *still* felt inadequate.

She smoothed a basted seam with her hand. Ashamed though she was to admit it to herself, Emily looked forward to getting out of mourning. She was utterly tired of wearing the same dark clothes day after day. The dye had helped the one ruined dress, but in some lights it still looked streaked. There were so many shades of black— some had blue undertones in them, some had red, and others brown. The dye didn't match the original color of the dress, and she'd had limited success in covering the orange. She sighed. Queen Victoria, that champion of morality, still wore mourning for her beloved Prince Albert, and he'd been dead for nineteen years. Of course, it would be easier if one were a queen. With royal wealth, one could wear a different gown every day, and never the same one twice. But that was a petty thought—she was certain that Victoria would trade her fortune to have her prince consort alive and well again.

But maybe Luke had been right—maybe it *wasn't* necessary to wear mourning clothes like a flag to advertise one's grief. In fact, if she thought about it, she might even consider it to be showy and ostentatious, instead of a private matter of the heart and soul.

With her dress draped over her arm, she borrowed the chair from the escritoire next to the sewing machine cabinet and sat down at the Singer. The desk's drop leaf was open, as if someone had been sitting there earlier, and she noticed a half-finished letter on the desk. Next to it lay a red stub of dull pencil, its eraser rubbed down to the nickel tip. She knew she shouldn't even try to identify the handwriting. It was personal correspondence that was none of her business. But as she guided the waist seam under the presser foot, her gaze kept straying to the lined writing tablet and the fuzzy gray words. Keeping her face pointed toward the machine, she lifted her chin and cast her eyes to the side, as if spying on the letter in such a manner would somehow be all right.

Dear Cousin Eunice . . .

Emily turned her head just a little more—it made the muscles in her eyes ache to pull them so far to the right.

How ar things going for yu in Casper?

She leaned sideways just a bit.

We ar all fine here mostly. Ecept Luke has gon and married a mail orderd bride . . .

So, this was Cora's letter. Her bad spelling made the lines difficult to decipher.

I dont no why he did it, we were getting along well enouff. You would think he would be true to poor Belinda's memory, after what he did to her. She would be a-live today if not for him. She would still be here if he had not . . .

A cold hand closed around Emily's heart, and her throat dried. *After what he did?* she thought, her feet pumping the treadle furiously. *What could he have done?* But the letter stopped there, unfinished.

When she looked down at her dress again, she discovered that she'd run the stitching off the seam line and into the gathered skirt.

"For heaven's sake," she muttered and removed her foot from the treadle. If she needed more proof that nosiness was a social sin, she had it here, in twelve inches of meandering thread that she'd have to tear out.

Carefully she pulled on the tight, close stitches with a hatpin. If she were too rough, she'd create runs in the silk, so she had to concentrate. But Cora's cryptic words remained with her as she corrected her sewing error. She realized that she had never been told how Belinda died, and it had never been mentioned in any of Luke's letters to Alyssa. People died all the time—illness, accident, childbirth. It had not occurred to her or her sister to wonder about the cause of Luke Becker's widowerhood. Of course, it would be too rude to ask. Cora's letter to Cousin Eunice stated that he was somehow responsible for her death.

And that reminded her of how little she really knew about Luke. He had not been very forthcoming about his life, and she'd assumed his past was too painful to discuss. But what if it *were* too ghastly—for darker reasons?

Emily realized that she had nothing to base this on except a cranky old woman's badly spelled, unfinished note, and she supposed that it was little better than gossip. But a cloud of doubt remained. She could ask Rose, but Emily knew she had no right to make a young girl answer questions that she was afraid to ask herself.

She tugged out the last bad stitch and positioned her dress under the presser foot again. The letter sat on the writing desk, a glaring indictment written in dull pencil.

She kept her eyes on her own business this time—the sewing machine needle rising and falling with each push of the treadle.

But it wasn't easy.

Cora pulled a rag-covered corn broom over the upstairs hall floor, dragging dust from the corners and woodwork. Maybe she didn't have Mrs. Becker's fine and fancy ways, but no one could accuse her of being a bad housekeeper. No sirree. She could cook and clean and wash circles around that high-flown etiquette teacher, and when people were hungry or dirty, a hot meal and line-fresh clothes were a lot more important than remembering which fork to use.

Listen to the racket down there—that treadle machine was getting a workout, with her sewing away on her new dress. And what had Luke been thinking of, spending all that money on a piece of yardage like that, when calico would have done just as well? A body would think that Emily was the Queen of Araby, to need such a swanky getup.

Well, maybe that dummy letter to Cousin Eunice would open Emily's eyes about her mail-ordered husband. Emily would probably think it was none of her business to read someone else's mail. But Cora knew human nature, too. She had left the tablet in a good place, and it wouldn't be very hard to read what she'd written there. It might take a while, but eventually Emily Becker would realize that she'd made a big mistake and pack herself back to Chicago. They would be done with her.

She continued her trip through the hall and into the rooms, dusting as she went. She was secretly disappointed to find Emily's bedroom as neat as a pin. Cora stretched her dust mop to the top of the doorframe—*no one* dusted the tops of doorframes—but her mop came away clean. She frowned.

Pushing open the door to Luke's room, she looked first for Belinda's vanity set and their wedding photograph. There they were, standing in their proper places, although the silver-backed hand mirror and brush were showing signs of tarnish. She would have to remedy that. At least Luke seemed to have given up stowing the keepsakes in a bottom bureau drawer. She'd fished them out often enough to prove that two could play the game, and she had won.

It was a spare-looking room, but what could a person expect from a man? It was neat enough, so she supposed she ought to be glad for that. He made his own bed and hung his clothes on the back of the corner chair. If he was sneaking around at night to be with his "bride," she couldn't tell.

In her own bedroom, she dusted her way in, stopping once to turn the cloth. Then she stretched a chapped hand toward Belinda's porcelain doll that sat on top of the bureau and tweaked a flounce on its dress. Luke had wanted to give the doll to Rose, but Cora had known it would just get dirty. This was a nice doll, not one made of rags or old socks that a child could drag around by its neck. Belinda's father had brought it home to her for her tenth birthday, which, in Cora's opinion, was the least he could do after he'd brought them out here, away from family and friends.

A paradise, he'd promised her. A fool's paradise, more like it. She'd buried her only boy on the trip out, after he fell from the wagon and got run over by the wheels. One of the iron rims had cut his arm clean off. She never forgave Wendell for that, and she never let him forget it, either, by God. She'd put all of her hope in Belinda after that. Belinda would find a good husband and not end up being just a farmer's wife.

Then Belinda had married Luke Becker. And now she was gone, too. Cora sighed heavily.

But she still had Rose, who was the spitting image of her mama. She left her own room and went to finish her dusting chore in Rose's bedroom. It looked as if a cyclone had been through here, with socks and underwear falling out of the dresser drawers and the good Lord knew what-all under the bed. One side of the pink gingham curtains was pulled askew, as if Rose had been trying to see to the pasture where her sheep grazed. Cora indulged her, though, because she knew that Rose loved her, even if *they* were trying to weaken the girl's loyalty.

She set the broom against the wall and went to the bed to pull the covers into place. How one small girl could make such a whirlwind out of a bed—and, God, now what was she sleeping with? She heard a crinkle of paper and searched the quilt and top sheet until she ferreted out a rolled tube of brown wrapping. Pulling it open like a scroll, she saw more of Rose's silly scribbling. How could Mrs. Becker believe that this was a worthy pursuit, this waste of time? It didn't teach the girl a thing about how to get a cow milked, or supper cooked, or floors mopped. Bah.

Holding the brown paper at arm's length, Cora studied the sketched figures more carefully. The drawing began on the left side of the roll and seemed to progress like the traveling pan-o-rama that came through town one time. That one had shown the story of Abraham Lincoln's as-sassination, an amazing and gruesome display.

She stretched her arms a bit more, trying to identify the pictures. Oh, that was better. There were Belinda, Luke, and Rose, all together in front of the farmhouse.

Then she'd drawn in a picture of Fairdale Cemetery with Belinda's headstone, complete with a tree and flowers. That gave way to a drawing of Luke, Rose, and Cora at the farm. She smiled at the image of the girl holding only her hand and not Luke's. Then Cora's smile faded. There was an unmistakable rendering of the boat dock in town, and a tall, skinny woman in a black dress. In the next image, only partly finished, Rose was holding Emily's hand.

With her jaws clamped, Cora rolled the paper into a tight tube and jammed it behind Rose's feather pillow.

That evening after dinner, Luke lingered at the table, trying to decide if he would take his whiskey bottle with him when he went to the barn. The lamb he'd brought home from Chester's had turned sickly, and he'd put both of the sheep in a back stall where it was warm and dry. Since Rose was out there now, sitting with them, Luke figured he'd better leave the bottle here.

He saw Emily pass through the hallway, her shawl around her shoulders. The front door opened and closed. He couldn't imagine what she'd want to do out there on the porch, except it was probably far enough away to escape the stink of the boiled cabbage that Cora had served for dinner. Luke grew the stuff, but he didn't like it at all. At least not the way that Cora cooked it.

He wanted to follow Emily and reassure her somehow. He'd sensed a coolness in her. She hadn't been any less polite or proper. He didn't believe that her notions of gentility would let her behave otherwise. But something about her was different. If the aloofness *was* there, he was responsible for it. He might have hurt her, and in doing so, had hurt himself, too.

Luke had allowed Cora to shame him into retreating to

his memory of Belinda, which had become more of a curse than a bittersweetness. Trying to force himself to ignore Emily, to forget the feel of her soft lips under his own was stupid and destructive—it made him miserable and discontented, and served no good purpose. At night he lay in his cold bed, married but not, knowing that she was on the other side of the wall, and wondered if she was thinking about him, too. Or he'd wake up in the darkness, sweaty and restless, dreaming of a blond woman with a willowy grace and long legs, which she wrapped around his waist as he took her with heat and tenderness. Luke had never been shy around women but the image in his head brought heat to his face even as it heated his groin.

His gaze strayed to Cora's broad back and the knot of faded red hair on her head. She stood at the sink pouring a kettle of boiling water over the washed dinner dishes to rinse them. Watching her, resentment welled up in him, as bitter and dark as gall. She'd probably be content—at least as content as that woman could be—to keep the three of them, Rose, Luke, and herself, here, frozen in place until they died, one by one. He pictured their headstones, all lined up next to each other at Fairdale Cemetery, and a chill flew down his back. Cora was a peevish old bag, but she wasn't in charge here. He was.

Goddamn it, he'd told Rose that life was for the living. It was time that he started following his own advice. He pushed his chair away from the table.

"Where are you off to now?" Cora demanded.

"I'm going to find my wife," he said. Her pinched expression gave him great satisfaction. He pulled open the back door and bounded down the steps.

When he came around the house, he found Emily sitting on an old stool on the side porch. He'd have to see about getting her a better chair, and maybe one for himself. It might be nice to sit out here on summer evenings and watch the twilight come on. The low evening sun fell on her fine features and made them as warmly luminous as an eggshell held before a candle. She was a very handsome woman, and she seemed more so with every passing day, he realized.

Her gaze dropped to him as he approached the bottom step. "Would you mind some company?" he asked.

"Um, no, not at all. Please—sit." She wasn't very convincing. She rounded her shoulders and glanced away. He sat on the step below her feet and leaned against the newel post. The pointed toes of her black shoes peeked out from beneath her black hem. "Is Rose still in the barn?"

"I think so. She's been nursing that lamb as if she were its mother." He tipped back his head to watch a pair of geese fly over, honking as they went. It was quiet here, and the smell of spring and new hope filled his head and soothed his spirit.

"I hope the poor little thing survives."

He shrugged. "It's not really a pet. Rose understands that animals die."

"But she's lost so much—I mean, her mother and all."

Even now, the pale ghost of Belinda's memory insinuated itself between them. Would it ever rest in peace? "Yes, I suppose she has."

Between twiddling with the ends of her shawl, Emily folded and unfolded her hands in her lap. From what he'd noticed about her, she didn't usually fidget like this. "Mr. Becker—I mean, Luke—"

He waited. She seemed to be struggling with a big request. God, he hoped she wasn't going to ask for more cash. After he'd bought the silk and given her money to order Rose's dress patterns and material, there just wasn't enough right now. He wouldn't see good income again until harvest.

"This is rather awkward, and ordinarily I would not ask such a question—" Color filled her cheeks and she entwined her fingers again.

Awkward. Damn, it had to be about money, he thought. In his experience, that was *always* an awkward subject. He and Belinda had often disagreed about money, usually after she'd been talking to Cora. Emily was reasonable, though. She had to understand his circumstances. If she didn't, he'd be obliged to explain what a farmer's year—

"Forgive me for asking, but how did the first Mrs. Becker pass away?"

If she had kicked him in the chest with her pointy-toed shoes, he couldn't have been more surprised. The call of frogs croaking down by the stream seemed as loud as thunder. "I thought you knew. Didn't Cora tell you?"

"Well, no, not exactly. And you've never mentioned it." Now her face was the color of the blood-red sunset.

No he hadn't. Because he didn't talk about it. "It was pneumonia."

"Pneumonia?" The tone of her question asked for more.

But he didn't want to go into the details that had led to Belinda's fever—he couldn't. He never discussed them. He was ashamed of himself and had borne the guilt these three years. Belinda shouldn't have died. The night that led her to her grave had begun a relentless string of shouldn't-haves.

"Yes, ma'am." He folded his arms across his chest and stared at her. He wasn't about to admit his sin to Emily, who seemed to have never done anything wrong in her life.

Emily started fiddling with her shawl again. "I'm sorry. I shouldn't have asked. It's just that . . ."

He waited for her to continue but she didn't.

"Just that what?"

"I—we know so little about each other." She sounded almost wistful.

He uncrossed his arms. "Yeah, I guess you're right. I'll bet I know even less about you than you do about me. After all, you had a chance to read about me."

She flushed, and he was sorry. He hadn't meant that the way it sounded. It was only the truth. "I mean, I never had any letters from you."

"Oh, yes, I see."

He leaned against the railing again and considered her. "What would you tell me about yourself if you were going to write to me?"

"What?"

"Well, if you had answered my advertisement for a bride, what kind of letter would you have sent to me?"

"You already know that I'm a teacher and that I worked in a girls' school. What else is there?"

"Shoot, there's a lot more. Describe yourself to me. What do you look like?"

She ducked her chin and stared at her lap. She was silent so long he wondered if she was going to answer. At last she said, "I see no need to be cruel, Mr. Becker." She took a deep breath. "I apologize again if my question was too personal."

God, now he really felt like a heel. "You don't know, do you?"

"Know what?"

"How pretty you are."

Her head came up at this and she looked at him with wet eyes that pleaded for mercy. "I know that you are lying." Her low voice shook. Now he really did feel as if he'd been kicked in the chest, right over his heart.

He scooted closer and took her cold hands in his. He wasn't going to say that she was the most beautiful creature he'd ever seen, because that *would* sound like a lie. "No, I'm speaking the truth. You're a fine-looking woman. Hasn't anyone ever told you that?"

She tried to pull her hands away but he held them fast. "Of course not! Alyssa was beautiful but—"

"Tell me what you look like," he insisted quietly.

"Why are you doing this?" Her voice held a tortured edge. "It's no secret that I am plain! I've never pretended that I'm not. I am too tall and I am plain. My hair is too light—"

"What color are your eyes?"

"They're green."

"Like the clover."

Her brows rose slightly.

"What color is your hair?"

"I told you, it's too light."

He shook his head. "Naw, that's not a good description, teacher. It's blond. Like ripe wheat, like a palomino in the sun. Like high grass at the end of summer."

She stared at him, tears overflowing the rims of her eyes. But she was intrigued, he could see that.

"I'm tall," she ventured in a small voice, as if waiting to see what good he could find in that fact.

"Yes, you are," he agreed. "And graceful like a birch tree in the breeze."

"But plain."

"Nope, sorry. That just isn't so."

"Yes, it is. I've seen it reflected in other people's faces when they look at me. And I've heard it more often than you can imagine."

"From who?"

"From Fran Eakins and Clara Thurmon, to name two.

And from my stepfather, from my mother—"

Clara and Fran, that didn't surprise him. But her own mother? "Your mother told you that?"

"Yes. 'I've never had to worry about you, Emily,' she said, 'you're a sensible female. There's no shame in being plain. Pretty women are decorative, but plain ones get the work done.' "

Damn but if that didn't sound like something Cora would say. "That may be, but you are pretty to me. And you can't change my mind." Her hands squeezed his ever so lightly, as if involuntarily.

Even though his background was about as different from Emily's as it could get, he'd never given much thought to his looks or how it might feel to be thought of as homely. Women had always been attracted to him, so he'd never pondered the problem. He remembered homely kids around town, though. They'd either been bullied and teased or ignored completely. He suspected that Emily had probably been the target of the same kind of treatment and it bothered him. This graceful female could use some compliments.

"Where did you grow up?"

"In Chicago."

He smiled. "I know that. Did you live in a big house or a little one?"

Emily couldn't believe this. No one had ever asked so many questions about her. She dabbed at her eyes with her handkerchief. She wasn't certain what Luke's motives were, but as unaccustomed as she was to personal attention, she basked in it like a cat in an afternoon sunbeam.

So she told him about her father, Captain Adam Gray, lost in a storm on the lake, and about being adopted by Robert Cannon when he married her widowed mother. "He was a successful businessman and owned several warehouses. We lived in a nice neighborhood." This was an understatement. The Cannons had lived on Washington Boulevard, a street of elegant homes with servants in every one. "Then Chicago caught fire in 1871." She paused a moment. "And that was the beginning of our end."

Luke sat back and listened, without interrupting or showing boredom, while she described the loss of Robert's business assets—he'd never believed in insurance—which eventually forced them to sell the elegant home and move to successively poorer neighborhoods.

"My stepfather never seemed to come to grips with his losses. After my mother died, he sank into melancholy, and became more and more apathetic. I think his one remaining hope was that Alyssa would make a good match and rescue the family from its despair. He had no expectations of me except that I support us with my teaching job while he waited. He died before that happened. Alyssa and I were the only ones left." She threaded her fingers together and looked out toward the stands of dark firs that bordered the property. "And of course, now there's just . . . me."

Emily leveled her gaze on Luke, smoke-eyed and handsome. She'd lived her entire life under the admonition "What will people think?" True feelings were never discussed, manners and deportment were paramount to all else. Hurts and disappointments were hidden behind masks of outward serenity. No one, it was believed, wanted to hear about another's problems or misfortunes, and it was considered bad form to discuss your own. Even when the Cannons had tumbled down to rented rooms on one of Chicago's back streets, gentility had been more important than anything else. She sometimes thought that Robert and Letty Cannon had died of shame, rather than the weak hearts the doctors had ascribed to them. They had tried to pretend that nothing was different. But ultimately, she believed, they couldn't cope with the loss of the world they'd become so accustomed to, or with the possibility of what their former friends must have thought of them after that loss.

Certainly Emily found nothing wrong with being kind, self-reliant, and forbearing. But a lifetime of pretending that everything was just fine—well, it was lonely. In all of her years she'd had only Alyssa to confide in, and even then, her sister had never understood what it was like to be seen as gawky and not well-favored.

How extraordinary, then, that she felt comfortable telling all of this to Luke, who sat at her feet and gave her his full attention. And how wonderful. She saw his gaze drop to her lips and down the front of her bodice. It returned to her mouth and hovered there. A spark of excited anticipation kindled within her.

"Daddy!" Rose's voice broke the spell between them and Luke turned to watch his daughter run toward them from the barn. Her face was flushed with excitement and she pulled on Luke's arm, trying to get him to his feet. "Daddy, come and look at Cotton, please? I think he's better."

"Cotton?" Emily asked.

"That's what I named the lamb. He looks like a puff of cotton." Rose beamed like a buttercup, and Emily felt her heart swell with joy.

Luke stood and stretched his back. "Well, let's go see how he's doing." He turned to look at Emily and smiled. "I'm glad we had a chance to talk. I'd like to make a habit of it."

Emily smiled, too, and watched Rose drag her father

across the yard, making him laugh as he went. As she watched them disappear into the barn, her smile faded. If Belinda had died of pneumonia, why did Cora claim that Luke was responsible for her death?

CHAPTER TEN

THE NEXT AFTERNOON, EMILY WAS SITTING BY THE WINdow in her room hemming the sleeves of her new dress when she heard a ruckus among the birds in the oak outside. She glanced up, expecting to see that a cat or some other predator had encroached upon a nest, threatening a bird family living in the branches. Instead, through the new leaves she saw a pair of goldfinches, their wings fluttering wildly as the brightly plumed male covered the plainer female in a mating that took only the blink of an eye.

Everywhere around the farm she'd seen the same life-affirming ritual repeated with other animals. Well, it was spring, after all. She bent her head to her task to take a small bite of fabric with her needle, then looked up again. Her hands stilled in her lap as a rush of realization and regret flowed over her. Perhaps that was why Luke had suddenly become so attentive to her. He had been widowed for three years, and even though he'd told her that there would be no traditional romance between them, she was a handy female living right under his own roof. And that was all there was to it. Man was supposed to be superior to animals and have dominion over them, but the truth was, all of human and animal kind were part of the same earth, with its ancient rhythms and cycles and primal urges. It wasn't a very flattering thought, but regardless of Luke's compliments yesterday, she knew that she was not attractive. She swallowed. Maybe spring fever had made him see her with a rosy glow that she didn't really possess. Wait until summer or fall came along.

But she had barely slept last night for remembering the way he'd looked at her, the kindness she'd seen in his smoke-colored eyes, and how her icy hands had felt warmed when he took them into his own. Everything feminine in her wanted to ignore her common-sense explanation of why Luke had sat on the porch with her, why she'd caught him watching her with a raw yearning that even she could recognize. In the deepest core of her, she felt herself responding to the same stirrings that the rest of the earth seemed to take in stride. She could easily imagine Luke covering *her* with his lean, hard body.

The very notion scandalized, and yet tantalized. In fact, her own yearning begged her to believe that there was more to his attentions than a basic animal drive. But doubt plagued and confused her. When she looked in the square mirror in her room this morning, she saw the same face staring back at her that she'd known for twenty-eight years. The past weeks on the farm had not transformed her so that Luke would see someone besides the tall, plain woman who'd arrived here from Chicago. Only her bridal veil could perform that kind of magic. Even that notion was a work of fancy, one that she was trying to let go of. How odd that even as a rational, mature woman, she clung to the idea, the hope.

And then there was still the matter of Belinda's death. . . .

Emily was alternately puzzling over these thoughts and whipstitching her sleeves when she heard Rose thunder up the stairs and slam her bedroom door. She was home from school already? Emily looked at the watch pinned to her bodice and realized how late it had gotten. Muffled sobs floated to her and she debated whether to intrude or not. She'd made good strides with Rose, but her role was still vague and undefined. No, she decided, the girl was suffering. Emily's protective instinct took over and she put aside her stitching with the intention of comforting her. Before could leave her chair, though, Rose darted out of her bedroom again and charged back downstairs.

"Rose! Where do you think you're off to now?" Cora's grating voice spiraled up the stairwell to Emily's ears.

"The barn."

"Well, missy, you just think about what I said. And since you and Mrs. Becker want to be family, you can make your own blamed supper." Emily heard the front door slam. It reminded her of when the servants used to argue in the kitchen on Washington Boulevard, but this was far worse. The servants had never yelled at her or Alyssa. *What in the world is going on?* Emily wondered. She didn't have to wait long for an answer.

"You! Mrs. Becker!" Cora's rude bellow came to her. "I'm going to sit with Bertie Richmond. She sprained her ankle and she can't get her housework done. I hope you know how to cook."

The back door slammed with enough force to rattle the windows. And Emily found herself alone in a suddenly quiet house.

"Miss Emily?"

Emily looked up from the pile of potatoes that she was peeling, and not very well, she had to admit. At the back screen door, Rose stood with a dirt- and tear-streaked face, clutching Cotton to her chest. She struggled with the lamb's limp weight. Its back feet dragged around Rose's knees, the little hooves brushing against the legs of her overalls.

"Rose!" She jumped from her chair and the potato she held slid out of her hands, bouncing across the floor. She ran to the screen door and held it open. "What happened?"

"Cotton is worse again! He's gasping for air. Daddy isn't back from the feed store, and I don't know what to do."

"Bring him in here." Without a thought for the potatoes or the clean dinner plates she'd put out, Emily pushed everything aside to make room for the sheep. His fleece was grimy with hay, manure, and dirt, but that didn't even cross her mind. "What did your father say is wrong with him?"

"He said something about congestion of the lungs, but Cotton was getting better, truly he was." Bewilderment and terror crossed her face in waves. "Only now—now—"

Only now the little thing seemed to be panting as if he'd run across a field, his sides heaving with the effort to draw one breath. Now and then, he issued a weak bleat.

Emily didn't know the first thing about animal medicine, but she had rudimentary knowledge of how to ease a human's breathing problems. "All right, we'll have to work quickly. Get under the table."

"What?"

"Go on. We'll make a steam tent, and you need to hold him. I have a bottle of eucalyptus oil upstairs that we'll use for an inhalant." Rose crawled under, and Emily picked up the lamb and handed him to the girl. Then she raced out of the kitchen and upstairs to her bedroom to get the oil. She opened her trunk and flung things right and left before she found the tissue-wrapped vial at the bottom. Galloping back down the stairs, she skidded to a halt in front of the sideboard, pulled open a drawer, and yanked out two tablecloths to make the tent. She flung them over the table, arranging them so that they reached the floor and created an enclosure underneath. Turning to the stove, she stoked the fire to a hot blaze, then pumped water into two big kettles and put them on the burners. From the kettle that always sat on the back of the stove, she poured boiling water into two crockery bowls and dripped over them the oil of eucalyptus. The aromatic vapor instantly filled the kitchen and gave it the odor of a sickroom.

"Rose, here are bowls of hot water. Be careful that you don't burn yourself." She lifted one flap of the makeshift tent and pushed the medicated water inside. "Try to hold his nose close to the vapors."

"Oh, he won't let me!" The lamb struggled in Rose's arms, apparently having enough life left to fight his nurse. Emily dropped to her hands and knees and crawled under the table to help.

"He's probably scared and doesn't understand that we're trying to heal him." She took the baby onto her lap and tipped his head close to one of the bowls. "Just hold him there."

Rose's fear showed in her pale cheeks and tear-wet eyes. "Please let him live," she prayed. "Please. He's so little. And—and I don't have much family."

Emily's heart clenched in her chest. "What do you mean, dear? You've got your father and your grandmother—"

"No, Grammy is mad at me. She found my drawing and she said I don't love her."

God, again? Emily thought wearily, struggling with the lamb's hooves. "What drawing?"

The girl dashed a dirty hand across her eyes. "I've been drawing a picture on that brown paper you gave me. Kind of like that tapestry you told me about, the By–Bygone one?"

"You mean the Bayeux Tapestry?"

"Yes, that's it. I've been sketching the story of our family on that long piece of paper. I started with Mama and Daddy and me in front of our house, and then I drew in Mama's grave." She went on to describe the picture as she'd sketched it thus far. "Then you come along in the story." Rose hung her head and her braids swung forward.

"And your grandmother didn't like that?" Emily could just imagine that she didn't.

The girl gave a tremendous wet sniff and Emily heard the agony of heartache in her voice. "She said that I must not love her anymore and that I'd better figure out which side my bread is buttered on. I don't know what that means, but it sounds bad."

Just then, footsteps sounded on the stairs and the back door opened. "Lord above! Good Lord above!" Cora had returned. "Are those *Belinda's* table linens?" Her voice climbed in volume with each word. Rose flashed Emily a look of fear.

She put the lamb back in the girl's lap and crawled out of the tent. Rising to her full height, she towered over Cora, who wore a battered blue straw hat and carried a knitting bag. "Yes, Mrs. Hayward. We're trying to save Rose's lamb. He's having trouble breathing."

Cora's contorted face turned scarlet and she made a series of inarticulate noises that raised the hair on Emily's arms. "The lamb? You ruined Belinda's beautiful table-cloths for a lamb? Have you lost your mind?" she screeched at last. "It's a good thing I came back for my favorite apron, or who knows what you'd do to the rest of the house. Didn't I tell you to keep your hands off Belinda's tablecloths? Didn't I tell you not to touch *any* of her belongings, *Miss Fine-and-Fancy-Manners*?" Her fleshy double chin wagged like a turkey wattle with every word she shouted.

Beneath the table, Rose began crying again and fury filled Emily's head like the eucalyptus vapor. "Can't you see how you're upsetting Rose? Your behavior is appalling and unacceptable, Mrs. Hayward," she replied, cutting off each syllable with fire and ice.

Cora would not back down. "Oh, is that right? Well, everything was fine between me and Rose before you got here. Then you came, uninvited, trying to change things, sticking your nose where it doesn't belong. You act like you own this place, lock, stock, and barrel. Well, you don't! You'll never belong here! This is still my daughter's house."

At last, Emily thought, it was out. The dreadful harridan had finally joined words with her graceless attitude. "Then maybe we should set a place at the table for Belinda every night!"

"Well! You have a lot of nerve, Mrs. Becker!"

"A living creature has more worth than an inanimate object like a tablecloth! The living must be given greater consideration than the dead!" Mercy, she was actually shouting back in this ridiculous but vicious argument. "Have you no heart?"

At that moment, Luke walked in. He'd heard the yelling from the yard and came up the steps in one jump. He didn't know what was happening, exactly, but one look at Emily's face told him that his mother-in-law had overstepped her bounds one time too often. He felt as if he'd plunged his head into the spinning blades of a windmill.

"Cora!" he barked.

"Tell her, Luke!" she demanded, whirling to face him. Her hat was askew on her head. "Tell her we don't need her here! She's done nothing but cause trouble."

All the years of resentment that he'd bottled up and tamped down, all the words he'd swallowed to keep the peace and give Rose a stable home, finally boiled over. Though his own home life had been one of constant arguing, his old man's drunkenness, and abuse, he'd fry in hell before he saw that happen to Rose. "The only person causing trouble is you, Cora Hayward, and I'm goddamned fed up. I want you to pack up and go home."

She pressed her hand flat to her ample bosom, wearing the look of insulted dignity that he'd come to despise so. "Me? You want *me* to leave?"

"The sooner the better, Cora. This day has been coming for months. I'm going to have peace under this roof. This is my house, not yours, and Rose is my girl, not yours."

"She's more my blood than she'll ever be yours."

"Cora." The warning in his voice carried a threat that no one, not even his thick-skinned, block-headed mother-in-law could have mistaken. Even Emily's eyes widened.

Cora lifted her nose. "Well, what should I expect from the man who killed my daughter?"

From somewhere under the table, Luke heard his own daughter sobbing. Cora had never come out and made that accusation until now, and he knew she was using it as a last resort. But she'd said it in front of Rose and Emily. God, would this nightmare never end? Luke wondered. And that smell, he thought irrelevantly, what the hell was it?

"I think we know the truth about that, don't we?" he ground out. "Whose house did Belinda die in?"

She gave him a poisonous look. "I'll be gone in the morning. And there's no point in trying to make me stay. I wouldn't live here now if you got down on all fours and begged me." With that, she spun on her heel and marched to the hall and up the stairs.

Rose's sobbing quieted to an eerie moaning.

Emily pushed aside a corner of the tent. "Cotton has taken a turn for the worse," she told Luke. "He can't breathe."

"He's not breathing at all now," Rose announced, her voice teary and yet dull-sounding.

Luke stooped down and looked at his daughter on the floor under the table. She had the lifeless, dirty sheep on her lap, holding his head over a steaming bowl of some concoction. "Oh, hell, Rose, honey—I'm sorry."

"Daddy, you'll save him, won't you? We've already tried everything we can."

The stricken, pleading look on her face made him want to promise just about anything, but he couldn't save Cotton. The animal was dead. He climbed under the table with her, trying not to bump his head. Rose's hair hung in dark, damp strands around her face. The air was thick with humidity and the combined smells of medicine and wet, dirty wool. He pulled Rose and the lamb onto his lap and wrapped his arms around them both.

"He's already gone, honey. I can't do anything for him." From the floor above, he could hear Cora opening and slamming drawers, and stomping around with great drama.

"Oh." Her chin began quivering again. "He was so little. What's going to happen to him?"

Luke's heart ached for his daughter. No child should have to endure the kinds of losses and turmoil she'd suffered. What could he do? How could he make this better?

Emily lifted the tablecloth and sat down cross-legged on the floor. It seemed so out of character for a woman who didn't even let the back of a chair touch her spine. "Rose, would you like to have a little funeral for Cotton?"

"Could we?" She turned to her father. "Oh, could we?"

Luke thought it was a silly idea, but blessed Emily for her kindness and insight into the workings of a small girl's heart. "Sure, honey. We'll have a funeral."

"Can we bury him beside mama?"

"What?" Luke started.

Emily shot him a look and then said, "Wouldn't you like it better if we bury him here on the farm, so he'll be close by?"

Rose thought about this and then nodded. She let Emily take the lamb from her arms. "Come on. Your father will help you find a nice piece of old blanket to wrap him in."

"Thanks, Emily," Luke said, and even though tears stood in her eyes, he swore there was a smile in them.

The sun was just a crimson ribbon on the western horizon by the time Emily made her way to the front porch. The evening stars were beginning to come out and she settled herself on the stool, feeling as creaky and tired as an old woman. Her black dress, the one that had already suffered through the visit to the chicken coop, was filthy again. Between holding Cotton and dragging her hem through the mud beside his grave, the dress was probably a loss.

Rose had chosen to put Cotton's gravesite under the oak. Luke had suggested something farther from the house, but in the end, he dug the hole under the tree and they'd had a brief service for the expired lamb. Rose had asked Emily to read a little Bible verse over Cotton, but she couldn't think of one. Instead, she'd recited a stanza by Cecil Frances Alexander that seemed appropriate.

> *All things bright and beautiful,*
> *All creatures great and small,*
> *All things wise and wonderful,*
> *The Lord God made them all.*

While she supposed that it might be sacrilegious to commend a sheep's soul to God's keeping, she had asked anyway. It comforted Rose, and what could it hurt? Emily held fast to her belief that kindness and consideration of others' feelings were not a "blame-fool" waste of time. They were part of what made life bearable. Patently, Cora Hayward did not share this belief. A miserable, manipulative woman, she seemed bent on making those around her miserable as well.

After Cotton's funeral, Emily had scrubbed the kitchen table and put together a quick dinner of cold roast beef sandwiches. It wasn't much, but no one's appetite had been very keen. Cora had not come downstairs, but Emily made a sandwich for her, too, and left it covered with a clean napkin on the table. Then she went out to sit on the porch.

What a dreadful day it had been. Until now, Emily's life had not been particularly happy, but it had been, for the most part, peaceful. Even though her circumstances had changed over the years from privileged to penurious, and had included a liberal ration of heartache and loss, voices in the Cannon household had been moderate and the emotional manipulations more subtle. She hadn't grown up in a family that had been demonstrative of temper or given to the kinds of outbursts she'd seen under the Becker roof. This was all new to her. She found it to be very disturbing and exhausting.

Behind her she heard the screen door squeak on its hinges. Luke came out and flopped on the top step near her feet. He set down a whiskey bottle and a glass on the porch next to his thigh. Emily supposed he'd earned the right to a drink. She half-wished that ladies were allowed to take a drink, too.

"How is Rose?" she asked.

"She's not asleep, but I think she'll be all right. God, what a day." He put his head in his hands for a moment, then began massaging the back of his neck. Watching this, Emily yearned to take up the task for him, to work out the tension in his muscles and feel his warm skin under her fingers. But it seemed too forward. "I guess I didn't do a very good job of picking out that lamb and ewe. He was probably sick before I brought him home. If we lose the mama, too, I don't know what it'll do to Rose."

"Is the ewe sick?"

"No, at least not yet. Maybe she'll be fine." He poured a half-inch of amber liquor into his glass and drank it down in one swallow. He sucked a low breath through his teeth and turned tired gray eyes up to her face. "I want to thank you for everything you did today. If you hadn't been here, well, Cora wouldn't have been any help." He stared at the step under his feet. "She wasn't before."

"I wasn't able to save Cotton."

He sighed and ruffled his hair with a big hand. "Oh, honey, he was just too far gone. No one could have helped him."

Honey.

Had it been an unconscious slip by a man too tired to know what he'd said? Emily wondered. Even if it had been, that didn't diminish the sudden warmth that flooded her, and the feeling of familiar belonging. Almost without thinking she crossed her palm with her thumb to feel her wedding band on her little finger.

"I guess you're right," she said, and then added, "Luke, what did Cora mean about Belinda?"

He tipped his head against the newel post. "You mean when she said I killed her?"

It was awkward to hear it so baldly put. "Well, um, yes—" She told him about the unfinished letter she'd found in the parlor, then realized how it must sound. "I honestly don't make a habit of reading other people's mail!"

His smile was a tired one. "I'd bet she left that letter there on purpose, hoping you'd find it. She hasn't had any contact with her cousin Eunice for years." He turned and faced her. "But you have the right to know the truth."

He told her about his youthful infatuation with Belinda, and in his voice she heard the ghost of a passion that made her heart sink. She knew he would never feel that way about her—Belinda had been the love of his life.

"That summer, Belinda was sixteen and I was nineteen. She wasn't interested in me." He shrugged. "I suppose I can understand that now. My brothers and I were pretty wild back then, and not too many parents wanted their daughters marrying one of the Becker boys. God knows I'd get out my shotgun if someone like one of us came courting Rose. Both Belinda and Cora wanted her to marry Brad Tilson. He was a doctor's son from Portland and had come out for the summer to work on one of the farms around here for a monthly wage and found. He was studying medicine, too, so I guess they thought he was a good catch. I saw him at grange dances and around town sometimes and I didn't like him—I thought he was a stuck-up rich boy and I could tell he was just leading her on.

"Of course, I was jealous as hell, too. But I knew he wasn't going to marry her. He'd go back to his rich-boy life in Portland and never think about her again." He hung his hands between his knees. "And that's just what he did. Cora thought I chased him off and ruined Belinda's chances with him. The truth was, she never stood a chance at all. Men like him don't marry small-town farm girls. And no matter what Cora would like to believe, I think she knows that truth, too. It's just easier to blame me—for everything."

Luke went on to explain that after Tilson left town, he stepped up his courtship of Belinda and finally won her over. "I think her heart was broken, and she didn't care who she married. But I didn't know it then. I just figured I was the luckiest guy in town to win such a beautiful girl."

He didn't mention Belinda's pregnancy and neither did Emily. After all, it was only a rumor she'd heard, and in any case, it would be unspeakably rude to bring it up. But if it was true, she wondered if Luke realized what a good man he was, even coming from a poor background, to accept his responsibility and marry Belinda.

The years had not been kind to their marriage, Luke continued, and always, always, Cora was an interfering influence. "She gave Belinda all kinds of reasons to be dissatisfied. Nothing I did was ever really good enough." He shook his head. "I think we would have been all right if not for her. But we argued a lot. Then one night just over three years ago, Cora came for Sunday dinner. She'd gotten her little digs in about a lot of things. By the time she finally went home, Belinda and I were like two cats spoiling for a fight. Cora seems to have that effect on people. I said things and Belinda said things . . . finally she got angry and said she was going back to her mother's house. I figured, fine, let her go. It would give us both a chance to cool off."

He rolled his whiskey glass between his hands and studied its empty bottom, as if looking at a window to the past. "But it was raining that night, and a fierce wind was blowing down the gorge. It had been a cold March. Belinda left without a coat, and when she got to Cora's she was soaked to the skin. She developed a fever. I didn't know she was sick, because I was angry and let my pride get in the way. I should have gone over there and brought her home. Cora put her to bed, but didn't think she was sick enough to send for Dr. Gaither. I found that out later. You probably got a sense of how Cora is. She thinks doctors are for weaklings, and didn't suppose he could do anything for Belinda that she couldn't do herself. By the time she changed her mind, Doc Gaither *couldn't* do anything for her—she was too far gone. I went to see her but she was unconscious—I don't think she even knew I was there." His voice was barely audible. "She died that night. And when she went, she took my heart with her."

"Oh, dear God," Emily murmured.

"I was mad as hell at Cora for letting Belinda suffer. She blamed me because she said I'd driven Belinda out of her own home and exposed her to the weather that made her sick in the first place." He shrugged. "She's right, I guess. At least, that's how I've been looking at it for the last three years. But, Jesus, Emily, at least I would have ridden for the doctor."

"Of course you would have," Emily sympathized. She thought for a moment, and then added, "But Luke, Cora must feel just as responsible as you do."

"Nope, it's been easier to blame me."

"But consider this—she thinks Rose's interest in drawing is a waste of time. And she told her that nice needlework is fine for a woman who sits around all day with nothing important to do. Yet she turned your home into a living memorial to Belinda, who apparently loved needlework. Look at the fuss she caused over the tablecloths. Yes, she might have been trying to punish you, and I have no doubt that she wanted me to feel unwelcome." Emily felt safe in saying that now that Cora would be leaving. "It's odd that she wanted a soft life for Belinda, even though she scoffs at it. Still, I don't think she'd have done all that if she didn't feel guilty, too."

Luke stared at her, comprehension dawning in his eyes, and a kind of relief, too, as if she'd conferred a benediction on his soul. "I never thought about it that way."

She nodded, as if praising a bright student who had worked out a complicated problem. "Sometimes when we're too close to a situation, it's hard to be objective about it. To see it as it really is. I'm an outsider so I can be a better observer."

"You're not an outsider, Emily," he said, and stared at the whiskey he'd just poured into his glass. "Your name is Becker now, just like mine, and just like Rose's."

A flush of confusion and gratitude swelled in Emily's chest. Sharing a name didn't necessarily make one part of a family—after all, Robert Cannon had given her his name, but she'd never really felt like his daughter. This was a step in the right direction, though. At least she hoped it was.

He drank the second shot of whiskey in one gulp, like the first, and set the glass upside down on the step next to him. "I never saw any of this coming when I got up this morning. Like I said, it's been a hell of a day."

Emily could see it in his profile. The weariness that always lingered behind his eyes seemed more pronounced than ever. "I can't argue with that."

He turned to look at her, a wry smile pulling at his mouth. A chuckle worked its way up from his chest and he laughed. "You're a rare one, Emily-gal. You're a rare one." Then without warning, he laid his head in her lap, as if too tired to sit upright any longer. Instinctively, she wanted to stroke his dark curls. The instant she felt his soft hair, she pulled her hand away, fearful of the heat that traveled up her arm and the tug she felt in her heart.

Luke wondered if he'd felt the caress of Emily's touch, or simply imagined it because he needed it so desperately. Upstairs, the window slammed in Cora's bedroom, breaking the soft spell of the balmy spring night. He realized that she'd probably been listening to every word he and Emily had said. He didn't care anymore. He supposed he should try to maintain some kind of relationship with her for Rose's sake, but too many things had been said. Too much had happened. Once Cora was gone—and he would see to it that she left because he intended to drive her home first thing in the morning—they'd have a little peace in the house. Suddenly, nothing sounded more appealing.

Much as he didn't want to, Luke lifted his head from Emily's comfortable lap and stood up. "I'd guess I'd better check the stock one more time and then get to bed. Morning will come soon enough." He turned to set off for the barn, then stopped and turned to face Emily. "I really did appreciate your help today." He took her smooth hand from her lap and pressed a kiss into her palm. It was soft and warm against his lips, and made him want to linger. But he couldn't. "I wish I had more to give you," he said. "More than my name." More than the shell of his broken heart. She deserved it. But he feared he would never love anyone again except Rose. He picked up the glass and the bottle and went down the steps.

He didn't see her press her palm to her cheek, as if to hold his kiss there. He didn't know about the disappointment on her face—an expression of hopes dashed—as she watched him walk away.

CHAPTER ELEVEN

"WELL, I'VE BEEN WAITING." CORA SAT ALONE AT THE
kitchen table, drumming her fingers. Luke stood in the
doorway, buttoning his shirt. He'd just come downstairs
to start his day. The sun was still only a promise on the
eastern horizon, and the morning stars had not yet blinked
out.

That was Cora. Surly to the end.

By her feet stood her valise and three years' worth of
belongings, including some of Belinda's things, tied up
with a length of rope like a cowboy's bedroll. He thought
that Rose might like to have her mother's keepsakes, but
decided to leave the subject be. Thank God Rose was still
asleep and Emily had chosen to stay upstairs. There was
no telling how ugly this could get if Cora had an audience.

"Waiting for what, Cora?" Not for his change of heart,
he hoped. She'd see the next blue moon before he'd ask
her to stay here.

"For you to drive me home, of course. Unless you expect me to walk." She started to push her chair away from
the table.

He sighed. "No, I don't. I was planning to take you."
He poured himself a cup of coffee from the pot she had
brewed and sat across from her. He drizzled a measure of
cream and spooned two sugars into the thick black murk

of hers that he'd learned to drink. "Look, I'm sorry about the way this has all turned out."

She responded by staying in her seat and pressing her thin lips into a white crease above her chin.

He hadn't expected this to be easy, and she wasn't disappointing him. He forged ahead. "I appreciate all your help over the past three years. You pulled us through a real hard time—we were the better for your being here." It was an exaggeration, but Luke wanted to be big about this. "I'll keep helping out around your place. That won't change. And if you need anything, just let me know. You're still Rose's grandmother and it's important that you and she stay close. I know she'll want to stop by after school sometimes, and come to see you when school lets out."

"Are you sure Mrs. Becker won't mind? After all, she's taken over now," she sniped.

Last night, both Rose and Emily had told him about her reaction to Rose's drawing. It had only reinforced his decision to send Cora home. He bracketed his coffee cup with his elbows. "What happened yesterday started way before Emily ever got here. Way before I placed that advertisement for a new wife."

She fixed him with her small, hard blue eyes. "You're right. It started the day you married Belinda."

He drew a deep breath. "Then it should be over now, shouldn't it? Belinda is dead and gone." It sounded harsh to his own ears, and yet freeing, too. It was the first time he'd been able to state aloud that his first wife had died. It was as if at this moment, his mourning ended and a new beginning waited for him.

That left Cora with nothing more to say. She adjusted her battered straw hat and stood up. "Dead and gone. Just like that. All right, I'm going, too."

He nodded. "I'll hitch the team and bring the wagon around."

Cora watched him go out the door and down the steps. He crossed the yard and she waited, her teeth snapped together like a bear trap. "But this isn't over, Luke Becker," she murmured. "Not yet."

From her bedroom window, Emily watched as Luke pulled the wagon out into the road. Pink and yellow fingers of dawn stretched out from the eastern sky, providing enough light to see the dark silhouettes of the wagon and Luke and Cora. Emily had remained upstairs, certain that her presence in the kitchen would not be welcome or appropriate. Maybe with enough time and healing, the four of them could reach a truce. Right now, though, there were hard feelings all around.

But Cora's leaving gave Emily a sense of a new beginning in so many ways. She stood at her square of mirror and braided her hair. Then she opened the doors of her wardrobe and studied one of her day dresses. Her period of mourning Alyssa was not fulfilled, but she let her hand linger on a lavender muslin gown with linen collar and cuffs. It would be cooler and more practical for household chores than the black crepe. And it looked better. It wasn't dirty or streaked with variegated shades of black.

"Alyssa, please forgive me," she murmured and pulled out the lavender dress. Perhaps those who were mourned were not as worried about appearances and dictums as those who did the mourning. Maybe—and this was a revolutionary and rebellious thought for Emily—maybe in heaven or wherever the souls of the departed flew to, the complex manmade observations of proper social conduct seemed as mundane and insignificant as the doings of microscopic beings seemed to humans.

So in the cool morning light, Emily dropped the broadcloth over her head, let it slide down her chemise and her legs, and buttoned the bodice. Then she tied her apron around her waist and opened her bedroom door.

Her first stop was Luke's room. She hesitated a moment, just as she had the one other time that she'd put her hand on his doorknob. She drew a breath and lifted her chin. Regardless of the arrangement between them, she was the lady of the house now that Cora had left, and with the title came responsibilities and obligations. One of those responsibilities included making beds. So with a sense of belonging and purpose, she turned the knob and walked in. But to her surprise, the bed was already made.

"Well, for heaven's sake," she muttered to herself.

She plumped the pillows and straightened the already-tidy quilt, feeling a little deflated. She tried to imagine sharing this room with him, but it was so small and austere, it didn't look as if a woman had ever occupied it. It was as plain and unadorned as always. This time, though, she noticed that Belinda's vanity set was gone. Only the wedding photograph remained and it was turned, as if someone had pushed it aside while reaching for something else.

She left the room and went down the hall to Rose's bedroom. Opening the door a crack, she saw that the girl still slept. Her dark head was barely visible in the nest of bedding. Poor thing, Emily thought. She'd lost her grandmother and her pet on the same day. Emily wasn't even sure if Cora had bothered to tell her good-bye. She hoped she had.

Emily proceeded downstairs and got breakfast started. She had to hunt for a while to find everything she needed since Cora had never let her do much in the kitchen. Finally she had a bowl, flour, salt, baking powder, and milk assembled on the table to make pancakes, then realized she would need eggs.

And that would mean a trip to the henhouse.

In Chicago, even when the Cannons had been forced to live in rented rooms, street vendors came by selling eggs, butter, and milk. Or she could buy eggs from one of the families that kept chickens in their backyards. Now the chickens were in *her* backyard and she was scared to death of them. At least, she was afraid of the hens. Her memory of that day in the henhouse—the stifling odor, the sharp beaks and claws, the flapping wings—was acute, like a nightmare she'd suffered only hours earlier. Every few minutes, she glanced out the window, looking for Luke and the wagon. Perhaps he wouldn't mind taking over the task of gathering eggs for her. After all, he'd scolded her for even going out there that day.

Cora is the only one who knows how to handle that mean old biddy.

Then she remembered how she'd resented being talked to as if she were a child. If she was going to do a proper job of running this house, she would have to manage the bad and the good. Luke had enough to do out in the fields. She wasn't afraid of hard work, and sometimes that meant doing dirty work. She knew full well that life consisted of more than just tea parties and nicely appointed dining tables, something Alyssa had never really had to learn, at least not for a long time. Yes, she'd been aware of their reduced circumstances, and had stood on the sidewalk and wept the day they left the house on Washington Boulevard. And Charles Walker had eventually called off his engagement to Alyssa when he realized that the Cannons had tumbled from their social position. But she had stayed home and taken care of their father while Emily had gone to work and supported them. In fairness to her sister, Emily didn't suppose that had been an easy chore, especially toward the end of Father's life.

She eyed the egg basket on its shelf next to the back door. To cook breakfast she would need eggs, and she would go get them, by heaven. She snatched the basket from the shelf and marched out the door and down the back stairs, full of grand resolve.

The grass and wildflowers that grew on each side of the wide path to the barn bore crystals of dew that sparkled in the early morning sun. Looking out across the plowed fields, she noted long, arrow-straight rows of new green plants, all well-tended, almost lovingly so. How did Luke make those rows so straight? she wondered. What landmark did he use as a guide? It seemed like an amazing accomplishment for someone working with the simple tools of a plow and a pair of horses.

The pastoral hush of the morning was an unexpected balm to her spirit. The house and the outbuildings were in good repair, and Luke put food on the table every night. Yes, he took a drink now and then, but his life had been hard and lonely, from what Emily could tell. He loved his daughter with a sometimes befuddled but fatherly devotion that she wished she had known in her youth. What, then, had Cora found so lacking in him? she wondered. She'd have thought that a mother would be proud, even relieved, to have such a son-in-law. But Cora's bitterness seemed to reach to the very core of her heart, like a tooth rotten to the roots.

As she approached the sun-bleached henhouse, some of her resolve evaporated. The coop chickens didn't pay her much attention, but those laying hens . . . God, those hens. She stood before the door, the basket handle over her forearm.

She squared her shoulders, determined to establish her dominance over the situation. "I'm coming in now!" she announced, and then felt rather foolish. She opened the door and a rush of warm, nasty odor washed over her. The chickens peered at her with their black-bead eyes and made distrustful clucking noises as they moved their heads in jerky motions. "I know I'm a stranger to you," she went on in her best schoolmistress voice, "but *I* am in charge now and we will become acquainted."

Luke had pulled the wagon up to the back porch, figuring he'd give Rose a ride into town after seeing Cora back to her own home. It had been a tense, stiff trip, and the mile to her place had seemed more like five.

He knew that Rose would be unhappy about the last twenty-four hours. He couldn't change or fix things, and he didn't even know what he would say to his girl to make her feel better. But he had to try. He hoped that some gem of wisdom would come to him between now and then. He hopped down from the wagon seat and had one foot on the bottom step when he heard a feminine voice coming from the henhouse. Curiosity turned him toward the source of the sound.

". . . got off to a bad start, but I'll be collecting your eggs every morning from now on and there will be no more nonsense about it. That's just the way things are going to be. I won't tolerate rude behavior or disrespect. Any of you who give me an unreasonable amount of trouble, well, she'll find herself in my skillet one Sunday afternoon. And I'm not joking."

Luke rounded the weathered henhouse and crept to the open door where he saw Emily, her spine straight, her shoulders back, addressing the ten chickens inside as if she were holding class. Her hair hung down the center of her back in a single yellow braid, and damn if she wasn't wearing a dress that wasn't black. It was the color of lilacs, he thought, some kind of pale violet shade. He was so completely enchanted by the sight and sound of her that he managed to keep from laughing at her technique of chicken-taming. She sounded so stern, he half-expected the chickens to step up and lay their eggs in the basket for her.

"All right, then, I believe I've made myself clear," she said, and stepped deeper into the structure. Luke heard some flapping and squawking, and Emily's sharp replies, but eventually she emerged wearing a triumphant expression. The morning sun made her skin glow like fresh cream.

"Oh! Luke, I didn't know you were back. Look!" She held out the basket for inspection. "I did it. I got the eggs away from those cranky birds."

He couldn't keep his chuckle to himself any longer. It felt good to laugh a little after the last day or so. He came closer and looked into her basket. A clutch of eggs sat inside, all unbroken. "Yes, you did. What about the old biddy?"

Emily pursed her lips. "She didn't have any to give." The subject of the hen apparently reminded both of them of Cora. "Cora is settled in her own home?"

His smile faded and he shrugged. "Well, she's there, anyway. We didn't talk much on the way. I promised her that I'd help out around her place whenever she needs it. And I told her that Rose understands she can go there anytime she likes. I wouldn't stop her from doing that."

Emily nodded and sighed. "Maybe it's all for the best. I'm just sorry that the situation became so, well, unpleasant."

He laughed again. Still the expert at the understatement, he noticed. With all the shouting, arguing, and recriminations thrown around the day before, the description hardly fit. "No, ma'am. Working in the rain is *unpleasant*, slipping on a cow flop or drinking burned coffee is *unpleasant*. Yesterday was flat-out hell."

She gave him a wry smile and didn't comment on his language. "I would be inclined to agree."

They turned and headed back to the house, and almost without thinking, Luke put his hand on the small of Emily's back.

She stiffened and turned her head to look at him.

He dropped his arm.

"Sorry—I didn't mean to—"

"No, it's fine, I'm just not used to . . ." She glanced away, giving him a nice view of her profile.

Damn it, he wasn't sure he even knew how to court a woman anymore. He'd probably been ham-handed and clumsy, and scared her. Then he realized the path of his thoughts. God, was he trying to court Emily, the tall drink of water who had more rules for living than Reverend Ackerman? Yes, he supposed he was. And he had been since the day he'd brought her the silk from Fran's store. Because there was a whole lot more to Emily than her manners and rules, and beneath her cool, composed exterior, he sensed a full-blooded woman trying to break out. Someone—certainly her stepfather and her mother—had squashed the confidence right out of her. He'd seen coquettish women in his time, females who could bring a man to his knees simply by giving him a hot, unspoken promise with their eyes. Sometimes it was flattering. In other cases, such as with Clara Thurmon and Fran Eakins, it was just embarrassing.

Emily had none of their clumsy guile, and none of an

accomplished flirt's, either. She wasn't heavily decorated or given to putting on fine airs, despite her way of doing things.

She was just Emily.

And that was fine with Luke.

He put his hand on her waist again, and this time he felt her lean against it as they walked back to the kitchen.

Emily turned Rose toward her reflection. She'd perched the girl on a stool so that she could see herself in the dresser's high mirror. "Well, what do you think?"

Rose stared at herself in the glass in her bedroom, her eyes wide. "Is that really how I look?" The pale blue broadcloth dress they'd finished together was a pretty outfit with simple lines and a white apron. Her own girlish beauty was allowed to shine through without having to compete with garish colors and oceans of flounces.

Emily smiled. "Yes, dear, that's you. Do you like it?"

Rose spun toward her, her face glowing. "Oh, it's *wonderful*, Miss Emily. Thank you so much!" It was so good to see her smiling again.

In the days that followed Cora's departure and Cotton's death, Rose had been barely more than a shadow moving through the house, as silent as a cat, barely speaking and picking at her food. Emily had worried about the pale violet smudges that underscored her dark eyes, and she knew that Luke had been troubled about her, too. He'd brought her a gray tabby barn kitten to keep in the house. Rose had shown only polite interest until Luke told her that the mother cat had rejected the runt. That had brought out Rose's nurturing instincts, and now the little cat she'd named Stripe slept with her in her bed. Thank God for children's resilience. Of course, there were scars that remained a lifetime—Emily knew that from personal experience. But youth made it a little easier to bounce back from some disappointments and hurts.

"I've never had such a pretty dress!"

"You had a lot to do with it, Rose. You worked hard and learned a lot." Emily had taken over those tasks that she knew would give a beginning seamstress trouble, like setting the sleeves and sewing the tucks in the hem of the apron. But Rose had done her share of pulling basting threads and stitching the straight seams on the machine, and she'd done a good job. "Do you think you like sewing?"

Rose turned back to the mirror. "Yes, ma'am! Can we make another dress?"

"Yes, we will eventually. But at least now you have something to wear to the basket social at church tomorrow night."

"So do you," Rose said, craning her neck to look at the back of her apron where Emily had tied the sash into a big bow. "Your dress is pretty, too."

It was. The teal grosgrain had turned out very nicely, and Emily had felt as giddy as a girl all week, thinking about the upcoming event. There would be music and dancing and dinner. She'd get a chance to meet some of the neighbors, hopefully without Cora there working to diminish her status. She would appear on Luke's arm in her silk dress with Rose beside them. The new Becker family. It would be wonderful. It would be terrifying. And it was coming tomorrow night.

Emily shook off the thoughts and looked at her watch. They still had work to do. "For now, though, we've got dinner to finish. Your father will be coming in from the fields, hungry as a bear. Change your clothes and come down and help. And don't forget to hang your dress."

"All right," the girl agreed and hopped down from the stool.

Emily hurried down the steps to the kitchen to baste the roast she'd put into the oven earlier. Opening one oven door, she spooned meat juices over the beef and the potatoes and tiny onions that ringed it. Their fragrant aroma filled the room and mingled with the warm, yeasty scent of bread and an apple crisp baking in the other oven.

Cooking hadn't been the daunting task she'd thought it might be. She had cooked for Alyssa and her father, but now she felt that she had to prove herself to Luke and Rose. What she hadn't expected was that they were so grateful for palatable food, she could have served them just about anything, decently cooked, and they'd have been pleased.

She had yet to learn to make butter, and Rose knew only what she'd seen Cora do, which was no better than Emily's own ignorance. So for the time being she'd worked out an arrangement with Jennie Manning, Chester's wife. Rose stopped by the Mannings' place once a week to pick up Jennie's butter, and in exchange, Emily gave the Manning girls some basic etiquette lessons. It buoyed Emily's spirit to know that not every farm wife thought that manners and refinement were a "blame-fool waste of time." Jennie was a pretty, practical woman who worked hard, but also recognized the value of developing her daughters' brains and beauty.

In her own home, Emily made a special point to set an attractive table for the family meals and to give the house her own little touches. She put wild lupines in a canning jar on the hall table, since she couldn't find a vase. She opened the windows in the parlor and aired it out, something she believed hadn't been done in three years. She washed and ironed the few of Belinda's table linens that

Cora had left behind and had used them for the one Sunday dinner they'd shared together thus far. And she put all of Cora's caustic homemade soap in a box and put it in the back of a closet. Now they were using white, store-bought bars from the druggist's. The soap was a new product that not only was mild, but also floated on the surface of the water.

With just the three of them in the house, Emily had been more acutely aware of Luke than ever. She knew what time he came in from the fields in the afternoons, and often caught herself wandering over to the side window to watch him wash at the pump. Guilty pleasure warred with a lifetime of moral lessons. She knew that none of the experts who had penned the tomes she used in her own classrooms would approve of her watching her husband strip off his shirt and lather his face and upper body with a slick bar of white soap. Mrs. L. H. Sigourney, who had written *Letters to Young Ladies*, a book devoted to deportment and character, would soundly denounce as vulgar her peeking at Luke through the lace curtains as he sluiced water over himself. Emily's fascination at the play of muscle across his back and chest, glistening wet in the low sun, would not be a reasonable excuse for her behavior. Miss Anna Fergurson, author of *The Young Lady's Guide to Knowledge and Virtue*, would probably wither in shame at Emily's furtive spying. But knowing all of this, she persisted. In fact, wasn't that the pump handle she heard right now out in the yard?

She ambled to the side window in the kitchen, telling herself that she was only looking for a gravy boat that she'd seen on a nearby shelf. Outside, as she'd expected, there was her husband briskly rubbing soap over himself, raising the suds into a high lather as he ran the bar up and down his arms and across his chest. She had made it a practice to leave a clean shirt outside for him, and it lay neatly folded on a crate beside the pump. Now Luke worked the pump handle again and stooped to let the water pour over his head and bare torso. Emily swallowed and glanced back over her shoulder. Goodness, but that stove put out a lot of heat, she thought. She returned her attention to Luke. The water streamed down his back in crystal rivulets and snaked their way into the waistband of his dungarees. Even from here, she could see the goosebumps erupt on his flesh when a breeze kicked up. What would they feel like under her fingertips if she were to—

Suddenly he turned and looked right at her, as if he'd felt her eyes on him. His knowing grin left no doubt that she'd been caught. Emily jumped back out of view and pressed her hands to her hot face.

Rose thundered down the stairs, through the hall, and into the kitchen like a runaway colt. "Okay, I'm ready," she announced, wearing her faded overalls and fortunately unaware of Emily's impure thoughts about Luke. She whirled and went back to the table, glad for once that Rose hadn't yet mastered the art of entering a room with grace.

She straightened and tried to pretend that she'd only been basting the roast and not her imagination. "Let's set the table the way I showed you. Remember, knife edges point toward the plates."

Rose went to the sideboard and took out dishes and silver while Emily transferred the roast and potatoes to a flowered platter. Just as she put them on the table, Luke walked in the back door. Flustered, she couldn't meet his eyes, and he only grinned like a fool.

Leaning over the platter on the table, he inhaled the aroma of their dinner. "Hey, something smells pretty good around here," he said, giving them both a good-humored smile.

And it might be him, Emily thought, before she could harness her musings. He brought with him the scents of fresh air, a clean shirt, and Ivory Soap. Mixed with those was his own male scent, one that she could not seem to ignore. His wet hair curled at the ends and at the base of his neck where it had begun to dry, and his smoke-colored eyes seemed to darken when he looked at her.

What had come over her lately? More than ever she fought to conquer her indelicate, unladylike instincts, and it seemed to be a losing battle. Last night as she lay in bed, she'd even found herself trying to picture what Luke would look like with *no* clothes, not just without his shirt. God in heaven! Marriage was not supposed to be about carnality. The ideal marriage was romantic, tender, and sentimental. Hearts and flowers. Love letters and devotion. Soft words and kind comments. Quiet evenings of reading and music.

All of her manuals stressed these virtues. They said nothing about wantonness of thought or the need for moral restraint. It was generally accepted that it shouldn't even be necessary to warn against such things. But Luke had been a wild troublemaker in his youth, not the suit-and-tie-wearing man that the books' illustrations depicted.

"Both of you take your seats," she said, trying to bring her attention back to the matter at hand. She cleared her throat. "Luke, will you carve the meat, please?" He caught her eye and gave her a secret little smile that only made her face flame again. He actually seemed to be enjoying her embarrassment. Emily turned back to the stove to pull out the bread and the dessert.

"Daddy, you should see my new dress!" Rose piped in mercifully. She put her napkin on her lap, just as Emily had shown her. "It's so beautiful, the beautifullest one I've ever seen."

"I guess we owe Miss Emily a big thanks for that, don't we?"

Emily put the sliced bread on the table and slipped into her own chair. "I was happy to help. And Rose is a good student. She learns quickly."

Luke took a bite of roast and closed his eyes as he chewed. Alarmed, Emily feared that he'd found something about the taste he didn't like. "Is it all right?"

He looked at her with a transcendent expression. "It's more than all right, Emily. It's wonderful. I can't remember the last time I ate so well. It's been years."

"Oh—I'm glad you like it." She ducked her chin.

Luke took another bite of roast and then buttered a piece of tender, piping-hot bread. As doubtful and apprehensive as he'd been the day he saw Emily Cannon on the dock in town, everything was working out. He'd hoped for a woman who looked like Belinda and he'd gotten the exact opposite. But it had begun to dawn on him that trying to replace his late wife wasn't a good idea. It just kept him living in the past, a past that hadn't been especially happy. It was a hard thing for him to admit, but he realized it was true.

Having a wife with fancy manners, who knew how to cook and set a nice table, wasn't such a bad thing, after all. Rose's snotty attitude had improved and she was learning from Emily. Even more amazing, he found his tall, blond wife's flowing grace as arousing as he'd once found Belinda's brunette petiteness.

Best of all, he saw Emily at the window every afternoon, eyeing him while he washed up. Today, he decided to let her know that he'd seen her watching him, and was amused and touched by her look of flustered surprise.

It seemed that she was interested in him, too.

"... fix for the social? Fried chicken? Potato salad? Chocolate cake?"

Luke realized that Emily was talking to him. "Sure, that all sounds good. I'll dress out a chicken for you."

She looked relieved. He doubted that she'd ever had to swing a flapping fowl over her head to wring its neck, or lop off its noggin with a hatchet. It was enough that she'd overcome her fear of the henhouse.

"Daddy, you're going to buy Miss Emily's basket, aren't you?" Rose asked. "We want to eat *her* supper, not someone else's."

"Yes, ma'am, I'll make sure we get it. I don't want Emily having dinner with some other man." Luke said this with a laugh, but he was telling Rose the truth.

CHAPTER TWELVE

EMILY TOSSED AND TURNED IN HER BED SO MANY TIMES that her nightgown had twisted itself around her legs like mummy wrappings. She didn't know what time it was, but she had watched a square of moonlight work its way down the wall to form a bright patch on the floor.

Every time she tried to drift off, she saw Luke, with his dark, curly hair and smoke-gray eyes, sending her looks across the kitchen table. Looks that seemed so obvious, she'd worried Rose would notice. Fortunately, the girl had chattered on about the upcoming church social and her new dress. If she missed Cora, she kept it to herself. In fact, since Cora had gone, it was as if a black pall had been lifted from the house. Newcomer that she was, even Emily sensed it. Luke smiled more, Rose was more light-hearted, and Emily felt a new freedom. She fretted less about touching things around the house, no longer fearful that the harridan would jump out suddenly and screech at her about handling Belinda's possessions.

So why couldn't Emily sleep tonight? Because she knew that Luke lay just on the other side of the wall, and her restless heart gave her no peace. She didn't want to care about him, beyond giving him the respect he was due as her lawful husband. A life of lonely sadness awaited her as the bearer of unrequited love.

Surely that was what she could expect, because Luke Becker was still in love with his dead wife.

And try as she might, Emily had not succeeded in tamping down the feelings she held for him. It was the finest type of torture.

She pulled the sheet up to her chin so that she could blot the tears that leaked from the corners of her eyes. She'd known she was taking a big chance by coming here in the first place, and so far, it had worked out much better than she'd originally hoped. Luke was kind and loved his daughter, he was thoughtful of Emily's feelings, and he'd defended her against his mother-in-law, ultimately ordering the woman from his house. His gift of the dress fabric had been a wonderful and unexpected surprise.

But, as he'd told her the day he'd met her, she'd never have his heart. He'd reminded her of it again, the night before Cora left. Well, for heaven's sake, she scolded herself, wasn't she being greedy? Until the day she decided to come to Fairdale, she hadn't expected to marry at all. So what if this wasn't a love match, a marriage made in heaven with valentine-bearing doves hovering over it? Luke was a good man, and many women entered marriages doomed from the start, simply because so few options were available to them. At least Emily had reached the decision on her own.

Exasperated with her weepy self-pity, she flung back the covers and decided to go down to the kitchen to brew a cup of weak tea. Maybe its warmth and a touch of honey to sweeten it would help her sleep.

She left her bed and padded barefoot to her bedroom door. Slipping quietly into the hall, she was surprised to find Luke's door open. Although the moonlight was faint in his room, she could see that his bed was rumpled and empty. He might have simply gone to the necessary.

Creeping to the end of the dark hall, she saw a faint light coming up the stairs. She was halfway down the steps when she heard him clear his throat. He was in the kitchen. What had happened? An emergency? She tried to decide if she should just go back to her room, or find out why he was up at this hour. Ultimately, her accursed curiosity won out and her feet carried her the rest of the way to the kitchen. There she saw him sitting at one end of the table. A single lantern burned at the other end. A whiskey bottle sat in front of him, its cork still in place, and a clean, empty glass stood next to it. He stared blankly at the bottle, as if his thoughts were miles—or years—away.

Just as he noticed Emily, she realized that she had come down wearing only her long nightgown and nothing else. Not even a shawl on her shoulders. He was dressed in dungarees and an undershirt.

He pushed a chair out for her with his foot, as if not surprised to see her. "Sit down, Emily." He seemed very pensive, more so than she'd ever seen him. "I hope I didn't wake you."

She took a tentative step forward. The floor was cold under her bare feet. "N-no, I couldn't sleep and I just came down to get a cup of tea."

He nodded. "Yeah, I couldn't sleep, either. But I had something stronger than tea in mind." Perhaps that was true, but he made no move to pour a drink from the dark brown bottle.

Her advice manuals told her that it was a wife's job to devote herself to her husband's comfort and well-being. In fact, she had a vivid recollection of one illustration that depicted a concerned wife sitting at her mate's feet, her hands clasped under her chin, while he lounged on what was probably the nicest chair in the house, his brow knitted with worry. Emily wasn't sure why, but she'd always thought that his expression looked rather guilty, as if he were about to tell her they were bankrupt, or that he no longer loved her and was leaving her for another woman. But the caption had commented about a wife's duty to ease her husband's troubled mind and make him forget the cares of the day.

Emily was a bit too independent to sit at anyone's feet, and Luke bore no resemblance to the husband in the picture. Still, if he wanted to talk—and his offhand invitation to sit made it appear that he did—it was her job to listen. She perched on the chair he'd pushed out for her and waited for him to speak. He stared at the tabletop for so long that she had to fight the urge to fidget.

Then they both spoke at once.

"Is there something—"

"I've been thinking—"

She nodded at him. "I'm sorry, please go ahead."

He breathed a deep sigh. "I've been doing a lot of thinking lately, especially since Cora left." He reached for the glass and idly turned it over in his hands. "You said you're supposed to wear mourning clothes for your sister for six months."

Emily jumped in, feeling as guilty as if she'd been caught stealing from the poor box at church. "Oh, dear—yes, I'm sorry—my mourning clothes are in such a state—"

He shook his head and stretched out his free hand to cover hers. "It's all right. I'm not blaming you for wearing regular dresses. In fact, I'm glad to see it."

"You are?"

"Sure. I told you that what's in your heart is more important than some rule about what clothes to wear. And it's good to see you dressed in some color."

Mollified, Emily asked, "Well, then, what are we talking about?"

He released her hand. "Your rules say you're supposed to mourn your sister for six months, but here, we've been in mourning for Belinda since the day she died over three years ago now."

She couldn't argue with that. It was so obvious. She nodded, waiting for him to continue.

"I've begun to wonder if it's been long enough. Cora pretty much kept it going as a way to punish me." He shrugged. "And maybe herself, too, if you're right about her feeling guilty for Belinda's death. It was probably more than she could accept. She lost Belinda's brother coming out here on the Oregon Trail—he fell out of the wagon and got crushed under the wheels. They had to bury him along the way in an unmarked grave."

"Oh, God." So Cora had lost both of her children.

"I *know* she blamed Belinda's father for that. Cora never wanted to come out here in the first place."

Emily remembered her first night at this table, when Cora talked about the miserable trip out here from Missouri.

"I loved Belinda." He stared at the tabletop as if he were seeing the years rolling past. "But I know she never really loved me."

"What?"

"It's taken me a while to admit it to myself. She was probably grateful at the beginning, but gratitude isn't the same as love, and it can't make a person happy. In fact, sometimes, it just makes a person resentful. That's part of what happened between Belinda and me."

The conversation had become intensely personal, and Emily was unprepared for the switch in their relationship. Until this moment, Luke had revealed almost nothing of himself beyond what she'd read in his letters and could see for herself. Now he was telling her that his wife—the sterling paragon to whom Emily had been compared time and again—had not loved him. "Grateful?" she repeated. Why on earth would a woman who seemingly had everything feel only gratitude for Luke Becker? Had Belinda been unhinged? Luke was, well, he'd been a hell-raiser, from what she understood, but it seemed like he'd done everything he could to prove himself worthy of Belinda Hayward.

His voice dropped to a near hush, as if he were going over a bad memory that he didn't want to remember too clearly. "I told you that she wanted to marry Bradley Tilson, but he went back to Portland."

Emily nodded.

"He left her with more than a broken heart. She was pregnant."

Emily gaped at him.

"Cora never would have let me marry Belinda if she hadn't needed a husband for her. After Tilson left, I came courting Belinda, but I was too, well, *dazzled*, I guess, to wonder why the Haywards were suddenly willing to marry her off to me when all of them, including Belinda, had seemed so lukewarm about the idea."

Emily was still trying to grasp what he was telling her. "You mean that Rose—she isn't . . ." She couldn't finish the question.

"Tilson is Rose's father. On our wedding night, Belinda broke down and told me that she was pregnant. I felt used and lied to. Betrayed," he added, as if trying on the word for size. He shrugged. "Hell, I guess I had been, no two ways about it. But after I had time to think it over, I decided I didn't care. I loved Belinda so much, I figured I was lucky to get her any way I could. I told her that I'd raise the baby as my own and no one would be the wiser. So that's just what I did."

She couldn't believe what she was hearing. "Rose looks so much like her mother. At least from the photograph I saw."

Luke slouched in his chair and rolled the empty glass between his hands. "Yeah, that was lucky. She got Belinda's features and dark hair, so it made things a lot easier. I don't know what people might have said if she'd turned out red-haired and blue-eyed like Tilson."

"I suppose that might explain why you started having trouble with Rose after her mother died."

"Why?"

"Well, since she knows you aren't related to her and her mother was gone . . ." she began, and his expression clouded over.

He put down the glass and stared at her as if she'd suggested that Rose must think he'd never wanted her. "She doesn't know I'm not her father."

She lifted her brows. "But shouldn't you tell her?"

He sat up straight. "Hell, no! Why would I want to do that? She already lost her mother—what would it do to her to find out that she's being raised by a man who's only pretending to be her father?"

Emily countered, "You aren't pretending to be her father. Robert Cannon *pretended* to be my father, even though I knew he wasn't. And he made a very poor job of it." She hadn't meant to say that. Luke had a way of getting information out of her without even trying. "You're a wonderful father. It hasn't mattered that you aren't a blood relative." She realized that how he treated Rose had a lot to do with how she felt about him. Every good thing he did for his daughter gave him a stronger foothold in her own heart.

He leaned forward. "All right. Give me a reason why we shouldn't go on as we always have."

"Well, what would it do to her to find it out from someone else? It's a risky secret to keep. Suppose one of her friends tells her or, or—"

"No one knows except Cora and me." The darkness in his eyes made her scoot back in her chair. "And now you."

"You know I would never say anything!"

"Then why should I muddy up the waters with the truth? What good would it do?"

She couldn't think of an argument to his logic. If only three people knew the real facts, maybe it didn't make any difference after all. And he was Rose's legal father, with the right to make the decisions about how she grew up. "You're right, I suppose. I guess I was just thinking of how I'd feel if someone told me that the man I believed was my father turned out to be someone else. But that won't happen to Rose."

Luke's brow relaxed and she hoped he understood that she had only Rose's best interests at heart. "I wish someone had told *me* that. I would have been relieved."

"That's a horrible thing to say!" The admonishment just popped out. Emily had heard only bits and pieces of Luke's background.

He considered her with hooded eyes. "Did I tell you that my old man used to beat me and my brothers whenever he was drunk? And he was drunk most of the time. He beat my mother, too, now and then, but didn't bother my sisters much. I'm not sure why. I don't think I even want to know."

Emily stared at him and Luke was fairly certain that regardless of how lonely or penny-pinching her life had been in Chicago, she never saw the kind of tenuous, hardscrabble existence he'd grown up with. He told her harrowing stories of his youth and watched her shrink further back into her chair. He spared only the most gruesome details. But she didn't turn away in disgust, as he thought she might. He didn't know why he went on, but once he got started, he couldn't seem to stop. It was as if he had someone to listen to him at last. Belinda had never liked hearing about his background. Or maybe he'd wanted to shock her and see how much she'd be willing to hear and still like him.

"Finally, after my brothers and sisters had scattered to the wind and my parents were both dead, I ended up here, a hired hand working for the Olstroms. Lars and Sigrid had kids—two boys and a girl, all under twelve, and all as blond as you. But they took me in, too, and treated me like one of their own." He smiled. "That probably wasn't easy. I had a smart mouth and a chip on my shoulder the size of a boulder. I watched them, though, the way they treated each other, the way that Lars and Sigrid respected and teased one another. They *loved* each other. They'd flirt and make calf eyes. I'd never seen that kind of life. Lars taught me about farming and animals—I never learned anything from my own father except how to swear and how to drink. They trusted me—they had faith in me." He shook his head, still amazed.

"Why did they leave?" Emily asked. "Cora said the house burned down, but couldn't they rebuild?"

He crossed his ankle over his knee and leaned back in his chair. "Yeah, they could have, I guess. But I don't think their hearts were in it. Six months earlier, Sigrid had a stillborn baby. When the house caught fire, they lost everything. We tried to put it out, but it had been a dry summer and it went up like a box of matches. God, it was an awful sight, especially afterward. Just a charred, smoking skeleton of what had been there before. The whole family had to move into the barn. It all added up to more than they could face. Sigrid became melancholy and started pining for the old country. Lars had put away enough money so they could go back to Sweden if the time ever came. And it did. They wanted to go home."

"Oh," she replied, her voice small and low. He heard a tinge of heartache in the single word.

"Lars offered the land to me first. I wanted to jump at the chance, but hell, I didn't have a pot to pee in—" Emily frowned slightly. "Um, I mean I didn't know how I would pay for it. He took me into Portland and introduced me to his banker. He even vouched for my character." Luke shook his head in wonder. "It was a big responsibility to live up to and I knew I couldn't let him down. He'd put all of his trust in me."

He unhooked his ankle and stretched out his legs. "When the Olstroms went back to Sweden, I stayed here and lived in the barn. I wanted to be a better man than my father was—it wouldn't have taken much effort. I saw what kind of marriage Lars and Sigrid had, and I knew I wanted that for myself. So I took a risk and went calling on Belinda. Tilson was gone, I had the land and some stability—you know, good prospects. I figured I stood a decent chance at winning her. Her parents still looked me up and down like I was the devil himself, but everything went forward and one afternoon, there we were, standing in front of Reverend Ackerman, getting married. The day we moved into this house, I could still smell the fresh paint." It seemed like a lifetime ago now to Luke. He'd brought home whom he thought was his virgin angel-bride, only to find out on his wedding night that she was carrying another man's baby.

"Early one morning six months later, Doc Gaither put

Rose in my arms, a little pink bundle of a thing who stared up at me like I was the grandest man on earth. And at that moment, I was. I'd come a long way from the shack that I grew up in on the river. I had my own farm, I had the wife of my dreams, and I had some respectability. But Rose made a man of me that day. I loved her from the first moment I saw her." He looked across the table at Emily. "How can I tell her that I'm not her father?"

Emily's green eyes sparkled with unshed tears. "Of course, you can't. I understand."

And he really believed she did. He glanced at the window and the darkness beyond. "We've only got a couple of hours till sunup. Shall we try and get some sleep?"

She smiled and nodded, and pushed herself away from the table. Her modest nightgown didn't do much to enhance her willowy shape, but Luke found it to be oddly arousing, like brown-paper wrapping that hid a wonderful secret.

He put the whiskey bottle back in the sideboard, grabbed the lantern from the end of the table, and held out the crook of his arm to her. Their shadows danced tall and flickering on the walls. She took his arm and they went into the hall and up the stairs. He delivered her to her door, wanting more than anything to follow her inside and make love to her, his shy schoolteacher wife. But the time wasn't right. He would try to court her, woo her, and win her heart. This time, things would be different.

Instead of following his body's nagging desire to touch her smooth, bare skin, he took her soft hand and pressed it to his cheek. In the low light from the lamp, he saw the surprise in her face. She smiled and ducked her head.

"See you in a couple of hours, Emily."

"Yes, g-good night, Luke."

"Emily?"

She lifted her chin again and he took it between his thumb and index finger. Then he pressed a light kiss on her tender mouth, but as soon as their lips touched he deepened the embrace. She clung to him suddenly as if he were the only thing keeping her from being swept away by a strong current. Tongues, soft lips, arms, and Emily's small, anguished murmur all blended together to fan the fires in Luke's body.

When he released her, she searched his face in the low light, then sped into her room. Her long, blond braid dangled down her back, and she closed the door.

Luke went to his own room and flopped on his bed, a heavy throbbing down low in his belly as his imagination showed him Emily's long, silky limbs and sweet curves. He wondered if he'd just guaranteed that he wouldn't sleep the rest of the night.

Saturday was unusually warm and humid, and was spent in a flurry of activity in the Becker household. While Luke did farm chores, Emily gave both her dress and Rose's a final inspection and pressing, and made sure that Luke's suit was clean and ironed.

Then she fried the two chickens that Luke had dressed out for her, and gave Rose the task of chopping up boiled potatoes, pickles, onion, and hard-cooked eggs for salad. The meal would be accompanied by fresh bread, spread thick with Jennie Manning's sweet cream butter. Dessert would be the chocolate cake Emily had promised and two quarts of apple cider.

All this work should have kept Emily so busy that she wouldn't have time to dwell on her late-night conversation with Luke. But she could barely think of anything else. Of all the things he'd told her, two stood out in her mind with knife-sharp clarity.

Rose was not his daughter, he had been duped into marrying her mother, and yet he loved the girl as much as any father could. This revealed more to Emily about his character than anything else she'd heard yet.

The other and most important thing he'd said was that he'd begun to question his mourning of Belinda. This fact, combined with the touch of his hand on hers and the hot, moist kiss he'd given her, put a different face on their marriage.

Now she was almost as nervous as she'd been the day she landed at the Fairdale dock.

Now she had hope.

A person with hope ran the risk of losing everything, or gaining the world. Even the writer Alexander Pope had made a pithy observation about it: *Blessed is the man who expects nothing, for he shall never be disappointed.*

But such a man would never know joy, either, Emily thought. Hope, joy, and disappointment were a tightly interwoven triumvirate. To live, one had to take chances.

So, late that afternoon, as she'd stood in her bedroom and dropped her new teal dress over her head, she knew that she must open her heart to him and take the chance that Luke would come to love her, too. Take the chance that they'd have a real marriage together. Certainly her attraction to him had never been a problem. She had heard him at the pump earlier, washing up just as he did every day, and had gone to the side window to gaze upon him. He glanced over his shoulder at her, and this time, she hadn't jumped back. She'd just smiled.

Now she heard him calling from the front of the house. "You women better get a move on if we're not going to be the last ones walking into that social! The food is loaded in the back of the wagon but I can't eat it all myself!"

With a last glance in her mirror, Emily grabbed her gloves and fan and scurried out into the hall. "Rose, come along. Your father is waiting."

Rose emerged from her room, and Emily looked her over, checking for missing items. The girl seemed to have everything—matching stockings, matching shoes, her hair was still neatly braided. She still owned no gloves, though. Emily hadn't had a chance to do anything about that, but her heart swelled. She could not have been more proud of her if she were truly her own daughter. "You look beautiful, Rose."

Rose beamed. "So do you, Miss Emily."

She smoothed her skirt. "Thank you, dear. Let's go show your father." Emily had taken special pains to keep Luke from seeing the dresses. She wanted to surprise him, and he'd played along, pretending to sneak peeks while they worked on them in the parlor, making Rose shriek with mock dismay.

That Luke had pulled the wagon around to the front of the house indicated that this was a special night. Most of the time, they came and went from the back door. When she and Rose stepped out onto the front porch, Emily thought the very air between her and Luke was electrified. He looked as handsome as ever in his frock coat, standing there next to the front wheel. He gave a low whistle as he considered first Emily and then his daughter. His dumbfounded gaze returned to Emily, where it lingered like a caress. Even with no experience, she felt the heat of his regard.

"Did I make good use of the silk, Mr. Becker?" she inquired playfully, the closest she had ever come to coy flirting.

His eyes traveled over her, from curled, upswept hair to hem. "Yes, ma'am, you sure did." He turned to his daughter. "And you, missy, you look so fetching—well, I'd better not catch any young farm boys giving you the eye tonight or they'll have to answer to me."

"Oh, Daddy!" Rose blushed furiously but her grin was as bright as daybreak.

Luke helped Emily up to the seat next to him, and then put Rose in the back, next to the wicker basket of food. "Everyone ready?" Nodding at his own question, he clucked to the horses and they set off for town.

As they made their way down the hill toward the church, Emily noticed dark clouds boiling up from the south. "A storm?"

"Looks like we might have some weather headed this way," Luke confirmed over the jingle of harness and rattle of the wheels. He studied the sky with a farmer's eye. "We can use the rain, but I hope it holds off till we get home tonight."

They passed the cemetery, and no one looked at the gate or the graves. Not tonight. Emily was too nervous, wondering how she would be received by the community, and whether Cora would be at the social. Rose, she suspected, was eager to show off her new dress, and Luke— well, she never knew what Luke was thinking. But the furrows that often marked his brow were absent, and she hoped that he was looking forward to the evening of fun he'd promised her when he first invited her to attend.

When they arrived at the church, the surrounding grounds were packed with wagons, buckboards, and a buggy or two. To see a carriage in Fairdale would have been so astounding, Emily suspected that its owner would be mobbed by curiosity-seekers, or perhaps even shunned as highfalutin.

Women came and went, toting boxes of food and dishes, flapping tablecloths over makeshift picnic tables, and setting out all manner of delectables for those who weren't participating in the box-dinner auction. A temporary dance floor had been built in the side yard and Jennie Manning had told Emily that music would be provided by the Duffy brothers, the same group who played at weddings, grange dances, and socials. They had a fiddle, a tin whistle, and spoons. If Tom Duffy had enough to drink, he might even bring out his uilleann pipes. Reverend Ackerman didn't hold much with drinking on church grounds, but he figured the Duffys were the pope's problem and not his. A string of lanterns had been rigged around the perimeter for late-night dancing. Luke had told her that dances sometimes went on until dawn, although that probably wouldn't be the case with a church social. Reverend Ackerman wouldn't want to give anyone an excuse for not being in their pews in the morning.

Children ran around, full of energy and high spirits, playing tag and bragging about their mothers' cooking. The men clustered in groups and engaged in discussions about planting, weather, and crops.

Luke stopped the wagon under a wide-branched maple and jumped from the high seat to help Emily down. Then he handed Rose out and unloaded the wicker hamper that Emily had packed.

"Mrs. Luke!" Emily turned and saw Jennie Manning waving at her from a group of tables on the north side of the church. A couple of the smallest Manning children, a girl and a boy, peeked at the Beckers from behind Jennie's skirt. "Mrs. Luke, come and sit with us."

Relieved to see a familiar face, Emily waved back, and Luke and Rose followed her to the table set up next to the Mannings'. "Mrs. Manning, how good to see you," Emily responded. "Carrie and Jack, it's good to see you, too." With a nudge from their mother, the youngsters made polite replies.

"My, my, but that dress made up so nice! You have a real talent with the needle," Jennie said. "And Rose, I see you've got a new frock. The Becker women look handsome tonight."

Emily thanked her, and opened the hamper to pull out her box dinner. "Luke, would you mind putting this on the table with the other dinners?"

He tipped her a private smile and said, "Don't forget what I said the other night. I'll make sure that you and I eat this—no one else."

Emily felt the blood rise to her face and she ducked her chin.

"Come on, Rose," he said. "Let's find out where they're collecting the boxes." Emily watched them walk away and when she looked at Jennie again, the woman was smiling approvingly.

They chatted for a while, then Jennie's attention was diverted to a minor squabble among her own brood. Emily was putting out her family's dishes when she saw Clara Thurmon coming toward her. She hadn't seen or spoken to the woman since that terrible afternoon at the general store. She smoothed out her checked tablecloth and waited for Clara to speak first.

"Well, Mrs. Becker, this is a surprise. I didn't expect to see you here at my basket social tonight."

Apparently Clara had recovered from their last encounter, enough to try and insult her again. Emily straightened and squared her shoulders. "And why is that, Miss Thurmon?"

"I figured this might be tame entertainment for someone used to big-city ways. We're just plain-speaking folks here, not given to fancy manners and fancy talk."

"Really? I've found that people are basically the same everywhere. One difference I've noticed, though, is that where I come from it's customary to make *everyone* feel welcome, especially newcomers."

Clara tightened her lips into a white line, obviously unable to think of an excuse for her plain-speaking rudeness. So she changed tactics. The sun glared off her spectacles, giving her a weird, eyeless appearance. Her gaze raked Emily up and down, taking in her new dress. "What a lovely outfit. Blondes usually look terrible in that shade. But it suits you."

Emily sizzled inside her "lovely outfit," trying to think of a reply. But nothing came to mind, and she was tired of the battle. "I'm sure you must have many important duties to attend to, Miss Thurmon, and I know I do. If you'll excuse me. . . ." She dismissed Clara, who had no option but to move on.

Jennie leaned closer, obviously a witness to the war of words. "Isn't she the most dreadful woman?" she whispered. "I hate talking to her—I never know where to look. All I can see is that silver mustache of hers."

The tension broken, Emily laughed. "I don't suppose it would be so noticeable if she had a nice personality that a person could concentrate on. For some reason, she's taken a grave disliking to me."

Jennie, her eyes sparkling with humor and good will, laughed, too. "Mrs. Luke, I thought you knew why!"

It was good to have another woman to confide in. She hadn't enjoyed that since she'd lost Alyssa. "I know that she and Fran Eakins make fun of my height and my way of doing—"

The other woman shook her head. "Oh, no, no, it's not that. Well, it might be part of it, but what's really eating them up is jealousy."

Emily stared at her. "Jealousy! Forgive me, Mrs. Manning, but that's impossible."

"Don't you think it's time you started calling me Jennie?"

She couldn't help but grin at the woman. Jennie Manning had known her share of heartache, loss, and hard work, but she hadn't let it conquer her spirit, as Cora had. "Yes, and you must call me Emily. But Jennie, I still think you're wrong about those women. What could they possibly be jealous of?"

Jennie pulled a stack of folded napkins from the crate she'd brought with her. "They wanted to marry your husband. And they hate it that he chose you instead."

Emily stared at her. "How do you know that?"

"Neither of them can keep a confidence to save their eternal souls. They've been talking about it in town ever since you got here. They were both sure that one of them would eventually drag Luke to the altar. Heaven knows what would have happened if he'd offered for one of them—they probably would have scratched each other's eyes out. He was the most eligible bachelor around here, with a good piece of farmland and a nice house. And it doesn't hurt that he's a good-looking man, either, almost as handsome as my Chester."

Emily suppressed a smile. Chester Manning was a devoted husband and a tireless provider, and she knew that Jennie adored him, but he looked like a scarecrow that had been left out for too many winters.

"Anyway, you pretty much settled their hash, and now they're sniping and resentful." She leaned closer. "If I were you, I'd enjoy it. No one has been able to put those two biddies in their place, and you did it very nicely."

Jealous. Emily could hardly believe it—was it really true? No one—*no one*—had ever been jealous of her. It seemed that she'd spent most her life trying to justify her worth as a human and a female. She'd never had anything that someone else wanted or envied. Until now.

She let her gaze drift over the crowd until she found her husband's dark head where he was in a conversation with a couple of other farmers. His stance was easy and naturally graceful, his profile clean and chiseled. His black frock coat emphasized his big shoulders and narrow waist, and she thought he was the handsomest man present. Just as when he washed at the pump, it was as if he felt her gaze on him, and looked in her direction. He gave her a smile and winked at her.

She realized that Alyssa would have made Clara and Fran just as envious. But Alyssa, God rest her, had never suffered the kind of social misery that Emily had. Before the Cannons' financial ruin, when they still attended parties and balls, Alyssa had taken her beauty and popularity for granted. She'd never sat unclaimed at a dance, hour after hour, like the last stale piece of pie on a plate, trying to make polite small talk with the chaperones and all the while wishing she were on the moon. In fact, when their social status had sunk and all the parties came to an end, Alyssa had been more baffled and unhappy than Emily. After all, she'd lost so much more, including her fiancé.

Now, though, Emily had a sense of confidence and strength that she'd never known before. She was married to Luke Becker, and as far as those women knew, it was a love match. But whether they believed that or not, Emily would be the one going home with him tonight, not either of them. And he had kissed her last night with a passion that made her feel as if molten honey drizzled through her. Only fear of her own response had sent her scurrying to her room.

As Emily unpacked the silverware, she overheard a group of farmers talking about the weather. Well, of course—it was a popular topic among people who lived off the land.

"We've had some wicked-bad rainstorms lately. But it's been warm. Been worryin' about the snowmelt in the mountains."

"Yeah, after the snowfalls we had last winter, the creeks and rivers are runnin' a little high. I ain't worried about my land, but the Edgertons planted on the side of that steep slope. That damn fool Paul, I told him it was a bad idea. The whole crop could wash down to—"

Reverend Ackerman interrupted all conversations when he clapped his hands for attention and used his best preaching voice to carry to all ears.

"Friends, thank you for coming out this evening to support our humble church. God willing, we'll raise enough money to put the new roof on before the fall rains set in." He went on to introduce and thank Clara Thurmon for organizing the social, to drone on about the joy of giving freely, and finally, to begin the auction so that everyone could start eating.

Several of the dinners were auctioned off, including the one prepared by Fran Eakins. Jobie Palmer, an arthritic old logger who lived in a cabin on Larch Mountain and rode a mule, bought her box of roast beef for the grand sum of one dollar. He was the only bidder. Everyone clapped and cheered Jobie on, and Fran, trying to keep her face from collapsing with disappointment, went along with him to dine at one of the tables.

"Now, let's see," Reverend Ackerman continued, "it looks like we have a meal here from our newest resident, Mrs. Emily Becker. She lists fried chicken, potato salad, rolls and butter, chocolate cake—sounds mighty good. Who'll start the bidding?"

"Five dollars!" A murmur rippled through the onlookers and Emily saw Luke emerge from a group of men. Five dollars was a fortune, an almost ostentatious gesture, especially for a farmer. It was only a little less than her weekly salary had been at Miss Wheaton's.

Reverend Ackerman chuckled. "Luke, I guess you know better than anyone how well your new bride can cook."

"Yes sir, and for the time being I intend to keep it that way. Good luck with the roof, Reverend." Emily blushed and everyone laughed as Luke handed over his money to buy his wife's dinner box. Everyone except for Clara, who seemed to be stewing in her own juices, and Fran, who was miserably occupied with gnarled, white-haired Jobie.

Luke looked around for Rose, found her, and gestured at her to follow him to their table. When he came back to Emily, he said, "I believe I have the pleasure, ma'am."

"Luke, that was a lot of money to spend," she murmured. "Can we afford that?"

He chuckled. "No. But I didn't want to waste time outbidding someone else. So I just took everybody out of the running." He said this as if he believed another man would actually have challenged him for the right to have dinner with her.

"Well, thank you. I am honored."

So the three of them, Luke, Rose, and Emily, sat down and enjoyed her fried chicken dinner. Emily felt awed, thrilled, stunned. Around her she could hear the sounds of silver clinking on dishes, of the other boxes being auctioned off, and the awkward moment when Reverend Ackerman himself finally had to bid on Clara's box because no one else did. It was all there, buzzing in the background. But what she heard in her mind, repeated over and over, was Luke saying, *I just took everybody out of the running.*

After everyone had eaten, Reverend Ackerman announced that with the money earned at this event, added to proceeds from earlier bake sales and bazaars, the church had achieved its financial goal and the roof could finally be replaced instead of patched. Applause and cheering rippled through the well-fed group, and Clara Thurmon took advantage of the moment to bow as if she had personally donated every penny and cooked every meal.

Then the Duffy brothers took their place at the edge of the floor and the dancing began. Luke held out his hand to Emily.

"What?"

"Come on with me, Emily." He tucked her hand in the crook of his arm and pulled her toward the dance floor. The drumming sound of feet on wood planking kept time with the lively music.

She resisted. "Luke! I can't do this." When she'd hoped that he'd ask her to dance, she hadn't realized how she'd feel if he actually did.

"Do you mean to tell me that an etiquette teacher doesn't know how to dance?"

"Yes, of course I do—at least I used to. But I haven't danced in a very long time. I'm not sure I remember."

He gave her a disbelieving look. "Yes, you do. You're just being shy again. Your shoulders are rounded."

She gaped at him. Had he studied her so closely that he knew her gestures?

"Come on," he repeated and twirled her out to the floor. She feared that she'd trample all over his feet, but he led her with ease, and the steps came back to her. How nice it was to be held in his arms, to be able to look up at his face instead of down, as had often been the case with the dance partners of her girlhood. Smelling of bay rum, soap, and fresh air, he was surprisingly graceful and light on his feet, and the music and rising stars combined to make it a magical experience. She was aware of everything about him—the way he looked, the texture of his wool coat under her hand, the warmth of his touch at her waist. Onlookers watched them with approving and admiring glances, and Emily, wearing her new dress and held in the arms of her handsome farmer-prince, felt like Cinderella at the ball. Haunting thoughts of Cora, Belinda, and the uncertainty of her position fell away with each passing moment.

"Did you get your money's worth at dinner?" she asked, before realizing how it sounded.

His smoke-gray eyes gleamed with a raw flicker in the setting sun. "I got enough food, if that's what you mean, Mrs. Becker," he said next to her ear. "But I'm still hungry."

She met his gaze, her mouth open slightly. There was no doubt, even in naïve Emily's mind, what he meant, and his words sent a delicious shiver of anticipation through her. His eyes touched her here and there, as blatant as a hand, yet unnoticed by others. Her heart throbbed, and though she supposed it might be due to the exertion of dancing, she knew it was more than that. The air seemed to grow very heavy, and the music and chatter around her faded away into the background. There was only Emily and Luke, waltzing under a twilight sky. If they were truly alone, what would he do? she wondered. She had only a vague idea, but it thrilled her just the same.

At last, the weather seemed to be working against them. The wind had picked up. Even the Duffy brothers gave up their spot by the dance floor. Napkins and loose tablecloths blew across the grounds, and the stiff gusts flattened women's skirts against their legs. People were gathering their belongings and children to head for home.

Luke glanced at the darkening sky. "We're going to get a storm. We'd better pack our things and get home. You don't want to get caught in the rain in your new dress."

No, she didn't. "Where's Rose?"

Luke looked around. "There she is, talking to Billy Reed."

Emily followed his gaze. "Billy Reed? Really?"

"Why, do you know him?"

"Um, no, I just heard his name once or twice." Emily had never told him about Rose's scuffle with the boy. She worried that they were fighting again. But when she spotted them, they were sitting on the church steps and seemed to be getting along just fine. Rose was even holding a pink wildflower. Emily smiled. She guessed that Billy no longer thought that Rose's dress looked like it came from a carnival sideshow.

"Rose!" Luke called. "Let's get going! That sky is going to open up."

"Aw, Daddy! Just a few more minutes?"

"Nope, now!"

With a last glance over her shoulder at Billy Reed, Rose came dragging over with great reluctance. Within a few minutes, good-byes had been said and they were in the wagon, heading up the hill for home. It was hours yet before midnight, Emily thought, but Cinderella had to leave the ball.

This time, though, Cinderella was leaving with her farmer-prince.

CHAPTER THIRTEEN

AFTER EVERYONE HAD CHANGED OUT OF THEIR SUNDAY best, there was work to do. Luke unhitched the team and went to feed the stock. Emily heated water on the stove, and she and Rose washed the dirty dishes they'd brought home from church. Then Emily sent Rose upstairs to get ready for bed.

Outside along the western horizon, a thin line glowed with a faint, eerie green-white light, and dark clouds had made night come on two hours early. The wind still rustled the trees and made one of the shutters on a henhouse window bang back and forth.

Emily searched for Luke from her own window, but she saw lamp light still pouring from the barn door. What would happen when he came in? She glanced at her own bed and wondered if she would sleep alone here tonight, or share it with her husband. Nervous anticipation shimmied down her spine. Would he be impatient and demanding? Gentle and patient?

Finally she changed into her own nightclothes and walked down the hall to check on Rose. The girl sat on the edge of her bed, brushing her hair. Well, ripping at it would have been a more accurate description. She still didn't have all of her ladylike behaviors down pat. But what an improvement had taken place in the last few weeks, Emily marveled. She still had her implacable moments—a whiny response, a loud, exasperated sigh, an occasional hint of sullenness—but since her father had begun spending more time with her, she'd made great strides toward becoming the well-behaved young lady that Luke so wanted her to be.

Emily paused in her doorway and watched as Rose tugged at a tangle, pulling out long dark strands with her impatience. "Here, let me help you with that. You'll go bald if you pull that hard."

"No, I won't," Rose said, giggling at Emily's exaggeration. She handed Emily her brush and turned her back. Emily pulled the bristles through the strands with long, gentle strokes.

"Did you have a good time at the social?"

"Oh, yes! It was so much fun watching people dance and seeing kids from school. Daddy hasn't liked to go to dances and things. Maybe he will now. Especially since he danced with you."

"Maybe. Did you make up with Billy Reed?" Emily asked.

Rose glanced over her shoulder briefly, giving Emily a view of a scarlet blush that reached her hairline. With supreme effort, she suppressed a grin.

"He said my dress looked nice."

"And it does. It takes a big person to admit when they're wrong."

"He didn't exactly do that."

"Perhaps not in so many words, but he made the effort. Apologizing is very hard for some people to do, and that's too bad. Sometimes people hold grudges, and that's bad, too."

"I told him *I* was sorry for beating him up."

Now Emily did smile. "I'm very proud of you." She

continued to work the tangles out of Rose's hair, and the child relaxed under the soothing touch.

"What's it like when you're in love with someone?" Rose's voice had turned low and sleepy-sounding.

Emily was unprepared for the question. What did she know about being in love with a man, anyway? "Why? Do you think you're in love with Billy?"

"No! But if it ever happens to me I'd like to know what to expect."

What to expect. What could she tell her, she, Emily, who had so little experience it was worthless? "When you find the right person, you'll know," she hedged.

"Like the way you feel about Daddy?"

The brush stilled in Emily's hand and she swallowed. "Well, I certainly like and respect him."

"But you *love* him, too." Obviously Rose took this for granted, despite knowing the circumstances that had brought Emily here.

"Y-yes, Rose, I do." It was an indisputable fact, she realized. She admitted this truth to herself while admitting it to the girl. She loved Luke. And she had for some time now.

"Well, how does it feel?" Rose pressed.

Emily put down the brush, unwilling to share feelings that she herself was discovering now, for the first time in her life. She wanted to examine her feelings and learn the answer in the privacy of her own heart.

"We'll talk about it later. It's a very personal subject, and one that deserves more time than we have tonight. Now you should be in bed. We've all had a busy day."

That seemed to satisfy Rose, and she climbed under the covers. "Will you stay for a while, Miss Emily?" She patted the empty space next to her.

"Of course." Emily smoothed Rose's dark bangs off

her forehead. She felt such a rush of motherly emotion for Rose, it was almost as if she were related by blood. That must be how Luke felt, she realized. It didn't matter that someone else had begun her life—she was theirs now, Luke's and hers. And she would do whatever it took to keep Rose safe and happy.

Luke came into the house after feeding the stock and rubbing down the team, expecting to find Emily waiting for him in the kitchen. When a search of the whole downstairs turned up no one, he climbed the steps. Maybe she'd gone to her room to wait for him. He felt pretty certain that with everything that had been said and implied at the social, this would be the night that he would consummate his marriage to Emily Cannon Becker. He'd even washed at the pump again in anticipation of a night spent in his wife's slender arms. He would carry her to his bed and begin by kissing her smooth throat, then work his way up to her lips and temple, and back down again to her breasts. Just envisioning his plan gave him an intolerable ache that only she could satisfy.

At the top of the stairs, he saw the lamp lighted in her room and her door invitingly ajar. Suddenly uncertain and a little self-conscious, he ran his hands through his hair. This was the damnedest spot he'd found himself in for a long time. Luke Becker had never had trouble making love to women. Except, it seemed, when his feelings ran deeper than his crotch, as they had with Belinda. And now, as they did with Emily. He didn't want to examine them very closely—it was still too new, too strange to think of caring for another woman besides Belinda.

He stopped short of buffing his boots on the backs of his pants legs and started what seemed like a very long walk toward Emily's bedroom. Halfway down the hall, he saw a light in Rose's room, too. Well, hell, was she still awake? That might put a real crimp in things.

He stopped in the open doorway and looked in. A hush fell upon his spirit and the feelings he'd been harboring in his heart surged forward. Rose was asleep, all right, his small, dark-haired princess. And next to her, on top of the blankets but sharing the pillow, slept his fair-haired princess, Emily.

Luke's smile was rueful as he studied them and realized that all of his amorous intentions had just been postponed for some other night. But he went to his own room with a full heart and a sense of contentment.

Rain. The first sound he became aware of was rain. Just a few scattered drops ticking on the roof and the siding. But that wasn't what woke him. Luke had been listening to rain all of his life. In this part of the country everyone was used to it. The sound was as much a part of the background as birdsong and the east wind in the trees.

A sudden flash filled his bedroom with the white-hot light of a thousand candles, followed almost immediately by a horrendous clap of thunder that seemed to explode directly over the house and rattled the glass in the window frames.

"Jesus Christ!" He jumped out of bed and looked out his own window. Along the top of the oak tree in the front yard, Saint Elmo's fire danced over the uppermost branches, outlining them in moving veins of blue light.

Another lightning stroke touched the earth, this time hitting the oak with a noise like a dynamite blast. A blinding flash lit the tree trunk from top to base as if it burned from within. The intense heat of the electricity incinerated the leaves and limbs as it split it like a melon. Half of the burning tree crashed onto the henhouse and even from this distance he could hear the squawking of the frightened birds.

"Daddy!" Rose screamed from the hall.

"Luke?" Emily's voice followed. "What's happened?"

He ran out to the hallway and met them there. The lamp still burning in Rose's room provided enough light for him to see his daughter clinging to Emily, her arms wrapped around her waist.

"The henhouse is on fire!" he said. He ran back to his room and pulled on his rubber boots, then charged downstairs and out the back door, dressed only in his drawers.

From one of the two windows in the old building he could see fluttering wings and high, leaping flames that were fed by dry straw in the nest boxes. The fallen half of the tree had crushed the roof, essentially destroying the little shed. Smoke poured from the gaping hole torn in the roof and the sickening stench of burning feathers, manure, and cooking chicken blew over him in waves. The henhouse was a loss but it was attached to the barn and he had to try to stop the fire's progress. He ran to the well and pumped water into a bucket. It was more than one man could accomplish alone and yet he didn't dare take the time to call for help. God, it seemed hopeless but he had to try. If the barn caught—

As he ran toward the fire, another fork of lightning lit up the sky and the yard, followed closely by a clap of thunder. High wind fanned the flames, making them rise and dance.

"Luke!"

He whirled and saw Emily and Rose illuminated by the orange-white glow. Emily had flung her shawl over her shoulders and Rose had tucked her nightgown into her overalls.

"Rose, can you work the pump? And Emily, grab the

pail next to it and the one from the back porch," he called over the roar of the fire and the wind and the thunder. They scampered to follow his orders, and soon they had a bucket brigade formed, such as it was, with only three of them to man it. The tree was green enough that Luke believed it would burn itself out, but the henhouse was just as old and dry as the barn wall it had been built against.

Luke poured bucket after bucket on the flames with a growing sense of despair. He felt as if they were fighting the fire with teaspoons of water. Only sprinkles of rain fell, barely enough to even dampen the soil. Sweat poured off of him in rivers, from the heat and the exertion. Even Emily, when he had caught a glimpse of her face, bore a gleam of sweat and a look of grim determination overlaid with a mask of soot. Minutes seemed like hours—hours of struggling in this inferno of heat, noise, and smoke. If this was what the end of the world would look like, with fire, lightning, and wind, Luke figured he'd seen everything now.

One of the henhouse walls, in a sheet of flame and heat, groaned and began falling toward him.

Emily screamed. "Luke!"

He jumped back just in time to avoid being caught beneath its burning weight.

Finally, flames began to creep up the barn wall. Luke decided he'd better rescue the stock from the barn while he still could. He backed away, putting his arm out to the side to keep Emily behind him.

"We have to let it go," he shouted over the din. "I've got to save the animals before the whole barn burns."

"Can I help you?" she shouted back, but he shook his head.

"Stay here and look out for Rose. Just in case." He

looped an arm around Emily's shoulders and kissed her. Just in case.

As soon as their lips met, it was as if fate had taken pity upon them. The sky, which had sent only pitchforks of fire and destruction, now opened over them.

It began to rain in earnest. Luke pulled away from Emily's lips and looked up at the darkness.

The rain came in heavy, wind-lashed torrents, quickly soaking everything and turning the barnyard into a sea of mud. The henhouse began to hiss and steam, as if a trap door to hell had been slammed shut.

"Oh, Luke—we shouldn't give up now, should we?" Emily asked.

"No! Rose!" he yelled to his daughter. "Keep pumping, honey! We might make it yet."

Rose, who'd left her post, ran back to it and began working the pump handle again.

The rain, cool and far-reaching, gave them a huge boost of help and courage. At last, the flames began to recede until he felt confident that the worst of the fire was out.

The downpour, a real gully washer, continued to fall, kicking up more steam and smoke from the ruined shelter. Eventually, the storm passed, heading in a northeasterly direction, and the moon came out to cast its gray-white light on the scene. All that remained was a charred, smoking ruin that had been the henhouse, and half of the century-old oak tree that had once shaded the house with its graceful limbs. Thank God the tree had fallen toward the barn and not the house. He didn't know what he would have done if the home he'd built with his own two hands had been destroyed.

Luke dropped his bucket, and Rose and Emily came to him. He picked up Rose and took them both into his embrace wordlessly. Briefly, they clung together, saying nothing, all shaking with fatigue, emotional weariness, and the chill of wet clothes.

At last Emily lifted her head from Luke's bare shoulder. "Just when I'd gotten the hang of gathering those damned eggs."

He looked at her, amazed at the language his prim wife had used. Then he threw back his head and laughed until tears came to his eyes. She and Rose laughed, too, half-drunk with shock and exhaustion. "Emily, you're one hell of a woman!" She beamed at him as if he'd told her she were the queen of the world. He shook his head and laughed again. "Thank God we're all safe and didn't lose anything else." He hugged them again, then set Rose down.

"Let's go back to the house and get cleaned up and into some dry clothes," Emily suggested, dragging her hand across her nose and smearing the soot.

"I just want to check that inside wall," Luke replied, pointing at the partially burned side of the barn. "I'll be there in a minute."

As he walked to the barn, Luke glanced over his shoulder to see that Emily and Rose made it to the house safely. There were none so brave as his young daughter, who'd handled the pump like a half-grown man. And his city-bred wife, covered in soot and grime from his barn and his henhouse. He doubted that Cora, or even Belinda, would have fought as hard to save everything as his strait-laced schoolteacher wife.

Emily helped Rose wash off the soot and grime, and shampooed her hair in the kitchen sink to get rid of the smoke smell. She planned to tuck her in and then bathe, too. She had just come downstairs from Rose's room when Luke walked in through the back door. His hair was wet, perhaps from the rain. But she thought he must have washed it in the icy well water from the pump outside. His face was still smudged, though. He'd found a shirt to put on and he'd left his boots on the porch, so now he was barefoot.

Emily was certain that she'd never seen a man so heroic, despite the fact that he was dressed only in knee-length drawers and an old shirt. Dear God, when that burning wall had collapsed, she'd been terrified for him. If he'd been crushed under it, she didn't know how she would go on. To finally love a man only to lose him—

That thought brought her up short. She loved Luke? God, she realized that what she told Rose was true. Every day that she'd been here, every look, every deed, had opened her heart to him and now she was in love with a man whose heart belonged to a woman buried in the cemetery. Fear and uncertainty twined themselves around her feelings.

"Rose is in bed?" he asked, dropping into a chair at the table.

She swallowed and then pumped water into the kettle to heat on the stove. "Yes. I hope tonight doesn't give her nightmares. I remember how long I had them after the fire in Chicago. Our house didn't burn but the flames stopped within two blocks of our yard. We didn't even need to light the lamps in the house, it was so bright. And it was hot and smoky. All those buildings burning at once—" She shivered. "I still remember it so vividly. You can't ever get that smoke smell out of clothes. And of course, after that everything changed."

He stood up wearily and took her by the arm to sit her down. "Here, you have a seat. I'm going to fix us a drink."

"A drink—do you mean spirits?"

"Yes, ma'am. But I'll put yours in hot water and add

some sugar and cinnamon, and you can call it a toddy if you like."

"Oh, I don't know . . . spirits . . . I don't usually, ladies don't—"

He smiled and went to the sideboard for his whiskey bottle. "Don't worry, Emily. I won't tell anyone."

She knew that some women took a drink now and then for their nerves, or for female complaints, or for various medicinal purposes. But to just have a drink for no good reason—well, it didn't seem right. Still, there was Luke, dressed in only his underwear and a shirt, pouring whiskey and hot water into a teacup, and fiddling with a couple of different spices from the rack over the stove. Maybe there was a good reason after all—she could drink a silent toast to the loss of her heart. And it would be rude to refuse after he'd gone to so much trouble. He handed her the cup, with a saucer, she noted, and said, "Here, see how you like this."

She took a cautious sip, the aromatic vapors reaching the tops of her sinuses before the hot liquid touched her tongue. The taste took her breath away. She sucked in a lungful of air through pursed lips, then pressed the end of her smoky shawl to them.

Luke sat down across from her. "Good stuff, huh?"

"Hoooo!" was all she could say, and she fanned her face with her hand.

He laughed and nodded. "Yeah, good stuff." He saluted her with his own glass and took a drink. "A little more sugar, maybe? More cinnamon?"

Emily shook her head. "No." Her voice was a bit rough.

"Take another sip. This one won't be as—surprising."

She cast a doubtful glance at him but did as he suggested, and found that he was right. The taste wasn't quite as sharp this time. And the hot water, spices, and whiskey seemed to flow through her veins, bringing warmth to her icy hands and feet. She took another taste, savoring the heat, and her tight, aching muscles began to relax.

He propped his bare feet on the empty chair next to her and sank low in his own chair to sit on his spine. "I want to thank you for helping me tonight. I couldn't have fought that fire by myself. If we had lost the barn—well, I don't know what I'd do."

Emily drank her toddy and considered Luke. He was soot-faced and tired-looking, but his eyes seemed to see through her dirty nightgown to her heart. In the distance, thunder rumbled across a faraway valley. "I don't know much about being married," she confessed quietly, amazed by her own loosened tongue. "I've read about it in books, and I've taught young women what those books said their duties and responsibilities will be when they become wives. I know how many forks should be set for all kinds of meals, the proper format for calling cards, and how to serve tea. I know a lot of intricate details about correct form." She set her empty cup on the table. "But in the end, I think marriage is about a man and woman working together to build a life, promising to take care of each other, and being true to their union. It seems to me that helping my husband fight a fire that threatened our home fits into all that."

He gave her a thoughtful, lopsided smile that touched her soul. "I think you're right, teacher. But I'm still grateful."

He drank his whiskey down in one gulp. Pushing himself upright in his chair, he got up. "How about another toddy?"

"Oh, dear, I don't think I should—" She was already giddy and light-headed from the first one. It was a very pleasant feeling, but who knew what it might lead to? An awkward slip of the tongue, an embarrassing confession of her heart's deepest secret? Her advice manuals forbade ladies from taking more than a sip of champagne at a wedding or a spoon of medicinal alcohol for those nervous problems and female complaints. She'd already broken that rule with the first toddy. Of course, fighting that fire had been nerve-racking.

"That's all right. I'll do the thinking for now." He picked up her cup and carried it to the stove. "Now, you drink this while I get a bath ready for you."

She stared at him. "W-while you what?"

"You worked hard all day, preparing food for the social, then with the fire and all, well, you deserve to soak for a while in the tub."

"But that's so much bother for you to—"

"Oh, and helping me save the barn was just a picnic in the park, huh?" He put the refilled teacup on the table in front of her and dropped his hands to her shoulders to keep her in the chair. "I'll bring in the tub and fill it for you. Wouldn't you like that?"

"Yes, but . . ." But it was so personal, it hardly seemed proper. She wished he wouldn't look at her that way. It made it hard for her to keep her thoughts straight. He was her husband, but even in traditional marriages—which they did not have, at least not yet—there were lines of propriety and intimacy that should not be crossed. Or so Emily had read in her advice manuals.

But a bath sounded wonderful. She had to wash off the soot and smoke, and dragging in the tub and filling it was a big job even on easier days. After the long day and frantic night she'd put in, to just sit and soak would seem like heaven.

Luke didn't wait for her response. He opened the door and dragged in the oblong, galvanized tub from its storage place on the back porch. Then he stoked the fire in the stove to heat pots and kettles of water.

"One of these years when the crops are really good," he said, "I'm going to buy a stove with a hot water reservoir on it so we don't have to go through this every time we want to wash."

He went about the business of readying her bath, pouring kettle upon steaming kettle of water into the bottom of the old tub, followed by a few pots of cold water. He even brought her a towel and a clean, white cake of Ivory soap, still in its wrapper, from the pantry. In her whole life, no one had ever waited on Emily, and she wasn't sure what to make of it now. It felt odd to sit idly while someone else pampered her.

"Well—" He gestured in the general direction of the hallway. "I guess I'll just go on upstairs and get washed myself," he said, suddenly seeming almost as awkward and bashful as she felt. "Don't worry about bailing out the tub. I'll take care of it in the morning when I get up. It's too heavy for you to lift, anyway."

Emily heard his footsteps on the stairs and she was left alone with an oil lamp and her bath. When she stood, she was surprised to find herself a bit unsteady, but she got her balance and stripped off the smoke-ruined shawl and nightgown. There would be no saving them. Just as she'd told Luke, the smell would never come out, no matter how many times she washed them.

Stepping into the hot water, she sank into its warmth to let it cover her shoulders. She barely noticed the corrugated bottom of the tub, which she usually found uncomfortable. Heated from the inside as well as the outside, she breathed a satisfied sigh.

Emily wasn't sure how Luke felt about her, but right now, her barefoot farmer seemed like one of King Arthur's knights.

CHAPTER FOURTEEN

LUKE STOOD AT HIS MIRROR IN DRY DRAWERS, SHAVING by the light of his lamp. This was such a dumb thing, he pondered, shaving at midnight, but he had a plan. And if that plan went as he hoped it would, a shaved face would be a necessary part of it. He'd already washed himself off once at the pump and then finished the job here at his washstand.

Plying a virginal woman with alcohol to get her into his bed probably wasn't the most noble deed he'd ever committed. But, what the hell, it wasn't the worst, either. He wanted to make love with his wife and he suspected that she'd be a little nervous. He knew *he* was. His insides were jumping around like a drop of cold water bouncing across a hot stove top. Night after night he'd lain awake, knowing that only a wall separated them, just a few feet of flooring.

But night after night, he'd wrestled with Belinda's ghost, as well. She'd risen in his dreams to accuse him of breaking his promises to her, of letting another woman into her house. In his nightmares, she hadn't moved her mouth when she spoke, but he'd heard a voice just the same. Cora's voice. Strange that when Cora moved out, the dreams stopped. He'd decided that Belinda wouldn't care what he did. Death was a final break with the living and whatever fate awaited departed souls was known only to them. In the meanwhile, Luke had Emily living under his roof as his legal wife.

And he wanted to make her his wife in fact.

Just thinking of her sitting in the old galvanized stock tank that they used for a bathtub set his pulse to racing. In his mind, the tank became a fancy copper tub, like he'd once seen in the window of a hardware store in The Dalles. Emily's long, pale hair would be draped around her in wet hanks, covering some places and letting others peek through. Her milky skin would be pink from the hot water, the lather from her soap would make it smooth like velvet dipped in cream. He imagined crystal sheets of water flowing over her as she rinsed away the bubbles, streaming over her breasts and belly—

"Goddamn it!" He muttered another curse and pressed his thumb to the nick he'd gouged in his chin with the razor. That was what he got for not keeping his mind on what he was doing. Hell, one wrong slip and he might take off his whole head, picturing Emily in her bath.

He managed to finish with no further mishaps. Just as he was wiping his blade on the towel around his neck, he heard soft, bare footfalls on the steps. He glanced at his bed, and then once again at his reflection. At least his chin had stopped bleeding.

"Emily?" he called softly and went to his open doorway.

She stood there in the light of the lamp she carried, poised for flight like a deer.

Luke swallowed hard.

She wore nothing but her towel.

It covered just her torso, leaving her arms and most of her long, slender legs exposed. Her hair was towel-dried, and twisted into a rope that hung over the front of her shoulder.

She clutched her flimsy covering to her, and the pulse pounding in Luke's head almost drowned out her words. "Oh! I—I didn't want to put on my dirty nightgown after my bath. I thought you'd be asleep and—" She seemed torn between making a dash for her own bedroom and running back down the stairs.

Luke stepped forward, took the lamp from her hand, and set it on a corner table. She smelled of soap and water and a sweetness that he'd never known on any other woman. Not even Belinda.

"Emily . . ." She still looked as if she might bolt. "Emily . . ." he repeated. "You're beautiful." And it was a simple truth. In his life, in all his experience with women, he'd never seen anyone as captivating as this tall, willowy female dressed in just a towel. The pulse thumping in his brain sent echoes through the rest of his body and straight to his groin. But rising within him, just as strong and hard, was an awe, a reverence, that Emily Cannon, decent, loving, steel-spined, and almost painfully attractive, was his wife. What if he'd sent her away that day on the dock? What if he'd been damn fool enough to let Cora chase her off?

All the smooth charm he'd used on those other women in his youth was forgotten. He hadn't loved them, but he'd loved Belinda, and now he loved Emily. The realization was both startling and a relief. He *could* care for someone again. He'd assumed that he had no room in his heart for anyone except his first wife and his daughter. That thought had haunted him these last few weeks, almost as much as Belinda's ghost had. It foretold a dreary future, one that he probably deserved. But damn, didn't a man also deserve some reward for changing his ways and working hard from sunup to sundown to make a home? Was it asking so much to love and be loved in return?

But he must win a place in Emily's heart. Words failed him—he'd always found his tongue tied when it came to expressing his feelings. That wasn't especially surprising, given the way he'd grown up. He'd learned to take his whippings without making a sound or shedding a tear. If the old man saw a hint of weakness, he'd flay Luke and his brothers with his belt even harder.

How could he tell Emily how he felt about her? Almost involuntarily, as if a heavy hand had landed on his shoulder and pushed, he dropped to his knees before her. If he looked foolish, he didn't care. With a light touch on her forearm, he asked, "Emily, will you be my wife?" He let his hand drift down her arm to take her hand in his. He lifted it to his lips and kissed it.

She looked into his face. "But, I *am* your—" Then she stopped. "Oh . . ."

Luke leaned forward and pressed his forehead against Emily's thigh. She thought her knees might buckle from shyness and surprise. Here was Luke Becker, her big, strong husband, a man wanted by every available woman in town—and perhaps even some who were unavailable— kneeling at her feet like a supplicant, begging for her favor.

He looked up at her again, that raw flame flickering behind his eyes. "Will you?"

She drew a breath. "Yes, Luke. Now and always." This promise meant so much more than the one she'd made in Judge Clifton's office. Now she was pledging her heart and soul. That day, she'd given only her word.

Luke rose to his feet and with no warning, picked her up in his arms. "I've been waiting for this night for weeks," he muttered against her ear, sending delicious shivers over her. Even in the face of her butterflies and the thrill of anticipation, she couldn't ignore the fact that in his embrace, she felt as light as swan's down and as delicate as the silk illusion of her bridal veil.

He stopped in the doorway to his bedroom and pressed a fevered kiss to her mouth, hot, soft, and demanding. It was nothing like the other kisses he'd given her. This one seemed to consume her breath, and made her heart thunder along all of her nerves.

He shut the door with his hip and carried her to his bed. Rain pelted the windows and she could just make out his silhouette as he loomed over her. The mattress sagged under his weight and she could feel the heat of him next to her even though he did not touch her. He kicked off his drawers and flung them across the room.

He covered her with soft, moist kisses, working his way down her arms and, dear God, up the insides of her legs. With each kiss, her heart gained another ten beats and her breath grew shorter.

At last she felt his hand at her waist, on top of the towel. "I've been looking forward to unbuttoning all those buttons of yours and unbraiding your hair," he said, his voice husky. "That will have to wait until tomorrow night, I guess."

His hand slid up from her waist to cover her breast, and a quiver of fear and excitement sizzled through Emily. She turned her face to his and he claimed her mouth with his once more, this time outlining her lips with his tongue. With one finger, he untucked the top edge of her towel and unwrapped her as if she were a gift. She remembered the crude comments she'd overheard at the general store about young Luke's prowess with women. She had nothing to compare this to, but suddenly her nervousness fell away. At this moment, all the hurts and slights in her past no longer mattered, and lying naked in Luke's arms seemed honest and right.

As if reading her mind, he whispered, "Are you scared?"

"No." She paused and then asked, "Are you?"

"A little."

But nothing about his actions gave it away. Why on earth he should be nervous made no sense to her, but it pleased her just the same.

He covered her nipple with his mouth, warm and moist, and tugged lightly, sending wave upon wave of gooseflesh over her body. She jumped, unaccustomed to the sensation, but Luke soothed her with more kisses and wordless murmuring that she found both exciting and comforting.

With one arm holding her close, he pressed his hips against hers to give her the feel of him. She stroked the length of his strong back, as she'd so longed to do every time she'd watched him wash at the pump. Beneath his skin, she felt hard muscles move and flex. It was all new, this touching a man, new and wonderful. A low moan escaped her and she felt like a wanton, reaching up to twine her fingers in his hair and twisting beneath his ministrations.

Somewhere in a cobwebbed corner of her mind, she knew that her behavior was shameful. Although marital relations were never discussed in her manuals, it was generally believed that it was a wife's duty to submit to her husband's more earthy—and dreaded—demands, and that from this submission she would know the joys of motherhood. So far, she'd found nothing about this to dread. Then all cognitive thought left her as his fingers skimmed the underside of her breast, trailed over her belly, down the insides of her legs, and up again to her most secret place at the apex of her thighs.

His fingertips delved the slick, hot folds of her, testing, experimenting, looking for exactly the right place to stroke her. When he found it, Emily let out a muffled cry and turned her face against his neck. Luke tightened his grip around her waist and murmured to her while continuing his torturous massage.

"I want it to be right for you," he whispered. "I want it to be good."

She thought her heart would burst from her chest, it pounded so hard against her ribs. Tongues of flame flicked through her, all gathering in the tight fireball that burned between her legs beneath Luke's questing touch. Her own hands began seeking him, feeling the hardness of his hipbone, the smoothness of his flank, the rigid maleness throbbing against her thigh. When she closed her fingers around him, he sucked in a breath and increased the friction of his touch on her. Suddenly, her body seemed to be spiraling into a vortex of heat and sensation that was almost frightening in its intensity. As if her body had developed an instinct of its own, her hips reached for his hand, reached for an ending or a beginning, she didn't know which. The vortex spun faster until it pulled her into a place where nothing and no one existed but she and Luke, as wave upon wave of spasms racked her body. She sobbed his name between breaths, weeping with the powerful sensations that had overtaken her.

At last the contractions subsided and she lay limp and dazed on the mattress, astounded by the feelings that Luke had coaxed from her. Her hair had worked loose from the rope she'd twisted it into and now fanned out on the pillows.

He rained more kisses upon her hot skin and wound his fist in her hair. "God, Emily, you're wonderful." His breath against her ear was hot and rapid. "I promise I'll be careful—"

Luke covered her with his sweat-damp body and parted her legs with his knee. He'd had a virgin just once before, and it had been so long ago he couldn't remember exactly what it was like. *Careful,* he told himself, *be careful.* She owned his heart. And she was his wife, deserving every consideration and all of his patience. But holding back wasn't easy. It took more self-control than he'd ever mustered to keep from plunging into her tender flesh, swollen and wet and waiting all these years for his entry. He probed her gently and heard her gasp when he breached her maidenhead. She tried to squirm away from him but he held her fast, smothering her protests with kisses and rough-whispered apologies. She lay still and at last he broke the seal of her femininity, pushing home into the tight warmth of her.

"Luke—" Emily wrapped her arms around him and pulled him closer to her.

A groan rose from Luke's chest at her acceptance. God, it had been years since a woman had lain beneath him, and even longer since one had received him with joy. The emotions churning in him were almost as strong as his basic instinct to couple with Emily. He would make this last, though, if he could. He wanted to savor every moment; he wanted to end this exquisite torment. He angled his body to give her the most pleasure. He knew that this first time probably wouldn't be as good for her as it was for him, but he would try.

Slowly, he began moving within her, push and pull, ebb and flow. Emily, his innocent with a spirit of fire and steel, adjusted her movements to match his, and the heaviness low in his belly increased. She lifted her hips and moaned, and he knew another climax was about to overtake her. Suddenly, rapid undulations grabbed him as she reached that instant of passion. His own need increased threefold and he pushed harder into her fevered body, seeking his own release.

Faster he plunged, bent on joining his soul to Emily's. He thrust forward one last time and tumbled into an abyss of white-hot convulsive tremors that shook him to his core. He poured himself into Emily, and it was as if all the pain, regrets, and sins of his past were released at the same time. In his mail-order bride, he felt reborn.

At last he lay exhausted and panting with his head on the pillow next to hers. When his breathing slowed, he asked, "Did I hurt you? Are you all right?"

Emily wanted to tell Luke that she loved him, but despite the intimacy they had shared, she felt shy about revealing her heart. She smiled in the darkness. "No, you didn't hurt me. Did—did I do it right?"

He rolled off her and pulled her into his arms. His chuckle was warm against her hair. "You did it better than right, Emily. You're beautiful."

Beautiful. There was that word again, applied to her, Emily Cannon Becker. Maybe he really meant it. After all, he didn't have to tell her that now—now that she'd already succumbed to his charm. She burrowed her forehead against the hollow between his shoulder and throat. "I have a wedding veil. Well, actually, it was my grandmother's veil." She told him the history of the length of silk and why it was now in her possession. "Because I was the plain one, I always had a fantasy that if I put on that veil, I would become beautiful, like the frog turned into a prince in the fairy tale. Except, I'd be a princess, of course."

"Well, what happened?"

"I've never tried it on. I thought I'd wear it on our

wedding day, but that was a pretty hurried event. I think I wasn't meant to wear it."

He turned his head and tried to look down at her. "Oh, hell, honey, you don't need a magic veil." She heard compassion and his heart in his words. "You're already a princess. At least you are to me."

She watched in the gloom as he interlaced his fingers with her own. "You know, you're a very remarkable man, Luke."

"Me? Naw. I'm just a farmer who got a second chance at life."

Emily's throat tightened and for a moment she couldn't speak. Then she reached up to touch his jaw and the words tumbled out. "I love you, Luke. And I'm so glad I was able to get up the courage to come out here in Alyssa's place. I worried sometimes that it had been a mistake, when Cora still—well, I worried."

He shifted on the mattress and resettled her against him. "I know that was hard—I should have done something sooner, I guess. But I didn't know how. Finally, I knew I had to ask her to leave."

"Now we have a new family."

Beneath her cheek, his chest rose and fell on a deep sigh. A silence settled between them. A married silence, was all Emily could think. That intimate moment between husband and wife when words were not necessary. She'd suspected her mother had had it with her father, doubted she'd had it with her stepfather. But now, she, plain but well-mannered Emily, was sharing such a moment with her own husband. A warmth filled her, one that had nothing to do with being pressed against Luke's naked body.

After a time he put a kiss on her forehead and said, "Morning is going to come pretty early, with a load of chores. And there's that henhouse to take care of."

He pulled the top quilt over them and it wasn't until Emily heard Luke breathing evenly in sleep that she realized he hadn't told her the one thing she'd hoped to hear.

That he loved her, too.

The hands on Luke's big alarm clock pointed at four twenty-five when dawn crept into the room. Emily peered at the clock face on the dresser and remembered that Luke had said daybreak would come soon. It certainly had.

Next to her, Luke still slept, turned on his side with his arm looped over her waist and his forehead pressed against her upper arm. He'd thrown a leg over hers on top of the quilt, and she studied his bare hip and flank. He was as beautifully made as a sculpture. Except he was flesh and blood, and he was her husband. She moved a little to get a better view of his face, relaxed in slumber. He looked younger. His curly hair was awry and all the lines that usually marked his eyes and brow were smoothed out. Her heart swelled with affection and tenderness for him. Then she thought about the night before and hot blood rose to her cheeks.

The prim etching of the concerned wife at her husband's feet in one of her advice manuals now seemed like an illustration from a child's book. Emily at last had knowledge that so many other women already had—what a night in a man's bed was really like. And it bore no resemblance to the chaste, brother–sister relationship that she'd once pictured. It was sweaty and violently passionate, undignified and intensely intimate beyond anything she had ever been able to imagine.

And Emily had reveled in it.

It wouldn't have helped if someone had tried to tell her about it before. She realized that it would be impossible to explain a sexual union to a maiden, even if that were permissible, which it most certainly was not. Ladies did not speak of such things, no matter how curious they might be. In any event, it had to be experienced to be understood. Especially the heart-stopping pleasure a husband's nimble fingers could bring to his wife's body.

Next to her, Luke tried to pull her closer in his sleep. As much as she wanted to stay, Emily knew she had to get breakfast going. There would be a lot of hard work to do today, and she wanted to give her family a good start.

She slipped from Luke's embrace and paused a moment to gaze upon him. Oh, she did hate to leave him, even for an instant.

Pulling herself away, she went back to her own room to wash and dress. Downstairs in the kitchen, she bailed out the heavy tub but decided to let Luke take it out to the porch.

She went outside to look at the remains of the henhouse and was shocked by the devastation. A chill skittered through her, and she knew it wasn't just from the coolness of the morning. The sky was still gray and low, although the rain had stopped for the time being. She crossed her arms over her chest and wished she still had a shawl.

In the light of day, she saw how close they had come to losing the barn. Only one corner of the little henhouse remained unscorched. The rest had been reduced to black, charred rubble that was still hot in some places. Here and there, she saw blackened chicken carcasses, almost indistinguishable from the rest of the debris. The huge old oak—nothing of it could be saved as far as she could see. It had been split right down the middle, and the smells of fresh and burned wood mingled together. It would take a lot of work just to clear away the wreckage. And where would the money come from for a new henhouse? she wondered. Maybe she could arrange to teach etiquette to other girls in the area, just as she did the Manning daughters. At the social last night, a few mothers had expressed interest in having their girls learn the finer points of proper deportment. Emily wouldn't be able to charge much, but every little bit would certainly help. And she would be able to make a real contribution to the rebuilding project.

Emily straightened her shoulders, as if mentally taking on her responsibility. She had never shied from hard work, and now she had something to work *for*.

She turned and went back to the house. With no eggs, she had to improvise breakfast. She stoked the fire in the stove, then sliced bacon and put it on to fry. She cut bread to put in the toast rack and got a pot of cornmeal mush bubbling. By the time she heard Luke's tread on the stairs, she had food ready on the table, the coffee brewed and fragrant.

He came into the kitchen and seemed to fill every corner of it. He grinned at her, and though the morning was cloudy, it was as if the sun had broken through. "Good morning, Mrs. Becker."

Emily felt her face flush and she stammered like a schoolgirl. "W-well, um, good morning, Mr. Becker." But she was grinning, too.

He walked to the stove and poured his coffee. "Did you sleep well?"

She ducked her chin. "Yes, very well."

He nodded and gave her a knowing look. "Me, too."

Rose followed soon after, dressed in overalls and yawning. Her hair was a dark tangle, probably because she'd gone to bed with it wet. She talked about the fire for a while and then asked Emily, "What's the bathtub doing in here? Are you going to take a bath?"

"Nope, I'm taking that out to the porch right now,"

Luke said, and picked up the tub as if it weighed no more than an empty soap crate. When he came back inside, he said, "That's a hell of a mess out there, isn't it? I'm not sure how I'm going to rebuild the henhouse." But even through this grim news, he smiled at Emily.

Emily directed Rose and Luke to their chairs to eat and doled out a big spoon of mush to each to go with the bacon and toast. "I was thinking about tutoring a few pupils." She told him about her idea to teach etiquette. "I thought I might be able to help the family finances."

"Let's wait and see what we're facing," he replied. "I don't want you taking on more than you need to. Being a farm wife is a lot of work on its own." But she could see he was pleased with the thoughtfulness of her offer.

Rose shifted her gaze back and forth between them, her porridge spoon stalled in her bowl. "What's everyone smiling about? Our barn almost burned down and you two look so happy." It wasn't an accusation—she sounded genuinely puzzled.

Emily exchanged a private look with Luke, and couldn't help but remember being held in his arms deep in the night, their bodies joined. She glanced away, certain that every detail of the memory was there on her face for anyone to see.

"Well, we're just . . ." Luke paused and rubbed his hand over his mouth and chin, as if he smothered a cat-licking-cream smile. Emily picked up her coffee and took a hasty sip. The strong, hot liquid reminded her of sharing the whiskey-laced toddy with him. She set her cup down with a snap. As if he had the exact same memory, Luke fingered the rim of his own metal cup as he continued with a tender light in his eyes, "We're just glad the fire wasn't any worse, Rose," he said.

Rose didn't look convinced, but she didn't ask any

more questions. Obviously she believed this was another of those instances where adults knew everything and children were left in the dark.

Under Luke's intense regard, Emily tried to eat more of her breakfast. Her heart thumped in her chest, but she kept her hand steady as she sliced a piece of bacon. Luke's gaze tracked her every movement, lingering on her mouth as she took the bacon between her lips.

"Since tomorrow is the last day of school, I thought I'd stop by Grammy's on the way home—"

Rose's abrupt statement reminded Emily that she was not at a private wedding breakfast with her husband. She dropped her gaze from Luke's and folded her hands in her lap.

"I've only seen her once since she left, and that was when Daddy went over there to plow her kitchen garden." Rose threw out this announcement as if waiting for either Emily or Luke to object.

"I think that's a fine idea, don't you, Luke?" Emily said, bending a meaningful look upon Luke.

He wiped his mouth on his napkin and swallowed a bite of toast. "Well, sure, honey, that's good. I know your grandmother will be glad to see you. You go visit her."

"Really?"

"Yeah—did you want me to say no?"

"No, but I thought you might."

He pushed away his empty plate. "Whatever problems Cora and I had don't have anything to do with how she feels about you, Rose. And I expected you to keep on seeing her. She's still your Grammy."

Emily released a quiet, relieved sigh. She hadn't supposed that Luke would forbid Rose from seeing Cora. But he had a right to feel bitter about his former mother-in-law. She'd caused a lot of trouble in the family, from what

Emily could tell, both before and after Belinda's death. She was glad that Luke was big enough to rise above those problems and not criticize her to Rose.

"Today, though, I'm going to need your help around here."

"Oh! What do I get to do?" Rose wore a look of responsibility and importance. Emily was so pleased that Luke had found a way to reach out to his daughter, and that Rose had responded to the gestures.

"We've got to start clearing away that tree and the ashes. Unless Emily needs you for something else?"

Emily shook her head. "No, you two go along. I can handle what needs doing around here. I'll bring you a snack around mid-morning, and we'll catch our meals as we can today. It doesn't look like we'll have a regular Sunday dinner anyway."

"All right, then, let's get going."

Luke stood and Rose jumped up, too. "Can I chop wood? I know how the axe works."

He winced slightly. "Yeah, well, I don't think I need you to do that to start. We've got plenty of other chores, though."

Just as they were about to go out the door, Luke turned and walked back to Emily. In front of Rose and God and the nation, he took her into his arms and gave her a long, soft kiss. "We'll see you later." Then he released her, winked, and went back to the door.

Emily felt almost as dumbfounded as Rose looked, with her jaw hanging open.

"Daddy!" Rose exclaimed, scandalized. "It's not proper to kiss a lady that way. Miss Emily said—"

"It's all right, Rose," Emily interrupted, a little dazed and dreamy.

"But you said public displays of grand affection between men and women are never acceptable."

"Well, this isn't public." She looked at Luke's mouth. "And anyway, I think I've been wrong about some things."

A broad grin lit up Luke's face. "See you later, Emily." His gaze lingered on her a moment and then he pushed Rose out the door ahead of him, before she could say anything else.

Luke Becker was a happy man. Even while he used a corn hook to pull down the charred, crumbling remains of the henhouse that he could barely afford to rebuild, he felt like smiling. Although it had started raining again and he was going to be soaked before this day was done, he couldn't stop the grin from coming. He had his daughter working beside him and a smart, pretty wife in the house. Why shouldn't he be happy?

"Rose, let's pile all the ashes we can into the wheelbarrow."

Rose worked with a little shovel. He didn't plan to let her stay out here very long. He just wanted to spend some time with her and let her feel included.

"Some of this is still hot. And—and there's dead chickens in there, Daddy."

A different warmth filled Luke at the easy way Rose once more called him Daddy. Maybe Emily was right. He didn't have to understand all the secrets of a young girl's heart, but spending time together would go a long way toward healing the rift between them caused by Cora and the last few years of pain. It didn't matter that she wasn't of his blood. With the way she looked at him, he knew that he was right not to tell her he wasn't her real father. He was her father in every way that mattered.

He straightened and watched to make sure she didn't

venture beyond the edges of the wreckage. "I know, you leave them be. I'll take care of them. Be careful not to burn yourself—we'll pour water on the pile again after we have a load ready to take to the garbage heap."

He'd gotten only about four hours' sleep, but he felt like he could climb mountains and conquer the world. It reminded him of how he'd felt when he thought he'd won Belinda's heart all those years ago. But it was different this time. Emily *loved* him. She had told him so. He hadn't had to pry it out of her. She'd volunteered her declaration with sincere passion. He felt a little guilty that he hadn't been able to tell her he loved her, too. His heart wasn't ready for that, not now anyway.

He hoped it would be someday.

Luke was tired, wet, and dirty that afternoon when he heard the sound of wagon wheels in the drive. He'd been able to clear out a good portion of the henhouse debris, and had sent Rose inside when he began collecting the dead chickens. Now he turned to see Chester Manning on the high seat of his own farm wagon, dressed in oilskins. Luke waved and the farmer pulled his rig up to him.

Chester's weather-seamed face reflected his astonishment. "By God, Luke, looks like that storm last night dealt you a dirty hand. Did you lose anything else?"

Luke leaned on the handle of his rake. "No, but I was worried for a while." He gestured at the scorched barn wall.

Chester nodded. "I heard that wind tore the roof off the outhouse at the Purcells' place. I guess Cyrus was busy in there at the time." He grinned and Luke laughed as he pictured three-hundred-pound Cyrus Purcell, sitting in the outhouse at the moment the roof took flight.

" 'Course," Chester added, "that don't compare to this. Can you rebuild before fall?"

"I sure as hell hope so."

"Well, try not to worry too much. Once folks hear about it, they'll pitch in to help. You know *I* will. I also heard talk the log bridge over by the cemetery is getting pretty shaky. You know the town council voted not to spend a dime to fix that damned thing last summer when they should have. With all this rain, I'm worried that someone will get killed before they let go of the purse strings."

This wasn't good news. "If that bridge washes out, all of us in this neck of the woods will be cut off from town. That creek underneath is just deep and swift enough to be a real danger."

Chester made a disgusted noise. "I know, I know. You'd think the council'd have to pay for the repairs entirely out of their own pockets."

"When the weather dries out, we'll have to go to the meeting and put some pressure on them to rebuild it. It'll probably be all right until then. It's seen a lot of rain and ice storms."

Suddenly, a muffled bleating noise came from inside Chester's big oilskin jacket.

Surprised, Luke looked up at the scarecrow of a farmer and laughed again. "Say, Chester, what's going on under there?"

The man unbuttoned his coat to produce a snowy lamb. "Jennie told me what happened to that other lamb I gave you, and I felt bad for not pickin' out a better one, especially since it was a pet for Rose. Sometimes those little mites are weak and need special tending. I wanted to make it up to her. I've got Mrs. Luke's butter, too. You know, she's a mighty fine woman, your wife. Jennie and

me are real pleased to have her givin' our girls some refinement. She's a blue-ribbon lady, and she's got a good
heart, too."

Luke was touched by the gesture and by the compli-
ment. He took the squirming lamb from Chester. "Thanks
very much. I know Rose will appreciate it."

Just then, Emily appeared on the back porch and waved
at them both. She looked both simple and elegant standing
there in a lavender dress and her white apron, and Luke
thought his shirt buttons might pop off with the pride
swelling his chest. "Mr. Manning, come in for coffee,
won't you?"

"I'd really like to, ma'am, but my wife's waitin' for
me."

"Next time, then. And bring the family, too."

"I sure will, ma'am. I sure will."

"Give them our best," she called.

He turned the wagon around in the barnyard and
headed off for home.

Holding the lamb and the butter, Luke watched him go
and then his gaze shifted to Emily on the back porch.

Yes, indeed, Luke Becker was a happy man.

CHAPTER FIFTEEN

———

THE RAIN CONTINUED OFF AND ON THROUGH THE NIGHT, but neither Luke nor Emily noticed it much. After dinner, time seemed to drag at a snail's pace. Emily washed the dishes while Rose dried, and Luke found a half-dozen reasons to come into the kitchen and brush past his wife at the sink.

When they'd finished the dishes, Rose wanted to spend time in the barn with Luke and the new lamb, which she had named Lucy.

"Lucy? What made you think of a name like that?" he asked her, helping her fill the lamb's milk bottle.

"Miss Emily has been reading *A Tale of Two Cities* to me. It's a book about some kind of war in France. A revolution, she said. People get their heads chopped off in something called a gee-o-teen. Anyway, there's a lady in the story named Lucy Mannett. I just like the way it sounds, I guess."

Luke scratched his head and looked at the lamb in her little pen. "Okay, Lucy it is." He had been a lousy student, himself. He couldn't remember a single book from his brief schooling. It wouldn't be long before Rose was better-read than he was. He chuckled to himself. Maybe Emily would tutor him as well. He had a quick image of lying naked with her, their limbs intertwined, his hand cupping her breast while she read to him in that prim schoolteacher voice she sometimes used. He reined in the thought and added more hay to the lamb's pen while he tried to focus on his daughter's rambling tales of all she would do with Lucy at her side.

After bedding down the lamb, Rose wanted to look at patterns so she could plan to make a couple of new dresses over the summer. She and Emily sat at the kitchen table, and Luke brought in a farm journal and joined them. The quiet ticking of the kitchen clock, the homey smell of brewed coffee, and the lingering aroma of the pot roast Emily had prepared for dinner added to the sense of family, of belonging that filled Luke. He'd worked hard for this dream, and here it was in his grasp, sitting at his kitchen table. His daughter's dark head was a sharp contrast to his wife's pale hair. Why had he ever thought blond was not for him? He'd been a blind fool, that was why. Beauty came from within, just like a man's true character showed in the way he treated his family and provided for them, not because of where he came from.

Once in a while, Emily and Rose would burst into giggles, glance at him, and mutter about how maybe they *should* be looking at new frock coats instead. He tried to look stern and uninterested, but it was hard with his heart in his throat. He tried to refocus on his farm journal, but that was just as hard when all he could think of was later tonight. Now and then, his eyes would meet his wife's across the top of the pages, and they exchanged urgent, unspoken promises that would be fulfilled later, after Rose went to bed, which seemed forever in coming. The anticipation was exquisite for Luke. He now knew how smooth her cream-colored skin was, he'd threaded his hands through her wheat-pale hair until it draped her shoulders in wild abandon. He knew that he could make that cultured voice catch, then call his name on a deep earthy cry.

Finally, eight chimes tolled on the mantel in the parlor and they could legitimately shoo the girl upstairs without making her feel as if they were trying to get rid of her.

Luke waited in his bedroom while Emily made sure that Rose was safely tucked in and dozing off. He washed at his washstand, and then washed again, wondering what was taking Emily so long.

When at last she stepped out into the hall, he pulled her into his room and closed the door. They fell into each other's arms amid a shower of kisses. As desperate and impatient as secret lovers meeting for an illicit tryst, they let their hands seek and stroke and unbutton. Lips met lips and brows and throats as each item of clothing fell away until they lay naked on Luke's bed.

He kissed each of her knuckles and then placed her hand over his pounding heart. "Can you feel it beating for you?" he whispered.

"Yes." Emily moved her hand and kissed the throbbing place just left of the center of his chest. "Yes."

Shyly, she took his hand and pressed it to her breast. "Can you feel mine?"

"Not yet, but let me keep searching." His fingertips grazed her soft flesh with exquisite tenderness, working magic and leaving trails of gooseflesh in their wake. Soon the search was given up in pursuit of more urgent pleasures, and though rain pelted the windows, they both forgot about anything else but each other.

The next morning, Emily saw Rose off for her last day of school. She stood on the back porch and waved to her, glad that the rain had finally let up a bit, because the girl was wearing her new dress. Rose wanted to show it off to her grandmother. Somehow, Emily didn't think Cora would appreciate that, but she said nothing to discourage her. Cora was a grown woman and she would have to come to terms with certain facts, including the one that Emily was now Luke's wife and was here to stay.

"Have a good day at school, and don't forget—come home by four o'clock."

"I won't," Rose called back over her shoulder.

What a difference the last couple of months had made. When Emily first met Rose, she was a sullen troublemaker who refused to take any interest in trying to look nice or be the daughter that Luke so wanted. With just a little help from Emily, but a lot from him, they'd turned Rose around to walk down the path toward becoming a decent, mannered young lady. She marveled at how much her own expectations had altered since that first day at the dock. She realized that some of the things she'd been taught were important, such as the value of reading and improvement of the mind. But others were silly or didn't apply to all circumstances, as she'd once believed. What did it really matter if a mourning dress had a pleat or a touch of embroidery within the first month of a death? If one took off one's gloves during a formal call, would the world really end? These rules and many others like them had been ingrained in Emily and she had trouble letting go of them. But after living on the farm, seeing the hard work Luke did from dawn till dusk to provide for them, then spending the night in his arms, well, she'd come to understand that relationships and responsibilities were just as vital as some rules.

She realized that having a gracious nature and generous heart were more important lessons, and they were what she wanted Rose to learn.

Emily waited until Rose disappeared around the bend

in the road, as proud as any mother could be.

Then she went back to the kitchen and to Luke.

"Grammy!"

Cora heard Rose's voice before she reached the front door. She looked outside and saw her precious duplicate of Belinda running up the road toward the house. It was almost as if her own daughter had returned from the grave. She hurried to the door and went out to the porch.

"Rose! Isn't this a nice surprise!"

Rose ran to her arms, the child she had missed and so yearned to have under her own roof to take away the sting of loss and betrayal. "Today was the last day of school so I came to visit after it let out."

"That's just grand. Come on inside. I've got lemonade and some cookies that I baked a few days ago." Cora's farmhouse wasn't as nice as Luke's, but that was fine and dandy with her. She didn't have some bossy new wife telling her what to do over here. Rose followed her into the kitchen. "Set down at the table, honey, and tell me all the doings."

"Well, the henhouse burned down the other night during the storm."

"Lordy!"

"Yes'm. Lightning hit the oak tree and it fell into the henhouse. We poured buckets of water on it until it started raining."

"I bet Mrs. Becker raced around like a blame-fool female running from a mouse!" Cora hooted, enjoying the mental picture.

"Oh, no, Grammy, I worked the pump and she took the buckets to Daddy. We all helped."

"I guess that means Luke doesn't have to gather the

eggs from the hens anymore. He probably wasn't too happy when he had to take over that job."

Cora was anxious for the news, certain that things couldn't be going well for Luke. After all, he'd kicked her out and let that city-bred priss stay. He'd come here to plow Cora's kitchen garden and even though she needed it to be done, she hated that he was the one doing it. She'd made it a point to ignore him the whole time he was out there and didn't bother to say hello or good-bye. He knew he'd made a big mistake sending her home. He knew. And she hoped he was stewing in his own juices over it. Cora put a chipped plate of gingersnaps in front of Rose and poured her a glass of lemonade. Then she sat across from her and leaned closer, putting her elbows on the table. "How's that etiquette teacher getting on now that she has to do all the cooking and cleaning?"

Rose took a sip of lemonade and made a puckered face. Sugar in lemonade just ruined the flavor, in Cora's opinion. The girl dropped her eyes to the tabletop.

"Come on, honey, you can tell me," Cora urged, encouraged by her reluctance. "I knew you wouldn't be cows in clover once I was gone. Are you getting enough to eat? Can that woman make decent soap?" Without Cora there to intervene for Rose, Emily was probably making her do all kinds of crazy things in the name of "good manners."

"We have good food, Grammy. We're getting along all right."

Cora straightened in her chair. "Well, there aren't any oysters on the half-shell out here in Fairdale. That's probably the kind of snooty, fancy food Mrs. Becker wants." She'd read about oysters once in a women's periodical, but she didn't really know what they were. Some kind of fish, it had seemed. "But she's making you do silly things like walk with a book on your head, and bawling you out for using the wrong fork, isn't she?"

"Um, no, Grammy."

Well, if the girl wanted to lie to protect the woman, there was nothing she could do about it.

"Look, she even helped me make this dress."

Cora sat fully back. The dress was as plain as an iron skillet and had none of the ruffles and flounces that Cora so loved. "Oh, she did."

Rose's face lit up like a Christmas candle. "Yes, and we don't use homemade soap anymore. Now we have *store-bought* soap. It smells so good, and it even floats in the water so you don't have to search for it!"

Cora led Rose along, asking more questions, trying to get a sense that life at the Becker farm had deteriorated since she'd gone. That Emily Becker was just a tall, skinny thistle with a lot of thorns. But Rose found nothing bad to say about her. She chirped along as happy as a bird.

"Miss Emily braids my hair and she's reading a book to me. And Daddy and her are always smiling at each other, like they have some happy secret."

A dark red anger began to grow in Cora, the same burning resentment she'd felt when Luke had run off Tilson and when she'd had to live with Luke's new wife. Mrs. Becker was just perfect, wasn't she? Cora simmered.

She pushed herself away from the table. "I'd better get supper going if we're going to eat. You're staying for supper, aren't you?"

"No, I can't this time. I promised I'd be home by four."

"Who did you promise?"

"Miss Emily."

So Mrs. Becker would even steal the chance for her to have supper with her own grandchild. Well, she'd see about that. "Then maybe you can come and stay with me for the summer now that school is out. How would that be? You could go home and pack up some things, and come back tomorrow. Wouldn't that be fun?"

"Well, but I have my lamb to take care of, and I want to hear the end of the story Miss Emily is reading to me. Then we're going to make another new dress for me."

"I thought that lamb died."

"Cotton did. But Mr. Manning brought another one for me. I named her Lucy and I have to stay home to make sure that nothing happens to her."

Cora sent her a reproachful look. "You care more about a blame-fool lamb and a—a storybook than spending time with your Grammy? What about your poor mama, Rose? I wouldn't be surprised if you don't ever think of her anymore. Mrs. Becker probably even rearranged the parlor, and uses your mama's special things willy-nilly."

Rose squirmed in her chair but said nothing. Cora could read the horrible truth in her granddaughter's averted gaze.

She felt cut off at every single turn. By God, Luke and his new wife would fix it so that Rose forgot her own mother and had nothing more to do with her grandmother. Well, she wouldn't stand for it. She'd bring her girl back to her hearth and her arms if it was the last thing she did today.

She stood over Rose and put her face in the little girl's. "Let me tell you something about your Miss Emily, Rose. She may be fancy, but she likes to gossip, just like the rest of us. She told me a secret that your father told her. I wasn't supposed to let anyone know, especially you. But I think your mama would want me to tell you. She was going to tell you when you were grown up a little more, I'm sure."

Rose stared at her fearfully, the half-eaten cookie on the plate in front of her forgotten. "What?"

"Your Miss Emily told me that Luke Becker isn't your real father."

"W-what do you mean?"

"Just what I said. Luke isn't your father and Emily Becker is the one who told me so. Your real father was a wonderful man, a doctor from Portland, but he died before you were born. Your mama was a respectable widow but Luke badgered her until she finally relented and agreed to marry him. He said he'd take care of her and be a father to you." Cora shook her head. "He acted like I couldn't take care of my own child. He's been pretending to love you all this time. *Lying* all this time. I never knew it. He's just a stranger. The only person around here related to you by blood is me. And I'll always love you."

A look of abject terror filled Rose's face, and the bloom faded from her cheeks. Cora felt a twinge of remorse about that, but in the end, it would all work out for the best. Thank heavens Rose was too upset to ask for more details.

"I don't believe it! I am too his daughter. Daddy wouldn't lie like that. He loves me—he told me so!"

Cora feigned great regret. "I wouldn't have thought so, either. But that's what Emily told me. You trust her, don't you?"

"N-no, I mean, yes, but—"

"Oh, Rose, honey, I know this is awful news." She reached out and stroked the girl's shoulder. "Don't you think you should stay here tonight?"

But Rose jumped up from the table, sobbing. "N-no. I need to go home! I need to find out why—" She ran out the back door, faster than Cora could move.

Cora went to the porch and called after her. "Rose! Come back here!" But all she could see were Rose's dark braids flying behind her as she ran down the road.

Another twinge rippled through Cora's bulky frame, this time one of worry. But the girl would be all right. Cora might have started a mighty big fight, but in the end she'd win. Luke had no legal right to keep Rose and when the truth came out, she felt certain that Judge Clifton would see it the same way.

Luke pulled the wagon into the road that led to the house. Behind him was a load of fresh-planed lumber to build the new henhouse. Bill Whinters, who owned the sawmill in town, had agreed to give Luke credit until harvest time. He hated going into debt, but they had to have chickens and eggs, and credit was a fact of farming life. Luke took a poorer grade of lumber to keep the cost as low as possible. And he'd made a deal with Bill to give him whatever he could salvage from the fallen oak. That helped keep the price down, too.

The planks in the wagon had some knotholes in them but he figured it would be cheaper to patch them than to pay the difference for first-quality wood. After all, chickens would be living in this place, not the family. If Luke kept the weather and predators out, that would be good enough.

The whole transaction had taken longer than he'd expected, and he knew Emily would be putting dinner on the table in a few minutes. He had just enough time to take care of the team and get washed up.

As he pulled around to the barn, Emily came rushing out to meet him. She was dressed in a soft, fawn-colored dress and she'd pinned her braid into a pretty knot at the back of her head. At first he thought she was just giving him another enthusiastic greeting—he could get used to those really fast. But her expression told him something else was going on.

She came out to the wagon. "Luke! You didn't see Rose on the way home?"

He frowned down at her, the lines still in his hands. "No, why?"

"Oh, I was hoping she was with you. I told her to be home from Cora's by four o'clock and it's past five. She knows we eat at five-thirty."

"Has she been home at all?"

"No, I haven't seen her since she left for school this morning." Emily wrung the corner of her apron in slender hands that shook.

He lifted his gaze and scanned the fields, as if he'd find her out there. But all he saw were plowed and planted rows. "Maybe she stayed late at Cora's. I'll go over there." Somehow, he suspected that Cora was involved in this, and her place seemed like the logical place to start looking.

"I'll stay here in case she comes back. Dear God, she's all right, don't you think?" Emily's face was a study of worry.

"Sure, she's fine," he said with a lot more confidence than he felt. "She probably just lost track of time. Or she's checking on the ducklings down at the creek. Kids are that way." He reached down and gave her shoulder a gentle squeeze. "I'll go get her and bring her home."

Emily nodded, and looked a little relieved. "All right."

Luke turned the wagon around in the barnyard and headed out again, this time for Cora's farm. He still had three good hours of daylight left if he needed them to search for his girl. But he knew he wouldn't. He'd get to Cora's and Rose would see the wagon and come running out, looking shame-faced and sheepish. He'd give her a little talking-to and make sure she apologized to Emily, and that would be the end of it.

But he kept a vigilant watch as he drove to Cora's, looking for any sign of glossy dark hair, or the flashing movement of a new pale blue dress covered with a clean white apron. He peered through the dense undergrowth that was still green from the rainfall, and over the tops of wild lupines that were nearly as tall as Rose. He saw nothing.

Finally he pulled into the road that led to Cora's place. When he neared the house, he saw that the door was open, but his girl didn't come running out. He set the wagon brake and wound the lines around the brake handle.

As he jumped down, Cora came out with her arms crossed over her chest, her very stance defensive and belligerent. It was the same one he'd seen so many times before. He felt as if he were reliving a bad dream. Except this time, his daughter was somehow involved. And this time, if Cora gave him trouble, she was in for the tongue-lashing of her life.

"Cora, I'm looking for Rose."

She uncrossed her arms. "Didn't she come home?"

"No. Is she here?"

"Of course not. She left here about two hours ago. She was upset."

He crossed the yard and climbed the porch. "Upset—what about?"

"She told me what Mrs. Becker said to her."

He sighed and pushed a hand through his hair. "Cora, I'm not in the mood for guessing games. What are you talking about?"

"Well, I thought you knew. Rose said that Mrs. Becker told her the truth about you—that you're not her father.

She left here crying and said she was going home. I tried to stop her but she wouldn't listen and just ran off."

Luke felt as if the painted planks beneath his feet tilted suddenly. "Rose told you that?"

"She did. I thought it was a cruel thing for your wife to do to the poor child." Cora's mouth flattened into a thin, white line. "She didn't need to know that, although Mrs. Becker seemed to think it was best."

Something about this all seemed wrong to Luke, like parts of a watch that wouldn't go back together. How could Emily do such a thing? Why would she? Then he remembered the night in the kitchen when he'd told Emily the story of Bradley Tilson. She hadn't agreed with his decision to keep it from Rose.

. . . shouldn't you tell her?

. . . what would it do to her to find it out from someone else? It's a risky secret to keep.

Emily was stubborn, and believed she knew it all when it came to teaching young girls. Well, this time she was wrong. Dead wrong. He didn't know what possessed her to tell Rose such a private thing.

Right now, all Luke knew was that his daughter was missing, and according to Cora, Emily might be the reason why.

He spun on his heel and ran back to the wagon. Cora called after him but he didn't hear what she said. He couldn't hear much of anything except the blood rushing through his head, driven by fear and anger.

As he lashed the horses to get back to the farm, the lumber slid around in the wagon bed behind him, and one plank bounced out. But Luke didn't stop. He couldn't think of anything except Rose and one other horrible fact. He'd been betrayed again.

Emily had betrayed his trust, just as Belinda had.

*   *   *

Emily sat on the porch watching the road, but she couldn't see very well from there. Every few minutes she ran down the drive to the fence, looking for Luke, looking for Rose, but she found neither. At last she gave up going back to the porch and climbed to the top fence rail to wait.

And the waiting was torture. God, it was like the fire in Chicago, not knowing if your world was about to end, or if everything would be all right. Or the moment when Alyssa had been hit. She'd prayed that her sister was alive, but she knew it couldn't possibly be true. Luke had said Rose was fine, but her heart told her something was horribly wrong.

Where was that girl? Was she with Cora, as Luke had said, or was she lost or hurt? Emily's head throbbed with worry. Everywhere she looked, she was reminded of Rose. The wild lupines that grew along the fence line, the twittering little birds in the trees, Cotton's grave next to the fallen oak—Rose's imprint was on this land and on her heart.

At last, when she thought she could bear it no longer, she saw Luke's wagon racing up the road. But he was alone in it, and he was lashing the team like the devil was after him. Oh, God, it must be something bad—

She climbed down from the fence and ran after the wagon as he drove it into the yard.

When she caught up to it, she was breathless and dizzy. "Rose—she—wasn't at—she's not with—"

"If she's not here, I don't know where she is." He barked it out, impatient, angry.

"What did—what did Cora say?"

He jumped down from the seat and advanced on Emily. The look on his face was so fearsome, she backed up, and stumbled over a rock half-buried in the soft dirt. "I'll tell you what she said. She said that Rose told her she knows I'm not her real father."

She tried to clutch her heart with her hand. "Oh, no! Did Cora tell her that?"

"No, Emily, you did. And after I told you I didn't want Rose to know."

She could not have been more surprised or hurt if he'd slapped her. "I did no such thing!" But it was as if he couldn't hear her.

"I trusted you with my daughter, the one person in this world who has made my life worthwhile, and this is where it got me." His handsome face twisted into a hideous mask of rage and frustration. "Damn it, I offered you a home and my protection when I could have left you standing on that dock in the rain. This is how you return the favor? Did you think because you taught at some fancy girls' school you know more about how to raise my daughter than I do? Well, I may have bungled it the last few years, but I've been part of her life since she was a baby. I know her better than anybody. You've known her barely a season. One more thing. Nobody hurts my daughter. Nobody." His smoke-colored eyes had turned black, and Emily actually thought he would strike her.

Instead he turned and began walking back toward the road.

She stood there stunned, her feet planted in the yard as if his harsh words had nailed them in place. He was leaving. She sprang into action and trotted after him, hard-pressed to keep up with his long strides. "Where are you going?"

"Where the hell do you think I'm going? I'm going to look for my girl!"

"Please—let me come with you. I want to help."

He spun on her again. "You've done enough, *teacher*.

Goddamn it, I never should have accepted you in your sister's place! I should have figured out a way to pay your fare back to Chicago, and get you as far away from us as I could."

He hadn't touched her, but Emily felt as winded as if he'd kicked her in the stomach. She stopped running after him and watched as he strode away as rain began falling again.

Back in the house, Emily took the wedding ring off her little finger and gently laid it on the kitchen table. Then she dragged up the stairs and went to the room she had occupied when she arrived. Her clothes and belongings were still there, along with her trunk and her canvas Gladstone bag, though she'd been spending her nights in Luke's room. She moved like an automaton, scarcely aware of her actions as she crossed from the wardrobe to the bed, laying out her things, from the bureau to her bag, carefully folding each garment and tucking away each belonging. She would leave here as soon she knew what had happened to Rose. How could she continue this sham of a marriage and stay with a man who did not trust her? Who believed that she was capable of hurting a child, and who so obviously had no feelings for her? Oh, she'd tried to fool herself for a while, telling herself that he cared, that their time together at night meant something to him. But he'd never stated anything as plainly as he had just moments ago.

I never should have accepted you in your sister's place.

It was the same refrain she'd heard all her life. She would never be what her sister was. Oh, she could dream about it, pretend for a little while in the dark with Luke, but the truth was, she was tall, gawky Emily, who used manners and rules as her only shield against being hurt.

But even that shield had been taken away from her. In the end, the one man who should have believed she would never violate such a confidence had so little regard for her or her integrity that he thought her capable of betraying his trust.

When she opened her trunk, she lifted out the bridal gown and veil, because they had to be packed on top. Like pouring salt into an open wound, Emily opened the clouds of tissue paper surrounding the veil and looked at it. She'd always believed it would be her lucky charm. Now she thought that it was her curse. She was cursed for wanting something she did not have coming to her, for wanting to be something she wasn't. It had been in her hands for a few precious days, only to be yanked away again. But just as Dickens's Jacob Marley was bound in death to carry the chains he'd forged in life, so was Emily bound to carry this gown and veil with her.

Tears ran like rivers down her face, blurring her vision, but she kept working, pausing only to swipe at her eyes with her sleeve. She had enough money to make it to Portland. Once there, she would sell the dress and the veil for passage to Chicago. Maybe then she would be free of her chains. Maybe she'd also find a sort of peace, as long as she didn't try to be more than she was.

As she laid the items in her trunk, she found the pink satin hair ribbon that she had given Rose and that Rose had rejected. She draped it across her open palm and looked at it. So many hurts had been piled upon Emily here. She'd been willing to brave them through because she thought that Luke and Rose had needed her. And she'd had hope.

The ribbon her sister had given her was one of the few keepsakes that she still had. She'd left everything else behind in Chicago to come out here, including her sister's grave. After the accident, Emily had gone to visit Alyssa at Rosehill Cemetery a few times because she'd had no one else to talk to.

Emily's head came up suddenly at the thought. Rose might be thinking the same thing—that she had no one else to talk to. And Emily knew exactly where she would go in such an event.

She had found Rose at the cemetery once before. Oh, the poor thing—there was a chance, a good chance—

Emily abandoned her packing, leaving the Gladstone bag and her trunk open. Charging downstairs, she dashed through the hall and the kitchen. Pausing to scratch a quick note to Luke, she then flung open the back door and ran outside into the rain.

"Rose! Rose, can you hear me?" Luke was nearly hoarse from calling his daughter. He'd left on foot to comb the dense vegetation along the roadsides, and then began to regret it. If he found her and she was hurt, he'd have no way to transport her. The creek edge had yielded no sign of Rose. Even the ducks had abandoned the ferns near its swollen waters.

He was soaked to the skin and the cloudy sky meant that it would get dark sooner than he'd originally considered. Where could she be? he wondered anxiously. Where would she run if she didn't go home?

He had retraced every foot of the route between the farm and Cora's, and he'd found no sign of her. He didn't know what to do except go home, change clothes, and get a search party going. He needed help. There was too much area for one person to cover, and alone, he might miss something. When Belinda had fled that night, he'd waited too long to go looking. He vowed not to repeat that mistake with his daughter.

As he trudged back to the farm through the mud, it occurred to him that he might even get Red Bailey to bring his bloodhound along. But it would all take time, and he felt like that was the one thing he didn't have. Every hour that Rose was out here—somewhere—was another hour that she might be hurt without help, or lost and scared with no one to turn to.

Unless, of course, she had come home. With that possibility looming before him in the rain, he picked up his pace and hurried to the house. When he got there, he saw that the back door was standing wide open.

He took a couple of running steps forward. "Rose? Emily?" But there was only silence. He trotted into the kitchen and found no one there. He called out again. "Emily?"

Upstairs in Emily's bedroom, he found her trunk pulled to the middle of the room, and open, empty dresser drawers. Draped over the trunk lid was a cloud of some kind of white fabric with a headpiece attached. Luke realized that this had to be the veil she'd told him about.

He put a finger on the delicate fabric, and remembered the shy hesitation in Emily's voice as she'd revealed her belief the veil would make her beautiful. In a sudden cascade of memories, he thought of all the things Emily had done to help Rose. Covered in chicken shit, her first concern had been to ask him about Rose's lessons. Then she'd braved Cora's wrath by using Belinda's tablecloth as a tent to try and save Rose's lamb. And last night, Emily had sat with Rose, listening to her girlish fancies about satin and lace gowns.

An icy hand of reason closed around his heart. Why the hell should he believe what Cora had told him? Why had he been so willing to accept as truth what she'd said, when he had years of experience with her manipulation and lying? God, he'd said horrible things to Emily, all based on what Cora had told him. What if it wasn't true?

What if—well, the answer to the *what if* was right here before his eyes. Emily was packing to leave. The only two people he cared about might be lost to him this very minute, thanks to that damnable bitch Cora Hayward, to the fact that he'd waited too long to stand up to her and that he'd held Emily back at arm's length because of his guilt over Belinda. He'd never felt more helpless in his life.

"Christ, get hold of yourself," he said, shaking off the inertia.

He went back downstairs, to try to decide what steps to take next, and saw Emily's ring and note on the kitchen table. His heart stumbled in his chest at the sight of the wedding band he'd given her and she'd just returned. He'd never even bothered to replace it with one that fit her elegant hand. He was a fool. He snatched up the paper, afraid of what he would find there. Instead, he smiled.

Gone to cemetery to bring Rose home.

How she knew where to look, Luke had no idea. But in some ways, Emily knew Rose better than he did.

He ran out to the wagon again and jumped up to the seat. He'd left the team out in the rain, something he never would have done under any other circumstances, and he felt rotten about it. He had a lot of things to make up for, if his hunches were right.

"If it's any comfort to you, I'm just as wet and cold as you are," he told the horses.

He urged the team down the road, which was getting soupier with every passing hour. Darkness would be upon him soon. As he passed the Manning place, he saw Chester in his oilskins, moving his sheep to a higher pasture. Chester flagged him down.

"Gotta move the flock, Luke. If you've got stock near the creek, you'd better get them away from it."

"Chester, can your boys move my stock?"

"Well, I s'pose—"

"I need your help. Emily and Rose are at the cemetery. I'm worried that they might get in trouble with that bridge."

"God almighty, what a time to go payin' respects to the dead!" He turned and called one of the boys out in the field. "Morris! You, Morris! Get Willie to help you move them sheep. Tell your mother I'll be back as soon as I can." Then, to Luke, he asked, "Have you got a rope back there?"

"Yes, and this lumber if we need it."

"All right, then." Chester clambered up to the wagon seat, his stiffly healed broken leg obviously hindering him. But he was willing, and Luke was grateful for it. He was a good neighbor and a good friend.

Luke slapped the lines on the horses' backs and they lurched forward toward the cemetery. Gripping the lines, Luke said a silent prayer for only the second time in his life, but it was the same one he'd said the night that Rose was born.

Please let my wife and child live.

Chapter Sixteen

———

Emily's wet skirts wrapped themselves heavily around her legs, impeding her progress as she hurried along the muddy road. She had an ache in her side and her feet squished inside her soaked shoes. But at least the cemetery was up ahead, and she was almost positive she'd find Rose soon.

She crossed the narrow log bridge that spanned the creek and noticed that the water was running high and fast. They'd had so much rain, and there had been that conversation she'd overheard at the social about mountain runoffs being high this year. The sky was low and gray and darkening, completely obscuring the view of the Columbia River that was usually visible from here on a clearer day.

She turned into the cemetery gate and looked for the elm tree that sheltered Belinda Becker's grave. Just as she suspected, she saw Rose's small figure huddled at her mother's headstone. Relief made Emily's knees like soft rubber.

"Oh, dear God," Emily intoned. "Rose!" She ran to the grave and found Rose wailing with her cheek resting against the chiseled letters of Belinda's name. "Rose, sweetheart, you have to come home!"

Rose looked up at her and Emily saw such heartbreak

in her small face, such disillusionment, that she thought her own heart would break as well. "Go away! I thought you were my friend—I *believed* you all those times you said my daddy—Mr. Becker—really loved me!"

If Emily lived another hundred years, she would never forget the horror of this moment. Luke could be blamed for taking Cora's word over hers—after all, he should know better. But Rose was only a child and thought that her grandmother loved her. She believed the lie she'd been told. How could she conceive that Cora really loved no one, not even Rose? Emily could barely fathom it herself.

She crouched next to Rose, trying to shield her from the weather but it was nearly impossible. Although the elm helped a little, the wind drove the rain at them as they huddled there. Rose's dark braids hung heavy and wet from her head, and her new dress and apron were sodden.

"We've got to get out of here now, sweetheart. Let me take you home. We'll talk there and get this all straightened out."

"I don't have a home! Daddy isn't my father, you aren't my mother—I don't have anyone except Grammy." Rose wrapped one arm around the headstone. "And Mama."

Emily sat down next her, heedless of the wet grass. "Luke Becker may not be the man who gave you life— you aren't related by blood—but he loves you with all his heart. He loves you much, much more than my own stepfather loved me." The child seemed unimpressed with this. "Rose, listen to me—I don't know what your grandmother told you, but she shouldn't have said anything. Luke didn't want you to know because as far as he's concerned you *are* his daughter. In all the ways that truly matter."

"She said that *you* told her about me. You told her that Daddy isn't my father." A gust of wind came up and blew her words across the headstones.

Cora's lie was as complicated as the proverbial tangled web. Emily shook her head and water fell from her hair, mixing with the rain. "I never told anyone anything. It wasn't my place. At first I disagreed with your father's decision to keep the secret from you, but in the end, I believed he was right. Do you love him less because you aren't related to him?"

"N-no." Rose swiped a hand across her eyes, smudging her face with mud and tears.

Thank God, Emily thought. The child was more reasonable than some adults she knew. "Your grandmother was wrong to tell you what she did. She's known all along that Luke is your father, too, you know."

Rose sniffled. "She has?"

"Yes, but I think you owe it to your father to let him explain it to you. He's the one who knows it best, and this all happened years before I came to Fairdale." She took Rose's icy hand in her own. "But remember one thing—both of us, Luke and I, love you very much. We want you to be safe and happy, and to have a good life. Do you believe me?"

A poor, drenched little urchin, Rose considered her with solemn reddened eyes. At last she nodded.

Emily smiled at her and reached out to touch her cold cheek where the carving had left a sharp mark. "Good, I'm glad. Now, please, let me take you home. It's miserable out here and it's going to get dark soon. Plus your father is beside himself with worry—he's out looking for you now on foot. We didn't know what happened to you when you didn't show up at the farm."

There was no point in telling the girl that Emily's grand

hope for family and home had fizzled away, and that she'd be leaving on the first steamboat she could arrange passage on. Rose had been traumatized enough for one day. Still gripping the girl's hand, she stood, and Rose gained her feet as well.

Emily put her arm around Rose's thin shoulders and pulled her close, then steered her toward the road. The rain began falling harder, and as they approached the log bridge, Rose looked down and then held back.

"What's the matter?" Emily asked over the wind and rain.

"The creek is awful high . . ."

"I know, that's why we must cross quickly so we can be on the home side. We don't want to be wandering around out here in the dark."

"Well, okay."

With Emily still holding onto Rose, they both stepped on the bridge at the same time. "It's not very wide. We'll hurry."

With just two more paces to go, the bridge suddenly heaved a tremendous groan and one of the support beams came away. Screams echoed off the hillsides, muffled only by the low clouds. Emily tumbled first and Rose followed. Emily twisted Rose so she would break the girl's fall and in the process scraped both hands on a log. They bounced down the short slope, roots, pebbles and vines grabbing at them, slowing their fall. After what seemed an eternity, they landed on a dirt shelf, stranded between the road above and the rushing water below.

Dazed, Emily sat up and immediately reached for Rose. Mud streaked the girl's face, and leaves dotted her hair. Emily cupped her shoulders and studied Rose for injuries. "Rose! Are you all right?"

"Yes, I think so." She looked around, at the log that

had dropped into the creek, and at the sheer wall behind them covered with ferns and grass. "Maybe I can climb up to the road and get help."

Emily was doubtful, but a girl Rose's size might make it up. "All right, I'll give you a boost." She interlaced her fingers. "Step here in my hands and see if you can grab that root sticking out of the dirt up there."

Rose put her foot in Emily's hands and Emily pushed with all her might to lift the girl high enough to grab the one handhold within their reach. Puffing and straining, she grunted, "Can you get it?"

"Y-yes," Rose grunted in reply, "but it's all wet and muddy and it keeps slipping out of my hand."

"All right, come down." Emily lowered her with a great exhale. "We don't dare risk losing our balance and falling into the water."

Rose was muddy and had grass stains on her wet dress. "How are we going to get out?"

"Your father is looking for us right now. He'll be here, don't worry."

Rose leaned her head against Emily. "This is how my mama died." Fear laced her voice as she wrapped her arms around Emily's waist. "In the rain. Grammy said so."

Grammy was full of hot gas, Emily had long ago decided. She returned Rose's embrace, trying to soothe the girl with long strokes on her back. "No, honey, your mother died of pneumonia. That's a sickness of the lungs. Rain can't kill anyone unless they drown somehow. When we lose someone we love, through death or for some other reason, all we can do is keep them in our hearts and go on living." They were brave words, but Emily wondered if she'd really be able to follow her own advice. She glanced down at the raging, swirling water and thought, oh so briefly, that life without Luke wouldn't be worth much. But almost as soon as the thought crossed her mind, it was gone again. She would have to be strong, but she was already strong. Hadn't she discovered that about her-self over the last few weeks? And she would be unhappy, but she would go on. She would try to find meaning in life again.

Without Rose.

Without Luke.

Emily felt her eyes well up and she struggled against it. She couldn't fall apart now and scare Rose. Emily had had no one to depend upon for so long, she knew she could count on herself. She must be strong for them both.

"What's that?" Rose cocked her head.

"What?" Emily asked. "I don't hear anything." Then over the sounds of the creek and the wind and rain, she heard a distant voice. It rose and fell with the gusts.

"Emily! Rose! Where are you?"

"Oh, thank God! It's Luke!"

They both started yelling at once.

"Here we are!"

"Daddy, we're down here! Down here!"

In a moment, two heads emerged over the edge of the fallen-away bridge. In the gathering gloom, Emily rec-ognized Luke and Chester Manning.

"Don't you worry, ma'am. We'll have you out of there in a jiffy."

"Are you hurt?" Luke called down.

"No, we're all right. Just dirty, wet, and cold," Emily answered.

"I'm coming down to get you. Rose first, then you, Emily."

Emily waited with her heart in her throat as Luke low-ered himself down the hillside to their little perch. Watch-ing his long lean body as he carefully threaded his way over the mud and roots was a special torture for Emily. She knew that she would never be held by those strong arms again, or cradled against that broad chest. Or ever hear him tell her he loved her. When he touched down, in the fading light she saw that he was just as wet and dirty as they were. He'd tied the end of a rope around his waist, and now he untied it and secured it around Rose.

"The other end of this is tied to the wagon. Chester!" he called. "Here comes Rose! Back 'er up!" From above and below, Luke and Chester guided Rose as she reached the road.

Emily watched anxiously until Chester reached over, grabbed the girl, and lifted her the rest of the way.

When Rose had both feet safely on the ground above, Luke turned to Emily. He gripped her shoulders in his hands while rain poured off his head. The storm seemed to fade away and all she saw were his dark eyes, all she felt were his hands on her once more.

"Emily, Emily, God I was such a fool! I saw the ring on the kitchen table. You can't leave us. I never should have listened to Cora. That wicked-hearted old bitch could have gotten all of us killed with that lie she made up. Please"—he squeezed her shoulders and looked into her eyes—"please try to forgive me. And *please* don't leave us. I'm begging you, as a man and as your husband. I love you and I need you. So does Rose." He released her shoulders and took her hands, kissing them through the mud and scraped flesh. "Until this moment, I wasn't sure if I could love anyone again. After I lost Belinda, I couldn't imagine caring for another woman. But I can't let you go."

Emotion and reaction set in, and Emily began shaking like someone with Saint Vitus' dance. She leaned against him for a moment, relieved, exhausted, elated. "Luke, it's all right, it's all right. I forgive you. I'll stay. Dear God, I'll stay. I'm so glad you don't hate me."

"*Hate* you," he repeated. "Honey, I have two shining lights in my life, two—you and Rose. I know I said awful things—I was worried and scared for Rose, and I—"

Emily put her hand to his lips. "Hush. None of that matters now. Let's just go home."

He kissed her hands again and nodded. Then he tied the rope around her waist and had Chester back up the wagon to pull her up. When all of them had been lifted from the creek, the two men stacked Luke's lumber order across the road, about thirty feet from the edge of the drop-off.

"We can't do anything about the other side. We'll just have to hope that no one comes along in the dark and falls off into the creek," Luke said.

Just as full darkness settled over the land, all four of them were safely back in the wagon and headed toward the Manning farm.

"By God, wait until that town council gets an earful of this," Chester grumbled as they reached his place. "I'll give 'em an ass-chewin' they won't likely forget. By the time I'm done with them, they'll not only offer to build a brand-new bridge, Luke, they'll be begging to name it after the Becker ladies. We'll get them to replace your lumber for that henhouse, too, and with first-grade stuff."

From the back of the wagon, Luke barely listened. He just kept his arms wrapped around Rose and Emily, kept them tucked against his heart.

Jennie Manning was waiting for them on her front porch, and when she learned what had happened, she had her children bring out blankets and hot coffee.

"Are you sure you won't come in?" she fretted. With her shawl wrapped tightly around her, she waded through the mud to the wagon to check on the Beckers herself. "I hate to send you off like this, wet and cold."

"Jennie, we appreciate it, but we've had a really terrible day." Emily glanced at Rose, then Luke. "We want to get home and clean up."

She nodded, obviously understanding, but worried just the same. "All right. But please be careful, and take care of yourselves. I'll come by tomorrow and see how you're doing."

They all waved good-bye and Luke got the wagon rolling again, this time for home.

This time, for good.

"This is where you belong," Luke said, as he entered Emily. The bed creaked under the weight of their bodies and his slow rocking. "You are the love of my life, and this is where you belong. In my arms and in my heart."

They had washed and eaten and had both shared the task of putting Rose to bed. Luke had given his daughter an extra hug, and promised to talk all she wanted in the morning. Then, to reaffirm their love and their lives, Luke had brought Emily to the shadowy stillness of his bedroom to make slow, sweet love to her.

She gasped with pleasure and a feeling of completion as he joined her. "Yes," she responded, rocking her hips toward him. "And this is where you belong. Always in my heart."

Emily had never felt so alive, so certain of the purpose of her existence, as she was at this moment. She had been born to love Luke Becker and to be loved by him in return.

He honored her with his body and spirit, with urgent, whispered words, the promise of a lifetime full of tomorrows. Pushing her to her climax, he held her while she wept his name and convulsed beneath him. Then he sought his own release and solace in her.

At last, when they lay spent and exhaustion was about to claim them, Luke rolled Emily to her side and pulled her snug up against his torso so they matched like spoons.

"We've had our share of disasters around here, haven't we?" Luke commented. His whisper lifted the hair at her nape. She snuggled closer. His arms tightened.

"More than our share," she returned. "What are you going to tell Rose?"

"What I should have told her in the first place—the truth. At least as much of it as I think she should hear for now." He put a kiss on her bare shoulder. "You were right all along, Emily."

"I wish that I hadn't been." She interlaced her hands with his. "If Cora hadn't known, you would have been safe to let things stand."

"Yeah, and I should have known better. She threatened me a couple of times over the years, that she'd tell Rose I'm not her father."

"What will you do about her, Luke? Will you still let Rose see her?"

"For now, Rose doesn't want anything to do with her, and who can blame her? Cora's idea of love is a twisted thing. If Rose changes her mind later, we'll talk about it. But as far as I'm concerned, our relationship with Cora Hayward is finished. She could have gotten you and Rose killed today."

The truth of his statement sent a chill through Emily, and they fell silent for a moment.

"I think the rain is finally letting up," Emily said at last. It wasn't pounding against the glass anymore. She felt Luke's lips against the back of her neck.

"That's good," he murmured, and then she heard the sound of his slow, even breathing and knew that he slept.

"Yes, it is. It's all good." And Emily released her hold on wakefulness to join her husband.

EPILOGUE

"CAN ANYONE PRESENT SHOW JUST CAUSE WHY THESE two should not be joined in holy matrimony?" From his place on Luke's front porch, Reverend Ackerman directed his question at the assembly of people gathered in the Beckers' front yard behind Emily and Luke. It was a beautiful day in late June—just about the time it stopped raining around here, Luke had told Emily. Birds twittering in the trees were the only response to the reverend's question.

"All right, then." Ackerman led the wedding couple through a traditional ceremony for a wedding that was anything but. "Luke, the ring."

Emily's heart sank. She hadn't been able to find her wedding band again after she'd taken it off and put it on the table that awful day. Luke had said nothing about it, but she knew he must have noticed that she wasn't wearing it.

Now he took her hand and pushed a beautiful wide gold band onto her ring finger. She looked up at him, surprised, but he just winked at her.

". . . vested in me, I now pronounce you man and wife. Luke"—he nodded at the groom—"kiss your bride."

Luke lifted Emily's fine silk veil, then took her into his arms and gave her a brief but heartfelt kiss. The neighbors behind him cheered and applauded.

Emily laughed, even as tears streamed down her face. Their neighbors crowded forward to wish them well, but Jennie and Chester Manning led the group. "I haven't seen a bride so pretty since I married my little gal, here," Chester said, pecking Emily on the cheek. "Luke, congratulations! I'm glad we all lived to see this day."

Luke pumped his hand and clapped him on the shoulder, overwhelmed by the feeling of support and belonging with his neighbors that he'd never known before. "Thanks for everything, Chester. Everything. I owe you the life of my wife and child."

The farmer looked embarrassed. "Oh, damn it, Luke. I was just payin' you back for saving *my* family last year. That's what neighbors are for!"

"Yeah, but you got the town council to replace the bridge and pay for my lumber, you organized this wedding, and got everyone to help with building the henhouse. God, that's more than any man could ask for."

Chester waved off any more thanks. "Now you just have some of Jennie's fried potatoes and enjoy your day. But watch out for the punch—I think old Jobie might have spiked it with that white lightnin' he makes up there on the mountain. So of course I'm having me a taste of that."

"Not too big a taste," Jennie warned, overhearing this. "I don't want any more broken legs around our house, after that fall off the barn roof last year."

"I wasn't drinkin' that day!" Chester protested.

"No, and look what happened," she teased. She pressed forward to take Emily's hand. "You look beautiful."

"I felt a little odd about wearing my teal dress with this veil, but I think it's all right."

"Of course, it is. Lots of brides are choosing wedding dresses that they can wear again, anyway."

"You *are* beautiful, Mama Em." Rose stood beside her,

lovely in her restored dress and carrying a small nosegay, as befitted the maid of honor. Her hair was tied back with Emily's pink satin hair ribbon. She learned from Rose that Cora had made her return the gift when Emily had given it to her. Emily was happy that it now belonged to Rose.

And they had decided that "Mama" must always be Belinda. But "Miss Emily" was too formal, and having a child call her by her first name was unacceptable to both Luke and Emily. So they decided on "Mama Em" as a compromise, and everyone was happy with it.

"Thank you, Rose." She leaned over and pressed her cheek to the girl's. "Someday you'll wear not only this veil, but the dress that goes with it as well, if you want."

"Ohh, really?" Rose beamed.

"Yes, when you find a man as good and kind as your father," Jennie said, tipping a smile at Emily.

"Everyone—" Chester raised his voice to be heard above the crowd. "We all know why we're here today—to see these fine folks married off right, and to build them a new henhouse. So let's eat our wedding breakfast and get to work. Afterward, the Duffy brothers will provide the dancin' music, and we might be able to coax our fine ladies into feeding us supper, too."

Everyone sat down to eat at the tables that had been set up, much like the ones that had been used at the church social.

It was a wonderful day, full of toasts and good wishes and more happiness than Emily had ever known in her whole life. She had a husband who loved her, a fine daughter, and good friends. If she had asked them which fork went with a seafood cocktail, she doubted any of them could have told her.

And what a relief that was.

*   *   *

That evening after everyone had finally gone home, Luke and Emily settled on the front porch to watch the sunset and gaze upon their new henhouse. She had a cup of tea and he had a glass of whiskey. They were tired and happy, mindful of the past and excited about their future.

"Wasn't that nice of Fran Eakins to give us the paint *and* the chickens for the new henhouse?" Emily asked.

"Considering what a miserly, sour pickle that woman is, I'm surprised she did it." He took a sip of the whiskey.

"Luke!"

"Well? Weren't you surprised?"

"Well . . . yes," Emily admitted, grinning. "She was sweet on you, you know. She wanted to marry you. So did Clara."

"God, what a thought, to be sitting here with either of them now instead of you. One of them staring at me from under those beetle brows, and the other congratulating herself and fishing for compliments." He shuddered.

"No, I wouldn't have liked that, either."

"So do you like your wedding present?" he asked. He'd given her two matching rocking chairs for the front porch. "You don't think they make us seem like old people, do you?"

"Of course not." She pushed hers into motion. "Besides, I plan to be here when I'm old, too. I'll still need a place to sit on the porch."

He leaned over and gave her a whiskey-flavored kiss that reminded her of the first night they made love. She inhaled the fumes and deepened the kiss, which he responded to in kind.

"Hmmmm, Mrs. Becker, I believe you're trying to seduce me."

She giggled. "What, me? The innocent old-maid etiquette teacher from Chicago?"

He dropped another soft kiss on her mouth. "Not an old maid anymore. Oh, before I forget—" He leaned over and picked up a roll of paper next to his chair. It was tied with a pretty blue ribbon. "This is Rose's wedding gift to us. She gave it to me just before the Mannings took her home to their place for the night." He handed the roll to Emily and she took it with the same reverence as she would a valuable museum piece. She knew what it was.

"I've seen this paper before. This is what my dress material came wrapped in. Rose asked me for it because she thought it would be good for drawing." Emily slipped the ribbon off the tube and unrolled the paper. "Oh . . ." Her eyes filled with tears.

"Well, would you look at that—"

The scroll, which was about seven feet long, was a history of the Becker family, beautifully drawn by Rose. Emily remembered how angry Cora had gotten when she found this. It began with Luke and Belinda holding hands in front of the house, and then Rose joined the picture. It progressed to depict Belinda's grave in the hillside cemetery, and Cora appeared in the drawing. Then Emily came along. It ended with Emily, Luke, and Rose standing in front of the house, the oak tree gone, and Cotton's grave in the background. Lucy scampered in a nearby meadow and a fat sun seemed to shine down on everything.

"I didn't know she could draw this well," Luke marveled.

"I did. I saw her work when I first got here." She told him about the Bayeux Tapestry and how it had inspired Rose to create this scroll. "If she wants to pursue art, I think we should encourage her, Luke."

"You're the teacher, Em, and an amazing woman besides." He kissed her again. "But you were wrong about one thing."

She chuckled. "What, just one?"

"Yeah, so far."

She poked him with her elbow. "And what was I wrong about, *so far?*"

He gave her a tender smile. "You didn't need that bridal veil to make you beautiful, honey. You just needed love."

Emily's throat closed, and she knew he was right. She had the love of a grand man and a wonderful daughter. If she had beauty now, they had given it to her.

And it was the best gift she'd ever received.